Eva *and* Skye's Magical Hair Solution

DARKE CONTEUR

Eva and Skye's
Magical Hair Solution

Special thanks to Rebecca Poole at Dreams2Media for cover art and formatting,
Annette Beatwell for the second pair of eyes,
and Elizabeth Hurst for editing.

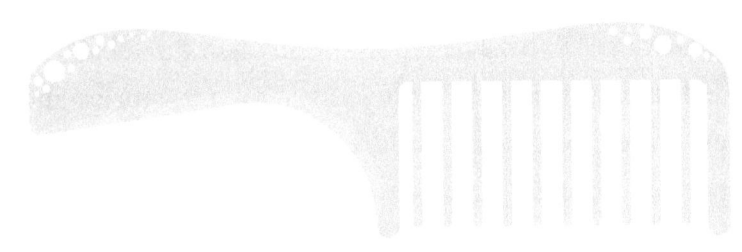

Chapter One

Tuesday, September 7th, 1982

The older she got, the less fourteen-year-old Evandra Shade was sure about anything, except that this is where she wanted to be. The teen stared at the long, two-level red brick building from between wispy black bangs and slowly exhaled. She was nervous, and the queasiness in her stomach got worse with each passing moment. She took a deep breath. This was it. What she begged her parents for, ever since the Council of Ministers said it would approve a special dispensation to allow her to continue her education outside of their community. Her elementary lessons in spellcasting were over, and she didn't want to spend the next four years travelling from community to community, hoping to earn an apprenticeship. She didn't know what she wanted to become and doubted travelling around the magical realm would solve that problem. After all, her older brother Dominik finished his four years of internship and received only one offer. Now they were stuck at home together while their parents went over the terms of his apprenticeship, and he was being a complete jerk about it. Getting away from him for seven hours a day was her only escape.

Evandra knew a little bit about the outside world from Dom's best friend Delano Allard. The Allard family had done business with the outside for centuries and she loved listening to stories about the places they'd been. She knew children were taught in places called schools; one for younger children and one for teenagers. The idea that children of the same age would all go to one place to learn fascinated her, and now she was old enough to go to a *high school*. What did they learn? Did they go from school to school learning? Did they focus on one skill or many? Did she have any skills other than spellcasting? She played with her turquoise choker. She wasn't allowed to use or talk about magic at all. The Council and her parents were adamant about that. Not unless it was a life-threatening event.

She pulled the collar of her hand-knit cardigan close to her neck, trapping some of her long hair under the wool. The sweater was knitted in an intricate pattern full of colour; one her great-grandmother made years ago for Evandra's mother. She pulled part of the collar close to her nose and took a sniff. It still held the faint scent of her mother's favourite perfume, the one her father made such a fuss about finding in time for last year's Winter Festival. That was the night he told them about his new placement and the move. He figured news about the move would go over better with her mother if he had an expensive peace offering.

She clutched a small linen bag tight to her chest. Her heart raced. For the first time in her life, she was venturing out beyond her tight-knit world. This was scary but in a good way.

The parking lot of Frontenac Collegiate and Vocational Institute was full of cars with barely enough room for the half dozen school buses to maneuver through. Music blared from the back of the last bus, with puffs of smoke that billowed out from a few back windows, accompanied by the faint scent of burnt tobacco. The main doors were just across from the parking lot. Now if she could get her legs to move...

The lobby of the high school was chaotic and loud. Dozens of students hung out in the large foyer, talking and laughing. Banners with bold letters in mahogany and silver hung on the walls with tables set up directly underneath, and everywhere she looked something exciting was going on. She smiled at a couple of older female students close by and was given the once-over by both. One, a pretty blonde with big, teased hair, and dressed full of denim and lace, scrunched up her nose and turned her attention back to her companion; a brunette who snapped a piece of gum and shook her head, which made the seashell earrings she wore clink.

"Oh, my, g*awd*," the brunette said, in a loud voice. "It looks like she raided a second-hand store."

The blonde glanced over her shoulder. "Gag me. I swear minor niners are so grody."

The corner of the brunette's mouth turned slightly upward into a sneer. "I wouldn't leave the house if I looked like that."

They headed toward Evandra. The blonde slammed her shoulder hard into her. "I'd kill myself if I looked like that."

Evandra trembled and glanced around the foyer. No one heard the comment, but no one noticed her either. Evandra narrowed her eyes. Her world had nasty people too, but they didn't go out of their way to be so insulting. She glared at the blonde and clenched her fist. All it would take was a couple of swipes with her index finger to create a spell and make that nasty person trip, and she was fast enough that she could do it without anyone seeing her, but she relaxed her hand and shook off the tension in her fingers. That would be breaking her promise.

A bell echoed through the school corridors. The sudden noise startled her, and within moments, the foyer swelled with students, and she had to back up to the front doors to keep from being swept away. She opened her bag and pulled out an envelope with the type-set smeared from water. She received the letter from one of their new neighbours the day before. They found it lying on the ground on the edge of a puddle. Inside were several sheets of paper. Damp spots on the first one smudged the typed words and made it impossible to read and the other sheets. What looked like a map of the school and a permission form were also ruined. The only one to survive was her class schedule.

According to the timetable, she had English for her first class. It seemed odd to learn a language she already knew, but it was com-pulsory and in room 224. She carefully opened the ruined map. Parts were legible, enough so that she concluded that all rooms that start-ed with the number one were on the first floor, so logically anything with a two would be on the second. She stepped into the stream of teenagers and followed them down a corridor and up a flight of stairs. Lower numbers were at the far end, so room 224 should be just a few doors down from the stairwell, but the last door was num-bered 219 and the one next to it 217. Panic set in as she frantically searched for any number higher than 219.

Lockers slammed shut and muffled conversations echoed all through the halls as she desperately tried to find her first class. She took a second set of stairs back down, but she was nowhere near where she started, and worse, the corridors swelled with more stu-dents making it difficult to go anywhere but in the general direction of everyone else. She stumbled into a few students and got pushed down a branching corridor. The tide of students carried her down to an exit, and moments later she stood outside at the back of the red brick building and a few meters away from a long, wood build-ing painted white. Several teen girls stood close by, smoking. She pulled her small bag close to her chest and stepped off the concrete walkway that led to a second building at the end. She swallowed a few times, trying to ease the growing knot in her throat. She was lost on her first day of school and it was all she could do to keep from bursting into tears.

"No smoking by the portables!" A man's voice shouted over the conversations of the students nearby.

The smoking girls rolled their eyes and dropped their cigarettes, grinding them into the gravel as the middle-aged teacher approached them.

He put his hands on his hips. "Really? That's your goal in life? To get suspended on the first day?"

Their faces scrunched up into sarcastic looks as he followed them back up to the walkway and waved to a small group of kids to move. "All right folks, two minutes until the final bell. I suggest you get a move on."

Evandra walked up to him. "Excuse me, sir." Her hand trembled as she held up the sheet of paper. "Where is room 224?"

He pointed at a group of boys. "I saw that Wilkins. I've got my eye on you." He faced the portable. "Ferguson. Class. Now." He took a passing glance at her. "Second floor. B building."

"B building? Where's that?"

"It's on your map."

She flipped over her schedule. "My map got ruined."

He pointed to the secondary building. "That's B building. I suggest you get to the office and grab a map. Your classes are going to be all over the school and until you get used to the layout, you're going to need one."

She nodded. "Where is the—"

"Go! Now!"

Evandra jostled her way back to B building, through the double

5

doors and into a smaller, very overcrowded corridor. The faint smell of cooking oil came from somewhere farther down the hall, and the wave of students took her down to a back exit with plate glass for walls and glass doors. Beyond the doors was a courtyard with three round cement tables and seating, several large trees that swallowed a third of the yard with their canopy, and the entire place was coated in a layer of gravel. The short, glass corridor continued past the doors, went three steps up, and connected a set of heavy metal doors that opened up to the brick part of the school. She stood by the glass wall. Hordes of teens stood around smoking and talking. The blonde and brunette were there as well, in the middle of a group of older students. The blonde made rude gestures to a small group of younger boys standing in the corner. She stared at the lit cigarette between the blonde's lips; watched as the white-blue smoke exited through her nostrils. She thought about the smell of the tobacco until she could almost smell it. It was a disgusting odour and smelled nothing like real tobacco. It was a nasty, choking, nauseating smell that needed to be cleansed from the air with a strong gust of wind. A few leaves blew into the grotto and twirled in the corner near the boys. Evandra focused on the smoke as it dissolved into the air and the breeze grew stronger. The bell on the wall above her gave out two quick rings. Evandra didn't jump this time, but a strong burst of air rushed through the confined area, throwing dirt and garbage all over before it quickly dissipated. People brushed leaves and garbage from their hair and walked toward the glass doors.

A female teacher came out from the office-type room just down the way and clapped her hands several times. "Second bell, people! Let's move!"

She blinked a few times, glanced down at her schedule, and approached the teacher. "I'm looking for room 224?"

She pointed toward a set of heavy double doors. "Go through those doors, take the stairs. 224 is at the top."

Evandra shook her head and followed a line of students up to the second floor. A small crowd of students waited at the top looked just as confused as she did. She glanced at the number on the door they stood in front of. At least she had found the right room.

A small group of male students roughhoused up the stairs and one bumped into her from behind. The impact knocked the strap off her shoulder and the entire contents of her bag, and his knapsack spilled onto the floor. She bent down and picked a few things up. A quick look over the sheets and she realized some of these weren't hers.

She held up a different schedule. "Sorry, this must be yours."

He was thin, slightly taller than her with dirty blonde hair and a bad case of acne. His jean jacket was covered in colourful patches and was almost as faded as his jeans. He grinned at her, and his eyes disappeared into two half-moons, but even when he stopped, they stayed partially closed.

"Whoops. Can't be losin' that."

His first class caught her eye. "You have English first period too?"

He nodded. "Looks like."

"Good thing we made it here in time."

He frowned. "We don't go here yet. Gotta go to homeroom first." He stepped back and glanced at the number on the door. "And unless you're in grade eleven, this ain't your homeroom."

Evandra's panic returned. "I don't know what my homeroom is or where it is."

"Should be on the top of your schedule." He handed hers back and pointed to the top of the page. "Right next to your name."

Her eyes followed the line from her name. "9F?"

He smiled and pointed to an open door just across the way. "Cool. We're in the same class."

"Where's that?"

He pointed down the hall at a room. "Right there." The bell rang out for a third time and was much longer that the previous rings. "We better boot-scoot, don't want to be tardy on the first day!"

Evandra followed quickly behind. At least she didn't have far to go.

Her homeroom had no windows with a pile of boxes stacked on a table in the far corner. Six rows consisting of wooden and metal desks lined up in front of a metal teacher's desk. Most of the seats were occupied, except for a few at the back. Everyone knew everyone else and sat in small groups together. She glanced over at the young boy who helped her. He'd already found some friends and was talking up a storm. Evandra made her way to one of the empty seats in the middle row. She put her bag on her lap and looked around, in awe of everything. She'd never seen so many kids her age all in one place before. The most she'd ever seen was five, and that was only because her father and a few other pa rents took their kids to the *Astrometry* to watch a Saturn/Neptune conjunction up close.

She smiled at a few girls who looked in her direction. A couple smiled back, but mostly they looked her over, giggled at each other and turned away. She tugged at the neck of her cardigan and tried to straighten out her pleated skirt. Her clothing didn't look anything like what they wore. Their outfits were full of bright colours, denim, or oversized shirts. A few girls had teased hair and wore bright makeup. No wonder they were laughing at her. She sat forward at her wooden desk and stared at the codes for her classes, trying not to look as awkward as she felt.

The classroom door closed behind a male teacher. "All right, settle down. My name is Mr. Grossman, and I'm your Homeroom teacher." He dropped a dark leather briefcase on the desk. "Welcome to your first day of high school."

Evandra put away her schedule. She never had a real teacher before, only her parents. A few kids behind her quietly made a few jokes about Mr. Grossman's name, and she giggled too.

"After today, you will come here for your first-period class," he continued. "I shut the door at the second bell. If you're not here by then, you're marked late."

He picked up a sheet of paper from the metal desk and stood in front of the first row. "This is a diagram of the class. Write your name down in the appropriate spot."

He strolled toward the second row. "This will be your seat for the year, and no, you cannot change seats once you're assigned, so if you don't like where you are, move now."

He continued to stroll along the front. "There will be other students occupying this room throughout the day, sitting at your desk, so *do not* leave anything of value behind."

Evandra leaned to one side and looked down. There was a small wooden shelf under her seat. The light-coloured wood was worn and chipped along the edges.

"There will be no talking during announcements. No chewing gum, and no eating. If you're hungry, I suggest you eat beforehand, or after Homeroom." He stopped in front of the fourth row. A girl sat with a set of headphones over her ears. Mr. Grossman yanked them off her head.

"No listening to music while you are in Homeroom. You are to be present and alert at all times."

The loudspeaker hummed and then crackled as announcements

9

began. It was a mix of school rules and regulations, the national anthem, and in-school promos for everything from football to volunteers for the school store. Evandra took in every word. She imagined herself trying out for the cheerleading squad or the yearbook committee. She imagined herself hanging out with other kids and talking about class, walking with friends to class—or maybe she'd go to a friend's house after school!

The placement diagram found its way to her, and she carefully printed her name in the appropriate box. She did a quick scan of the other boxes and found the name of the boy who helped her. It was Keith-something? She could barely read his handwriting. It was a few more minutes of listening to Mr. Grossman before the bell rang again. The class emptied into the hall, along with students of the half dozen other classes on the same floor. She stood nervously outside room 224 when Keith came up behind her and gave a curt nod.

"How did you know about going to homeroom?" she asked.

"My sister's in grade eleven." The class door opened, and students filed out. The mean brunette from the foyer shot a quick, nasty glare in her direction before she slammed one shoulder into Keith. He rolled his eyes as she plowed through a small group of students, shoving several of them out of her way. "That's her. She's so totally heinous."

"I have an older brother. He can be a real jerk too."

They inched closer to the classroom. "When I was little, she forced me into my toy box and sat on it so I couldn't get out. Then she put heavy stuff on top and left the room." He shook his head. "No one could hear me call for help, and it was almost an hour before my mom found me."

Evandra nodded. "Sometimes, my brother would put dirt in my lunches. The first time he did it, he was babysitting me."

"He had you right where he wanted you."

"The worst part was my parents didn't believe me."

Keith exhaled. "They never do."

After English, which to her surprise was about reading books, she had three more classes and then lunch, or as her schedule put it, 'second lunch'. After overhearing a few kids make plans to eat in the cafeteria, she decided to follow them and joined a wave of students through the metal double doors, where the smell of cooking grease and something sweet surrounded her. Her stomach growled. She glanced down at the paper bag inside her pouch and peeked inside. It didn't smell as wonderful as the other aromas that came from the kitchen, but for today, it would do.

The long tables were packed with students talking and eating. Everyone seemed to know everyone else and didn't give her a second look as she stood at the front of the room and looked for a place to sit. At the back corner sat an empty chair at the end of a long table. Six male students were gathered at one end. They protectively hovered over a few dozen Alf trading cards as she walked past. At least the chair was close to a window, and she'd have something other than people to look at. She made herself comfortable and stared outside. The football team was holding tryouts, and off the field, young girls in cheerleader uniforms in school colours jumped and cartwheeled across the grass.

Her gaze drifted across the crowded cafeteria. Everyone knew someone here, and for the first time today, she wished she was back at home with her father doing her lessons. It might have been private and boring, but at least her family was friendly to her. Well, her parents were, but right now she'd willingly put up with her brother's horrible attitude, rather than be ignored by an entire school full of teenagers.

She took out her lunch and placed it on the table in front of her. A banana, and two pieces of thin, flat, white bread with a brown spread in between. Her father offered to send her with something a little more familiar, but she wanted to fit in and be like the other students. Dom's best friend called this a *sandwich* and assured her it was what teenagers ate for lunch. It looked nothing like the colourful sourdough buns and savoury meat *au jus* she was used to. She peered back inside the bag hoping to find something more, like a few *pirozhki,* but it was empty. She bit into her sandwich and immediately made a face. She spat her mouthful onto the paper bag. Flecks of dirt mingled with the spread. Her eyes teared up and she blinked them back.

She stuffed her food into the paper bag and slammed it against the back of her seat. Her stomach still growled, and a banana wasn't going to satisfy it. The aroma of something savoury drifted around her as one of the boys at the far end devoured a plate of thin, cooked strips of potatoes covered in a brown sauce. She stared at the plate. It looked interesting and smelled so good. He dropped some coins into the side pocket of his knapsack. She wished she'd brought some money. Her father had offered her some before she left, but she'd refused.

Evandra rubbed her abdomen. She couldn't go to the rest of her classes hungry. She could pass out from starvation or something. The students at the tables on either side of her got up and left leaving a large vacancy. Her gaze fell on a trio of girls several tables away with plates of the same potato strips and brown sauce in front of them. She glanced down at her food. Dom's friend was wrong. This sandwich was *not* what teenagers ate, and as the aroma teased her senses, she quickly concluded that this could develop into a life-threatening event.

She waved at the boys until she got their attention. "Excuse me. How much did that plate of food cost?"

He gave her a quick look over as he pushed his glasses up the bridge of his nose. "A dollar fifty."

She pulled out a sheet of paper from her bag that had several rows of circles of different sizes. It was given to her by Delano and she'd studied it feverishly for several days. A dollar fifty could be broken down into six quarters, or four quarters and five dimes, or fifteen dimes, or ten dimes and ten nickels, or—

She shook her head. There were too many ways to come up with one dollar and fifty cents. Her stomach growled again, and this time it hurt. She checked the clock on the wall. She had forty minutes for lunch, and she'd already used up half of it.

She closed her eyes and thought about the potato strips with brown sauce. She imagined a small pile of silver coins in front of her. Not a lot, just enough to get a small serving. She wasn't greedy. Just hungry. She imagined the small pile of coins that the boy had put in his backpack. That would be enough. The aroma of food made her stomach growl, and she had to really focus.

It's just a small spell. Money for food.

She opened her eyes, leaned forward and carefully drew lines with the tip of her index finger on the underside of the table. A faint outline of zig-zag lines with a circle appeared on the surface. It wasn't bright enough for anyone to notice, but she watched the other students just in case. A girl at the far end of the cafeteria screamed and the image disappeared. She inhaled and focused again. More shouts from close by broke her concentration again and she exhaled in frustration. Maybe this was for the best. She wasn't supposed to do magic here, but when her stomach growled again, she attempted a third try. The image shone briefly again as she focused on the image in her mind.

Money for food.

She opened her eyes. The sigil was bright and gently blew on it. It broke down into small twinkling pieces that were carried away with the air current and disappeared a few inches above the table.

Now all she had to do was wait!

She opened her small milk carton as a couple of older male students entered the cafeteria. A small group of senior girls waved at them from the next table. The guys were burly, solid teens with football jackets in mahogany and silver. One glanced her way; a quick look from beneath the red quaff hairstyle that swept to one side, but he didn't acknowledge her. They came within a couple of meters of her table when he tripped and fell into the group of boys huddled at the end. Garbage, backpacks, notebooks, trading cards—everything flew back over the table or onto the ground.

The students at the surrounding tables roared with laughter. Evandra's ears perked up at the sound of coins hitting the floor.

The laughter subsided as the boys picked up their stuff. They were shaken and embarrassed, and quickly gathered their things. None of them noticed the small number of coins left on the floor.

Evandra carefully slid the coins closer to her with her foot. She scooped them up, grabbed her pouch and headed for the kitchen.

The lineup was long, and the kitchen area was hot with so many good smells. White boards on the wall listed food items and the price. She mentally counted the coins in her hand. If her calculations were right, she had just enough for a small plate of that wonderful-smelling dish. When it was her turn, she pointed to a tray with food just ahead of her. "I'll have one of those, please."

Her plate of food was put on a tray and handed to her. When she reached the cash register, she picked out the right amount of coins and handed them to the student cashier.

"This smells so good," she said.

"Yeah," the student said, "Fries and gravy are the best here."

She stepped back out into the cafeteria, only to find it full of students. Even her spot at the back was taken. With her stomach still grumbling, she left and headed out into the hall. She walked slowly toward the glass doors, looking for a comfortable place to eat. Outside, the cement seating was full, but a few students were sitting on the ground.

The smell of cigarettes struck her the moment she stepped outside, but it faded as she walked away from the building. Soon all she could smell was the gravy and grease from her lunch. She found a quiet spot on the dirt under one of the trees and ate her food. It tasted just as good as it smelled. She sat back and watched the cheerleaders perform their routine. It looked so fun; tumbling around, and jumping, but the uniforms were a little on the short side.

A female voice broke into her thoughts. "Don't forget to put your garbage in the trash can."

Evandra looked up at a girl about her age. Her long hair was dyed a shocking pink and hung down to the middle of her back with two thin braids dyed bright green at the sides, but she could see blonde roots on top of her head. The clothing she wore looked different than what she'd seen the other students wear. Evandra didn't feel so bad about her outfit anymore.

Evandra blinked. "Pardon?"

The girl pointed at the empty paper plate. "Your garbage. Don't just leave it there. Put it in the trash can."

"Okay." She reached over and picked up the plate. She folded it in two and stuffed it into her paper lunch bag. "Are you the caretaker?"

"No, I'm trying to keep this place clean. People are lazy and they leave their trash all over the place." She crossed her arms. "It's up to each of us to do our part to keep this planet clean."

The girl was so dramatic. Evandra smirked. "Okay."

"It's not funny!"

"Sorry."

Evandra grabbed her bag and stood. The girl was a little taller than her, and she opened her mouth to introduce herself but was cut off by a familiar snarl.

"Oh, *gag* me." The mean blonde and Keith's sister walked toward them. The blonde wore a cheerleader outfit. "If it isn't ugly and uglier." She crossed her arms and stood in a defiant pose. "And look at you Skye. Trying to make friends." She glared at Evandra and looked her over. "Figures you find this freak."

The young girl glared back. "Fuck off, Carla."

The sneer on Carla's lips remained as she and her friend walked past and joined the squad at the edge of the football field.

Evandra stayed quiet until they were out of earshot. "You know her?"

"That's Carla Hanson, and unfortunately, she's my cousin." The young girl kept her focus on the older students and shook her head. "She thinks she's so rad because her family's, like, totally rich, but my mom says money isn't everything and it doesn't make you happy."

"Who's her friend?"

"Shelly Clery."

Evandra remembered how Keith described her. "She's . . . heinous?"

The girl nodded. "Totally."

"Her brother is in my English class."

"Keith? He's cool. We went to the same school." Her face softened. "I'm Skye Daniels."

Evandra smiled. "Evandra Shade."

Skye chuckled. "Wow, and I thought my name was weird."

"It's a family name, but everyone calls me Evie."

"That's worse! What about just Eva?"

Evandra smiled. "I like that."

The class bell rang out and echoed off the outside walls. Both girls headed toward the doors.

"What school'd you go to?"

"I didn't. I stayed at home and my dad taught me."

"Home-schooled?" Skye snorted. "That's what my mom wanted to do, but I said *not*! It's bad enough I had to share my room with my sisters, but to be around them all the time?" Skye opened the door for her. "See ya around, Eva, and don't forget to put your garbage in the bin." She disappeared with the wave of students to the left, leaving Evandra slightly excited and wondering if she'd just made her first friend.

The middle of the afternoon felt more like evening as Eva stepped off the city bus. Her first official day of high school was over, and despite the few rough spots, she counted it as a good day. She even made a few friends, maybe? It amazed her that so many kids went to the same place for education. All the talking and laughing. How did anyone get any lessons done with so many distractions? She cradled her bag in one arm and headed toward a lone street that jutted into a heavily wooded neighbourhood. The bag was stuffed full of papers given to her by her new teachers. It was the only thing she had to carry all the work. At least she didn't have to bring home any of the textbooks they assigned. The one for her geography class weighed a ton.

High limestone walls hid the trunks of centuries-old trees and the residential properties from the rest of the city. There were no sidewalks here, only well-manicured lawns right to the road. The few dozen houses of a contemporary design sat a good distance from each other, allowing for ample space between the wood or stone fences that marked off the property. The street itself looped through the neighbourhood and came close to the shore of Lake Ontario. A large jut of land extended out into the water, with a neglected split-level ranch house set close to the road. It was surrounded by trees and thick brush and looked much older than any of the other houses in the neighbourhood, especially with the crumbling cobblestone walkway that led to the enclosed porch. It was an odd mixture of limestone, brick, and siding with several small windows on one side bricked up.

Between the trees and the homes, the neighbourhood was quiet with only the sound of birds and the breeze in the leaves. Kingston was much smaller than the community she grew up in, but it held a charm about it that Eva could get used to.

She stood in front of her home with its skillion roofs. A large window on the first floor had a dark frame and both it and the front doors were detailed with protective sigils. A horde of small gargoyles were scattered across the wood shingled roofs, hiding in the shadows. She smiled at their clicks and growl sounds, and wondered what the neighbours would think if they ever heard them howl. Gargoyles howled when there was danger, and it was a sound you would never forget.

Lush ivy grew along the banister and trellis of the enclosed balcony. It was so thick that it blocked out most of the sunlight on the porch. The heavy, wood double doors creaked on their metal hinges as she forced them open and stepped inside. From the outside, the house looked spacious and bright, but inside was altogether different. The foyer was large with a library to the left, a parlour to the right, and a curved staircase straight ahead. The parlour connected to a dining room and a hall that led from the foyer to the kitchen at the back of the house. A large fireplace sat in the corner next to the stairs, with two high-back chairs facing the hearth. Wallpaper of heavy Gothic influence covered all the walls on the first floor, and dusty old curtains hung from brass rods over the windows. The staircase had a strip of worn carpet running down the centre, and a large stone archway built into the wall underneath, with a centre made of solid granite.

"Hello?"

The house was quiet. Unusually quiet. Usually, her brother Dominik would play his tunes all day long. Loud, raucous music that her father said could make his ears bleed, so the silence was a nice relief. She walked to the parlour entrance. The old room was packed with furniture just as old and dusty as the rest of the house, with portraits of relatives alive and dead scattered across all four walls.

"Anyone home?"

She turned to head back and came face to face with a black crystal skull the size of her palm mounted on a dark wood walking stick and held by a young man a few years older wearing only pajama pants. His shoulder-length hair was the same raven black as hers and the square of his jaw was sharp. She let out a yelp and jumped back.

His eyes narrowed as he forced the skull closer to her face. Two crimson dots sat in the centre of the eye sockets.

"Did you cast any spells today?"

"Dom!" She slapped the skull away. "Don't point that thing at me. Where's Mom'n Dad?"

His intense stare made his dark eyes look darker. "Dad's not home yet and Mom had to go back to work." He brought the sceptre close to him. "But she brought you a Fae wing pastry. It's on the kitchen table." A smile crept across his lips. "Well, did you?" He held the skull back in front of her. "The *cherep* wants to know."

She gripped the wood below the skull. It was cold. Very cold. Like ice, and a deep chill leech into the palm of her hand. She quickly let it go. How could he hang on to it for so long?

She raised her chin in defiance. "I'm not saying anything."

He held the sceptre close to her again. The crimson dots grew and illuminated the entire sockets. A sly smile creased his lips. "Looks like the *cherep* thinks you did."

Her eyes narrowed as she headed toward the kitchen. She wasn't sure how it knew, but the fact that it did bother her.

"I wouldn't've had to if you didn't put dirt in my food."

Dom followed. "Evie, you know Mom'n Dad will find out." His tone was taunting.

"How? It was so small it wouldn't even be considered a spell."

"Ha! I knew it." The sly smile returned. "Tell that to the Ministry."

The hall opened into a bright but small kitchen with appliances that were close to a century out of date. She dropped her over-stuffed bag on the counter and went to the fridge and pulled out a glass bottle filled with milk.

Dom rested against the door frame. "What was it? A rune? A friendship spell? A curse?"

She opened the cupboard next to him and removed a glass.

"What do you care?"

"I'm just curious."

She looked over her brother with skepticism and then poured

milk into the glass. "Why don't I believe you? Oh right, because you put dirt in my food."

Dom brought the skull close to his face and examined the crystal.

"Lighten up, Evie. It was just a joke."

"I didn't think it was very funny."

"That's because you don't have a sense of humour." He walked over to the counter and pulled out some of the sheets of paper from her pouch. "What's all this?"

"That's called homework." She put the bottle back in the fridge. A spark of excitement raced through her. "Lessons I have to finish at home, and I have to buy supplies for my classes." She walked over and pulled out a small piece of paper. "These are all the things I need. Lined paper, coloured pencils, pens, binders—"

"You need all of that?"

She sat down at the kitchen table in front of a plate of ornately decorated cookie. "I guess."

There was a look of contempt as he leaned over the table. "You told Mom 'n Dad you researched all of this. That you knew what it was all about. How could you not know about purchasing all these supplies, Evie?"

She pulled apart the delicate pastry, trying to avoid his glare. "I knew I'd have to buy *some* things, but this is a lot more than I thought there would be."

"Well, you'd better not quit. Not after they buy all these supplies."

"I won't."

"You sure about that? Seems like this high school might be more difficult than you thought." He grabbed her class schedule. "Are these your lessons?"

"Yes."

He was quiet as he looked over them. "I don't know, Evie. Looks like a lot to handle. You might not be ready to do this."

She snatched the schedule from his fingers. Her eyes narrowed. "I said I would do it, and I will."

His sly smile crept across his lips as he sat at the table next to her. "Okay, but don't say I didn't warn you."

"I *can* do this."

"Care to make a wager on that?"

Eva perked up. "What kind?"

He put the sceptre on the table and relaxed into the chair. "Well, if you quit before you've finished the school year, you have to—" He glanced around the room. "—do all my chores for a whole year."

Eva mulled the idea over. She hated chores, especially cleaning, and she couldn't cast spells to clean either. It was disrespectful to *Sem'ya* to clean using magic. She went to speak but Dom cut her off.

"But I still get my allowance."

Eva's mouth dropped open. "That's not fair!"

"Seems fair enough to me."

She clenched her jaw. "Fine, but if I do the whole school year—" She thought about what he would do. It had to be something he didn't like. Something that she knew he wouldn't do unless forced. A smile creased her lips. "You have to take me out to dinner."

He snorted. "That's it?"

"At a really fancy place *here*. In this world. No Mom 'n Dad. Just you and me. And we have to dress up."

He looked as though she'd punched him in the gut before the devilish look returned. "Okay, it's a deal, but I'm making this so you can't back out." He jumped up and grabbed a knife from the block. He poked the index finger of his left hand with the tip. A small drop of blood beaded on the wound as he took her right hand and turned it palm up. With the tip of his finger, he drew a sigil on her palm in blood. Once he was done, he handed her the knife. "You still want to do this?"

Eva cautiously took the handle and pricked her finger. A Blood Oath was one of the strongest forms of magic, and it meant that he was serious about his bet, which meant she had to be just as serious. To break a Blood Oath spell would bring harsh consequences. The worst she heard was some poor boy who lost the ability to speak for a whole year after making an oath with a friend about keeping a secret. He could make noises and everything, just couldn't form words.

He tilted his head to one side. "Having second thoughts?"

She grabbed his right hand and turned it palm up.

"You're going to buy me dinner."

She pricked her finger and traced the same sigil on his palm, and they held their hands just inches from each other. Dom took his injured finger and circled their hands as he spoke.

"Blood is blood. Blood is light. I bind my blood to seal this rite."

Light emanated from the tip of his finger and swirled around their hands a few times before it disappeared.

Eva held out her pricked finger and moved it in the opposite direction.

"Blood is blood. Blood is light. I bind my blood to seal this rite."

The sigils glowed a deep amber before their hands slammed together. They closed their eyes. Eva imagined her and Dom out at a fancy dinner. They laughed and ate fancy food, and she drank a fizzy drink in a tall glass. She smiled. She'd make this happen.

Their hands were forced open, and Eva shivered as the sigil disappeared into her skin.

Dom rubbed the centre of his palm. "I'll give it two months, tops, before you give up."

"You better do your homework on restaurants," She rubbed the palm of her hand. "And put cherep back before Dad finds out you

23

were trying to use it on me, or he'll never let you leave the house again."

He scoffed. "I'd never use it on you, and besides, his magic isn't that strong. He'd never know I touched his stuff."

"He will, Dom and he said he'd punish us if he found out we did."

Cherep was Black Magic, and it bothered her that it was in the house, even if it was locked up with protection charms. Eva had seen the artifact when she helped unpack. Her parents didn't say a lot about it, just that it was dangerous and not to be toyed with.

Dom scoffed and got up from the table. "Yeah, well Dad says a lot of things and then doesn't follow through."

Eva rolled her eyes and sat back at the table. "What does that mean?"

"Nothing, just that he said he'd talk to Minister Jarsdale about his offer of apprenticeship with the council but didn't."

"He's busy with his new position." She took a bite from the pastry. "He's a senior field agent now. He's got a lot on his plate."

"He's not that busy." Dom strolled to the exit as he examined the sceptre again. "Delano's father had that same job and still had time to look after his son's interests." His eyes flared as he spoke. "He's stalling because he knows I have a shot at becoming someone really important in the realm. Something he could never be." He turned away from her. "He's a weak Spellcaster, and everyone knows the only way he got that job was because Delano's father retired and recommended him." His anger boiled over. "He's holding me back because he doesn't want me to make him look bad!" He curled his fist and hit the wall.

The house groaned and banged as chilling wails echoed from behind the walls. The paint in the kitchen went from faded yellow to dark red, and Eva quickly ran to a wall and stroked the surface. Dom backed slowly into the kitchen doorway.

"It's okay," she said, placing her cheek against the wall and closing her eyes, "You know he doesn't mean any disrespect when he lashes out like this."

Dom nodded his head vigorously, watching the walls as they shifted into darker shades of red. "I'm sorry, Sem'ya. I really am." He put the sceptre on the counter and went to touch the wall. A small charge of electricity snapped out from the surface and hit Dom's palm. The young man yelped in pain and rubbed the center of his hand. "Please forgive me. I didn't mean to hurt you."

The pictures on the walls shook as the house shuddered and returned to normal. Dom cautiously stepped back into the kitchen and picked up the sceptre as Eva relaxed but kept stroking the wall.

"You have to control your temper."

Dom didn't reply, but stared into the skull and then turned and quickly left the room.

Skylark Eloise Lorelei Daniels let several tubes of rolled cardboard drop to the ground as she got out of the front passenger side of her parents green Ford LTD station wagon. Her four siblings scrabbled out almost the moment her father stopped the car and were halfway up to the old farmhouse before she'd opened the door.

As far as first days go, this one wasn't bad. She'd had worse, like the first day of sixth grade when a female classmate put gum in her hair. She said it was an accident, but Skye never really believed that.

She stepped out of the car and threw her backpack over one shoulder. All her classes sounded so interesting. Canadian History, English. She especially loved her art class and was thrilled when the teacher said she could come in during her lunch and use the supplies to finish up assignments. Not like middle school where all the paints and equipment were locked up and the teachers grilled you on why you wanted to do art outside of class. High school teachers didn't treat you like a baby, and that made her feel a little more grown up.

"Hey kiddo, need a hand carrying all that in?" Lennon Daniels was of average height, a little too round in the middle, with puffy jowls and a receding hairline of light brown hair. Skye got her bright green eyes from him, as well as the gap in her two front teeth, but that was about it. His blue short-sleeved shirt was a few shades lighter than his Bermuda shorts and the car keys jingled in his hand as he walked.

She bent down and grabbed the posters off the ground. "Naw, I got it."

He walked past her and toward the front door. "Good, and don't let me see them lying around the house either. You're in high school now. You're responsible for this stuff. You're too old to have your mother and I constantly cleaning up after you."

The Daniels' home was a mixture of old-world meets last century with a hint of the twentieth century for good measure. The right half of the house was a story and a half made of limestone with one medium sized framed window next to the entrance and a smaller one right above the front door. The old tin roof slanted toward the front of the house with the dormer sitting very close to the edge. The left side was also a story and a half but built with red brick that started a foot from the entrance. This side of the house had a large colonial slider window covered with plants on the inside, and the worn, black, shingled roof extended as far back as the tin, and right in the center of the roof was an addition covered in tan siding with a newer-looking shingled roof. The foundation was covered by bushes that had grown wild and matched the front lawn of field grass and wildflowers with a smattering of odd toys for good measure.

A large old barn and several smaller buildings sat two hundred metres from the house. A small herd of goats and a mule wandered around a closed pen attached to the barn, while some chickens clucked in the adjacent coop, and it all sat on twenty acres of property covered in oak, maple, and ash with a handful of evergreens dotted in between. To the north sat a conservation area, the airport to the east, and had a beautiful view of the Saint Lawrence River to the south. Other than the animals, the only other sound was the wind in the trees and crickets in the long grass, until an airplane flew overhead.

The front door opened into a large kitchen with a long dining room table just to the right and cupboards with the fridge and stove at the back. The large front closet with bi-fold doors was overflowing with boots, coats, and backpacks that spilled out onto the doormat. To the left of the closet sat the curved entrance to the living room with a narrow set of stairs that lead to the second floor at the back of the kitchen behind the closet. The inside still had a lot of its original structure with wood beams and hand-crafted mouldings along the door frames worn with age, but along with the old, faded wallpaper in the kitchen, it all added to the charm of the home. A large stone fireplace sat against the west wall in the living room. The red brick of the hearth was visible through the black scorching and was deep-set and trimmed in dark wood. A chocolate brown sectional was positioned south to face the TV floor cabinet and the stereo system, and Mr. Daniels was already seated in his favourite lounge chair in front of the television.

"There she is!" Melody Daniels flipped some of her permed, blonde hair past her shoulders, but a few wispy bangs fell over her forehead. Her large glasses did nothing to enhance her small eyes, and only accented the fact her nose came to a bit of a point. Skye looked a lot like her. All except for the eyes.

"And how was your first day of high school?" She smiled and walked to the dining room table with a plate of cookies in her hands. A bright streak of pink stained a small portion of her hair and started just behind her ear. Skye chalked up her flare for dramatics, which included a multitude of different hair colours, along with her blonde hair, from her mother.

"Good. I found a couple places where I could set up my protest." Skye dropped her backpack on the floor next to all the others and walked toward the stairs. "And I can work on my posters in art class."

"Skye," Her mother's voice hung on the vowel as she turned from the table and put one hand on her hip. "Just remember what we talked about."

Skye slumped a bit as she reached the bottom of the stairs. "I promise I won't do anything to get into trouble."

"Good. You're in high school now, and you have to be more mature and act responsible."

Skye rolled her eyes. "Geez, Mom, I know."

She hurried up the stairs before her mother could say anything else. Just because she'd had a few 'incidents' last year didn't mean the same would happen this year. It was a new school with new students, and none of them would burst into tears if they saw her posters with depictions of dead animals on them. She could draw whatever she wanted now.

Skye's room was a few feet longer than it was wide, with enough room to fit a twin bed, a dresser, a desk and a few other furnishings comfortably. A small table sat in the corner with a record player on top and a milk crate on the floor next to it, full of record albums. She dropped the cardboard posters on the floor in front of the window and grabbed a shoe box from her open closet. She took one of the sheets of cardboard and unrolled it on her desk. There were a few outlines of wounded animals and one hand-drawn picture of the Earth. Lines with stenciled words made up the bulk of the poster, and she carefully traced out one of the letters in black.

The sound of a pot slammed against the counter downstairs echoed in the stairwell. A moment later her father's voice bellowed something from the living room, followed by her mother yelling back. Skye stopped tracing and stared at the cardboard. This had to be a record for them. He wasn't home ten minutes and already they were fighting.

The argument got louder until it sounded like they were fighting right at the bottom of the stairs. She noticed her four siblings hanging around the swing set not really doing anything, looking upset. They could hear them too, even through the stone walls and she wished, just for once, they'd fight where she couldn't hear. Skye got up from her desk and slammed the door to her room.

Eva sat at the antique writing desk in the library and read the math sheet in front of her. A dozen loose notes sat in a messy pile at the head of the desk. Geography, science, math, history—these were subjects she didn't know existed until now, and her mind reeled from information overload. What was the Canadian Shield? How did the Hudson's Bay Company come into being? She picked up one of her math sheets.

"If Johnny got on Train A in Toronto and headed west at two-hundred kilometres per hour, and Tommy got on Train B in Kingston travelling east at one-hundred kilometres per hour, how long would it take for them to pass each other?" She frowned. "Where are they going? Do they know each another?"

She lowered the paper and turned to the entrance. It was hard to focus on her homework. Dom's outburst bothered her. They'd been here almost two months and he just got worse every day. He lashed out at her and had been mouthy to their parents, but today was the first time he'd disrespected Sem'ya. That was something you just didn't do. She stood up and headed for the stairs. He was a pain, but maybe there was something she could do to help?

The second floor held a half dozen rooms, with cream-coloured heavy drapes over each door frame. There were four bedrooms on the floor, and each had their own bathroom. The remaining two doors were always locked. Dom's room was at the far end. He said he wanted to be away from everyone else, and at first, she thought he was kidding as their bedrooms in their other home were next to each other. Now, things were different.

She stared at the black drapes around the entrance to his room. They were ripped in places, frayed at the bottom and barely attached to the black, wrought iron rods bolted into the frame. She glanced back at her doorway. Sem'ya slowly turned the curtains around the frame from a dark to a pale orange. Her confidence was waning today, but she figured everyone did on the first day at a new school.

A radio announcer's voice boomed from inside his room. She gently knocked on his door.

"Dom?"

His footsteps were heavy, and they didn't come anywhere near the door.

She knocked harder. "Dom!"

The shadow under the door moved closer. He swung it open and glared at her.

"What do you want?"

"Is everything okay?"

He scrunched up his face. "What do you care?"

"I know you're mad at Dad, but he doesn't deserve it."

His dark eyes narrowed. "You sure about that?"

She snorted. "I get it, you're mad because he hasn't talked to Minister Jarsdale, but this is important, and he just wants to make sure it's the right path for you." She glanced around his room. "And Dad's promotion. Do you think moving here was an easy decision for them? Transversing Sem'ya from our old place to here? Having to be out interacting on the outside?"

He stormed toward her. "You really think Mom wanted to up-root Sem'ya from our *ancestral home* and live in some crumbling old house on the outside?"

Her temper flared. "He's a field agent, Dom. Do you think he had a choice? His job requires him to be here. Mom knows that."

"Yeah, well I don't have to be here."

"Then go back to Wynden. You can live with Delano for all I care. Go back and live with them and accept your stupid job."

His temper calmed as he walked over and fell back onto his large double bed. "I can't. Dad put a charm on the portal. Only him and Mom can go through."

Eva was shocked. "What? When?"

"After I got here. He *claims* the doorway's not stable, but I don't see him doing anything to fix it."

"How would you know? You lock yourself away in your room all day. Maybe he did fix it."

"I doubt it." He bounced off the bed and went to his record player. He removed the record and tossed the cover on the bed. He carefully placed the needle on the vinyl. "Now Minister Jarsdale will be looking for a new intern and my life is over."

Before she could speak, the room filled with the raging sound of electric guitars. Dom jumped around the room thrashing his head from side to side. Eva left, not wanting to get thrown into a wall. The door slammed behind her. At least she had an idea of what was bothering him.

She went downstairs and sat in one of the old chairs near the fireplace, confused by her father's actions. It didn't make sense. She thought their father would be excited that Dom was offered such a good position. Minister Jarsdale was a well-respected person with connections all over the magical realm. Dom would do very well under him.

The House groaned around her. Different tones and muffled sounds came across as drawn-out words that she thought she could understand. Her father once told her it was Sem'ya's way of talking to other ancestral homes, but not in this neighbourhood. There was an inter-dimensional connection between all ancestral homes, and as far as she knew, her home was the only one in this city. Which meant they were the only Spellcaster family too.

A soft chime rang out from a small wooden box high on the wall. Moments later, the granite centre of the old archway near the fireplace dissolved into a light blue whirlpool of energy. With a flash, a well-dressed, middle-aged man came through the portal. His expensive-looking grey suit was hidden under a grey cloak of the same material, and his raven-coloured hair was neatly slicked back and as dark as the well-trimmed facial hair. He held a walking stick in his hand with a large clear crystal embedded at the top. His brow rose when he noticed Eva in the chair.

"*Malyshka*," he said, and placed his walking stick in a nearby holder. His Russian accent was refined and soft. "You are waiting for us? Is something wrong?"

"No." Eva stood and hugged him. "I just like to sit down here and think."

Egori Shade frowned at his daughter. "Thinking is good."

"I know what's bothering Dom."

He nodded and headed down the hall. "Good. Tell your mother. She is at her wits' end with him."

The portal appeared again and this time a woman emerged. Her long brown hair was neatly swept back into a loose, messy braid that draped over her shoulder, and her one-piece pantsuit was more shoulder pads and belt. Her patchwork cloak was embroidered at the seams and hem, and the gold thread glimmered in the light of the room. A look of frustration on Venera Shade's face turned soft when she saw her daughter.

"Eva? How was your first day at the high school?"

"Good, but I need a few things for my classes."

She kissed Eva on the top of her head. "Can we find them in Wynden?"

"I don't think so."

They walked to the parlour. "That's fine. Your father exchanged some coins at Delano mercantile today. You can go out later." She motioned her daughter to sit with her. "Is the school all you hoped it would be? Did you make any friends?"

"The school is very confusing, but I think I made a friend, maybe, and an enemy."

Her mother waved the comment away. "Oh, don't say that."

"It's true. A girl by the name of Carla. She and her friend Shelly are just totally *heinous*."

Venera looked confused. "I beg your pardon?"

"Mean."

"They didn't hurt you, did they?"

"No."

"Do you want us to speak with the principal about these girls?"

"No that's okay. They're older so I won't come across them again."

"Good but remember your promise. No spellcasting."

She swallowed. "I won't."

A loud crash came from the kitchen and Venera winced. "Egori? Everything all right?"

There was a bit more commotion before her husband answered. "Sem'ya still will not allow the metal cooking box to ignite." His footsteps hurried down the hall and stopped a few feet from the entrance to the parlour, looking slightly frustrated. "Remind me again why preparing meals in our home is easier?"

"Sem'ya will get used to the new accommodation." She smiled sympathetically at her husband. "Meal preparation is different here, remember? We can't go out for all our meals."

He glanced back at the kitchen. "Then dinner will be late." He nodded toward his daughter. "Did Evie tell you she has discovered the nature of our son's bad mood?"

Eva exhaled. "He's mad because he lost the apprenticeship under Minister Jarsdale, and he's blaming it on Dad."

Egori's brow rose as he headed toward the stairs. "Then perhaps it is time he and I had a chat."

Venera looked worried. "Go easy on him, Love. He doesn't understand."

"Then I will make my reasons clear." Egori headed to the top of the stairs. "He is an adult now. He needs to stop sulking like a child."

Eva watched her father head upstairs. "What is he telling him?"

"The right things, I hope." Venera stood and motioned her

daughter to follow her. "Why don't we see if we can convince Sem'ya to start the stove, and you can tell me what you need for school."

Chapter Two

The second week of school ended on a muggy note. Temperatures were well into the hot and sticky range, which made sitting in a classroom almost unbearable. Every window in Eva's geography class was open, but the barely existent breeze was just as uncomfortable.

Eva's desk was right next to an open window that faced the busy roadway in front of the school. Outside, students dodged traffic to get to the burger place on the other side. Everyone went there, but she hadn't mustered the courage to go over yet. Especially by herself. A car honked and was met with shouts and a slew of swear words that were more than audible. She smiled at the wave of laughter that followed.

"Eva," a male voice whispered from the desk behind hers. "Do you have a maroon pencil crayon I could borrow?"

She blinked a few times to allow her eyes to adjust to the classroom light before she looked down at the rainbow of pencils next to a photocopied map outline of the world in front of her.

"Will wine do?"

The young boy shrugged. "I suppose."

She turned in her seat and glanced down at his map. "Brad, you've got seven different colours. There's supposed to be five. One for each continent."

Brad Carlson was a slightly portly teen with a good complexion and brown eyes and hair that was combed off to one side. He dressed nicely, with button-down shirts and dress pants. She rarely saw him in jeans like the other boys and was polite to her and very smart.

He didn't make eye contact as he shaded in the black outline of South America. "I don't care what the teacher says. There are seven continents, not five."

"But he's the geography teacher."

His dark eyes watched her for a moment. "Well, he's wrong."

Eva gazed at the wisps of facial hair on his top lip. They looked uneven and there was a slight rash under his chin.

"Did you shave?"

Brad's coloured pencil froze, and he kept his focus on the worksheet. "Maybe."

"Will it grow in thicker now?"

He started colouring again. "I hope so."

Eva sensed the teacher's presence behind her. "Is there something interesting on Mr. Carlson's desk?" His voice was deep and very irritated.

She turned back and faced forward. "No, sir."

"Then it must be Mr. Carlson you're interested in."

A few of her classmates giggled and Eva felt her face grow hot. She hunched down over her worksheet and forced herself to ignore the snickers. When the class ended, the room erupted into a chaotic mixture of conversation and laughter. Eva tossed her worksheets into her binder and raced for the door, but the swell of students in the hall blocked her from making a fast exit and was forced into a slow march down the corridor to the stairs.

She hurried through the main foyer and down the corridor to the right. A light odour of engine oil and sawdust permeated the hall at the end. She broke free of the wave and stood in front of her locker. It was just down the hall from both the cafeteria and the grotto.

Someone shoved her hard against her locker, and her head hit the metal door hard.

"Loser."

From the corner of her eye, she watched Carla pass with a group of girls and head toward the cafeteria. The blonde looked back and gave her a nasty look as the others around her laughed. Eva clenched her jaw and tried hard not to spell cast something nasty at her. Maybe if she told her parents what was going on, they'd let her have an exception.

She rotated the lock combination, threw open the locker door and exchanged binders and textbooks. If she didn't have to visit her locker so much, she could avoid Carla. She reached into her new blue and red Adidas bag and pulled out her black material pouch. Inside was a small amber glass jar. There were a dozen small white pills inside, and she popped one into her mouth. Her head hurt from the impact with the locker, and she pressed her forehead against the metal.

A female voice spoke beside her. "You sick?"

She kept her head on the locker but turned toward the voice. "No."

Tina Salisbury was a pretty brunette with a round face and long brown hair that was pinned back with a couple of barrettes. They were assigned as locker partners in Homeroom, but they never really talked much. Tina tilted her head to one side, eyeing Eva with a look of irritation. "Are you done?"

Eva moved away and the girl stepped up to the locker. "Yes."

"Oh, is it okay if my friend puts some of her books in here too?"

Tina dumped her things on the bottom shelf. "She's got a class down here and it's easier for her to come here instead of going all the way back to her locker."

"Sure, I guess."

"I'll give her the combination, so she doesn't need me to get it."

"We're not supposed to give people the number."

Tina scrunched up her face. "Then how is she supposed to get her stuff?"

"Can't you just get it for her?"

Her face melted into a look of sarcasm. "Um, no, I just told you why."

She grabbed a binder, shut the locker and left without saying another word.

Eva's stomach growled. The line-up in the cafeteria was short and she got in before the lunch rush swelled the kitchen. Fries and gravy were her favourite now, and this time, she brought her own money. The dining area was full with just a few seats at a table at the back of the room, but the cheerleading squad and the junior and senior football teams were taking up most of the tables and made it hard to get through. She headed for a small opening between the junior team at one table, and seniors at another. She was almost through when her path was blocked by one of the cheerleaders.

"Well look who it is."

Up close, Carla stood a few inches taller than her and smelled of stale cigarette smoke. She put her hands on her hips as her eyes narrowed. "I have a question. If I dump water on you, will you melt?"

A roar of laughter from the students around them brought a smug grin to Carla's face.

Eva's jaw muscles tightened as she stared at her. The promise she made to her parents rolled through her mind, but the temptation to make all of Carla's blonde hair fall out was growing.

"Aw, did I upset you?" Carla's voice dripped with sarcasm. "Maybe you should find another place to eat." She held up her arms to her side. "Since the entire cafeteria is full."

"Yeah," Shelly said, and stood next to her friend, "Maybe you should go outside and eat."

Carla feigned a surprised look. "That's a great idea. Eat outside—" Her face went hard. "—with all the other losers."

There was another round of laughter.

Eva clenched her jaw and forced herself to calm her growing anger. She turned but was blocked by a few of the older football players, and for the first time, wished her older brother was here. Dom might be a butthead, but he'd take care of these guys, and it wouldn't involve magic. After a few more taunts, the football players let her pass and she raced to the cafeteria doors and down the hall to the glass doors.

The Grotto was full of students. Most were smoking but there were a few who were eating. She disliked eating outside. All she had to sit on was either the ground or the cement seating and both were uncomfortable. There was no shelter from the elements other than the trees. It seemed almost barbaric. She found a spot on the steps of the large doors that led to the auto shop and put her food on her lap. She loved fries and gravy, but she was too upset to enjoy it and had to force herself to eat.

On the far side of the grotto, the girl she met yesterday—Skye—was setting up some kind of display. Eva watched as the teen battled with homemade cardboard signs with hand-drawn pictures of the planet, animals, and sea life. Other students watched her with bored curiosity. Eva stood with her plate of fries and walked over.

"What are you doing?"

Skye turned and one of her posters fell over. "Setting up my protest."

Eva read a few of the posters. "What are you protesting?"

"We're ruining the planet!" Skye put down a cardboard poster next to a megaphone and reached for a stack of printouts near an old, worn backpack. "Did you know we're killing the planet with acid rain?"

Eva blinked a few times. "No, I didn't."

Skye handed her one of the sheets. "It's caused by gasoline from cars. You know that blue smoke that comes out of the tailpipe? That floats up into the clouds and comes down as acid rain."

Eva read over the first few lines on the sheet. "Really? I've never heard of it before."

Skye was astonished. "Where have you been? It's been going on for, like, decades." Skye turned back to her display. "It's all over the news."

Eva handed back the paper. "I don't watch the news."

The teen shot her a disgusted look and didn't take the sheet back. "Then maybe you should. Every day another lake dies because of acid rain, and if we don't do something now, the whole planet will die."

Skye put up another poster with a hand drawn picture of a lake. Small fish with 'x's over their eyes floated on the surface. "Some scientists think that's what happened to Venus." She turned to Eva. "Do you want our planet to end up like Venus?"

"No," Eva said, barely above a whisper.

There was a wild look in her eyes. "Then stand with me and we'll boycott all the products that pump out acid rain."

Carla and Shelly walked past them toward the far end of the grotto. Skye grabbed the megaphone and brought it to her mouth. "Like fancy cars!"

Carla turned and gave them the finger.

Skye went back to her posters. "I can't believe you've never heard about what's going on with the lakes."

Eva opened her mouth to reply, but Skye spoke instead.

"Look, if you don't believe me, ask your parents. They watch the news, right?"

"I guess?"

"Trust me, they're adults. They watch the news. Ask them about it."

Eva nodded and walked back to her spot on the cement step. She read over the sheet. It had several paragraphs about what caused acid rain and how it destroyed the environment. There were several pictures of dead animals scattered through the text. Animals that looked like something had burned them. The caption under each claimed they died from drinking poisonous water. She dropped what was left of her lunch in the garbage. She didn't feel like eating anymore.

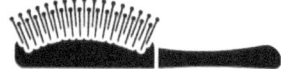

Eva sat on her bed and stared at the ceiling. Several multi-coloured swirls shimmered and distorted across the surface, but she wasn't paying attention. Her mind still held the crude images of burnt animals, and Skye's words echoed in her ears. Was this acid rain really a thing? Why hadn't she heard of it before now? The Regency Council had to know this was going on. It was too big for them not to know.

She sat up and went to her window. Outside, the clouds moved slowly across the sky. Above the clouds was the stratosphere, and the more she thought about it, the more it frightened her. She went to her bag, found the flyer and ran out of her room.

Halfway down the stairs, she saw Dom sitting in the parlour. "Where's Mom 'n Dad?"

"At work." He didn't look up from the large, leather-bound book he was reading. "Why?"

She held out the sheet of paper. "Do you know about this?"

Dom gave it a quick look over. "What is it?"

"There's a girl at school who says acid rain is killing all the lakes and if we don't do something about it, it's going to kill everything on the planet."

He closed the book and leaned forward. "Really?"

"Yes. She says there's proof too."

Dom closed his eyes as he struggled to find his words. "Proof it's going to kill everything or proof that it's real?"

"Yes!"

He frowned and looked slightly confused. "Who said this?"

"Skye, a girl from the high school. She's handing out papers and doing a protest about it at school and said I should ask Mom 'n Dad about it."

"But they're not here."

"I know!" Eva exhaled in frustration and flopped down in the Queen Anne love seat across from him. "Did they say when they'd be home?"

Dom shook his head and picked up the book. "Not until late."

"Do you think the Council knows?"

He shrugged.

She folded the paper back up and stuffed it in the pocket of her sweater.

"Dad would know for sure. He has to report to the Under-Secretary for the Council of Ministers. He *has* to know if this is true or not." She sat up. "Maybe that's why he works late all the time?"

Dom grunted an acknowledgment, and that was the end of their conversation.

Eva took a slow look around the parlour. In between the family portraits, a marble fireplace housed two mahogany curio cabinets. One housed several more books like the one Dom was reading, while the second held small old knick-knacks. She couldn't help but think that all these things would be destroyed.

Dom peered at her from over the top of the book. "Why are you still here?"

"Can't I just sit here?"

"No. Go sit someplace else and leave me alone."

Eva stormed out of the parlour and toward the portal arch. "Maybe I'll just go talk to them." She grabbed a dark blue cloak from the wooden coat rack that stood a few feet away from the arch and swung it around her shoulders.

"Dad's charm is still active." Dom's voice taunted her from behind his book.

Eva scrunched up her face. "Still?" She reached out and touched the granite centre of the archway. She glanced at him over her shoulder. "So, you haven't been through yet?"

"No, I went through yesterday."

"But you just said—"

"Dad said it was stable, but he's leaving the charm on, just in case."

She drew a sigil on the surface of the granite. The image burned a bright orange-red as smoke billowed up from the mark. Within moments it was gone. Nothing happened. She frowned.

"What happened?"

Dom let out a frustrated sigh. "I *just* told you. Dad's charm is still active."

She walked back over to the parlour and flopped down in the Queen Anne chair again.

"So, I can't go, but you can? That's not fair."

"Life never is."

She watched him for a moment. "Will you open it and come with me?"

He frowned over the top of his book. "Why?"

"Because I really need to talk to them, and you need to get out."

"I don't like going out."

"Since when? You went out all the time in Wynden."

"Maybe I had more things to do."

Eva looked sorrowfully at him. "Just get me through the door-way, please!"

He slammed the book shut and stood. "Fine, I'll take you through, but you can go to the Crypt yourself."

Eva let out a squeal and headed for the doorway again.

Dom followed. "The sigil's changed and I've only done it once, so it might not open right away." His sigil took a straight line left and then a sharp right with a few lines and a circle. The image glowed white, and a light blue dot churned from the seams of the wood until it engulfed the granite. It swirled in the centre and spread out within the frame.

Eva jumped toward the exit, but Dom grabbed her before she had a chance to pass through.

"Hold up," he said, as he draped a black cloak over his shoul-ders. "I opened the portal. I get to go first."

She swatted his hand away. "I don't think so."

She rushed through the doorway before Dom could grab her again.

Passing through the portal sent a slight chill and the sensation of bubbles bursting along the length of her body under the cloak. She felt the currents of energy tug on her. The ebb and flow of the barrier between worlds, and if she didn't have the cloak on, it would pull her off her chosen destination set by the Rune and drag her to parts unknown. The cloaks were enchanted and were the only thing that kept travellers safe through a dimensional portal. The journey lasted only a few moments, and she knew well enough to keep going forward until she felt the warmth of the other side on her face.

The portal opened into a small foyer with stone walls and exposed wood beams. It was constructed during Medieval times and was the house her ancestors lived in when they were indoctrinated into the realm. It was one of the oldest houses in town, and for a while, was a part of a historical walkabout for visiting citizens. She walked to the entrance of the rustic parlour to her left. Large windows opened up to a view of the property from two sides, something she was told was done by her grandfather's mother, so she could have flowers bloom inside. To her right, a spiral stone staircase led to a second floor with the stairs continuing on to the basement. Two chairs sat in front of a large stone hearth, identical to the ones that sat in the front hall of the other house. The walls were bare, but the windows were draped in a sheer material that hung to the floor, and a thin layer of dust had settled on all surfaces.

Eva paused and looked around. This had been their home for as long as she could remember. She hurried through the foyer and out a set of heavy wooden front doors. The building was small compared to the others around it, with colourful, flowery bushes, overgrown herbs, and ornamental trees that followed a slate stone walkway to a wooden gate. There wasn't much property connected to the building and was surrounded by a tall stone wall. Other homes were visible beyond the canopy of trees that scattered the property, and it gave some privacy from the neighbours.

Eva pulled on the wrought-iron rings and opened the gate. The narrow tree-lined street had a few pedestrians, with bright coloured flowers in planters next to tall oak and maple trees. None of the other houses along her street were the same as hers. Most were constructed in the Georgian or Victorian style and were grand in their design. Their ancestral home looked as out of place as their home in Kingston.

The aroma of baked goods hung in the air from the bakery at the end of the street. There were several food shops lined up in a row on either side of the bakery and offered everything from full-course meals with dining rooms, to small treat and drink stands. A large Victorian-era courtyard lay in behind and was a bustle of activity. Colourful birds chirped from the canopy and the gas streetlamps flickered and came to life. She felt the tension drain from her as she walked toward the far end of the street and a stone bridge. Off in the distance, tall, spindled buildings cut into the skyline, with dozens of narrow streets that branched outward from the center; each with a courtyard and adjacent eateries. The farther from the spiralled buildings, the larger the property lots became. This was Wynden, and she felt as though she hadn't been here in years.

She turned to Dom as he came up beside her. "I miss this place."

He tugged on her shirt. "Come on. I'll show you a shortcut."

They walked a few side streets that took them farther from the main road, and the farther they went, the quieter it became until the only sound was evening insects. The last path led down into a ravine, and the back of a building that barely rose above the trees. The atmosphere here was heavy. Eva stopped short of the heavy stone staircase that led to a wrought-iron gate.

"Where are we?"

"The back entrance." He pushed her. "Go on. You wanted to see Mom."

"Maybe I'll just wait for her out here."

He gave her another shove. "Oh, no. You wanted to see her, so go see her."

She stared at the heavy gate lock. "I'm scared."

"Don't be a baby. Nothing's going to hurt you." He stepped right up behind her. "Although, I did hear that some bodies are buried close to the steps, and sometimes they reach out and grab people."

He grabbed her hand and Eva let out a scream. She turned and slapped him hard on the arm. "Not funny!"

"I'm just joking. Go on. Nothing'll grab you."

"Will you come with me?"

"No."

"Then wait here till I get down there."

He exhaled and nodded.

With each step down the air grew heavy and damp. The musty smell of dead vegetation along with dirt swirled around her and she kept a close eye on the sides of the stairs. A few of the rocks that made up the wall were missing, and in her imagination, hands reached out to grab her. Her heart pounded wildly by the time she reached the bottom and the heavy gate.

"Okay, I'm—" She turned to the top of the stairs, but Dom was gone. "Jerk."

She pulled the string that rang a bell on the other side. She turned back and stared at the stair walls. The late afternoon sky quickly seeped into twilight, and she pressed herself closer to the gate.

"Evandra?"

Eva jumped at the mention of her name and turned to face a middle-aged man on the other side. He was short, not much taller than her, with thinning hair that barely covered his head and emphasized the roundness of his face.

"Mr. Nithercott. I didn't hear you walk up."

The old man genuinely surprised. "Evandra Shade? What are you doing here?"

"I came to see my mother. That's allowed."

"Yes, I know, but why didn't you come in through the *front* door?"

Eva scrunched up her face, trying to look bashful. "Because Dom showed me a shortcut?"

With a loud clang, Mr. Nithercott unlocked the gate. "Still, that's no reason to come in the back entrance." He stepped to one side and let her walk past. "There's no way you'd catch me coming in the back gate at this time of the day." He closed the gate behind her. "Walking down those steps at night? It's enough to set your imagination off."

As unsettling as the back entrance to the Crypt was, once Eva got inside the building it was a whole different atmosphere. The large antechamber was full of shelves with potions and dried herbs. Dozens of candles flickered in their holders on the walls in between glass canisters. A large cauldron sat in the middle of the room in its cradle, with the fire underneath burning low. The strong smell of sandalwood and rosemary filled the air, and Eva inhaled the scent as she marvelled at the shelves.

"Your mother is busy trying to prepare someone for internment," Mr. Nithercott said as he strolled past her.

"Maybe I shouldn't disturb her."

"Oh, no. She's having a heck of a time with him. Maybe you could convince her to leave it for the night and go home." He turned to one of the shelves. "He'll still be here in the morning."

Eva frowned. "Why is she having a hard time?"

"I'm not sure, but sometimes it's harder with younger guests."

Mr. Nithercott's posture slumped. "The young always have a hard time dealing with death."

He walked to a worktable and rolled open a scroll. "A strong young man, too. From what his family has told us, he was a bit of a recluse in life, and usually, all that bravado and arrogance dissolves when they detach from their physical body."

He picked up a quill and dipped it into a small vial of red ink. "The fact he refuses to tell her what he was doing hunting down an *Amarok* troubles me." He lifted the quill from the parchment. "Perhaps if I speak with the creature itself."

He carefully placed the quill back in its holder. "Excuse me. I need to do some reading. Your mother is down the corridor to the right. Third-last crypt on the end."

Eva smiled and headed out of the room. "Thank you."

Outside the antechamber, the hallway separated into three long corridors. The corridor straight ahead led up to the main foyer, with rooms for families to view their loved ones, along with the Mourning Stones of the more prominent Spellcasters of their community. The corridor to the left led to a vast library full of books on all types of magic. Her mother took her there once, just after she started her job, and she got lost in the long aisles of bookcases, but the corridor to the right was the worst. It was creepier than the short flight of stairs leading to the back entrance. This was the part she hated; the maze of halls and stairs that led to the final resting places. Some were important; they were the discoverers of spells or advanced Spellcraft. The Historians, Alchemists and Wielders whose knowledge was still sought even after death. She'd gotten lost down here once too, and even though she was found quickly, the panic of being around all the dead bodies still haunted her.

Eva kept to the centre of the corridor on the right as she walked toward the far end. Stone archways with stairs leading down deeper into the ground lined the hall every few metres, and occasionally she could hear voices coming from somewhere in the dark. Fifty metres in, the hall branched off into two more corridors. Eva stood at the crossroads.

"Keep going!" Mr. Nithercott's voice echoed off the stone walls. "All the way to the end."

Eva gave a quick nod and went forward. On the other side, instead of stone archways, now lay rooms that held a lone table with wooden high-back chairs all around. A few candles lit the rooms, and she followed the brighter light from a room up ahead. She heard the faint sound of her mother's voice echo down the hall and a wave of relief washed over her.

Venera Shade stood several metres back from an open coffin, her arms crossed, with most of her body weight on one foot. She wore a long, hooded black robe with gold embroidery along the hem and cuffs. In front of her stood a casket in wrought-iron brackets that kept it in an upright position. The well-dressed, young male in the casket looked as though he had been through a grinder, with deep wounds all over the exposed parts of his body. Most of them were around the neck and chest area. Eva watched as her mother lit some incense in a bowl and placed it on the floor in front of the casket. She could see her lips move, but her words were too soft to hear. Venera slowly circled the coffin, directing the smoke with her hands as it rolled over the body. As she waved smoke near the head, the spirit face of the male scrunched up his nose, and an ethereal arm tried to wave it away.

"Get away from me with that foul stench."

"Not until you release all the anger you still hold inside." She waved the smoke around his head. "You must let it all go."

"Easy for you to say, you're not dead."

She walked to the front of her table next to the casket. "You wouldn't be either if you took the simple precaution of telling someone where you were going."

The spirit wiggled in the coffin. "And have them try to talk me out of it? Not a chance." His ghostly arm brushed across the flesh arm and jerked it slightly. "At least untie the spirit knots so I can, at the very least, move around."

"Not on your life."

"Very funny."

Eva giggled from the doorway. Both her mother and the male looked at her. Venera frowned. "Evie, what are you doing here?" She quickly walked toward the exit. "Better yet, how did you get here?"

"Dom brought me." She stepped inside the room. "How come he can come through now and I can't?"

Venera turned to the casket and smiled. "We'll talk about that later, Evie." She looked awkwardly at her daughter. "I would like you to meet the late Mr. Fernsby."

He nodded to her. "Just Mr. Fernsby will do, thank you."

Eva strolled into the room. "Nice to meet you."

Venera placed her hand on Eva's shoulder. "Why aren't you at home?"

"A girl at school told me there's acid rain that's killing the lakes. Is that true?"

Venera stared at the girl with a blank look. "Acid rain . . ."

"Yes, and it's killing all the lakes and fish that live in them!"

"Yes, I understand that, dear."

"Then you know about it?"

Mr. Fernsby's spirit sat straight. "What is she talking about?

Venera picked up the incense bowl. "I don't think this is the right place for this type of discussion."

"Why not?"

"Because it's complicated."

"How?" Both Eva and Mr. Fernsby asked.

She put her tools down and walked toward the corridor, motioning her daughter to follow.

"Do I know about the acid rain? Yes, and so does the Regency Council." Eva went to speak but Venera held up a finger. "But that doesn't mean that we discuss things like this out in the open."

"Are they going to do anything about it?"

Her mother crossed her arms. "Of course they are, don't be so silly."

"But—"

"Eva, stop." She stepped through the doorway into her room. "The right people are aware of the problem." She took a step toward her and put her hand under Eva's chin. "Take comfort knowing that things are under control."

Eva was disappointed. "Okay."

Venera walked toward the coffin. "I'm almost done with Mr. Fernsby. If you want, you can wait for me back at the cottage. I shouldn't be much longer."

That was all Eva needed to hear and hurried through the corridor and back to the chamber. Mr. Nithercott sat at his desk, quill in hand and scribbled on a long piece of parchment paper.

"Would you like a cup of tea?"

"No thank you. I'm not staying long."

He looked disappointed as he lay his quill down.

"Oh, I'm sorry to hear that. I wanted to have a chat with you about your studies. Your mother told me you're going to a *high school*." He looked at her with curious eyes. "And how is that going?"

"All right, but it's just been a couple of weeks."

"It must be hard, being in a place where you don't know anyone."

She flopped down in a nearby chair. "I know a few people."

"New friends? That's good. I was concerned when your parents petitioned the Council to let you go. Not many from our world would want to mingle with the outside." He tilted his head. "Are you sure you wouldn't like a cup of tea?"

Eva nodded. "Positive, thank you."

The old man took a cup down from a shelf. "You know, the outside world has always fascinated me. Even as a boy, but I was never allowed to mingle with them. My parents forbade me to ever leave our realm."

"That doesn't seem fair."

"I thought so too." He poured hot water from a kettle into his mug. "Once, when I was about your age, I snuck out and went to a *diner*, I think they called it." He walked to the condiments on a nearby table. "I had the most delightful lunch. A toasted Swiss cheese sandwich and iced tea."

"Sounds wonderful."

"It was." He sat on his chair. "I remember thinking they weren't all that much different than us. Of course, they do not know the secrets of Spellcasting, but what they lack in magical talent, they make up for in other ways."

"My brother's friend, Delano, says the same thing, that's why I wanted to find out for myself. I don't know how to live my life without magic. To not be able to use it has been very interesting."

The older man gave her a sideways glance. "And most difficult. The temptation to cast a spell for the smallest of things is a hard urge to ignore."

Eva swallowed. She'd been careful, except for that one time, but her father said the Council had ways to learn if she'd broken her promise, and nothing had happened to her yet . . .

He went back to preparing his tea. "Of course, the Council would understand if there was a small mishap or two. After all, even adults are prone to making a mistake every now and then. Just as long as it was nothing truly serious. You are a lucky young lady. Not every parent would allow their child to embark on such an adventure as this." He looked upset. "There were some who questioned your parents' decision to allow you to petition the Council for special dispensation." He frowned and his mood grew dark. "I know your father well enough to not question *anything* about the man." He chuckled and turned away. "They have no idea who they're dealing with."

Eva frowned. "Pardon?"

Mr. Nithercott waved again. "Oh, nothing. I was just rambling. So, you said you made any friends?"

"Not really. I talk with other kids, but I wouldn't call any of them friends." She paused. "Not yet."

"Don't worry, I'm sure it will happen. Just remember, worthwhile things are never easy, and sometimes you have to be brave and make the first move." He got up and strolled to a workbench. "If you put yourself out there and be yourself, like-minded others will make themselves known to you." He gave her a quick wink. "And that's when the fun starts."

She bid him a good night and left. The night air was cool as the last bit of light had disappeared below the horizon. She liked Mr. Nithercott. There was something about talking to him that always made her feel better, and walking up the back stairs didn't bother her anymore.

Bessy the mule nudged Skye as she stood by the barn door and stared at the sky. It was a beautiful shade of robin's egg blue, and she wondered what lay out past that. Out past the clouds, to the stratosphere. Would the sky still look this way if all the trees were killed by acid rain? Would the stratosphere be there? Would they be able to live in homes or would they have to live in domes? Would she be able to see the stars through the dome?

The animal nudged her again, as if to say, 'stop daydreaming girl and get back to work.' Skye rubbed Bessy's forehead and gave her a kiss on her muzzle before scooping out the remaining dirty contents and replacing it with fresh straw. She liked working around the animals, and wished they had more, but her father wasn't keen on the ones they already had, and she doubted he would agree to getting any more.

Once her chores in the barn were done, she wandered through the long grass to the backyard. A large area of the field grass was kept at a manageable level for the back yard, and the kids had worn a path from the barn to the yard.

The smell of grilled meat drifted across the yard along with the smoke. Music played from a small transistor radio plugged into an outside outlet with an old protest song blasting from the speaker. Her father poured sauce onto three large chunks of ribs on a small, round griller, singing softly to himself as he brushed the meat. Skye recognized the song right away. It was one of her favourites, and she hummed a bit as she walked up to the covered picnic table.

There were some pickles and cheese already placed, and she popped a cube of cheese into her mouth before she spoke.

"You're in a good mood."

He turned to her and smiled. "Yeah, well I had a good day."

"Work was cool?"

He chuckled. "Very cool."

She shook her head. How working for a delivery service could be cool was beyond her.

He glanced back at her. "Did I ever tell you the time we went to see this guy in concert?"

"Yeah, a couple times."

Lennon picked up a bowl of barbecue sauce and brushed some on the meat. "Back in my college days, before your mom and I were dating."

"I know, and you met her at a Vietnam protest."

He chuckled. "I guess you have heard that story before."

She sat at the table. "Yeah, and that's why I'm protesting the acid rain. Your generation stood up to the evils of war. You felt you had to do it, and that's how I feel about the world."

"Yeah, but I was a lot older than you are when I did that. You're lucky, young lady. Do you think your grandfather would have put up with me protesting at your age?"

She slumped in her seat. "Probably not."

"You're damn right. He'd have whooped my ass." He turned back to the grill. "But I don't mind you doing this. You have to do what you think is right, as long as it doesn't interfere with your schoolwork."

She perked up. "I promise it won't." Off in the distance, a dog barked. She eyed her father as he flipped the meat. Maybe, with him in such a good mood, this would be a good time to ask for something? "Dad, now that I'm in high school, and being, like, totally more responsible, do you think we could get a dog?"

Lennon chuckled out loud. "You just started high school. Let's see how it goes first."

Skye smiled. This was the first time he didn't flat out say no.

The back door swung open, and her mother stepped out carrying a large bowl of potato salad, with all four of her siblings behind her, each carrying something for dinner. Her brothers—Ash and

Stoney— almost a year apart in age and several years younger than her, carried more food, paper plates and cutlery, with her twin sisters—Summer and Rain, who just started first grade this year—last out and holding drinks, cups, condiments and napkins. Everyone gathered around the picnic table as the boys hastily laid out the table. They looked more like their mother than Skye did with the same pointed nose and small eyes, while the twins looked like their father but didn't have the gap between their teeth, and all of them had the same colour hair as their father. Only Skye was blonde like her mother.

Grilled spareribs and potato salad were accompanied with coleslaw, deviled eggs, dinner buns, and the cheese cubes with pickles. The table was just big enough to fit the kids along the bench, and the parents at either end. They talked and laughed. It had been a long time since Skye had seen her family act like a family. It felt good.

As the boys finished off the rest of the food, her excitement about getting a pet overcame her. "Dad said we could get a dog!"

Everyone erupted into shocked and happy shouts, except for her father.

"Just hold on, Skye," he said and held up one hand, "I never said anything like that. I said I'd think about it."

"But that's as good as saying yes," Ash said.

"No, it isn't."

"But that's what you said when we asked for a goldfish." Summer spoke with a small pout.

Their father leaned onto the table and clasped his hands. "And what happened to the goldfish?"

"Oh Lennon, stop it," Melanie said. "It's not the kids' fault the poor thing died."

He frowned. "Of course it was. None of them bothered to look after it. If you didn't feed it every day, the damn thing would have died in a week." He focused on Skye. "You spend a lot more money on a dog and it comes with a lot more responsibility."

"We could always adopt one from the pound," Melanie said. "They're inexpensive."

"Or we can get another goldfish," Ash said.

"Can we get another goldfish?" Stoney asked.

"I don't want goldfish," Summer whined. "They're no fun."

"We want a dog," her twin said with a pout and crossed her arms.

Lennon slammed his hands down on the table. "Enough!" The empty dishes on the table jumped with the impact. "I don't want to hear another damn thing about dogs or fish or any of it!"

Melanie's eyes narrowed. "Don't yell at them. They were just excited at the thought of having a pet."

"Well now they can stop being excited."

Skye jumped up from the table. "Can I be excused?" She didn't wait for an answer and ran into the house.

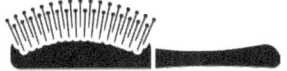

Fireflies twinkled in the night air as Eva walked toward the main road. Not as many people were out now, and the sun had all but set on the horizon. Streetlamps chased away the dark and she took a deep breath and let the cool night air fill her lungs. All of the street vendors were gone, with the few remaining shops open for a more mature clientèle.

She found Dom sitting with a young man on the steps of a gazebo in a park across from a tavern. Both were drinking from tall glasses.

"Thanks for waiting for me," she said, as she stopped a few feet away and crossed her arms. "Some brother you are."

Dom didn't look the same. His eyes were partially closed, and he swayed a bit, even though he was sitting. "What? Something grab you on the stairs?"

He and the young man snickered.

"No, but you know how much I don't like going there. You could have at least waited for me to go inside before you abandoned me."

The young man stretched out on the steps. He was nicely dressed, with his shoulder-length blonde hair slicked-back. There was a smug grin on his thin lips as he rested on one elbow. Delano Allard was her brother's best, and oldest friend. His family was wealthy and did some of their business with the Outside. Most of the time she liked it when he was around. Mostly because of the stories. He talked about places where his family does business, but lately, his absence in her brother's life had been noticeable.

"Oh, come now, Evie. You're a big girl. You don't need your brother to hold your hand."

She glared at him. "What are you doing here, Delano?" She took a step toward him. "I thought you didn't have time for Dom now that we've moved."

He relaxed back on the stairs. "For your information, I have been learning my family's business." His condescending look added to her anger with him. "Besides, your brother is a good and loyal friend, and that is something you don't give up so willingly." He took a sip from his glass. "No matter what other people might say."

Eva stormed past them and forced her way up the stairs, content with his explanation, but she couldn't help but think that if he'd been around more, her brother wouldn't be so angry.

Dom jumped up from the steps and hurried across the grass. Both Eva and Delano watched as he closed in on a group of teens close to the edge of the park.

Delano hastily put his glass down on the step as he jumped to his feet. "Dom! Don't!"

A few of the males in the group stood in a line in front of a few girls the same age.

Eva looked worried. "What's going on?"

"Alisha's dating someone new," Delano said, and hurried after his friend, "He just found out tonight."

Eva hurried behind Delano as her brother grabbed one of the males in the group and threw him to the ground. Another two grabbed Dom, but before they could do anything, Delano pulled them apart. Eva's heart raced as she ran up to her brother and tried to drag him away.

Delano turned to Eva. "Get him out of here, Evie."

She pulled on his arm. "Dom, come on."

He broke her grip on him and stormed up to a short red-headed girl standing in a circle of other girls.

"You told me there wasn't anyone else!" His body was tense with anger as Delano and Eva tried to hold him back.

The redhead glared at him. "There wasn't!"

"Bullshit!"

Alisha Jarsdale flipped her red hair over her shoulder. Her face was stern, but she had soft features. Eva always wanted to be like her, but now, not so much.

"You want to know what's *bullshit*, Dom? You said you were coming back. That your dad made a mistake denying your internship, and he'd let you come back and apprentice under Daddy." Her glare hardened. "But you didn't."

"So, you decided to go and start dating other guys?"

"I didn't know if we were together anymore. When I asked you to go places, you give me some sorry excuse about not being able to leave your home."

"I couldn't because—"

"Because your father put a charm on the gateway. You told me. You also told me your father's magic was weak and you could break the charm."

"It is, but—"

"Did you even try?" She looked away from him. "I'm tired of the lies, Dom"

"I'm not lying."

"I need someone who wants to be with me, no matter what." Her look softened. "And that's not you. Not anymore."

Another teen stepped forward and put his arm around Alisha. His dark hair was short all around except for a patch on the top of his head that flopped over his eyes. He glared at Dom.

"Looks like it wasn't meant to be, Domin—o."

Delano put his hand on the teen's chest. "Back off, Leander. Give the guy a break."

Eva pulled on Dom's arm, but her brother wouldn't budge. After a few tense moments, the guys backed away and headed for the bridge. The girls followed behind, and Eva and Delano blocked Dom from following.

"Leave it, Dom," Delano said, as he stood toe to toe with his friend, "She's shown her true colours. She's out of your life. Be thankful for that."

Skye laid on her side on her bed and stared at her open closet. Everything was going fine until she opened her big mouth about the dog. Why'd she do that? She knew better, but the excitement of getting a dog—she always wanted a dog and there was more than enough room for one—was too thrilling. He or she would have all the yard and the woods to run around in. Now her dad was back to the 'no more pets' stance. She tucked her chin close to her chest. She'd ruined it for everyone.

A gentle rapping at her door didn't make her roll over. The door-knob clicked and the squeak of the hinges made her tuck deeper into her little ball.

"Sweetie," her mother's voice was soft as her footsteps as she made her way to the bed. "I brought you up some dessert."

"No thanks," Skye whispered.

"But it's your favourite. Devil's Food muffins." She sat on the bed and put her hand on Skye's shoulder. "I'm sorry you had to see us fighting like that."

"Kinda used to it."

"I know, and I'm sorry about that, but your dad, well he's just acting that way because he's sad."

Sky rolled over. "About what?"

Melanie smiled softly. "You're growing up and not his little girl anymore."

"That's why he yells?"

"Well, not all the time, but I think you going off to high school made him realize that all you kids are growing up, and sometimes, that's hard on a parent."

Skye sat up and took one of the muffins off the plate. She bit into it and it was still warm in the centre.

"I get that," she said, after she'd swallowed. "But he can't keep yelling at me all the time. He's gotta respect who I am."

"And I'm sure he does. You just have to give him a little more time."

Skye reached for another muffin. "Yeah, sure. Whatever."

Melanie jumped up from the bed. "Oh, I almost forgot. I was

out today and saw something I thought you'd like." She motioned for her daughter to follow her out into the hall. At the long row of closets, Melanie opened one of the bi-fold doors and pulled out a bag. "I found this little store downtown that had some natural ingredients to dye your hair and I thought you'd like some." She handed the bag to her. "The colours are tame to what you're used to, but I'm sure you can mix something together."

"This is awesome! Thanks, Mom." Skye took the bag back to her room.

Melanie followed her. "Well, I was out with Aunt Shelia today and she when we passed by this place, I had to go in."

Skye hurried to her closet and put the new items with the other odd ingredients. "This is totally awesome."

"Maybe you could do up a batch of something and I could do your hair?"

"Sounds good."

Melanie sat on the side of the bed. "I do have a favour to ask of you."

"Sure. Anything!"

"I want you to stop being so mean to your cousin."

Skye froze. "What?"

"Aunt Sheila said you've been really mean to Carla at school."

Skye spun around. "She's lying. I haven't been mean to her at all."

Melanie's brow rose. "Did you say the F-word to her?"

Skye was silent for a moment. "Yeah, but she deserved it."

"Skye, what have we told you about swearing?"

"Mom! She's so heinous."

"She's your cousin."

"You don't know what she's like at school."

"Oh, no, I probably do. She's just like her mother, but this is her last year and she's under a lot of pressure to get good grades so she can apply to university, so if she's lashing out, it's just because she's under a lot of stress."

"Yeah, and I'm under a lot of stress having to be nice to her."

"Skye. Please. For me."

She rolled her eyes and slumped. "Fine."

Melanie smiled. "Thank you." She stood and walked around the bed. Just as she got to the door she turned back. "And don't forget it's your turn to take the food scraps to the compost."

"I won't."

"Do it now, that way it's done and over with."

Skye got up and followed her mother down the hall and to the kitchen. The other kids were gathered all around the table quietly doing their homework, and Melanie walked up behind the twins and looked over their shoulders.

The night was cool, and the smell of condensation and dirt hung heavy as Skye took a bowl down to the far side of the property by the tree line. Crickets chirped at an almost deafening level, but the sound soothed her and helped to clear her mind. The sun hung low on the horizon, but there was just enough light to light up the woods. She tossed the raw food scraps onto a pile of grass and sticks and turned back to the house.

Something hooted from a tree branch above her. She stopped and looked up. A massive pale brown owl with plump, rounded ear tufts sat perched on the lowest branch of a maple and watched her with inquisitive yellow eyes. Skye couldn't stop looking at it. It was so big. She'd never seen anything like it before in the few years they'd been living in the house.

She swallowed. "Hi."

The owl hooted.

A large grin washed over her face. "Nice to meet you. I hope you like the woods but try to ignore my parents fighting."

The owl hooted again, spread its wings and took flight. Skye watched as it disappeared into the darkness of the woods.

Chapter Three

The last week of September saw more leaves change from green to bright red, yellow and orange. The mornings were just a little cooler; the sun was a little less bright. Eva was used to the forty-five-minute bus ride both ways now. She had a routine. Once off the city bus, she and a large group of students split into two groups; one headed to the coffee shop on the opposite side of the street, and the other walked the half-block to the school. The coffee shop was the place to hang out before, after, and for some, during school, but Eva opted for a more solitary start and would sit in front of her locker until the first bell. After morning classes, she'd return to her locker for lunch. Not that she didn't like to go to the cafeteria, but she didn't know anyone well enough to sit with them, and most of the time the place was packed. Besides, lunch gave her a chance to finish up any lingering schoolwork, so she didn't have so much to bring home.

Laughter echoed from down the hall as a small group of older students turned the corner and walked past. Right in the middle of them was Carla. The others collected around her like drones around a Queen and from the look on her face, she knew it. She glared at Eva with a sneer as they passed but decided to bully another first-year student instead.

Eva ignored her and continued with her schoolwork. Science wasn't her favourite class, and her lessons caused her mind to drift off more than once. She flipped through the pages of the heavy textbook. She just wasn't into doing this right now.

"Hey." Her locker partner Tina gently tapped her on the thigh with her shoe. "I need to get in."

Eva shuffled down a bit. A moment later they were joined by two other girls, and all dropped their books in the bottom of the locker. Tina glanced down at Eva. "Janice and Mel are gonna use our locker too, so they have the combination."

A spark of anger raced through Eva. "Why don't they use their own locker?"

Tina shrugged. "Cos they're my friends and I said they could use it."

"That's not a reason."

Tina's eyes narrowed. "Yeah, well, maybe when you get friends you can let them use our locker too." Janice and Mel giggled, and they shot her mean looks as they all walked away.

Eva clenched her jaw and slammed her pen down on her binder. Between Carla and now Tina, she couldn't focus. Why was everyone so mean to her? Maybe coming here was a bad idea after all. The palm of her right hand itched and she rubbed it with her thumb. The faint pink outline of the sigil was still there, and so was the promise she made. Dom said she wouldn't make it through the first two months, and here it was not even the end of the first month, and she was thinking about quitting. There had to be something she could do to make being here bearable. A friend would do. A *real* friend. Mr. Nithercott's words echoed in her mind; she had to make the first step. She put her books away, grabbed a paper lunch bag from the locker and headed for the grotto.

The smell of cigarettes hit her hard as she walked across the yard toward the grass on the other side. A few of the cheerleaders were practicing, and she sat on one of the cement curbs to watch and eat her lunch. A small group of first-year girls, including Tina, sat on the grass and watched as they went through the routine. Today must have been try-outs. Being a cheerleader was a good way to meet people, but as Carla walked toward them, she quickly put it out of her mind.

"WE HAVE TO SAVE THE PLANET!"

The blaring announcement made Eva jump. Everyone within earshot turned to see Skye standing in front of several posters on the far side of the courtyard.

"THE LIVES OF MILLIONS OF CREATURES DEPEND ON US!"

Eva smiled. Skye's hair was a bright blue, and she had the mega-phone by her mouth as she stood in front of homemade posters depicting the world on fire.

"WE ONLY HAVE ONE PLANET! IF WE DON'T SAVE IT WHO WILL?"

A few students walked past, and she tried to hand them fliers, but they either ignored her or took them and crumpled them up and tossed them to the side.

"WE NEED TO ACT NOW! SIGN MY PETITION TO ASK THE CANADIAN GOVERNMENT TO STOP ACID RAIN!"

Eva picked up her lunch and walked over. She un-crumpled one of the fliers from the ground. It was a hand-drawn picture of fish skeletons in a sea with red and black lines streaming up from the water. The picture was crude, but it got the point across.

Skye came toward her. "Did you ask your parents?"

Eva kept her focus on the picture. "Yes."

"And?"

"My mom said it was real."

Skye's eyes went wide. "Awesome!" She handed a bunch of fliers to her. "So, you have to come and help me spread the word."

Eva was surprised. "Really? You want my help?"

"Duh, yeah! The more people who hear us, the more people will sign my petition." She grabbed a few of the posters and pointed to the ones that remained. "Grab them and follow me."

Eva did as she was told. "Where are we going?"

Skye opened the door to the school. "To the one place where everyone will be able to hear us."

Eva had a hard time keeping up, as the posters and fliers slipped through her fingers. By the time she reached the doors to the cafeteria, Skye was already on the far side setting up her display. Eva maneuvered around tables and chairs and stood off to one side and watched as she carefully placed her hand-drawn posters against the wall. When everything was in its place, Skye grabbed a chair and stood on the seat. She was the tallest thing in the room.

Eva winced as Skye brought the mouth of the megaphone up to her lips.

"WE HAVE TO SAVE THE PLANET!"

She put her hands over her ears. She was *a lot* louder inside.

"THE LIVES OF MILLIONS OF CREATURES DEPEND ON US!"

A few of the older male students shouted obscenities at her, but Skye continued. "IF WE DON'T SAVE OUR PLANET WHO WILL? SIGN MY PETITION TO THE CANADIAN GOVERNMENT TO STOP ACID RAIN!" She lowered the megaphone and turned to Eva. "Grab some fliers and hand them out."

Eva hurried to the pile and grabbed a small stack. She held out a few, but no one took any.

"You gotta be more forceful." Skye jumped down off the chair and took a few from Eva's stash. She shoved them in the hands of the closest students. "Don't take no for an answer!" She climbed back up on the chair and brought the megaphone to her lips. "THIS IS THE ONLY PLANET WE HAVE AND IT'S UP TO US TO PROTECT IT!"

More obscenities were hurled their way, and Eva dropped fliers in front of everyone she could reach. A few students took them; a few more even read them, but the majority either ripped them up or crinkled them into balls and threw them around the room. A few hit Eva in the face.

"WE NEED TO STAND TOGETHER AND LET THE GOVERNMENT KNOW THAT WE MEAN BUSINESS! STAND WITH US TO PROTECT OUR WORLD, FOR OUR CHILDREN AND OUR GRANDCHILDREN!"

A few of the older students called Eva and Skye names, but Skye didn't seem to care. She was putting herself out there for a worthy cause and wasn't going to let anyone stand in her way, just like Mr. Nithercott said, only Eva thought she'd be the one doing it. It never occurred to her that it could be the other way around. Nothing stopped Skye. Not even when food was thrown in her direction.

"STAND WITH US! PROTECT THE PLANET!"

An empty pudding cup hit Skye on the leg and fell at her feet. She jumped down from the chair, picked it up, and held it high in the air. "WE ARE RUINING THIS PLANET FOR GENERATIONS TO COME! SIGN OUR PETITION AND LET THE POLITICIANS KNOW WE HAVE A VOICE AND WE'RE GOING TO USE IT!"

Half of a bologna sandwich flew through the air and hit her on the side of the face. Half the cafeteria burst into laughter. Skye lowered the megaphone and stared at the pieces of sandwich on the floor. More garbage was thrown, and it collected at their feet.

Skye looked defeated. "Why don't they care?"

Eva walked up to her. "Don't take no for an answer, right?" She grabbed the megaphone and jumped up on the chair. "WE HAVE TO SAVE THE PLANET! ACID RAIN IS KILLING OUR LAKES AND STREAMS!"

Skye's eyes lit up as Eva spoke into the mouthpiece. She grabbed some of the fliers and handed them to the nearest students.

"IF WE DON'T SAVE THE PLANET WHO WILL? WE NEED TO STAND UP FOR THE PLANET NOW BEFORE IT'S TOO LATE!

A few empty chocolate milk containers flew across the room, followed by paper plates smeared with ketchup. A few ketchup-coated French fries hit one of the posters, and Skye hurried to salvage her artwork. Crusts from sandwiches, half-eaten pizza slices, garbage and plastic utensils were hurled through the air as a free-for-all food fight broke out. Eva jumped down from the chair and tried to protect a few of the other posters as more food splattered the wall.

"This is totally awesome," Skye said, a wide grin on her face as she gathered some fliers off the floor, "Everyone's gonna be talking about this."

"Why is that a good thing?"

"Because it brings awareness to the cause." Her face beamed with pride. "People are gonna say, hey, did you hear about the food fight? And someone else will be, like, yeah, I heard it was awesome. How'd it start? And they'll be, like, it was because of Skye and Eva and their protest!"

Eva wasn't sure what made her happier; that she was a part of something everyone would be talking about, or the fact Skye called it *their* protest.

The football player with the red quaff hairstyle walked up with a full plate of fries and gravy. He stood in front of a poster with dolphins in the water and squashed the food in the centre. The cafeteria erupted into a thunderous cheer, and he turned to the cheering crowd and raised his arms in a victory pose.

Eva's eyes narrowed as she picked up the paper plate and scooped up what was left of the food off the floor. It was one thing to shout at them, but he purposely ruined Skye's hard work! With the plate and the remains of squashed fries in her left hand, she focused on the back of the player's head and walked toward him; her right hand clenched tight in a fist with a slight glow and whispered,

"Gravy on fries. Fries on hair."

She flicked the plate with her right hand, and it flew into the back of his head and smeared into his hair. His look of disgust was mixed with anger as the crowd went wild around them. Skye laughed along with a few of his teammates.

He turned to Eva. His face was red with anger. "You bitch!"

Skye jumped to Eva's side. "What's wrong, Donnie? Can dish it out, but ya can't take it?"

A chorus of jeers taunted the player. He stepped toward Skye. Eva jeered. "Yeah—" She said, taking a quick look at Skye, "—Donnie."

He frowned at Eva. "Shut up, y'stupid loser."

The doors to the cafeteria burst open. Vice-Principal Banta was an older, pudgy man with a long white beard, and hurried in along with several teachers. "All right break it up!" The player backed away and melded in with his teammates as the teachers spread out along the front of the room. The crowd quieted down immediately. With his hands on his hips, the older man slowly walked toward Eva and Skye.

"Who started this?" He glanced at Skye, and then at the posters covered in food. "Did you have something to do with this, Miss. Daniels?"

"We were just protesting, Mr. Banta, and they started throwing food and stuff at us."

"So, your answer is yes."

"Yeah, but—"

"To my office."

"But—"

"To my office, Miss Daniels."

"But—"

He pointed to the exit. "Now!"

Eva picked up the megaphone. Mr. Banta held out his hand. "I'll take that, thank you."

She hesitated and looked down at the instrument.

"Miss?"

Eva held the megaphone up to her mouth. "MY NAME IS EVA SHADE AND WE HAVE TO SAVE THE PLANET!"

"Give me the megaphone, Miss Shade."

"NO. NOT UNTIL YOU HEAR WHAT I HAVE TO SAY."

A low murmur of shock swept through the cafeteria crowd. Mr. Banta wasn't amused, and he ripped it from Eva's hands and handed it to one of the teachers. "Fine, Miss Shade, you can explain yourself when you join Miss Daniels in my office." He turned to the crowd. "As for the rest of you, I suggest you go find something better to do."

Eva walked up to Skye with a smile. Mr. Banta turned to the small group of football players heading for the exit. "Hold on, gentlemen. All of you are staying here and cleaning this mess up."

The group let out a loud protest. Mr. Banta held up his hand. "You're a team, and I know for a fact that if Mr. Woodrow participated then he was egged on by the rest of you." He stood defiantly. "Or do you want me to call each of your parents and explain to them why their sons aren't playing in the game this Friday?" He turned his attention to Eva and Skye. "Ladies, I suggest you get to my office before I do."

They nodded and headed out. Skye stopped a few metres from the grotto entrance. "That was so awesome. They're gonna be talking about this for, like, years!"

The wood panel walls of the vice-principal's office reminded Eva of her father's study. The desk was large and had a dozen files on top with a few pictures and odd items that sat centre-right. If there had been a large bookcase on one side, it would be exactly like her father's study, but instead, there were plaques, diplomas and a few awards neatly spread out evenly across the wall. The 'Father of the Year' mug that sat on the far side of the desk made her smile.

The door to the office was open, and the muffled conversations from the main office echoed outside the room. It was mostly chattering among the half-dozen office staff about one thing or another; how their day was going, family problems, and the odd complaint about a student. There was a brief discussion about what happened in the cafeteria, but a hushed voice ended the discussion.

"This is awesome!" Skye moved around in her seat. "This will totally get the cause noticed." She turned to Eva. "I think we should protest at the game Friday. We could totally get, like, more people involved."

"How?"

"Just ask them. Say, hey, we're gonna protest again, wanna join?" She said facing straight ahead. "After what happened in the caf, we'd get a lot of people, for sure."

"Psst-"

Eva and Skye turned. A few feet from the office was the exit into the main corridor, with Keith and Brad standing in the partially opened doorway. Keith took a look around. "Is it true? You guys started a food fight in the cafeteria?"

Eva glanced at Brad standing behind Keith. He looked worried. "Well?"

"It's true!" Skye beamed with pride. "It was so awesome."

Brad poked his head past Keith. "Why'd you start it?"

"We didn't start it," Eva said, "It just kind of... happened."

"Yeah, well, my sister is *pissed*," Keith said. "She's supposed to meet up with Donnie for lunch, but now the whole caf is shut down and he's locked in there cleaning up."

"Good. He squashed fries all over my poster." Skye crossed her arms. "Him and his dumb friends."

"Yeah, well she knows it was 'cause of you two. I'd be careful."

Skye snorted "I'm not afraid of your sister, Keith."

"No, but I am, and she'll make my life fucking hell just cos I know you two."

Brad stepped past him and into the waiting area. "What'd you think Mr. Banta will do?"

Eva shrugged.

At that moment, Vice-Principal Banta strolled into the waiting area with two files in his hand. "Gentlemen, if you're waiting for the ladies, you'll have to do it someplace else." He closed the door as Brad and Keith scrambled to get back out into the hall. He turned and headed into his office. "All right, let's talk about your behaviour in the cafeteria today."

Eva took a quick look back at where the boys had stood. Brad stood close to the embedded window and still looked concerned. She gave a small smile.

"Don't worry, Miss Shade. I'm sure you'll see Mr. Carlson again." He said as he shut the door to his office.

He walked around to the chair behind his desk and sat down. Both girls sat straight and focused forward as Vice-Principal Banta opened the top file. "So, Miss Daniels, this is your second offense with your protest."

"Yes, sir."

"I let you off with a warning last time, but it seems you didn't adhere to my words."

"This is serious, Mr. Banta. The world is dying, and no one seems to care."

He glanced at Eva. "Well, Miss Shade does, otherwise she wouldn't be here with you now."

Skye pleaded with him. "We have to make people aware of the ozone."

"I understand that, but as I told you the last time, you're going to have to do it off school grounds."

"But I can't do it any place else."

"What about that small strip mall on the other side of the school?"

Skye slumped in her seat and crossed her arms. "It's private property. I'd need permission."

Vice-Principal Banta exhaled and opened the second folder. "Miss Shade. It says here that you were home-schooled. How did you get mixed up with all this?"

Eva opened her mouth but stayed silent as her gaze jumped between him and Skye.

He looked down at the file. "Never mind."

"I think it's important."

His gaze lifted to meet her. "Do you?"

"Yes."

Everyone was silent as he read over the files. Eva wondered what was in the file on her. Did it say she was from a magical society? Did it have information on her primary lessons in Spellcasting? She sat straight up and tried to read the few notes that were upside down. When he switched back over to reading her file, she quickly sat back in her chair.

He exhaled and closed the folder. "It seems we're at an impasse, ladies." He pinched the top part of the bridge of his nose. "I admire the strength of your conviction, Miss Daniels, and I agree this is a very important thing to be protesting."

Skye looked confused. "You . . . agree with me?"

"Completely. If this were a different situation, most likely I would join you, but as it is, we cannot allow such disturbances on school property. You have to understand that."

Skye nodded feverishly. "Yes, sir."

He turned to Eva. "Do you?"

"Yes."

"Good. Now, since this is so important to you, I am inclined to ask Principal Jarred and the school board if they would allow you to continue your activities at a later date."

Skye and Eva squealed with joy.

He raised his hand. "On a limited basis, and there would be conditions. I don't want either of you to protest for the rest of the semester. There's a board meeting in the new year. I'll petition the officials on your behalf if you can do *one* more protest." He continued, putting a strong emphasis on the number. "Now, don't get your hopes up. This isn't a simple matter of asking permission and receiving it. It could very well be that they say no."

"But they won't," Skye said, with a wide smile, "Because they know how important it is for young people to get involved with causes that will save the world."

He gave her a strange look, and she lowered her excitement.

She turned to Eva. "My Dad told me that once. He and Mom used to protest in the 60s."

He closed the folders with a heavy exhale. "Well, that explains a lot." He sat back in his chair. "But, returning to the matter at hand. I'm afraid I can't let what happened in the cafeteria slide."

"We understand," Eva said as she stood. "And we'll go help clean up the cafeteria."

"No, that's not your punishment." He motioned her to sit. "Mr. Woodrow probably did what you said he did, pushed on by his friends, no doubt, but your punishment must fit *your* crime, so to speak." He sat up in his chair. "Miss Daniels, this is your second time in this office on the same offense, and Miss Shade, even though you are new to the school, I don't want you falling into bad habits, so I am giving you the same punishment as a deterrent to further activity. One-hour detention. Today, after school."

Both girls sat quietly and stared at him. A small flicker of panic stirred in Eva. Getting into trouble so early in the school year might change her parents' minds and the Council's about letting her continue, just when she finally found someone she connected with. Her gaze wandered. If her parents stopped her from going to school, then did that mean she lost the bet with Dom?

Her heart pounded as the possible repercussions of this flooded her mind, but all she could do was sit in her chair with a stupid, shocked smile on her face, and she didn't mean to, but she let out a little giggle.

Skye gave her a strange look, and a moment later she giggled as well, and within moments, they both kept giggling.

"This isn't a laughing matter, ladies." His face contorted in anger. "This is serious and goes on your permanent record." He scribbled on a few sheets of paper in front of him. "I'll expect you to report to room 224 for detention after school."

"We will," Skye took her slip, trying to keep calm. "We really will."

He waved them away. "You're free to leave, but don't think I'll forget about this. I'll be checking on you after school to make sure you're where you're supposed to be."

They quickly hurried out of his office and into the school corridor. Skye pulled Eva down the hall a few metres and they burst into laughter.

"No, no, no," Eva said and forced herself to stop. "You heard what he said. We have to take this seriously!"

"Then why did you start laughing?"

"Why did *you* start laughing?"

"I was laughing because *you* were laughing."

They chuckled a bit more and Skye's expression changed. "Thanks for standing up with me. I'm sorry you got into trouble, though."

"It's okay, and it's a serious matter."

"Yeah, but we, like, don't hang together, so that was really cool of you."

Brad and Keith came up to them from the foyer.

"What happened?" Keith asked.

Skye held up her slip with pride. "We both got an hour detention after school."

Brad looked impressed. "That's not bad."

"But we're not allowed to protest for the rest of the semester," Eva said.

"But—" Skye interrupted. "Mr. Banta said he'd ask the principal and school board if we can do another protest next semester."

Keith nodded. "That's pretty cool of him."

"*If* he does it," Brad said. "He might just be saying that, so you won't do it anymore."

Skye clutched her detention sheet to her chest. "We'll see."

The bell rang in two short bursts and the halls filled with students. The four moved to the far side of the corridor to keep from being swept up in the wave.

"Where's your last class?" Skye asked.

"Out in the portable. History."

"I have gym." She looked over the piece of paper. "Detention is in 224." She frowned. "Where is that?"

"Back building," Keith said. "Eva and I have English there."

Skye nodded. "Okay, I'll meet you in the grotto right after class and we'll go together."

Eva nodded. "Okay."

She took a few steps away before turning back. "You should call your parents and let them know you'll be late."

Eva thought about who would be at her home in the afternoon. No one but Dom. Did she need to tell him? He'd ask all kinds of questions and she wanted to tell her parents about this herself.

Skye and the boys walked into the wave of students. Brad took a quick look back at her and smiled.

Eva smiled back. It was nice of them to wait outside, considering she didn't know them well. Keith was in a few of her classes, but Brad was only in one, and she thought he was kind of cute. She stepped into the corridor and followed the crowd to the foyer. Two pay phones were attached to the wall in the small entranceway right before the foyer. Eva froze in front of them. They had a phone number, but she couldn't remember what it was.

The doors to a narrow corridor stood next to the booth and she quickly went through and hurried down the hall. Entrances to the gymnasium were at both ends, with the girls' change room in between. She hurried inside and went to the small mirrors over the sinks. She stood in front and calmed herself. She had to be relaxed to do this and right now, and between the protest, the food fight, and detention her excitement levels were too high. She inhaled and slowly released the air a few times. She had to do this quickly before anyone came in. She held up her hand and drew a straight line from the lower right-hand side of the mirror to the upper left-hand side, and then a shorter line across the top of it.

"Open a doorway to my home."

The sigil glowed a cool blue and she slid her finger from the horizontal line along the surface of the mirror. The blue hue engulfed the mirror and shone brightly for a few moments before it disappeared. The reflection in the mirror was gone; replaced with a view of the entranceway of her home.

She leaned forward over the sink. "Sem'ya, is anyone home?"

The view quickly changed to show the kitchen, then the parlour, the front hall, the upstairs hall, and then Dom's room. He sat on his bed reading the same leather-bound book he had been reading in the parlour.

"Dom! Where's Mom 'n Dad?"

"Not home yet."

"If they get home before I do, can you tell them I'm still at school?"

He swung his legs to one side of the bed. "Why? What are you up to?"

"Nothing, I'm just going to be late."

Dom's face was right close to the mirror, and he looked around. "Where are you?"

"In the girl's locker room at school." She touched the top right-hand corner of the mirror and made a slashing motion to the bottom left-hand side, and Dom's confused expression disappeared; replaced with her reflection.

Eva waited in the grotto for Skye to arrive. The movie they watched in her history class took up most of the time and the teacher gave them the follow-up assignment as homework, so it didn't take her long to make her way across school to the hangout. When she passed the cafeteria, she couldn't help but smile a little.

A small group of students dressed in black, tall with black hair and a couple who had heavy black and white makeup turned and pointed at her. Eva felt uncomfortable under their stares. More so as a young girl from the group came toward her.

She was a bit taller than Eva, with long dyed black hair and a long face with thick black eyeliner around her eyes. "You and that weird blue-haired girl were doing that protest thing in the caf today, yeah?"

Eva nodded. "It's to bring awareness to the ozone."

The girl shrugged. "Whatever. I heard Banta caught you. What'd he do?"

"We got detention."

The girls' eyes went wide. "That's fuckin' harsh! Just cus you were doin' whatever that thing was?"

"Well, and partly for the food fight."

"You guys started that? Bitchin'!"

Eva nodded. "Yeah. Bitchin'."

The girl nodded and walked back across the grotto. "Later."

A moment later, Skye walked outside with Brad and Keith. "Hey."

Eva nodded. "Hey."

She motioned to the group on the other side. "I think you were right about all that attention stuff. That girl just came up and knew we got into trouble and asked me what happened."

Keith waved to her. "That's Runi. She's in my geography class."

Skye's eyes lit up. "See I told you. I bet the next protest we do, we'll have loads of people wanting to join."

"You hope," Brad said, standing next to Eva, "You still don't know if Banta is going to say anything."

"He will. I just know it."

They headed back inside and up the stairs to the detention room. All classes were empty, but the halls still had a fair number of kids hanging around by the lockers. They sat at the first four desks closest to the door. Skye sat behind Eva and the boys in the next row.

Skye took a long look around the room. "The room is so small without windows."

"Yeah, all the classrooms are like this," Keith said. "I have homeroom, English, and math in this building." He slumped in his seat. "It so totally sucks."

A few more students wandered into the room and sat at the far side. The group eyed them for a few moments and then Brad turned to Eva. "So, have you had detention before?"

Eva shook her head. "What's it like?"

"Boring," Keith said. "Like all you do is just sit here and veg the whole time."

Skye opened her backpack. "I need to plan out the next protest."

Brad leaned close to Eva. "What are you gonna do?"

She shrugged. "Homework, I guess."

Mr. Grossman hurried into the room and dropped his briefcase on the metal desk. "All those who aren't supposed to be here, please leave now."

Brad and Keith stood. "Catch ya later."

"Close the door on your way out, please." When the door closed, Mr. Grossman walked around to the front of the desk. "You are here because you've done something that warrants detention." He looked over at the girls. "A few of you should feel lucky you weren't suspended." He crossed his arms and rested against the desk. "For the next hour you will sit quietly and do whatever it is you plan on doing, but you will do so without making noise." He pointed at Skye. "You, you're too close to the other girl. Take your things and move a few seats away."

Skye piled her plans into the backpack and headed to an old wooden desk two seats back. She gave Eva a weak smile from her new spot.

"If you are unable to follow the rules, I'll see you again tomorrow after school." He walked back around and opened his briefcase. "Note that we will be here for a full hour." He brought out an egg timer and placed it on the desk. "Which means your hour detention starts when I say it starts." He cranked on the timer and placed it so it faced the desks. "And it begins now."

Eva turned and looked back at Skye. The young girl sat forward and stared down at the desk. She tapped the end of her pencil against a binder.

"Turn around, Miss Shade." Mr. Grossman's voice held a distinct hint of anger.

Eva faced forward and stared at the blackboard. This wasn't what she thought detention would be like. She reached down and brought out her homework from her last class. Most of the questions were easy, and she took her time answering each one. When she was done, a quick look at the clock on the wall told her she'd used up fifteen minutes. She exhaled and rested her head on the desk. She had no other schoolwork to finish. There was nothing to do but just sit there and wait for the hour to run out.

Mr. Grossman sat behind the metal desk, his briefcase open and a pile of tests in front of him. Eva watched as he wrote on several with a red pen and could only imagine what he was saying. She traced a few scratch marks on the desk with her finger, until a crumpled ball of paper landed in front of her. She looked at the teacher for a brief moment before glancing behind her. Skye pointed to the ball of paper.

Eva carefully straightened it out.

Where do you think we should hold the next protest?

She picked up her pen. *Not the cafeteria. We could get in trouble again.*

She picked up her book bag, placed it on the desk and carefully balled up the paper inside. She brought the wadded paper to her lips and whispered.

"Secret message, so mote it be. For only Skye and me to see."

She placed it on the palm of her hand and flicked it hard. The ball flew through the air and landed right in front of Skye.

Skye straightened it out, read it, and nodded. A few moments later, it appeared again in front of Eva:

Maybe we should do it in the main foyer at first lunch.

Flick.

Isn't that too close to the office?

Flick.

Yeah, maybe, but a lot of people walk through there to get to the caf.

Flick.

What about the grotto?

Flick.

Naw, too smoky.

Flick.

Eva thought for a moment. There had to be a perfect place where they could get a lot of kids to see. An idea came to her, and she quickly wrote it down. She was about to flick it back when Mr. Grossman suddenly appeared at her side and grabbed the paper ball from her hand.

He glared at Eva. "Is there a reason you're not turned around sitting forward in your seat, Miss Shade?"

She cowered under his glare and slumped forward. "No, sir."

He held up the wadded paper ball. "And what's this?"

"Nothing."

His brow rose. "Are you sure of that?"

Eva slowly looked at Skye.

He crossed his arms. "Sending notes maybe?"

Eva glanced at Skye. Skye's eyes were wide with fear. "No. I was just . . . bored and . . . made a paper ball."

Mr. Grossman snorted as he straightened out the sheet. His brow furrowed slightly, and he dropped it on the desk between them. Their conversation lay bare for the world to see, but he turned and walked back to his desk. "Find something to occupy your time that's less distracting."

Skye's look was a mixture of confusion and joy.

Eva took the sheet of paper from the desk and stuffed it into her book bag as Skye melted into her seat with a look of relief.

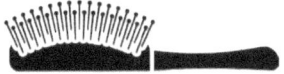

The last half hour went by faster after Mr. Grossman sat back down, but they didn't risk another round of notes, just in case. The school felt different with no students around. The frantic tension was now a lonely quiet as they walked up to the stairwell that took them down by the Grotto entrance.

"Can I put my posters and stuff in your locker?" Skye asked. "My locker partner leaves drinks in ours and she's already ruined one of my good ones."

"Sure."

They hurried down to the far end of the main school building. Skye's locker was set out of the way, in a short corridor with a large window set in the outside wall. She grabbed the posters, some markers and other craft items and slammed it shut. "Can I put this other stuff in there too? I swear, she uses my stuff for her art class."

"Sure," Eva said. "If Tina's friends can dump their stuff in there, so can you."

"Fer sure."

It was a quick walk past the cafeteria and the grotto to get to Eva's locker, and once the posters and art items were inside, they hurried out of the building.

Skye pushed open the door to the corridor that led to the girls' side of the gym. "That was totally worth it. I could so handle detention every day if I had to."

"But you don't want to, do you?"

"If that's what it takes, yeah." She exhaled and stopped by the door to the girl's change room. "But I doubt I'd get detention again." She shifted her backpack onto her shoulder. "Hey, do you want a ride home?"

"Thanks, but I catch the bus."

They headed toward the outside exit at the far end. "Where do you live?"

"Down by the prison."

"That's pretty far."

Eva shrugged. "I don't mind."

The bus ride home was long but sometimes Eva did a doorway spell in the bathroom at the transfer stop at the mall. She probably could do one using the stalls at school, but she liked the atmosphere of the mall with all the people.

They went down the small roadway that lay behind the strip mall at the edge of school property and crossed the street to the plaza that housed the coffee shop.

"When is your dad picking you up?"

"Not for a while." Skye dropped her backpack on the edge of the narrow cement sidewalk that ran the length of the coffee shop. "Usually, my mom picks me up after she gets my younger brothers and sisters, but she can't leave them alone to come and get me."

"Where do you live?"

"On Old North Road, just past the airport."

Eva shook her head. "I don't know how far that is."

"Far enough that my mom can't leave my brothers and sisters alone to come and get me, which is why I have to wait until my dad is done work."

"What are you going to do?"

Skye shrugged. "Don't know, but I told him I'd hang out here."

Eva started toward the intersection down the road. Her bus stop was just on the other side, near the drive-in on the far side. "I can wait too. If you want."

"But you'll miss your bus."

"You don't know when he'll get here, and you're waiting by yourself?" She bent down and opened a small compartment on the side of her book bag. "I've got some money left over from shopping." She brought out a twenty-dollar bill. "We can have a drink and wait."

Skye's eyes went wide at the sight of the bill. "How'd you snag that?"

"They never asked for it back."

Skye rolled her eyes. "Must be nice. I asked for five dollars once to get something, and my dad made me give back *all* the change."

They walked into the coffee shop and sat at the counter away from everyone else. Eva ordered two hot chocolates for them and two large chocolate éclairs. The éclairs were larger than the mug the drinks came in.

Skye swiped her finger through the cream filling. "Thanks, and not just for the food. For standing with me, even when I got you into trouble."

Eva shrugged and took a bite from her food. "It was worth it."

"How mad are your parents gonna be 'cause you got detention?"

"I don't know if I'm going to tell them."

Skye looked concerned. "You're gonna lie to them?"

"No, I wouldn't do that, but they're hardly home anymore, so they won't know what time I got home."

"Your mom works, eh?"

"Yes, she just got a job working at-" Eva froze.

Skye waited for a moment before asking. "At?"

Eva couldn't tell her that her mom worked at the Crypt. Other than the fact it was creepy, she couldn't reveal anything about their world. "At a place . . . where she works with a lot of old people."

"What? Like an old age home?"

"Yes."

"So, she a nurse?"

"No, just someone who helps them when it's time to...move on."

Skye's expression became serious. "Oh. Like when they're gonna die, and stuff."

Most of the people Eva's mother attended to were already dead, so, "Yes."

"That's harsh." She took a sip of her drink. "My mom doesn't work. She just says at home and looks after us."

"I wish my mom didn't. I never see her anymore."

"I wish my mom did. She's always there trying to be my buddy and stuff."

"Yeah, but if she did, who'd look after your brothers and sisters after school?"

Skye exhaled. "Me."

They sat in silence for a few minutes.

"So," Eva said, as she took a sip from her mug, "What do you want to do when you're out of school?"

"I wanna go places and do things, y'know? Get out and see the world."

"We went to Europe once."

"Really?"

Eva concentrated on faint images of being in the woods. "Yeah, but I can't remember it."

A small grey box of a car drove up to the donuts shop, with Donnie Woodrow driving. Carla sat in the passenger seat. They looked friendly enough as they walked into the shop and didn't notice Skye and Eva back in the corner.

Eva tried to hide. "Did they see us?"

"Who cares?"

"She hates me."

Skye scoffed. "Carla hates everyone who doesn't bow down and kiss her ass." She eyed the couple closer. "Where's Shelly?" She took a quick look around. "That's Shelly's boyfriend, but I don't see her."

Eva looked out the window at the car. "She's not in the car."

"He's cheating on her? What a prick!"

"You don't know that."

Carla stood on her toes and planted a long kiss on Donnie's lips. Donnie paid for their drinks, and they left. Carla snuggled up next to him in the front seat as they pulled away.

Skye shook her head. "Shelly's gonna *so* wig out when she hears about this."

"You're going to tell her?"

"No." She emphasized the vowel. "But she's gotta know what an asshole he is."

Eva stared out the window where Donnie's car had been. "Poor Shelly."

"Poor Shelly?" Skye choked on her drink. "She's heinous the way she treats Keith."

"Doesn't mean she deserves to be cheated on."

Skye slumped in her seat. "Yeah, I guess not."

They were silent for a moment before Eva spoke.

"Maybe you could tell Keith and he could tell her."

"I doubt he'll say anything to her." She gave a small smile. "Hey, you know Brad, right?"

Eva took a large bite of her éclair and the filling dripped down the side of her mouth. "Yeah, what about him?"

Skye leaned closer. "He likes you."

Eva was stunned. "How do you know?"

"He told Keith and Keith told me."

"Why would he tell him?"

"Cos they're, like, first cousins. Pretty close too." She nudged her. "So, you like him?"

"I don't know. He's cute, but…" Eva wiped the filling from her mouth with a napkin. He did have a nice smile, and he was very smart. "I guess."

"Well, you gotta know for sure. You don't wanna *say* you like him, and, like, *not* like him."

"Are you sure? Really for sure?"

"That's what Keith says."

Eva looked out into the parking lot. She'd never liked a boy before, not that she didn't like boys, but she never thought a boy would like her, but maybe he did? After all, he did look back at her when they all split up after leaving the office and he did smile at her.

"So, are ya gonna go for it?"

"I don't know."

"You should. He's a really nice guy." Skye ate the last piece of her éclair. "I've known him and Keith since grade one."

They sat quietly for a while. Eva was lost in her thoughts about Brad, and her silence seemed to signal to Skye to start working on plans for the next protest. The sun was almost behind the trees when a station wagon with wood panelling pulled up to the coffee shop. Skye grabbed her things off the counter and shoved them into her backpack.

"That's my dad," she said and swung her pack over her shoulder. "I'll ask him if he can give you a ride home."

The air was cooler now and Eva wrapped her arms around herself as they stepped outside. Mr. Daniels's pudgy face looked tired as he sat behind the wheel and motioned his daughter to get in. Eva couldn't hear the request, but a nod and a polite smile from him meant she was leaving too.

She got into the car behind Skye. "Thank you."

"Dad, this is Eva Shade."

Mr. Daniels nodded. "Nice to meet you. So, where am I going?"

"Carlington Park Place."

He faced forward but then turned to her again. "And where's that?"

"On King Street, just past the prison."

He put the car in drive and pulled out. "King street? And you go to F.C.V.I?"

"Yeah, they were the only ones who would let me register late."

Mr. Daniels looked both ways before he pulled out onto the main road. "Never heard of that before." He pulled up to the intersection. "So, detention, eh?"

"Yeah, but it was awesome, Dad, now everyone is gonna know about our cause!"

"That's not always a good thing, sweetie."

Eva turned to face him in her seat. "Yeah, but the more people who know about acid rain, the better, right?

"Sometimes, if it's the right people." He turned to his daughter. "Have you two had anything to eat?"

"Just a donut."

"Why don't we get something to eat, and we can talk about this ozone protest of yours. See what we can do to keep the both of you from getting into trouble again."

He drove them to a fast-food place, and they went inside. Over burgers, fries, and pop, Skye laid out her plans for what she wanted to do and how she was going to do it. Eva watched father and daughter interact, and it reminded her of when she was younger, and her parents would talk to her about everything in her life. Dom's too, but that was in the past. Ever since they moved things weren't the same anymore, and she missed the chats they'd have at the end of the day.

An hour later, Mr. Daniels pulled up in front of the Shade home. The old mansion was dimly lit at the front door, and the few outside lights barely shone a visible path to the house. The old crumbling brickwork was patched up, and the stones in the walkway were fixed, with small multicoloured flowers growing along the path.

He put the car in park and stared at the house. "You, uh, sure your parents are home? Looks like the place is empty."

Eva grabbed her book bag and opened the door. "It always looks like that. They're in there somewhere."

"Well, I'll wait here until you're inside."

"Thanks."

Eva headed toward the house. The walkway lights shone as she approached, and she could hear the gargoyles on the roof skitter around in the shadows. She looked up at one close to the edge and could just make out the wild look in its eyes.

"Getting ready for rain?"

It shivered and scurried off toward a shadow in the corner.

"Hey Eva, wait." Skye ran up to her, and the walkway lights grew brighter. "So, like, I told my dad we still have a lot of planning to do, so I asked if it was okay if you come for a sleepover Friday night."

Eva stared at her. "Really?"

"Yeah. I gotta ask my mom too, but dad said okay."

Eva smiled. "Okay. I'll ask my parents."

"Cool."

Skye ran back to the car as Eva forced open the heavy front door and waved to them as they drove away, a wide smile on her face.

Inside, Dom stood by the side window peering through the curtains. "Who was that?"

She gave him a smug look as she walked up the stairs. "My new friend."

Chapter Four

It was only two days until the weekend, but for Eva, it felt like an eternity. Her classes felt longer, the ride home on the bus took forever, but it didn't feel as long as the conversation she had with her parents when she got home the night of the food fight. She had to tell them about her detention. It felt wrong to lie to them, especially after Dom gave them her message. It was two hours of listening to her parents lecture her about what could happen if she was seen spell casting. Outsiders were dangerous and could get violent if they saw her. Her father went on to list all the reasons why their world had to be kept a secret; Outsiders were to violent. Outsiders were too greedy. Outsiders were too primitive. After the fourth reason she tuned him out. She'd heard all this before, and besides, she'd just cast small spells. Nothing significant.

Not surprisingly, her parents were a little concerned about Eva spending the night in a non-magical house. Not that they worried for her safety, but more fact that their daughter might again, cast a spell.

"I promise," Eva whined at the breakfast table Friday morning. "I won't cast any spells while I'm at Skye's."

Dom snorted next to her. "You shouldn't have done it in the first place."

"I didn't have a choice, thanks to you."

Egori froze. The old cast-iron frying pan hovered over one of three plates on the counter. A few pieces of scrambled egg dripped off the edge. "What is this?"

Dom glared at her. "It's nothing."

Their father carefully placed the pan back down on the old turn-of-the-century stove. "No, no. I distinctly heard her insinuate that you are the reason behind her carelessness." Egori's Russian accent was strong when he became cross. Mornings always saw him in a good mood, but this conversation was becoming the exception. He turned away from the stove and glowered at his son. "Is she right?"

Her brother's eyes went wide. "I didn't force her to do it."

"You put dirt in my lunch. I didn't have anything to eat!"

"Doesn't mean it was my fault that you spellcast."

"I had to eat something!"

Egori rubbed his brow with the hand that held the spatula. "Dominik, why did you put dirt in your sister's lunch?"

The teen shrugged. "I don't know. It was just a joke."

Egori's brow rose. "A joke? Please. Explain to me the punch line." He inhaled. "Evandra, do you understand the severity of what you have done?"

She shifted in her seat. "Yeah, I mean, they were just little spells." She glared at her brother. "And, I was careful. No one saw."

He turned away from the stove. "No, *dochka*, I saw, as well as Perrin Nithercott and Council member Kaige."

She froze in horror. "They did? How?"

Dom snorted under his breath. "Cherep."

"This was an experiment, of sorts, and the Council wished to keep a close eye on you." He exhaled deeply. "Even though you see what you did as insignificant, you did break your contract and there will be consequences."

"Does this mean I can't go to Skye's for the sleepover tonight?"

"No, you can still go." He walked toward the kitchen table as Eva brought over two plates. "Your mother will attend the council meeting and discuss a proper punishment, but I cannot stress to you how important it is not to spellcast outside of our community."

She looked down at her plate of food. "You're not going?"

"No. I will stay here." He focused on Dom. "The night alone with your brother will give me the opportunity to refine his sense of humour and help him to understand where he went wrong with his last joke."

Apart from the sleepover, there was a second reason to be excited for the weekend; the grand opening of a new mall out in the township. It was hailed as a two-level sprawling shopping centre that boasted more 'hip' stores than the old one level mall closer to the city centre, and everywhere Skye looked, students had fliers from popular stores, coupons, or were eagerly talking about the opening ceremony later that day.

This weekend was going to be awesome! She finally had someone else to talk to about the ozone, and the best part was, Eva seemed excited about it. Tonight, they'd spend some time getting ready for the next protest and her head was buzzing with new ideas.

She went up to Eva's locker. Her new ally was trying to shove an over-stuffed Adidas bag inside the narrow compartment.

"That's a lot of stuff. What'd you bring?"

"Just my night clothes and toothbrush and stuff."

Skye frowned. "What are nightclothes?"

"What I wear to bed."

"You mean pajamas."

Eva's face held a hint of fear. "Yeah. Pajamas." She gave it a final shove and quickly slammed the door shut. She looked over and smiled. "Your hair's pink!"

"Yeah, I did it last night." Skye grabbed one of her long pink braids and brought it forward. "I wanted to do something special since the new mall opens today."

"I know." Eva clicked the lock closed. "I got some money from my dad in case we go."

"Oh, we're going. Dad said he'd drop us off after supper." They headed down the hall. "Keith said him and Brad are gonna go too."

Eva's eyes went wide. "Really?"

"Duh, yeah! Keith said Brad wants to go cos he thinks you're gonna go, so we have to go." They turned and headed toward the main foyer. "And I heard there's gonna be a big sale on Bristol board and stuff too, so I wanna pick up more for posters."

The rest of the school day flew by. Eva met Skye out front of the main doors and they waited excitedly for Skye's mother to show up. A line of school buses drove past, loaded with students, with puffs of cigarette smoke coming from the back few windows.

The familiar station wagon pulled up in front. Mrs. Daniels waved at them with a large smile as Eva and Skye headed toward the car.

"How was school?" she asked, as Skye got in the front passenger seat. Eva climbed in and sat behind her.

Skye shrugged. "Okay."

Mrs. Daniels looked back at Eva through the rear-view mirror. Her permed, blonde hair was extra curly today and she wore large, white frame sunglasses that hid almost her entire face. "And how was your day?"

"Good."

They pulled out onto the main road. "So, what exciting things happened?"

"Not a lot," Skye shrugged again. "It was pretty boring."

"Toby Gillis threw up in my math class," Eva said. "It took a half hour with the windows open before the smell was gone."

Skye turned to her. "That's so gross."

"Well, maybe he couldn't help himself?" Mrs. Daniels said, in a somewhat cheerful tone.

"No, he asked the teacher if he could go to the washroom, and Mr. Canto said no."

Skye shook her head. "He's such a jerk."

"Well now, the teacher must have had a good reason not to let him go."

"No mom," Skye's tone was condescending. "Mr. Canto is just *heinous*."

"Totally," Eva said.

"He doesn't give you any time to do your work," Skye continued. "And if you don't have your homework done, he writes your name down and puts a line under it."

Eva nodded. "When you get three lines, he gives you detention."

"Well, what does that tell you?"

Skye shot a sarcastic look at her mother. "That he's a rotten teacher."

"Or maybe, he's just trying to get you all to take responsibility for your work." She glanced back at Eva. "You two are in high school now. It's up to you to finish your assignments *on time*. You want to be treated like adults, then you have to start acting like one, and that means handing in your work when it's due."

Skye rolled her eyes as she looked back at Eva. "Oh, my gawd, you sound like dad."

They waited outside Skye's old public school for her brothers and sisters. It was a tight squeeze to fit the additional four kids in the car, even if they were smaller. The twins were split up with Summer in the back seat and Autumn in the middle seat up front, and the boys arguing over who got to sit in the back cargo area. In the end, Mrs. Daniels let them both sit back there, as long as they stayed still and didn't move around. With that settled, everyone piled their backpacks in the middle of the backseat.

The drive to the Daniels home was anything but quiet. The boys bugged Summer, which caused their mother to shout at them, and Autumn wouldn't sit still and kept poking her older sister. Skye swatted her hand away, which caused a small fight.

Mrs. Daniels swatted them both. "Stop it!"

Skye took a quick look back at Eva. The girl sat pressed against the door with a look of confusion. Skye rolled her eyes. It was just like her siblings to cause a scene. Now Eva probably thought she was part of a mad house or something. At a stop light, the boys rolled around in the back area and the vehicle rocked. Their mother threatened no dessert after supper, groundings, and even no television, but none of it seemed to work. It was too many kids in too small a space.

Once the car stopped out front of the house, the doors swung open, and the younger children jumped out. Mrs. Daniels sat quietly in the driver's seat for a couple minutes with her door closed. Eva got out and grabbed her Adidas bag.

"Skye, sweetie, can you keep an eye on the twins while I go pick up your dad?"

Skye let out a frustrated exhale. "Why can't the boys look after them?"

"Please. I don't want to be late picking him up from the office."

Eva grabbed her bag and handed her a few of the backpacks.

"Fine."

They unloaded the car and Mrs. Daniels drove away. Skye stood at the edge of the gravel driveway as the station wagon disappeared behind a cloud of dust. It wasn't fair. The boys were old enough now to look after the twins and she had a guest over. Why'd she have to keep an eye on them?

Eva came up to her. "You okay?"

She wasn't. Usually, her dad picked them up after work, but he'd been staying later the last few days. Ever since she asked if they could get a dog. They'd stopped fighting too, at least in front of them, but she could still hear them sometimes, late at night in their room arguing about something stupid. She blinked back a tear before facing her guest and shrugged.

"Yeah, I guess."

A low rumble echoed from the north end of the property. Moments later a middle-sized plane flew by.

They both looked up.

Eva held her hand up to block out the sun. "That's annoying."

Sky headed for the house. "You get used to it."

"Really?"

"Yeah, and they don't fly by all the time."

Skye hurried to the door, but Eva stayed back and looked around the property.

Inside, Skye tossed her handful of backpacks onto the floor in front of the bi-fold closet. Everyone was in front of the television with afternoon cartoons on.

"I love your house," Eva said, as she came inside.

"Really?" Skye walked across the kitchen and dropped her back-pack on the table.

"Yeah."

"It's been in my dad's family for generations." She paused. "It was here before the airport." She walked to the refrigerator. "You want something to eat? It's probably going to be a while before supper."

"No, thank you."

Skye grabbed a slice of cheese and let the fridge door slam shut. She grabbed her backpack on the way past. "Come on. I'll show you my room."

Eva followed her up to the second floor. Skye took a quick look at the stairs that led to the addition. The bedroom door was closed. She swallowed. They never closed the bedroom door.

The narrow hallway was cluttered with antique hall tables, chairs, and the walls held photographs of the family. Some were a century old.

Eva held up her hand and placed it against the wall and closed her eyes.

"My room is down here." Skye opened a set of double doors and turned to Eva. "What are you doing?"

Eva inhaled and stepped back. "This place would be perfect."

Skye frowned. "Perfect for what?"

"It's a generational home." Eva slowly gazed around the hall. "I bet the energy that lives here is really strong."

"What energy?"

Eva stared at her for a moment. "Uh, you know, energy from your family."

"Okay. Whatever" Skye turned away and walked into her room. "What about your place? It looks pretty old."

"Yeah, but my dad says it's like twenty years old, or something like that."

"Twenty years old, eh? My mom says old houses like this have character," Skye said. "Whatever that means. I think your place has *a lot* of character."

Eva looked deep in thought. "You have no idea."

"Just put your stuff anywhere." Skye dropped her backpack on the far side of her bed and went over to the record player. "What'd you wanna listen to?"

Eva shrugged, glancing at the milk crate. "I don't know."

Skye grabbed a Duran Duran album in the stack and lifted the clear plastic lid. "I love this band. Carla played it at a barbecue over the summer." She carefully placed the needle on the vinyl. "You gotta hear the second song. It's totally wicked."

As the music started, she bobbed her head and flopped on the bed.

Eva placed her Adidas bag in the corner by the window and looked outside. "My bedroom looks out over the lake too." She turned to her friend. "Sometimes I open it and just listen to the sound of the water hitting the shore."

Skye shrugged. "I can't hear anything from up here. Just the wind" She got off the bed and went to her closet. "Mom said you can use a sleeping bag tonight." She opened the bi-fold door and dragged out the camping equipment. "It's pretty big and warm." She straightened out on the floor at the end of her bed. "Dad's got an inflatable mattress to put underneath 'cause the floor's too hard. He said he'd blow it up when he got home from work."

Eva stared at the green sleeping bag. "Okay." Her gaze drifted inside the closet to a pile of partially empty jars of different colours on the floor. "Is this what you use on your hair?"

Skye turned. "Yeah."

"Wow, you've got a lot here."

"Yeah I make it myself."

Eva picked up a jar half full of pink cream. "Really?"

She nodded and took the jar from her. "It's really easy, but I gotta do it every week to keep it." She grabbed some of her pink hair and let it fall from her fingers. "It's easy enough and it doesn't take me long."

Eva turned to the mirror. "Would it work on my hair?"

"Maybe, but we'd have to bleach out your natural colour first." A big smile appeared. "Do you wanna dye your hair pink?"

"Can we do it before we go to the mall?"

Skye's smile disappeared. "No. Bleaching it out and everything would take too long."

There was a loud *crash* from the bottom of the stairs. Skye raced over and threw open her bedroom doors. "Oh, my gawd! What did you do?"

She hurried out of the room and down the stairs. Of course, the little monsters would break something. She got to the bottom of the stairs and found the boys looking innocent at the kitchen table.

She stomped over to Ash. "What'd you break?"

"Nothing!"

"Then what was the crash?"

"Summer broke one of mom's vases," Stoney said.

"I did not!"

Ash's face twisted into a knot. "Don't lie. We saw you do it."

"I'm not lying. You're lying."

Skye rolled her eyes as they continued to bicker. "Where's Autumn?"

"Still watching tv," Ash said.

Skye went to the living room entrance. "You're supposed to be doing your homework."

"I wanna watch tv."

"You gotta do your homework." She bent down and hooked her arms under the girls' armpits. Autumn screamed and thrashed around.

"Lemme go!"

"No. Dad said everyone's supposed to do their homework when they get home."

The child thrashed around until Skye let go.

"You're not doing your homework."

"I am in my room."

Autumn dropped back down in front of the tv. Skye rolled her eyes and walked out.

She turned to her brother. "Why can't you just behave?"

"We didn't do anything!" He turned and pointed at the twins. "They broke the vase."

Summer stuck out her tongue.

Skye hurried to the broom closet. "Take this and clean it up." She pulled out a broom and dustpan and handed it to the boys.

Ash scrunched up his face. "Why do we have to do it?"

"Because I have a guest." She headed back to the stairs. "Get it cleaned up before Mom'n Dad get back."

Her stern voice echoed from the stairwell as she stormed back to the bedroom and slammed the door.

"They are such a pain in the ass! I can't wait to move out." She went to her closet.

Eva looked tense. "Are they all right?"

"They're fine. Just totally being a pain." She stood quietly facing the hanging clothing. Why wasn't her mother here to keep an eye on them? Why did she have to do it? Then it dawned on her. The dog. The argument. If she'd kept quiet none of this would have happened. She sniffed and wiped away a tear. She had company. She couldn't bawl like a baby in front of Eva.

"Vikki and Beth said they'd meet us at the mall. Vikki really likes Keith, so I told her we'd find out if he liked her too."

"Does he like her?"

"Dunno. I asked Brad but he didn't know either." She pulled out a mesh tank top and put it on. "What do you think? I got it when we went to Toronto this summer." She stepped in front of an oval floor mirror. "I'm gonna wear it tonight."

Eva tilted her head to one side. "It looks good."

Skye turned to her. "What are you wearing?"

Eva looked down at her outfit and tugged on her multicoloured, hand-knitted sweater and black skirt. "Just this."

Skye's eyes went wide. "Just *that*?" She turned back to her closet. "You can't wear that. Everyone is gonna be at the mall. You gotta look cool."

"Why?"

"Because if we look cool, then people will think we're cool and wanna hang with us." She pulled out a long, black lace cardigan and handed it to her. "My mom wore this for my grandpa's funeral. I borrowed it for a Halloween costume last year."

Eva tried to put it on over her sweater.

Skye laughed and shook her head. "Take your sweater off, first."

Eva wrapped her arms around her torso. "No."

Skye rolled her eyes. "No one's gonna see. I wear a bra all the time."

Eva looked away.

Skye's eyes went wide. "You don't wear a bra?"

Eva shook her head.

"I don't have one you could borrow." Skye went to her dresser and routed through the top drawer. "But I might have something you could wear underneath." She routed through a pile of

107

undergarments. "You must be the only girl in the ninth grade who doesn't wear a bra."

"My mom says I don't have to if I don't want to."

"My mom is, like, totally opposite. She says I have to now that I have boobs."

Eva pulled the neck of her sweater away from her body and looked down at her chest. "My mom wears a corset."

"That's kinda like a bra." Skye pulled out a thin, black camisole top and handed it to her. "Here, try this on. I only wore it once. To my grandpa's funeral." Skye walked to her bed. "You know, there's nothing wrong with *not* wearing a bra."

Eva turned away and pulled off her sweater. "I don't have one."

"If you want, we can look for one at the mall?"

Eva looked uncomfortable. "I don't know." The camisole was snug to her body, but it covered her small breasts. She put on the lace cardigan and stood. She scratched her neck. "It smells funny."

"Yeah, sorry. It's the closet. It's old." Skye gave a small smile. "That, like, actually looks good."

Eva tugged on the neck of the cardigan. "It's scratchy."

Skye took off her mesh top. "Try this one."

Eva examined herself in the mirror. "No, I'll wear this." She pulled at the neckline again. "It's not *that* bad."

Skye went and sat down on her bed and let out a sigh. "I'm sorry about all that yelling. My brothers and the twins are always getting into things."

"That's okay. I get it."

Skye looked away. "I hate looking after them. They never listen to anything I say."

"Well, as someone with an older brother, I can tell you it's no fun being looked after."

Skye was quiet for a moment as Eva continued to admire herself in the mirror. "So, have you figured out if you like Brad?"

Eva faced her. "I don't know. He's cute and smart, but I don't know if I like him like that."

"Don't you want a boyfriend?"

"I don't know." She sat on the end of the bed. "My brother and his girlfriend just broke up and it hurt him a lot."

"He must have really loved her."

She nodded. "She's dating this new guy, and it's so hard on him. I like Brad, but I don't know if I want to get hurt, and what if he doesn't like me?"

Skye pursed. "Then we'll just have to find out."

"Do you have a boyfriend?"

"No, not yet. Right now I'm busy with my protests, but I'd like to have a boyfriend. You know, someone you can hang out with and talk about stuff."

Eva nodded. "Yeah, that would be nice."

Skye stood. "Plus, I'd have someplace else to go other than here, especially when my parents are fighting."

"I've never seen my parents fight. If they do, it's not in front of Dom or I."

Skye frowned. "Who's Dom?"

"My older brother."

"Cool. What grade's he in?"

"He doesn't go to school."

"Must be nice."

"He's looking for a job though."

"Your parents don't want him to go to college or university?"

Eva shrugged. "No, not really. He was up for this really great job, but he lost it, so now he's moping around our house complaining all the time."

109

"That totally sucks."

"Yeah, it does."

The twins started to yell from the living room, but before Skye could get to the door, she realized that her parents were home. They ran down to greet them and were surprised to see several pizza boxes on the kitchen table. They gathered around the long table, and everyone grabbed a piece. Skye and Eva sat next to one another, while Mr. Daniels and the other kids went off into the living room.

"Don't get any on the sofa," Mrs. Daniels' called out. She turned to the table and grabbed a slice of pizza. "So, what are your plans for tonight? Doing each other's hair? Makeup? Maybe telling ghost stories?"

Eva picked up a slice of pizza. "Ghosts don't have stories. At least none that are interesting."

"Dad's taking us to the mall." Skye took a bite of her food. "Can I wear the earrings Grandma left me?"

Mrs. Daniels frowned. "Goodness sakes, no. Those are for special occasions."

"But this is a special occasion."

"I said no. They're too valuable. They're an heirloom, you know. Pure gold. Made before they put all that other junk in."

Shouts and screams came from the living room. Mrs. Daniels jumped at the sound.

"Oh, what's going on now?"

She hurried into the living room. Moments later an argument erupted between Skye's parents. One of the twins dropped their food and now there was a mess on the living room carpet. Arguing over who made the mess led to a heated discussion about letting the kids eat in front of the television.

Skye dropped a few more pieces of pizza on her plate and motioned Eva to do the same. There was another fight coming. She could tell from the tone of her parents' voices. Fights always started off this way.

"Mom, Eva and I are going to go upstairs and eat in our room."

Skye didn't wait for an answer and hurried up the stairs.

The mall parking lot was packed as Mr. Daniels pulled the station wagon up to the entrance. People hurried in and out of the mall. Most of them were teens, and everyone had a shopping bag with them. The girls got out of the car through the same door and stood on the curb. There was excitement in the air and it added to their already hyped up enthusiasm.

Eva was glad to be here. They'd spent the rest of the evening in Skye's room. She could easily tell the heated discussions going on downstairs were upsetting to her friend.

"Hey," Mr. Daniels said, as he waved them closer to him. "Mall closes at nine. I want you both out here and waiting. Understand?"

Skye nodded.

"Good." He reached inside his wallet and pulled out a twenty-dollar bill. "Here. Take this. Now have a great time and don't buy out the stores."

Skye stared at the money in his hand before grabbing it. "Thanks!"

They hurried into the mall and down the large aisle toward the centre of the building. Glass partitions encircled a large opening and let them look down to the lower level and the fountain that served as a focal point. There was a small food court between the supermarket and the main corridor. People crammed the mall, but most were just there observing the new shops. They followed the crowds to an escalator. On the ground floor across from the fountain stood an arcade.

Skye looked around the food court. "Do you see anyone?"

Eva shook her head. "Did Keith tell you when they'd get here?"

"No. Just to look for them." She pointed to the arcade. "Let's look in there."

The arcade was almost pitch dark with only the lights from the games. They pushed their way through the crowds to the back. Loud music from the wall speaker blared above them and made it impossible to talk to one another, so Skye made gestures to leave.

Just as they were about to exit, someone grabbed Eva by the shoulder. She turned to see Brad standing next to her, and Keith next to him.

"We saw you on the other side," he yelled. "We waved but you didn't see."

"It's too dark. I can't see anything." Skye stepped out into the mall and the others followed. "When did you get here?"

Keith shrugged. "About an hour ago. Got a ride with my sister and Donnie. Her and Carla wanted to do some shopping."

Eva and Skye shot concerned glances at each other.

Keith frowned. "What's that look for?"

"I'm thirsty," Eva said and headed toward the food court. "Let's get something to drink."

They noise from the arcade was drowned out by the noise of the mall. The small food court had a half dozen places to eat, and they each grabbed a drink from one of the burger places. A family got up from one of the tables, and they quickly ran over and grabbed their seats.

"Did you see anyone else?" Skye asked.

Keith shook his head, looking around. "No, but a few guys from my gym class said they were gonna come." His face lit up and waved his arms. "Over here!"

A small group of teenage boys walked through the food court tables toward Keith. Eva had seen them around school but didn't have any classes with them. One boy wore a jean jacket with patches of rock bands all over. He nodded to Brad when they approached.

Keith smiled as they clasped hands. "Hey, DevDude!"

DevDudes led a group of older teen males who all wore the same outfit. His mullet of dark brown hair hung past his shoulders and spiked in the front.

"Dude. Is this place bitchin' or what?"

"Oh, fer sure," Keith said. "Did you check out the record store?"

"Not yet. Anything good?"

"Totally better than downtown."

The teen nodded. "Cool." He took a quick look at Skye before he nodded at Brad again. "Catch ya later." He and Keith did a hand clasp before walking away.

Skye leaned across the table. "I didn't know you knew him."

"Dev? Yeah, we're in Shop class together." He turned to Brad. "Well, I'm in Shop. He only shows up half the time."

Skye turned toward him as he and his friends disappeared into a crowd.

Keith let out a guffaw of laughter. "What? You *like* him?"

She shifted uncomfortably. "I don't know. Maybe."

"Dude's in grade eleven and gots, like, piles of chicks after him."

Skye turned back to the table. "Whatever."

Shelly walked up to Keith and slapped him hard on the arm. "Hey, asshole. Gimme some money."

He frowned and rubbed his arm. "No way. You have your own."

Shelly scrunched up her face. "I spent it."

"Not my problem." He tried to avoid more of her slaps. "Go ask your boyfriend."

"I already did, but he says he needs it." She paused for a moment. "Please? I'm really hungry."

Brad turned to her. "I thought Donnie was taking you out?"

Shelly looked uncomfortable for a moment. "Yeah, well he didn't."

Keith stared at his sister and then reached into the front pocket of his jeans. "Okay, but I want the change back."

Shelly held out her hand. "Sure."

He pulled out a ten-dollar bill and was about to give it to her when he pulled it back. "Never mind, I'll buy it. Whad'ya want?"

She reached for the money. "I can get it."

He pulled the money out of her reach and stood. "Hardly. This way I know I get my change back." He walked toward one of the food stalls. "Whad'ya want?

Shelly's exhale was a mix of anger and frustration as she followed behind.

Brad shook his head. "Donnie's such a jerk."

Skye took a quick look at Eva. "Right? And he's cheating on Shelly."

Eva's eyes went wide. "I thought you weren't going to say anything?"

"I said I wasn't going to tell *her*."

Brad blinked a few times. "What?"

"He's cheating on her. We saw him and Carla together at the coffee shop by the school."

"So? Doesn't mean he's cheating—"

"They kissed," Eva said.

"On the lips," Skye continued. "And not in a friendly way. More like a boyfriend-girlfriend way."

Brad sat back. "You really think Donnie's cheating on Shelly?"

Both girls nodded.

"That sucks. Keith says she really likes him."

"Are you going to tell Keith?"

"I dunno."

Eva nodded. "I think you should. She deserves to know." Something on the far side of the food court caught her attention. She stared at a family as they stood by a stall, but it was who was behind the family that interested her. After a moment, the family moved. "Oh, my gawd!" She picked up her drink and tried to hide behind it.

Skye frowned. "What's wrong?"

"My brother's here." She took a quick look again. "And his best friend."

Skye strained her neck. "Where?"

"Over by the fried chicken stall. Sitting down on the bench."

Brad turned around. "I don't see anyone."

Eva put her drink down "He's wearing all black. You can't miss him." She looked again but he was gone.

"Okay, maybe that wasn't him." She sighed. Maybe it wasn't Dom?

"How old's your brother?" Brad asked.

"Eighteen."

"So, he's done school, or is he doing grade thirteen?"

"No, he's finished." She took a sip from her drink. "He did have an apprenticeship, but that didn't work out."

Skye took a sip from her drink. "Is that the job you were telling me about?"

Eva nodded.

"That sucks, but he could always go to college."

She shook her head. "I don't think he wants to do that."

"My dad didn't go," Skye said. "Got a job right after high school, but my mom went. That's where she met my dad. My grandpa said him not going to college is why he never got a good job." She leaned close to Eva. "And it's why we had to move in with them and live by the airport."

"Yeah, but it's a really nice house," Eva said, trying to sound sympathetic.

Skye shrugged. "Yeah, I guess."

Keith walked back to the table as he stuffed some money into his front pocket. Shelly was right behind him and sat at the adjacent table. He grabbed four small pie containers from her bag and gave one to each of them.

"They were four for a dollar."

The smell of apple pie filled the air, along with Shelly's burger and fries. She bit into her burger and pulled it away from her mouth. "There's bacon and cheese on this."

Keith shrugged. "Yeah, so?"

"That's extra."

He nodded. "I know."

She gave him a soft smile as she chewed her food. "Thanks."

Brad waved for her to come closer. "Pull your table over to ours."

Her gaze bounced between the four of them. "You sure?"

"Yeah." Keith motioned with his head. "You look like a loser sitting by yourself."

She gave him a dirty look but stood and pulled the small two-seater up to their table and sat down next to her brother.

Keith looked at everyone. "So, what are we doing?"

"Talking about Eva's brother," Brad said.

Carla and Donnie walked up to the table, side by side, laughing. She had several bags in her hands and dropped them by the table.

"What's up, losers!" She sat across from Shelly and took a few of her fries. "I so totally got more than I should have, but thanks to your boyfriend here, I found the perfect gift for Anthony."

Shelly looked hurt at her boyfriend as she ate a French fry. "You were with her?"

Donnie shrugged and leaned against another table next to them. "She needed my help."

Skye shot Brad a 'told-you-so' look.

Carla giggled. "I had to drag him from the arcade but wait until I show you what I got Anthony." She dug through her bags. "I found the cutest sweater!" She pulled it out and held it up. It was a tight crew neck in a brick wall pattern, with different shades of brown and heavy dark lines that defined the pattern. She smiled as she displayed it. "I think he'll love it."

"*Kakoy urodlivyy sviter.*"

Dom's voice was low as he and Delano walked up to the table. Dom's hair was slicked back, and the solid black outfit he wore was a snug fit.

Delano turned to his friend. "*YA by ne stal nosit' eto, skol'ko by vy mne ni platili.*" They both chuckled.

Eva's eyes went narrow. "What are you doing here?"

Delano slapped his friend on the back. "I asked him, what does a fun time in Kingston look like." He looked around the food court, unimpressed. "And he brings me here."

"Then he can take you someplace else."

Delano frowned and took a quick look at everyone. "Evandra, don't be rude. Introduce us to your companions."

Eva rolled her eyes. "Skye, Brad, Keith, Shelly, Carla and Donnie, this is Delano, and my brother Dom."

Carla sat up in her seat and leaned forward, trying to expose as much of her low-cut top as possible. "Very nice to meet you."

Delano nodded. "We all knew Evie was doing well in her new school, but to have so many friends." He turned to Shelly. "And attractive ones as well, now that is a surprise."

"Hey asshole," Donnie said and stood. "That's my girlfriend. Back off."

Dom stepped up to the table. "Skye? Is this the one that got you into trouble?"

"She didn't get me into trouble, and why are you even here?"

Dom held out his arms. "It's a grand opening, isn't it? Why shouldn't we come out and celebrate?"

"Because you don't like being around people, remember?"

Carla sat back in her seat. Her gaze jumped between Delano and Dom, but it lingered on Dom. "So, what language were you speaking?"

"Russian," Delano said.

Donnie stood close to the table. "You're a Ruskie? What the hell are you doing in this country?"

Dom went on the defensive. "What business is it of yours?"

Shelly slapped him. "Knock it off, Donnie."

Carla focused on Dom. "You wanna join us?"

"No," Dom said. "We have things to do." He turned to Eva. "Stay out of trouble." And then to the rest of the table. "Nice meeting you all." His gaze rested on Shelly for a few moments, and then gave a short nod and walked away.

Delano smiled. "It was very nice to meet you all." He hurried off to meet up with Dom.

Everyone at the table was silent for a few moments. Carla leaned to one side. "So, Evie is it? That was your brother?"

Eva clenched her jaw at the sound of her nickname. "Yeah."

"He's quite the hunk." She turned to Shelly. "I think he likes you."

Donnie exploded. "Well, she's got a boyfriend, so he can fuck right off."

Carla's eyes flared. "Oh, someone's jealous. Not a good look for you."

Donnie stood. "Come on, Shelly. We're outta here."

Shelly pushed the tray of food away and followed him, as Carla's face held a wicked grin.

Keith stood. "God, Carla, you're such a bitch."

Carla took a few of Shelly's left-over fries. "Hey, I was just having a little fun."

He tapped Brad on the shoulder. "Come on. Let's get outta here."

Brad nodded and they left, leaving the girls alone with Carla.

The older teen rolled her eyes. "Fucking wimps."

Skye reached over, took Shelly's tray and scooped up all the garbage. Carla reached out and grabbed Eva by the arm. "Hey *Evie*, find out if your brother likes me."

Eva broke her grip. "Why? You have a boyfriend."

Carla's gaze drifted past her. "Not one that looks like him."

Eva walked to a nearby garbage can. It all went in, but Shelly's empty drink cup slipped off and landed on the floor. She bent down to pick it up and bumped into someone.

"Oh sorry." She stepped back and recognized the goth girl from the grotto. "Hey."

The girl nodded. "Hey."

They both reached for the same spot on the handle. For a brief moment, their hands touched and a large jolt of static erupted from the gentle brush-up. It forced both girls back and made Eva's ears ring.

Eva rubbed her ears. "Wow, what was that?"

The girl looked just as bewildered. "Must be really staticky in here."

Eva looked down at her hand and clenched her fist a few times. Her hand tingled as the ringing slowly subsided. It had to mean something. Strange things like that always did, but she had no idea what.

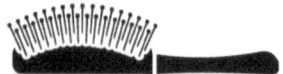

The mall patrons thinned in the last hour the mall was open. Even the arcade was less crowded as the girls played a few rounds of Pac-Man. Eva peeked over Brad's shoulder next to her and watched him play some cartoonish game of a gorilla throwing barrels. Keith stood on his other side and shouted and pointed at the screen. She didn't care about the game, she was focused more on Brad; the way his face contorted as he swatted the red buttons on the machine, and the way his eyes flared in the sterile light of the monitor. In this light, he looked kinda cute.

Skye's game ended and she dropped her arms by her side. "Well, I died. Again. I hate those ghosts." She turned to her friend. "Your turn."

Eva didn't say anything and just stared at Brad.

Skye glanced at the boys, and then back at Eva, and nudged her. "Your turn."

Eva blinked. "I don't want to play anymore."

Skye looked up at the clock on the wall. "Yeah, we should get going. Dad'll be here soon, and he'll freak if we're not out waiting for him." She turned to the guys. "We're gonna go."

"' K, see ya," Keith said, not taking his eyes away from the game.

"Yeah, later," Brad replied.

"You want a ride home with us?"

The synthetic game music played a finale. Both Brad and Keith slumped. Brad turned to the girls. "No thanks. We'll get a ride with Shelly."

Skye motioned him to move away from the game as Keith took his spot. When they were at a safe distance, Skye leaned closer. "Are you going to tell him about Donnie cheating on his sister?"

Brad balked. "Why do I have to?"

"Well, somebody has to."

Eva nodded. "Did you see how hurt she was when Carla showed up with him?"

Brad looked back at his cousin. "I dunno."

Skye shook her head, disgusted. "Whatever, but Donnie's an asshole." She turned and walked toward the exit.

Eva gave a short wave and followed behind. "See you Monday."

Brad waved with a small smile. "Yeah. See ya."

The mall was a mixture of shoppers, janitors, and teens in the food court as the girls headed to the escalator.

"This place is pretty cool." Skye held out her hand to the thin mist that surrounded the fountain. "A lot better than the other mall."

Eva shrugged. "I guess."

They stepped onto the escalator. Skye turned to her. "You ever been to the Eaton Centre in Toronto?"

"No."

"I've been once. When we went to Toronto for my uncle's wedding. That place is awesome. They have everything."

On the main floor, Shelly sat with Carla and Donnie on a bench near the exit. Carla admired the sweater she bought, and Eva snickered as her brother's words echoed in her mind.

"Hey," Shelly called to them. "Where's my dork of a brother?"

"In the arcade."

"Oh, just leave him," Carla said, and folded up the garment to put it back in the bag. "Let him walk home."

"He's playing that stupid game, isn't he?"

Eva nodded.

Donnie stood in a huff. "Go get him, or I leave without him."

Shelly rolled her eyes and walked off.

Outside, the night was cool with a clear sky and the moon almost full. The parking lot had a few cars near the far end, but the Daniels station wagon was nowhere to be seen. Away from the entrance, they sat on the cement ledge of an outside garden. Eva kept her gaze skyward and stared at the stars above.

"It's almost a full moon," she said.

Skye looked up. "Looks full to me."

"Nope, not quite."

The girls were still for a moment. Skye focused on her friend. "Should we have told Brad about Carla and Donnie?"

"If he's cheating on her, that's pretty horrible, and she does have the right to know."

"But what if he's not?"

Eva frowned. "We saw them in the donut shop, and that kiss was pretty intense."

"Yeah, but Carla's always flirty like that. She's always been popular. Maybe it meant nothing?" She looked away. "I mean, Carla can be a bitch, *fer sure*, but Shelly's her best friend. I don't think even she'd have the balls to do that."

"You know them better than I do, but I know what I saw."

They sat silent for a few minutes. Skye's serious look never faded. Only when Mr. Daniels arrived and beeped the car horn, did her mood change.

"So, how was the grand opening?" he asked, as they got into the back seat.

"The place is awesome, dad." Skye reached for her seatbelt. "They've got so many new stores. Nothing like the other malls."

Mr. Daniels nodded. "That's good." He looked at Eva. "And what did you think?"

"It's okay, but I don't go to malls that often."

He chuckled. "Never thought I'd hear a teen say those words."

He pulled away from the curb and drove around the mall to a far exit. A grocery store on the bottom level had an exit, and as they drove past, Eva saw the guys with Shelly and the others. She pointed. "Look, there's Keith and Brad."

Shelly walked behind Carla and Donnie with her brother. Carla looked more than just friends with him as she jokingly shoved him away from her. Skye turned to Eva. "I think we did the right thing."

Eva nodded. "Me too."

The ride back to the house was quiet. Eva was tired from the night and was looking forward to sleep, even if it was in a sleeping bag. The road to the Daniels' house had no streetlights, with only the car headlights shining up the road. The soft glow of light from the old house was a welcome sight as he pulled onto the property and parked near the front porch.

Everyone got out at once. The night air was much cooler near the water, and it sent a shiver through her.

"We've got a fire going out back if you girls want to hang out for a while." Mr. Daniels headed toward the house. "Your brothers and sisters are in bed, so it'll just be you two."

Skye nodded. "Thanks, dad."

They walked around the side of the house toward the backyard. "Is this a farm?"

Skye nodded. "Yeah, back when my grandparents lived here. They lived off the land and grew all their own food." A whimsical smile came over her. "I used to love playing with the animals they had."

"What happened to them?"

"Dad sold most of them off after Grandpa died. He said we needed the money to fix the place up." They walked across the short grass in the backyard. "They didn't have running water or hydro."

"Really?"

"Well, not like it's supposed to be. It was weird with hand pumps and really old glass fuses and stuff. Dad said it was a fire hazard and how they didn't burn the place down was beyond him."

They sat by a fire pit that still held enough burning embers to keep the chill of the night away. There were six old lawn chairs scattered around the pit, and the garbage remains of a s'mores-fest. Eva leaned back and looked up at the sky. This place brought a sense of peace to her that she had never felt before.

The back screen door slammed shut as Mrs. Daniels walked toward them with a tray loaded with goodies. "So, did you girls have fun at the mall?"

"It's so great," Skye said, as her mother put down the tray. "Everyone's gonna be hanging out there."

"Well, I'm not sure why we needed another shopping venue, but I guess that's what happens when a city grows." She sat next to her daughter. "Did you see a lot of your friends there?"

"Some." Skye picked up some of the gooey s'mores. "Even Eva's brother was there."

Mrs. Daniels's brow rose. "Oh, you have a brother?"

"Yes, but I don't know why he was there. He hates places like that." Skye frowned and stuffed the treat into her mouth. "His friend didn't seem to mind it."

Eva shrugged. "Delano's family owns a big business, and he goes all over the world. A small shopping centre like that is nothing compared to shopping in European cities, but I think he was trying to get Dom in a better mood."

Skye turned to her mother. "He got dumped by his girlfriend for another guy."

Mrs. Daniels put her hand to her chest. "Oh, the poor dear. I bet he's heartbroken."

Eva nodded as she bit into her treat. "He is."

"What a good friend your brother has."

Skye put her plate down. "I was gonna ask you earlier, what did your brother say?" Skye turned to her mother. "Carla was showing off this sweater she bought for her boyfriend, and Eva's brother said something in Russian."

Mrs. Daniels' brow rose. "Russian?"

Eva wiped some melted marshmallows from her face. "My father's from Russia, but Dom can speak it better than I can."

Mrs. Daniels smiled. "What did he say?"

Eva mulled over Dom's words. "He said it was the ugliest sweater he'd ever seen."

Skye let out a laugh and spit s'more crumbs. "That is so awesome!" She looked at her mother. "It was a totally gross sweater, Mom. Looked like a wall of bricks."

A scream of pain from somewhere inside the house was followed by shouts and more screaming. Mrs. Daniels let out a heavy sigh and stood up. "I thought they were asleep." She bent down and kissed the top of Skye's head. "Don't stay out here too late and dump that bucket of water on the embers before you come inside."

"Night, Mom."

"Goodnight, dear." She smiled at Eva. "Have a good sleep."

More shouts and screams echoed from the house and her mother hurried her pace, and once inside, loud threats of grounding and no television quickly quieted everyone down.

Skye shook her head. "They are such a pain in the ass."

"At least they're younger," Eva said. "Dom does one mean thing to me every day." She relaxed into the chair and grabbed another treat. "He says it's his duty as my older brother."

Skye had a wicked grin on her face. "I can see that." She picked up one of the glasses of pop from the tray. "Tired?"

"No, just relaxing." She sat up and examined the trees. "This place is really quiet."

"Yeah. It's nice."

An owl hooted somewhere off in the distance. Its low call cut through the stillness and Eva thought she saw something move from the edge of the tree line. Another series of hoots and she sat up and listened with more interest. "That's an owl."

Skye chuckled. "Yeah, we have a bunch of them that live in the old barn."

Eva listened intensely. "No, that's a *horned* owl." She stood. "You have horned owls on your property?"

Skye frowned. "So?"

"So?" A flare of excitement raced through her. "Do you know what that means?"

"No."

"It means that—" Eva caught herself. Horned owls were guardians that watched over woods and forest areas and companions to the Elementals that inhabited the wild places. If a nest of these owls were here, that meant this property was protected by something magical and there were several she could think of off the top of her head, but she couldn't tell Skye. Her new friend wouldn't believe her and maybe think she was some kind of crazy person, and that would be the end of their friendship. She sat back in her chair, disappointed. "It means that they feel safe here." She turned to stare at the embers. "That's a good thing."

"I guess. Dad likes them here cos they eat mice and other small things that would try to get into the house."

Eva stood. Being in the presence of a horned owl was a rare gift, and she had to know where it was. She walked slowly past the pit and toward the trees. The owl let out another series of hoots, but it seemed to be farther away than she thought.

"Where are you going?"

"I want to try and find him."

"Why? It's just an owl."

Eva got to the tree line and stopped. Elementals were very protective of their territory. If one was here, exposing it could bring problems to Skye and her family, especially as none of them knew how to interact with one.

Herself included.

Something lifted off from a branch above her and glided deeper into the canopy. Eva squinted to see if she could make out the bird but saw nothing. She turned and headed back to the pit. "It's gone."

Skye picked up the bucket of water. "Everyone's in bed, so we can watch TV." She dumped the water on the embers and the smoke billowed up into the night sky.

Skye picked up the empty dishes and put them on the tray and popped a small piece of treat into her mouth. "We can get more of these inside. Mom made a ton of stuff for us to eat for later."

Eva headed to the back door behind her friend, when a gust of wind blew through the back yard. Skye didn't notice other than it made getting inside a bit more difficult, but Eva knew exactly what it meant. She turned around and faced the darkness of the yard. A few moments later, her mother stepped out from the tree line with Mr. Nithercott behind her, and she ran to them immediately.

"What are you doing here?"

"We've concluded our meeting with Council member Kaige," Mr. Nithercott said, "And he has come to the conclusion that you do not understand the severity of what you've done."

"But I do. I know it was wrong, and I won't do it again."

Mr. Nithercott pulled out a small scroll. "While your mother and I believe you, I'm afraid the councilor is less trusting." He unrolled the parchment. "We've been asked that you sign this formal contract."

She frowned. "What is it?"

"It's just a statement saying that from this point on, you will not partake in any spellcast outside of your home, big or small."

She turned to her mother. "Do I have to sign this?"

Venera was stern. "Yes, you do, and to keep you honest, I've created a little something to help you keep from spellcasting while you're at your school."

Mr. Nithercott removed a quill that had been rolled up in the parchment and handed it to her.

Eva took the quill. "I don't need anything. I've been good."

"None-the-less," her mother said, as she watched Eva scribble her name at the bottom of the parchment. "You need help ridding yourself of the temptation." She opened a cloth bag that hung from her wrist and removed a small glass vial. "Drink this. It's a Blocking potion. It's nothing serious, but it'll keep the idea of casting a spell out of your mind."

Eva finished writing. "Mom, I don't need it!"

"It's just for a couple weeks, until you get used to not spellcasting."

"This is so heinous!"

Venera balked. "Actually, considering the circumstances, I think it's acceptable, and it'll wear off by *Soween*."

"You can still cast spells when you're in the realm, or at

home," Mr. Nithercott said, and took the quill from her. "The purpose of this is for you to understand when and where you should spellcast."

Eva rolled her eyes in a huff. "I can't cast spells, we can't do our protest. This is so harsh!"

Venera frowned. "What protests?"

Eva shook her head. "Doesn't matter now."

An owl hooted from the branch above them. Both Mr. Nithercott and Venera took an interest, but Eva couldn't care less.

The old man pointed. "Is that what I think it is?"

Venera smile. "I believe it is."

He looked around the property. "Very interesting."

Eva exhaled. "Can I go now?"

Her mother motioned to the vial. "Drink the potion first."

Eva pulled off the small cork and brought the glass to her lips. The liquid floated around her mouth, and she swallowed quickly. It had a blueberry aftertaste, and it made her body shiver.

Venera nodded. "Good. Go and have fun with your friend and we'll see you tomorrow."

Eva hurried to the house. At the back door, she turned and took a look back, but they were gone. A faint hue of light blue quickly faded into the black of the woods. Another hoot echoed in the darkness, and it was closer. It flew from its perch in a large pine tree and sat on the back of one of the lawn chairs and stared at her. Beyond the backyard, the trees bent to one side, as though something very large was walking by.

The back porch light flicked and the tall field grass at the far side of the house swayed in an unseen breeze. Eva stared at the grass and a trampled spot near the fire pit. A gentle wind blew through the property, and the field grass straightened up.

Something big just passed by. She raised her hands to cast a revealing spell, but rolled her eyes and dropped her arm.

Skye came to the door. "What are you doing?"

Eva shrugged and pulled on the screen door. "Nothing, I guess."

Chapter Five

Over the weeks, the girls kept their promise of no protests to the vice-principal, but that didn't mean they couldn't plan them. Skye bought several binders and filled them with slogans she thought would catch people's attention, diagrams of displays, a map of the school grounds and where they could protest as well as several lists of what hand-drawn art she would use, and more research topics. Eva didn't know the first thing about any of this, but knew this was the right thing to do, and helped where she could. This cause had become important to her as well, even if it seemed that most people didn't care.

They sat together in the cafeteria during one of their shared lunches. Skye had her binder open with sheets of paper spread out before her. Her peanut butter and jam sandwich were cut into quarters and lay to her right.

"I don't think we should go with the soft touch," she said and bit into her food. "People have to understand how important this is." She picked up one of the more gruesome poster ideas. "If we show people we're serious, they'll take it seriously too."

Eva took one of the more disturbing mock-ups from her. She understood what her friend was trying to accomplish, but this was too over-the-top.

"I don't know. This looks more scary than serious."

"It's supposed to be scary." She flipped to the back of the binder. "I need more paper. Do you have any?"

Eva shakes her head. "I gave all of it to you." She shoved a fork full of fries and gravy into her mouth. "We'll have to go to the mall to get more."

"I'll pick up more binders too."

Eva frowned and took a quick look at the stack in front of her friend. "Don't you have enough?"

Skye looked as though Eva had called her a freak. "We need to be organized." She piled the binders on top of one another with a look of pride. "If we're not, something could go wrong." The smile melted from her face. "Shit. Carla's headed our way."

Their tormentor wore her cheerleader outfit and smelled like expensive perfume. The scent tickled Eva's nose and she quickly rubbed it.

"Well look who it is." Her fake tone was noticeably condescending. "My favourite cousin and her best friend."

"What do you want?"

Carla shot a nasty look at Skye. "Nothing from you. I need to talk to Evie."

Eva cringed at hearing her nickname.

"She has nothing to say to you."

"Just shut up." Carla turned to Eva. "Tell Dom to meet me at our usual place so I can give him another driving lesson, okay? Around ten tonight."

Eva squirmed. "Okay."

She leaned in close to Eva. "Don't forget, because I know how to make your life even more miserable than it already is."

Skye pushed Carla away from their table. "Knock it off, Carla. You got what you wanted, so go slither back under your rock."

The older girl sneered before returning to Eva. "Ten o'clock."

She gave them both one last nasty look and walked away.

"What does he see in her?" Skye sat back down. "Does your brother have a mental problem, or what?"

Eva looked down at the remaining fries on her plate. "I don't know. My parents are happy that he's getting over his last girlfriend." She picked up her can of pop. "And my dad thinks that studying to get his driver's license means he's accepting that he lost his apprenticeship."

"That'll be cool," Skye nodded. "He can drive you to school and stuff, but he has to know what she's like." Skye was serious. "She cheated on her last boyfriend with Donnie, and she's so mean to you."

Eva glared at Carla across the lunchroom. She was horrible, and she needed to be exposed for the bully she was and she couldn't let her hurt Dom. Not after what Alisha did. He was family and you watched over family. Maybe something small like a slip tongue spell or—

"Eva?"

Hearing her name jolted her back to Skye's conversation. She shrugged. "Whatever. It's his funeral."

The walk to the mall took close to a half-hour, but with a chill in the air, they made it there in twenty. There were a few more new stores, but the parking lot was practically empty. They headed to the food court and bought two hot chocolates from a kiosk. Bright-coloured posters depicting the autumn season were everywhere, with a few stores already displaying holiday items.

They finished off their drinks and headed out into the mall. The stationery store was across from the record store, but Eva stayed outside and wandered by the adjacent shops. It was nice to have the mall quiet for once. The large crowds made it hard to shop. Tonight, there were just a few patrons walking the corridors. Most of the shop staff looked bored and didn't pay much attention to her as she browsed their merchandise.

"Hey, Eva." Brad stood at the entrance of a kid's clothing store. "You shopping too?"

Eva smiled as he came closer. "I'm just here with Skye."

Brad chuckled. "Lemme guess, Bristol board and binders?"

"How'd you know?"

"She's always buying that stuff."

Eva motioned to the bag in his hand. "What'd you get?"

Brad looked down at his purchase. "It's a birthday gift for my sister. Mom said I had to buy her something, but I didn't know what to get her."

"Let's see."

Brad opened the bag and brought out a girl's top and held it up. It was a heavy sweater with a floral pattern on it. "Her favourite colour is blue, but I couldn't find anything blue."

Eva stared at the top. "It's cute."

"That's what I thought too." They walked to the record store. "I was thinking about buying that new Aldo Nova album. It's really wicked."

They walked to a display just inside the store. There were a dozen albums lined up along three shelves with their rank in the lower left-hand corner.

Eva pointed to the one she'd seen at Skye's place.

"That one's pretty wicked too."

Brad picked it up. "Duran Duran." He flipped it over. "They're all right, I guess."

Eva took the album from him.

"The second song is awesome."

He leaned close to her.

"Really?"

Eva looked at his face. A few patches of stubble dotted his chin and lower lip.

Brad gave a slight grin.

"You have a nice smile," she said.

Brad quickly looked away.

"Thanks."

"Hey." Skye's voice came from behind them. "I've been looking all over for you."

"Sorry. I was just wandering around."

Brad nodded at her. "Hey."

"Hey." She walked up to them. "Well, you should have said something. I thought you bailed on me."

Brad looked over the large bag she carried. "More Bristol board and binders?"

Skye opened the bag. "And some paper, and markers."

He nudged Eva. "Told you."

Eva giggled at Skye's confused look.

Skye motioned to Brad's purchase. "What's that?"

"Birthday present for my sister."

"Let's see."

He took the sweater out of the bag. "I think she'll like it."

Skye made a face. "It looks kind of . . . young."

He frowned. "She's eight."

"Yeah, but does she wanna dress like an eight-year-old?"

"Why wouldn't she?" Eva asked.

Skye rolled her eyes. "The twins *hate* the clothes Mom gets them. They're always trying to wear my stuff."

Brad stuffed the sweater back in the bag. "Maybe I should get her something else." He looked across the corridor to the kids' store. "I don't wanna go back in there."

"You got her something," Eva said. "I'm sure she'll like it."

He looked torn. "Yeah, I guess."

They stood silent for a while as Skye rummaged through her purchases. Eva tried not to look at Brad, but when she did, he was looking at her and they both smiled.

Brad broke the silence. "You guys hungry?"

He bought them all fries and burgers and they tasted even better than they smelled. They sat at a small four-seater table near the fountain with all of Skye's purchases taking up the open seat.

Brad popped a French fry in his mouth. "So, you guys haven't done a protest since?"

"Nope." Skye was a little disappointed. "I'm keeping my end of the bargain."

"My parents aren't thrilled that I got detention," Eva said. "I don't think they like me doing them."

"But you're still gonna do them with me, right?"

She nodded vigorously. "Oh, fer sure."

"But what if you get in trouble with your parents?" Brad asked. "If they're not happy you did the last one, they won't be happy if you keep doing them."

"But this is important," Eva said. "I'll have to figure out something."

"Have you tried talking to them about it?" Skye asked.

"Not since my mom and I talked about the acid rain."

"Maybe you should."

"Maybe you *both* should," Brad said. He motioned to Skye. "I know your parents get it, but if you both talk to Eva's, tell them what you wanna do and how important it is. That might help them to understand."

"He's right," Eva said, as she took a sip from her pop. "I think we need to tell my parents together."

"And how are we going to do that?" Skye asked. "Your parents are never home."

"But they'll be there if I tell them you're coming for dinner."

Skye dropped her food on the wrapper. "After what happened, I don't think they wanna see me sitting at their kitchen table." Skye popped a French fry into her mouth. "And they could still say no."

"You don't know that," Brad said.

Eva smiled. "Then let's make sure they don't!"

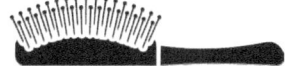

Eva was a nervous wreck. Her parents agreed to the dinner that weekend so they could discuss the protests, but that wasn't what made her nervous. Rather, it was the possibility something magical would happen and she'd have to explain to her friend that she and her family were part of a magical world that no one knew about. There was always the possibility someone on the outside would discover just how 'special' their home was but considering most people didn't believe in magic, it was easy to brush off any mishap as a flight of imagination, but Skye was single-minded. Eva worried that some ridiculous excuse wouldn't be enough.

She sat in her room and stared out the window. The days were getting much cooler now, and a strong gust brought some of the colourful leaves across her view. Even the dark grey water of Lake Ontario looked anxious. Dom's music blasted from down the hall, some dark and depressing beat that added to her anxiety.

She left her room and headed downstairs. Sem'ya turned the normal Gothic red wallpaper into a skull fresco in grey. She went to a wall and pressed her cheek against the paper. "Please, Sem'ya. Don't let his music get to you. Try to be in a better mood. For me? This dinner needs to be perfect."

The house moaned and groaned for a moment and slowly the treatment went from the depressing abstract to a more subtle tone of large fading flowers.

Eva stood back and examined the new design. "I suppose that's better."

Black mist tumbled from the stone archway as Egori and Venera walked through the portal. His Victorian-era tailcoat jacket and shirt accompanied a more modern looking pair of pants, with Venera's jumper being more in style.

"Good evening, Evie. Apologies for taking so long," her father said, and quickly headed off upstairs.

"That's okay. I'm just glad you're here now."

Egori spoke louder from the top of the stairs. "I will be just a few moments."

"Stop worrying." Venera hugged her daughter.

"I'm not worrying."

"Yes, you are." She kept her arm around Eva's shoulder and led her toward the kitchen. "Everyone has promised to be on their best behaviour for tonight. We are just as concerned about keeping our secret as you are."

"Her life is so different." Eva flopped down at the kitchen table. "And the energy is so alive."

Venera took a step toward the fridge. "I was surprised at the energy of the property. How many generations live there?"

"Only one, but it's been passed down at least three times."

Her mother took out a bag of dumpling and put them on the

counter. "Perrin said the owl we saw, it's one of the rarest in the world. There's something special about that place."

Eva went to the counter. "*Varenniki*?" A slight pang of anxiety came over her. "Did Dad make this...here?"

Her mother gave a quick wink. "What do you think?"

Eva relaxed. "He went to Kyiv."

Venera noted the disappointed look on her daughter's face. "What's wrong?"

"I just thought we'd have something a little more, you know, normal."

"This is normal."

"For us, yeah, but what if she doesn't like it?"

"Then we will make her something else." Venera cupped her daughter's chin. "Relax, Evie. Everything will be fine."

Eva went back to the kitchen table. "At least Dom won't be around."

"He's been quite the social butterfly as of late."

"Yeah, he's dating that girl from my school."

Venera cocked her head to one side. "Your school?"

"Yeah. The one giving him driving lessons." Eva thought about telling her how horrible Carla was, but he'd been in a good mood since they started going out, and she was tired of him being nasty all the time.

"She's made quite an impression on him. I never would have thought he'd be interested in anything to do with this world, but going for his license so he can drive her around, that is something." She paused and shook her head as she turned on the old cook stove and brought out some pots.

"I think he's tired of Shelly always picking them up for stuff."

Venera sighed. "I only hope this isn't some kind of rebound from Alisha."

Dom came down the stairs sounding like he was taking the entire staircase with him. He stormed into the kitchen and to the fridge. An air of musk followed him, and Eva waved her hand in front of her nose.

"What's that smell?"

Venera stifled a smile. "You look very handsome, Dom."

The teen brought out a plate of food. "Don't know when I'll be back. Don't wait up."

"Where is this party?"

He sat at the table next to his sister. "No idea."

"Do you know anyone else who'll be there?"

"Yup." He shoveled a fork full of food into his mouth and glanced at Eva.

Venera leaned against the counter. "When do we get to meet this Carla?"

"Hopefully, never," Eva said.

Her mother frowned. "Eva, don't be rude? You never used to be this . . ."

Dom looked at his sister. "Childish?" He scooped more food into his mouth. "It's the high school. I think it's a bad influence on her."

Eva swatted him hard, which got her a stern warning look from her mother. Footsteps came from the foyer as Egori entered the kitchen. His dapper suit from earlier was gone, replaced by a pair of jeans, a denim shirt, and a jean jacket. He did a curt twirl in front of his family. "What do you think? Luca Allard said this would make me look more like one of them."

Eva blinked with a straight face as she looked over her father's outfit.

Venera went to her husband's side. "Sweetie, that's an awful lot of denim."

Egori glanced down at himself. "Luca said it was a tuxedo."

She turned away. "Well, now I see where Delano gets his sense of humour from."

"You do not like it?"

Dom smiled. "You look good, dad."

"Yeah, dad," Eva said. "You really do."

Egori gave a short bow and went to the stove. "It is oddly comfortable."

The doorbell rang and Eva jumped to her feet. "That's Skye!" She raced off to the foyer and opened the heavy front door.

Skye stood on the porch, just a bit back from the door. A wide smile creased her face when she saw Eva. "Hey!"

"Hey." A car horn beeped from the street and Lennon and Melanie Daniels waved from the passenger side car window.

"Hi, Mr. Daniels!" Another car pulled up behind the station wagon. Shelly's small red car with Donnie in the driver's seat. "Dom. Carla's here."

He raced past them and down the steps. The back door opened, and Carla got out. Her outfit barely covered her body, and she flirted with Dom before they both got inside.

Donny pulled away from the curb and drove off, squealing the tires around the corner. Eva shook her head. "He such a loser."

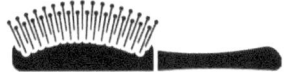

The parlour and the library doors were closed for obvious reasons, but the dining room was set for guests with candles and the good china. Eva's parents sat at either end, while the girls were placed across from one another near the centre. Egori served them a four-course meal consisting of all Russian dishes, and to Eva's delight, Skye enjoyed each. The dinner conversation consisted of Skye explaining her protests in great detail. Every question was answered with an intelligent response, and Eva could see her parents were coming around. The protest talk lasted most of the dinner, diverting a few times to classes or Skye's family. Venera asked a few questions about Carla and her family once she discovered she and Dom's new girlfriend were related.

Afterward, the girls went up to Eva's room. Skye was awed by how large it was, with its separate bathroom and windows that overlooked the water, not to mention the middle window with its sitting ledge and pillows.

"I wish I had this in my room," Skye said, as she sat on one end of the window bench. "I think I'd just sit here all day and read."

"Maybe your dad could make one?"

Skye shook her head. "I doubt it. You should have heard him swear when he had to fix the cupboards in the kitchen." She looked around the room. "So, what else do you do? You got any hobbies or stuff?"

Eva didn't do much outside of schoolwork, so there were no hobbies she could show off or talk about. She shrugged. "Just schoolwork."

"Do you got any records we could listen to?"

"No." Her face lit up. "But Dom does." She got to her feet. "I'll go get the record player from his room."

"Are you sure he won't mind?"

Eva shook her head as she headed to the door. "He's gonna be gone for hours. I'll put it back and he won't know a thing." She left the room and headed down the corridor. "I'll be right back."

Dom's room was a mess, with clothing thrown all over the bed and floor. She unplugged the player and laid it on the bed before going through his records. They'd never really talked about music before, so she grabbed several albums from a shelf on the far wall of different bands. The light in the room went dim. Sem'ya moaned and the walls shook.

Eva glanced up. "It's okay. I'll put it all back before he comes home."

Sem'ya continued to groan.

Eva exhaled. "Sem'ya please! Stop making such a big deal out of this."

"Who are you talking to?"

Eva turned to see Skye standing just outside the doorway. "Uh, no one."

Her friend frowned. "No, you were talking to someone."

"Oh, just to myself."

Skye moved to take a step forward. A flash of light burst from the entrance and threw Skye several metres backward. She slid down the hall and stopped just by Eva's bedroom door.

"Sem'ya!" Eva dropped the records on the bed and ran out of the room. "Skye, are you okay?"

The girl lay on her back. Blonde hair with a hue of green covered her face and she stared up at the ceiling. "What happened?"

"You're not hurt, are you?"

Skye sat up. "No, I don't think so." She tilted her head to one side. "It was like something…pushed me out. Hard." She focused on Dom's room. "Really hard. Like, I felt it hit my chest."

Eva crouched down by her friend. "I'm so sorry."

Skye's brow rose. "Wait, I'm right?"

Eva kept quiet.

Skye jumped to her feet. "Fine. I'll just go into his room and—"

"No!" Eva grabbed her by the arm. "You can't."

"Why not?" Skye crossed her arms. "Because I'll get thrown out again, won't I?"

Eva stood and swallowed. This was just what she didn't want to happen. She should have told Skye to stay in her bedroom. She wouldn't have followed her and Sem'ya wouldn't have protected Dom's room. The secret was out, and she knew Skye well enough that she'd keep pushing it.

"Sem'ya takes a while to warm up to new people."

"I was right! You were talking to someone." A satisfied smirk creased her lips. "So who's Sem'ya?"

Eva gave a weak smile. "It's really hard to explain."

Skye glanced down the hall. "Something hit me. I felt it." She turned to Eva. "Is that the energy you were talking about at my place? Is your house haunted?" A bright smile lit up her face. "Is my house haunted?"

"No, my house isn't haunted. It's more like an essence."

There was a look of disbelief. "Your house has an essence?"

"It's nothing. Really." Eva's anxiety grew. "Nothing special, I mean."

Sem'ya groaned and the walls shook as the wallpaper turned to a myriad of grey skulls and crossbones on a blood-red background.

Skye stared in shock at the spectacle. Turning around several times through the change. "Eva, I think your house essence is *really* upset."

Eva froze as the wallpaper all down the hall turned different shades of dark red. Eva closed her eyes. This wasn't happening!

She hurried to the wall and rubbed the wallpaper. "Sem'ya, I'm sorry. I didn't mean that." She turned to her friend. "Don't worry, Sem'ya won't hurt you." There was a pleading tone to her voice.

Egori and Venera hurried up the stairs, keeping a close eye on the walls as they continued to change colour. They stopped short when they saw the girls in the hall. Egori came forward. "Evie. What happened?"

Eva swallowed several times as she tried to ease the knot in her throat. Her eyes teared up and she let out a small sniffle.

Venera went past her husband. "Skye?"

Skye turned to Eva and then to her parents. "Is this house haunted?"

Egori sent a quick glance at his wife. "No, nothing like that."

Venera took another step closer to their guest. "Our home has a certain bewitching characteristic to it."

"Bewitching," Skye repeated. "You mean, like magical?"

Venera glanced back at her husband. Egori gave a slow nod.

She looked to Skye. "Yes."

The girl took a sideways look at Eva. "So, that means you're magical too?"

Egori took a step closer and raised his left hand. "Our whole family is."

Skye had a look of fear when she saw his hand in front of her. "Are you going to hurt me?"

Venera placed her hand gently on top of Egori's. "No, but he can make it so you won't remember any of what's happened, if you prefer."

Eva was openly crying and rubbing the wall. Why did she insult Sem'ya. She knew better! Ancestral entities were always sensitive, but she didn't mean to upset it.

Skye frowned. "Why would I want to forget?"

"Because," Venera spoke softly. "Most people don't believe that magic exists, and those who do sometimes have a difficult time accepting it."

Skye turned to Eva. "That day in detention, you whispered something into the ball of paper. I thought it was weird, but then the teacher didn't see anything we wrote."

Eva nodded between sobs and wiped her eyes. "It was a privacy spell. I cast it because we'd get into more trouble if he saw we were passing notes." The confession popped out before she could think about what she was saying.

Egori shot a stern look at his daughter.

"Have you done other stuff like that?"

Eva shrugged. "A few."

Skye's eyes went wide with excitement. "Really? When?"

"Skye," Venera said, coming closer. "You do understand that we must keep this a secret?"

She nodded. "Yeah, but I don't think anyone would believe me anyway." She looked at Egori. "Are you gonna make me forget?"

Egori lowered his hand. "Not unless you want me to."

Her face lit up. "Really?"

"Our conversation at dinner showed us that you are someone who understands the world around you better than most." He walked past her to his daughter's side. "I have no objection to you retaining the knowledge of this place, as long as you keep it to yourself." He put his arm around Eva. "If that is what you wish."

Skye smiled. "I think it sounds like fun."

He nodded. "Good. Then perhaps you can help our daughter to keep it a secret as well."

Eva choked out a laugh in between sobs. "I promise Sem'ya won't do that again." She turned to her father. "Right?"

He lowered his arm. "Why don't you take your friend outside, and we will ease Sem'ya's mood."

Eva took Skye by the hand and led her downstairs and through the kitchen to a very small back balcony that overlooked a half-acre of land against the shore of Lake Ontario. There was nothing in the yard except for a few juniper bushes, rocks and the shore. A short dock jutted out several metres into the water. It was old and looked worn and unstable.

"Is your house gonna be all right?"

Eva nodded. "Dad knows how to calm Sem'ya down."

"What's out here?" Skye asked as they headed toward the dock.

Just the lake, but "I want to show you something." Eva stepped onto the wood plank. It wobbled slightly and she waited until it stopped to continue. "It's really awesome."

Skye stood on the shore. "That dock doesn't look safe."

"It is." Eva motioned her to follow. "It's just a little shaky, but you get used to it." She waited until her friend took the first step before she continued. "I think you'll like this."

Skye carefully walked behind her. "What are you going to do?"

Eva turned to her and smiled. "Magic." She faced the lake and closed her eyes. "Real magic." She held up her right hand and traced a large circle in the air clockwise.

"Thought and breath mix as one, let water and fire combine, create a window in this place, and reveal to us what can be seen." She turned her head slightly toward Skye. "Spells don't always have to rhyme."

A soft breeze blew off the lake and onto the shore. Skye gazed out over the lake. "I don't see anything."

"Just wait."

The breeze grew stronger and caused ripples along the surface of the water. A moment later a thin stream of water rose from the end of the dock and into the air. It spun clockwise and formed into a circle and filled the center with a thin sheet of water.

"That is so cool."

The circle grew in size until it was a good metre in diameter. Skye reached out and touched the circle. The water brushed past her hand and continued in the loop.

Eva held up her hand. "Show me the family of my friend, Skye Daniels." She touched the center of the circle. Waves rippled outward from the thin sheet of liquid. "This is one of the first spells I learned."

With each ripple an image became clearer. It was of Skye's family at the kitchen table playing a board game. They couldn't hear what was said, but judging from the laughter, they were having a good time.

Skye stood in awe. She blinked a few times and reached out to touch the image. "Is it real?"

"Very real."

"Can you make it so we can hear them?"

"No, that's a more advanced spell that I could learn when I get older."

A longing smile crept across Skye's face. "That's the twins' favourite game. They got it for Christmas last year."

"Reveal Dominik Shade." Again, she touched the center of the circle and the waves rippled until the image of her older brother and others around him came into focus. He sat on an ottoman at the far end of a large sectional sofa. Carla sat on the edge of the sofa with Donnie next to her, and Shelly next to Donnie. Donnie and Carla were having a good time, drinking and talking to others around them. Shelly sat with a drink in her hand and looked uncomfortable. Dom just looked miserable.

"Looks like a fun party," Eva said.

Skye snorted. "Your brother isn't impressed."

"He never is."

Skye reached up and touched the image. "Shelly looks so sad."

Dom yawned and glanced in their direction. He frowned, and then stood and quickly walked toward them.

"He can see us?" Skye asked.

He flicked the center of the water circle and the entire thing collapsed back into the lake.

Eva sighed. "Yes. Magic sees magic."

"How much?"

"About as much as we could see of them."

Skye giggled. "So, he saw, like, a ring of water with two floating heads in the middle of the living room?" They laughed at the absurdity of it for a few moments and then headed back toward the shore. "So why don't you know the spell to hear conversations?"

"That's a special incantation, and it's only used by certain people," Eva said, as they walked onto the shore. "There are people in my world whose job is to keep our world safe from outside threats, but it has its limits too."

"Cos magic sees magic?"

"And hears it too." She took a quick look back at the dock. "But that? Everyone learns how to do that."

"Can you do magic anywhere?"

"Yes, well I could."

Skye frowned. "You can't now?"

Eva squirmed. "I wasn't supposed to do spells outside of home, but I did a few and got into trouble."

"From your parents?"

She nodded. "And from the ruling council, but because it was just small spells I didn't have to go before a Tribunal."

Skye spoke eagerly. "Cool, 'cause that seems kind of, like, harsh."

"Yeah, it was just one Council member, my sponsor and my mom."

"What was your punishment?"

"They gave me an elixir to keep the idea of spellcasting out of my head, but just for like when I'm not at home."

"Harsh!"

"Fer sure."

They got to the steps at the end of the deck. Eva's fear was gone, and she was glad Skye was so accepting about all of this. She thought for sure that the girl would run away screaming and never talk to her again, but Skye was pretty cool.

"So can you cast, like, evil spells?"

Eva stopped. "That's Black Magic. No one does that."

"Really? No one?"

They sat on the side of the deck. "Well, some people can, but it's not widely practiced."

"Cos it's bad?"

Eva looked over at her friend. Never in a million years did she think she'd be explaining to *anyone* what Black Magic was. Especially an Outsider. "Black magic, well, you have to hurt a living creature to complete the spell."

"Like cut them and make them bleed?"

She looked out at the water. "And worse."

"What happens if someone does a spell like that? Do they get punished?"

Eva shrugged. "I don't know. I don't know anyone who's done it before."

Skye looked out over the lake. "Wow. This sure does beat s'mores and a fire pit."

Chapter Six

The rest of the weekend Skye thought of questions to ask Eva at school, and it drove her crazy that she couldn't talk to anyone about it. She understood why. People were dumb and did dumb things when they were scared, and people would definitely be scared if they saw what Eva did at the lake. She wandered around the top floor of her home Sunday afternoon, carefully examining the walls for signs of anything. Eva said that her house had good energy. Maybe they had something like Sem'ya too, just waiting to reveal itself?

She placed her ear against the wall. "House. Are you there?"

Her mother appeared at the top of the stairs with a laundry basket full of clothing. "Who are you talking to?"

Skye pulled her head back. "No one."

Mrs. Daniels gave her one of those looks that mothers do when they don't believe you. "Whatever you say, but don't let your father catch you talking to yourself. You know Nana Daniels started doing that and they had to put her in a home." She planted a gentle kiss on the top of Skye's head as she walked by and went off into the boy's room. Nana Daniels was her father's grandmother, but she died a few years before Skye was born. She and her husband built the stone part of the house, but that's all she knew about her. She gazed at

Nana Daniels' picture on the wall. Stone faced and full of wrinkles. Maybe she knew something about the house that the other family members didn't?

Something scurried from behind the wall. She got all excited until she realized it was probably just a mouse. If there was something special about this place, she sure didn't see it. She sat on the first step that led to her parents' bedroom. The door was shut again. Her gaze fell over all the photos on the wall. Pictures of her grandparents, and their parents and photos of kids and people she'd never met. There was good energy here, Eva was sure of that, but Skye wondered how long it would last if her parents kept fighting.

On Monday, Skye had a bunch of questions for Eva and met her in the Grotto.

"What happens if you're not in the mood to cast a spell? Do you have to start over if you sneeze?"

Tuesday, she thought of something in second-period science but had to wait until she passed her in the hall before first lunch because they didn't have any classes together.

"How did you learn these spells? Is that why you were home schooled or is there, like, a school you go to? Can anyone learn how to use magic?"

Wednesday, it was more of a reflection as they walked from the coffee shop to school.

"I think I'd want to know how to do that weather magic. You know, use the natural stuff to fix the planet."

Thursday, as they walked to History, Skye was more contemplative.

"You have to be very mature to use magic. It's too tempting to just wanna change stuff or help people all the time."

On Friday, Skye passed her in the corridor outside the office at the beginning of first lunch.

"Can you make the principal give us permission to do the protests?"

"I guess, but do you really want to influence someone to do something they wouldn't normally do?"

Skye pursed her lips. "No, I guess not."

"Good, because forcing someone to go against their will would be a Black Magic spell."

"Even if it was something small?"

Eva thought for a moment. "I think it depends on what it is. If you wanted them to, like, buy you something, that's not Black Magic, but forcing them to do something that is the complete opposite of who they are. Yeah, that is."

Skye was in awe. "How do you keep it all straight?"

Eva turned at a connecting hallway. "We have a set of books called a Grimoire." She stopped in front of a classroom. "I gotta go."

At lunch the following Monday, they met up in the back of the cafeteria. Her art class was cancelled so they were able to have lunch together.

"How did you do that money spell? Was it spell casting or conjuring?"

"Rune magic," Eva said and bit into her sandwich. "I used a sigil to get the money."

"So, there's spell casting, incantations, rune magic. What else?"

Eva thought for a moment. "There's spell casting, conjuring, rituals and sigils."

There was a spark of excitement in Skye's face as Eva named off all the ways of magic.

Skye leaned close. "Do you think I could do a conjuring spell?"

Eva blinked. "I don't know."

"You could tell me what to do, so you won't get into trouble."

"But you don't come from a magic family."

"How do you know? You said there was something about my house. Maybe we are and just haven't done any in a while."

Eva was wary. "I don't know."

"You're not gonna to get into trouble because you're *not* doing it." The more she thought about it the more excited she became. "Maybe I could get enough for a couple plates of fries with gravy?" She shot a disgusted look at Eva's food. "Or are you really enjoying that sandwich?"

Eva stopped chewing and put it down on the brown paper bag. "Not really." She moved her lunch out of the way, picked up her Adidas bag off the floor and placed it on the table. "Okay, but just this one time. If it doesn't work, it doesn't work."

Skye's eye's lit up with excitement as she put her backpack next to the Adidas on the table. "How much should I ask for?"

"It's not about asking. It's about intent."

"Okay, so how much should I *intend* to ask for?"

"Just enough for two plates of fries and gravy."

"What about drinks?"

"You want a drink too?"

Skye shrugged. "I could go for a soda."

Eva leaned in close to her. "Okay, close your eyes. See the plate of fries and gravy on the table."

"And soda."

"And soda. Smell the gravy on the greasy fries and hear the bubbles in the pop."

Skye imagined the last time she had a plate of fries and gravy. It was hard to keep the image in her mind with all the noise around her.

"Okay, now what?"

There was a pause before Eva spoke. "Open your eyes and draw this on the table."

Eva held up a piece of paper with a drawing on it. It was a strangely shaped angle with just two sides.

"Keep the image in your mind as you draw," Eva said. "And keep repeating in your head, money for food."

Slowly, Skye ran her finger along the surface of the table. Her gaze jumped between the crude image Eva had drawn and her finger. She closed her eyes again.

Money for food.

The image of the food became clearer in her mind.

Money for food.

She saw herself pay the cafeteria cashier with a five-dollar bill.

Money for food.

She saw her and Eva sitting at the table enjoying their meal. After a moment she opened her eyes.

"Now what?"

Eva shrugged. "We wait. How much did you imagine you got?"

"I dunno. Five bucks?"

"You have to be precise, but that should cover it."

Skye stared down at the table.

Eva giggled. "It's not going to appear *right* in this spot."

"Then how?"

"I don't know. Last time Donnie tripped and fell into a knapsack with change in the pocket. The important thing is, the sigil energy is directing money to come to us."

They looked around the cafeteria. Skye wasn't sure how this would manifest. Most of the students around them had either already eaten or brought their lunch so someone dropping a five-dollar bill didn't seem likely.

"Hey, there's Brad and Keith." Skye waved at them, and they quickly headed toward their table. Eva smiled as Brad sat next to her. He smiled back and Skye thought she saw her face go red before she turned away.

"How long have you two been here?" Keith asked.

"Not long," Skye said, still looking around.

Brad tapped Eva gently on the arm. "Have you eaten?"

She pointed to her paper lunch bag. "Just half a sandwich."

"Dude," Skye slapped Keith on the arm. "Here comes your sister." She sunk low in her seat. "And she doesn't look happy."

"Yeah, she's been in a crappy mood since the weekend."

Shelly stormed toward them and held out a five-dollar bill to her brother. "Here, this is the money I owe you."

"For what?"

"The food at the mall Friday night, remember?"

Keith pushed it away. "I don't want it."

"Take it anyway."

"No."

She dropped it on the table. Right where Skye had traced the sigil. "Just shut up and take it, dork."

Before he could pick it up, she walked away.

Eva and Skye stared at the money and started to giggle.

Keith frowned. "What's so funny?"

"Nothing." Eva picked up the money and held it out to him.

"Naw, she's my sister. I don't want it."

Skye snapped up the money. "Then how about we split two large plates of fries and gravy?"

"And two pop," Eva added.

Skye got up and headed to the kitchen. It worked! She couldn't believe it worked. Oh sure, she hoped it did, and she read somewhere that keeping positive while you do things helps to make it happen, but to actually do magic? She definitely wanted to learn more about it.

It didn't take long for her order, and she hurried back to the table.

"Are you going to the dance?" Brad asked, as Skye put the tray down in front of them.

"The Halloween dance? I don't know. I've got English and Math tests that week."

"Dances are boring," Keith said, with a look of disgust. "You just stand around and pretend like you're having a good time."

"We used to have them at our old school." Brad sent a warning look Keith's way. "Yeah, it's kinda boring, but it'll be better than going to some dumb party."

"There's a party?" Skye asked.

"DevDude is throwing one the same night as the dance," Keith said. "And I'm going."

Brad had a look of disgust on his face. "Why? You said his last one was boring. Everyone just sat around, smoked dope, and listened to music."

Keith gave him a sarcastic look. "Yeah? So?" He smiled at Eva. "It was a totally bodacious party! I got so stoned."

Eva turned to Skye. "Are you going to the dance?"

Skye shrugged as she opened one of the pop cans. "I dunno." She looked over at Eva. "Do you wanna go?"

"I've never been to a dance before."

"Ever?" She snapped her fingers. "That's right. You were home-schooled."

"Then you should go," Brad said, as he stabbed a long fry with his fork.

"We should all go," Skye said.

Keith didn't look enthusiastic. "No can do. I'm not missing De-vDude's party."

Brad shook his head. "You can miss *one* party."

"Not a Halloween one."

Brad rolled his eyes. "Whatever." He looked at the girls. "I'm in."

Skye's smile lit up her face. "Awesome!"

Tina Salisbury approached the table with Vikki Harrington and Beth Holland in tow. Skye went to grade school with all three of them, and they were okay, but they never really hung out together. They were too preppy for her and they had nothing in common.

"Hey!" She gave a curt wave as she held on to the last vowel. "So, my parents said I could have some people over before the Halloween dance, and I'm only inviting people from homeroom." She turned to Keith. "Did you want to come?"

Keith didn't look up from the food. "Nope."

Tina was silent for a moment. "Oh, well, that's okay." She turned to leave.

"Eva's in your homeroom," Brad said.

Tina turned back around looking completely put out. "Fine. Do you wanna come?"

Eva glanced at Skye, who nodded her head.

"Okay, sure. When?"

"Come around six. The dance doesn't start until seven so we can do some stuff before, and all go together." Her gaze fell on Brad with a soft smile. "You can come too if you want."

He looked awkwardly at her. "Maybe."

Tina shrugged. "Whatever." She turned and the three walked off.

Skye smiled. "This is gonna be a blast!"

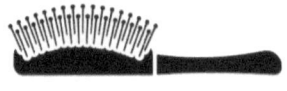

Skye could barely contain her excitement as she went with her father to pick up Eva in town. Eva had on the same outfit she wore to the mall opening, but the cooler weather made her wish she wore a sweater instead and she rubbed her arms to keep them warm. Skye was dressed in a combination of denim and neon outfit, which included a bright scrunchy that held up her fading pink hair.

Skye got out of her parent's station wagon and met Eva half-way down the walkway. There were no lights on inside, and the porch light flickered like a candle.

"Your house looks like the creeps," Skye said.

"Yeah, my parents went out for the night."

"Halloween party?"

"Soween celebration."

Skye frowned as they headed toward the curb. "What's that?"

"It's this big celebration where we visit our dead relatives."

"That's gross."

Eva nodded. "No, it's kinda cool. You tell them what you've been up to since last Soween, family gossip. You know stuff like that."

Skye stopped. "Wait. I thought you said they were dead?"

"They are, but, it's complicated."

"You so gotta tell me about it later!"

Mr. Daniels drove them out to the township and a few streets away from F.C.V.I. The houses in the subdivision were smaller, mostly one level, and the sidewalks were full of young children in costumes running from door to door. Skye wanted to ask if she went out Trick or Treating before, but with her father being I the car, she didn't want to break her promise.

A few streets later, one of the houses was overly decorated with a spooky theme.

Mr. Daniels put the car in park. "Here ya go, girls. Have a good time."

They thanked him for the ride and got out. Skye stared at the kids hanging out on the front lawn as her father drove away.

"I hate being so late," she said, "I knew we should have left sooner."

"It's okay," Eva said. "I'm sure she'll understand."

There were Halloween decorations up all over the property, with a thin fog coming from a machine hidden in the bushes. They walked past a tall Grim Reaper, and it screamed at them. Eva jumped.

Skye smiled. "Now that's cool."

Eva stared at the two small red light bulbs for the eyes and shivered. "Okay."

They followed a few other kids into the backyard. The in-ground pool had a cover over it and was roped off with caution tape. A small bonfire burned in the centre of the yard, with tables set up for food and drinks. Under an awning, a small group of kids danced, while others sat on patio chairs and talked.

Skye leaned close to Eva. "This is what a dance is like, but picture it inside the gym and more people."

Tina walked over to them. She wore a cheerleader outfit with the school colours on it. She didn't acknowledge Skye and frowned at Eva. "What's your costume supposed to be?"

"Costume?"

"Yeah, like, what are you dressed up as?" She gave a quick twirl. "I'm dressed up like a cheerleader 'cause I made the squad."

Eva looked down at her clothing. "I guess I'm dressed up as myself."

Tina snorted. "That's totally lame." Beth and Vikki came up behind her, both wearing costumes. "This is a costume party, Eva."

The snark in her voice was evident in the curl on her lips. "You're supposed to dress up, not come as yourself."

Skye frowned. "You never said anything about costumes."

"Duh. It's Halloween. What else would it be." She looked past them and her face lit up. "Hey, Keith. Did Brad come with you?"

Keith walked up wearing a vampire cape and stood next to Eva. "Yeah, he's just out on the front lawn."

He looked at Skye. "Where's your costume."

Skye rolled her eyes. "I thought you weren't coming."

Keith shrugged. Yeah, I changed his mind."

Eva slumped, hurt. "You knew about wearing costumes?"

He frowned. "Yeah, I mean, it's Halloween, right?"

A smug look came over Tina as she and the other two girls pushed past them. "Told you, but don't worry," Tina said, trying to hide her amusement. "You can just tell everyone you're dressed up like a home-schooled loser."

Eva felt miserable. "I didn't know."

Keith looked over his shoulder at Tina. "She told me in Science, and I told her to say something to you too."

"She didn't." Eva stepped back and leaned against the side of the house. "I feel like such a jerk."

"Can't you buy something?"

"I don't have any money."

Skye gave her a knowing look. "Or do you?" She grabbed Eva by the arm. "We'll be right back."

She led her into the house through the back door. There were more kids inside, and they walked past several groups on their way upstairs and to the bathroom. Skye closed the door. "You can do another money spell, we'll go to the mall and grab some cheap costumes."

"How are we gonna get there?"

"I'll call my mom and tell her what's what, and she'll take us."

Eva shook her head. "That'll take too long, and I've never done it for a large sum of money." She turned to the mirror over the sink. She drew the same sigil she did in the girls' change room. Again, the reflection in the mirror changed to that of the inside of her home.

Skye stood behind her in awe. "That is so cool."

"Sem'ya, find Dom."

The image changed multiple times until it stopped in his room. He sat on his bed with a pile of brochures around him. "Dom, I need your help."

He didn't look up. "What for?"

"Are Mom'n Dad still home?"

"Mom's already gone. Dad's still here, why?"

"Can you go ask him for some money for me?"

He looked up. "For what?"

"Tina's having a costume party and I need money to buy one."

"She didn't tell her," Skye said from behind.

Dom got up off the bed and dropped his reading material. "So your friend invited you to her party, but didn't tell you it was a costume party?"

"Yeah."

"Doesn't sound like much of a friend."

"Are you going to ask him or not?"

He winced before replying. "I really don't want to bother him. He's been locked up in the study for a few hours now. Something about old artifacts he's asking an old Sorcerer about. We're heading to Wynden soon."

Eva fell onto the toilet seat. "I'm busted."

His face appeared in the mirror. "What would you go out as anyway?"

"I don't know. Something other than myself."

He disappeared from the mirror.

Skye sat on the side of the tub. "Why don't we just head over to the school?"

"But the dance doesn't start for another hour, where are we gonna go?"

"The donut shop?"

"We don't have any money."

Skye slumped. "Oh yeah." She stared at the floor for a moment. She felt bad for Eva. This was her first Halloween party, and it was all messed up. "Maybe I can do that thing to get some money again. Maybe enough to get a donut and drink?"

"No, I don't think we should try that again."

"Don't look so pathetic." Dom's face appeared in the mirror. "Nothing wrong with going as yourself." He brought up a large black velvet bag and shoved it through the mirror.

Eva stood. "What's in it?"

"That dress mom bought you for Sow'een, and that pair of her boots you like."

She opened the bag and brought out each of the items. "I don't know."

"Mom wanted you to wear it tonight. Just because you're not going to Sow'een doesn't mean you can't wear it." He stepped back and pushed through a large brim-black hat with a pointed end. "And this was Alisha's. She left it at the other place, and it got packed with my stuff. I was going to burn it, but you might as well have it."

She took the hat. "Thanks."

"Just don't get those boots dirty or Mom will kill both of us." He waved his arm in front and the mirror returned to its normal reflection.

Eva quickly changed out of her outfit into the new one. The dress was solid black with lace sleeves and a lace skirt that started just above the knee. Her mother's boots were flat with ties and a zipper, and the oversized hat added perfectly.

Skye crossed her arms, impressed. "If you don't look like someone who casts spells, I don't know who does."

Eva stuffed her other clothing into the velvet bag, and they walked out of the bathroom. The brim of her hat was overly wide, and it hit a few people as they walked down the stairs to the living room.

Keith and Brad stood just inside the front door talking to Tina, and her friends. They didn't notice the girls as they walked toward them.

"Sorry," Eva said, and fixed the hat. She turned and looked at the other kids in the room. "I just wasn't sure if this was a *real* costume party or not."

"Wow," Keith said, with a wide smile. "That's a bodacious witch costume."

"Yeah," Brad stepped toward her and stood by her side. "You look so cool. You should totally wear that to the dance."

Eva nodded. "I was thinking about it."

Skye swatted at the brim. "But not this hat."

Everyone's eyes were on Eva, and for a brief moment, Skye felt uncomfortable, but she pushed it away. Eva looked good and Brad thought so too. There was an evil look on Tina's chubby face and it made her smile.

Brad turned to Tina. "Now that's a Halloween costume."

Keith looked at his watch. "We should boot-scoot. It's gonna take us a while to get to the school."

"You don't have to go right now," Tina said and reached for Brad's arm. "And my parents can always drive us if you wanna stay."

Brad shook his head. "Naw, I'd rather walk, thanks."

Skye gave Tina and her friends a quick wave. "See ya."

They walked out of Tina's house and headed down the driveway. A breeze swept across the road and sent a chill through Skye. Her body did a quick shake, and she wrapped her arms around her torso.

"I should have brought a jacket."

Brad turned to Eva. "You cold?"

"Just a little."

He unzipped his jacket "You wanna wear this?"

"Sure, I guess, but just till we get to school."

He took it off and draped it over her shoulders. Skye swatted at her and gave her a thumbs up. This night was working out perfectly.

The dance was in full swing when they arrived. The main auditorium was full of students dancing, while groups of kids hung out in the halls or outside. Chairs lined two sides of the room, but mostly kids sat in the cement bleachers at the back. A disco ball hung from a wire and twirled while strobe lights flashed near the stage and the local radio DJ and his equipment. Pictures of haunting creatures lined the walls, with a large Halloween banner draped over the curtains on the stage. Eva stood and took it all in.

"So, what do you think?" Skye asked as Eva took a slow look around the room.

"This is pretty awesome!"

"It's all right," Keith said.

"It's better than Tina's party," Brad said. "You know, she was just showing off 'cause she got on the cheerleading squad."

Skye shook her head. "No duh."

Eva gave Brad his jacket back. "Thanks."

He smiled. "Anytime."

Keith held up his hand.

"K, folks, I'm gonna take a tour. See ya later."

"Come on!" Skye dragged Eva across the floor, and into the small crowd of kids who were dancing. Eva wasn't sure what to do. She started with small movements, trying to mimic the other kids until she felt more confident. They left the floor when it came to a slow song and headed for Brad and a few unoccupied chairs near the entrance to the girls' change room.

"Having fun?" Skye asked.

Eva nodded vigorously and tucked her hat under the chair. "Yeah." She turned to Brad. "You?"

He shrugged. "I'm not much of a dancer."

Skye tugged on the sleeve of Eva's dress. "There's a lot of kids here. Even some seniors." She motioned with her chin. "Ugh. Tina and her little gang are here."

At one of the entrances to the gym, a small group of six girls stood huddled together. Eva saw Vikki and Beth, but the others she didn't know. In the middle stood Tina, still in her cheerleading uniform. After a couple of moments, Tina saw them and headed over.

"Why is she headed this way?" Eva said.

"I'll give you one hint why," Skye said. "And it starts with the letter B."

"I thought you said she liked Keith?"

Skye shrugged. "Guess she changed her mind."

"Hey, guys!" Tina's normal voice went up a pitch. Skye rolled her eyes. "Mind if we join you?"

"Sure, I guess," Eva said. She got a shrug from Skye.

166

Tina grabbed a chair and sat right next to Brad. The others did the same but spread out around Tina.

Skye leaned toward Tina. "I don't think you're allowed to wear your uniform outside of practice and games."

Tina scowled at her. "What do you know?"

"A lot, since my cousin, *Carla*, is the squad captain." She sat back in her seat. "She sees you in here wearing that, and she'll kick you off the squad."

Tina kept quiet and pushed her chair closer to Brad. She tapped him on the shoulder. "So, have you been here long?"

"Not long." he shrugged and looked away.

A fast-beat song came on.

"Oh, my, God!" Tina's eyes flared with excitement. "This is my favourite song!" The other girls squealed as she tapped him on the shoulder again. "Do you wanna dance?"

"No, thanks."

Beth rolled her eyes and pulled Tina onto the dance area. "Come on!"

Eva and Skye watched as more kids got up to dance.

"So what else do we do here?" Eva asked.

"This is about it," Skye said. "Just dance and hang out." She leaned very close to Eva. "Probably not as exciting as you're used to. You know, being magical and all."

"We do some magic tonight," Eva said, watching a couple of good dancers close to them. "It's more about our honouring our ancestors."

"I thought you said that you were going to talk to your dead relatives?"

"It is. That's part of it."

Skye frowned. "How do you talk to the dead?"

167

A fast-beat song came on and a roar of cheers erupted from the dance floor. Skye jumped to her feet. "Never mind. I love this song!" She grabbed Eva. "Come on."

They raced through the dancers, into the middle of the floor. Eva moved and swayed to the rhythm of the song, feeling light as a feather and as free as the wind, as Skye moved in ways that resembled a barn animal. When the song was over, the DJ played a slow song and the girls returned to their seats.

"I need a drink." Skye grabbed Eva by the arm and dragged her to one of the long tables with small clear plastic cups with an orange drink inside. She handed one to Eva before taking one herself. "I think Brad is gonna ask you to slow dance."

"Really?"

"Fer sure."

Eva headed off the floor. Skye grabbed her arm. "Where are you going?"

"I have to use the washroom."

"Yeah, I gotta go too."

Eva nodded and they ran for the change room. The place was empty except for one person who sat at the far end between the shower stalls. Eva walked into a stall as Skye walked up to her and gave a quick nod.

"Hey, Runi. I didn't think you'd come to the dance."

The raven-haired girl looked up and shot her a disgusted look. "I'm not. This place is quieter than the art room, so I hang out here."

Skye walked over to a stall. "How far are you on Mrs. Baptist's assignment?"

"Almost done."

"Seriously?" Skye groaned inwardly. Their art teacher gave them an assignment at the beginning of the school year, and it was due the end of next week, but she'd been so busy with her protests she'd barely had a chance to work on it.

"You're not done?"

"I've been busy."

"Yeah, I heard."

The music from the dance suddenly grew louder in the changeroom.

"Oh. My. Gawd!" Tina's voice boomed through the noise. "I can't believe he's sitting with *her*. Like, doesn't he know how much of a *loser* she is?" This was followed by several people agreeing with her and adding to the 'loser' title. "And, like, what's with that dress? And those boots? She looks like a slut."

Skye peered through a small slit between the door and the stall wall. Tina, Beth, and Vikki stood straight across at the sinks and fixed their hair in the mirrors.

Tina's hand was on her hip. "Look at me." Her voice was an octave higher. "My name's Evandra Shade—" She exaggerated the last half of her first name. "—but you can call me Eva." She lowered her arm. "Bitch."

There was another round of agreement and more shaming. Eva kept quiet in the stall next to her, but Skye wanted to jump out and tell them off.

"When is she going to leave?" Tina said and slammed the door a few stalls down. "How am I supposed to talk to him when she's always right there?"

"Maybe you could, like, spill something on her and then she'd have to leave," Vikki said.

"Like what? There's not enough in those stupid drinks at the table to ruin anything."

"What about a can of pop?"

"Do you got any change?" Beth asked. "A whole can of pop would do."

"No, I don't." The stall door creaked as it opened. "Gimme some money."

Skye waited until their footsteps left the change room before she opened the stall door. She stepped out and stood in front of Eva's stall.

"Hey."

No answer.

"Don't let her get to you. She's just a stuck-up bitch."

Eva's stall door slowly opened. "Why's she so mean?"

Skye made a growling sound and went to the sink. "She's like Carla. Thinks her shit don't stink. She's always been like that. Even when we were little. She'd walk around like she's hot shit, but she's cold diarrhea."

Runi burst out laughing. "Oh my gawd. That's fuckin' funny!"

Eva nodded, but it was obvious what Tina said really bothered her.

"Tina's a skank," Runi said. "She was on my case at the beginning of school. Just ignore her."

Eva nodded again.

Skye went to Eva's side. "She's just jealous, you know, and I doubt she'll pour pop all over you."

"But she might?"

"Not if she wants to stay on the squad. If she does shit like that, that's unbecoming of a cheerleader, and Carla'll pull her for sure." Skye crossed her arms. "Only reason Tina's on the squad is because Carla kicked a girl off. Trust me. When it comes to the squad, Carla doesn't mess around."

Eva sniffed. "Really?"

"I heard Tina's trying to make Brad jealous by going after Keith," Runi said. "But it didn't work 'cause Brad's really into you."

Skye's face lit up. "See! I told you!"

Eva smiled. "Really?"

A smirk appeared on Runi's lips. "Fuck yeah. His friends like you more than her, too. Tina and that fucking cheerleading squad. I'd like to shove those pom-poms up her ass."

Eva took a deep breath and wiped away the wetness from her face.

Skye placed her hands on Eva's shoulders. "Don't let her get to you. She's not worth it."

Eva nodded. "You're right, and I'm going to ask him to dance."

"Hell yeah," Runi shouted. "Show that bitch who's boss."

They walked toward the change room door, when Carla stumbled forward through the entrance as Skye pulled the door open.

The older teen focused on Eva. "Just the person I wanna talk to."

"Not now, Carla." Skye tried to push past her, but Shelly blocked the exit.

Shelly forced them back into the room as Carla stumbled over to the closest mirror.

"So, did your brother tell you that he dumped me?" Her words slurred as she spoke.

Skye caught a whiff of alcohol. "Have you been drinking?"

Carla glared at her. "Oh run home and tell mommy, y'little loser." She focused back on Eva. "He dumped me. He. Dumped. Me."

Skye crossed her arms. "Good."

Carla turned to her. "Why are you even talking?" She turned back to Eva. "And he won't return my calls or anything."

"So?"

"So—" Carla poked her. "—we're meant to be together."

Skye tried to keep from laughing. "Yeah, well I guess he doesn't see it that way."

Carla shoved Eva further into the change room. "Well, you're gonna make him see it that way."

"I can't force Dom to go out with you."

"You'd better or I'll make your life miserable."

Shelly stepped up beside Carla. "We *both* will."

Skye jumped in between Eva and Carla. She'd had years of dealing with her bullying, but Eva was new, and it was worse now because she was drunk.

"She's not doing anything."

Shelly shoved Skye back toward the stalls, and she hit them hard.

Carla came within an inch of Eva's face. "Convince him that he made a mistake dumping me, or I'll beat the shit outta you."

"Oh, that's good," Runi said. "Threaten the sister of the guy you like. That'll really make him wanna date you."

Carla glared at Runi from over her shoulder and pointed at her. "Shut your mouth, bitch, or you're next."

She focused back on Eva and grabbed her by the hair. Skye charged at her cousin, but Shelly blocked her and grabbed her by the arm, twisted it behind her back and slammed her up against the wall of a stall.

"You just stay out of this."

Runi stood but Carla pointed a finger at her. "Back off, freak." She yanked on Eva's hair. "Tell him to go back out with me or I'll make your life a living hell." She threw Eva back against the sink.

Furious, Skye broke free of Shelly's grip and charged at her cousin until there was two feet between them. She could smell the alcohol on her. This was the last straw. Carla was beyond evil, she was vile.

Eva jumped behind her and raised her left arm. She glanced back at her friend. Eva's face was full of rage, and she knew exactly what her best friend was about to do. Something that would definitely get her into trouble. She put her hand over Eva's fist and forced it down. A warning look in her eyes.

"Don't." She turned and glared at Carla. A smug grin on her face. "Back off, Carla. Or I'll tell Grampy what you're really like." She tilted her head to one side when she saw a flicker of concern. Shelly jumped right to Carla's side and grabbed her by the front of her outfit. Skye ignored her. "He fought in World War 2 against bullies, but how'd you think he'd take it if he found out his favourite grandchild was one?" She leaned in closer. "Or can your parents pay for all those years of university?"

Carla's eyes narrowed as she pointed a finger at Eva. "Tell him. Got it?"

Shelly let Skye go and with a smirk and shoved her back into Eva.

Eva rubbed the small of her back that impacted the sink but kept quiet.

Carla stepped back, a smug look on her face. "Mebbe you need a little incentive, just so you know I'm not fucking around." She winked at Shelly, and they left.

Eva looked bashfully at her friend. "Thanks."

Skye gave a small chuckle. "That felt good."

Eva fixed the top of her dress where Carla had grabbed her and glanced over at Skye. "Any suggestions about how to deal with your cousin?"

Runi walked up to them. "Yeah, stay the fuck off her bad side."

The girls didn't talk about what happened in the change room. Skye knew some of the students thought she was a loser, especially after what happened in the cafeteria, and if they told a teacher then they'd both be labelled squealers.

They stood by the refreshment table in front of the stage. Skye rotated her shoulder. It was really sore from Shelly pinning her against the stall. She didn't like the sound of Carla's threat. Either of them, but she didn't know what her cousin would do to make good on the second one.

"Do you think Dom would go out with Carla again?" Skye asked.

"I don't know. He doesn't talk to me about stuff like that."

Skye turned toward the set of chairs they had sat on. Tina was right next to Brad now, chatting, and he looked like he was having a good time.

Eva's voice was weak. "Do you think he wants to go back out with her?"

Skye balked. "Not likely." She scanned the room for Brad's best friend. "Where's Keith?"

"Maybe he left?"

"I'm gonna go look for him. Tell him what happened."

Eva grabbed her arm. "No, don't do that. I don't want anyone to know."

"He's Brad's best friend. If that bitch is messing with him, he has to know." Skye finished her orange drink and slammed the cup down on the table. "Stay here. I'll find him and come back."

As Skye crossed the gym floor she glared at Tina and her friends. Who the hell was she to go after Brad? They went out together in grade eight, and she didn't treat him well. She was always making fun of him because he got good grades, and was in dorky clubs, but that's who he was. She'd known him since first grade. He was always into stuff like that. Skye was so happy when she heard they broke up, she made him a cupcake with a candle in it to celebrate.

The halls outside the gym were empty and she wandered outside. The smell of burning tobacco hit her hard and came from a small group of students at another entrance to the school. In the dark, it was hard to see who was there, but Keith's guffaw of laughter she knew all too well.

She hurried toward the group. He had to know what Tina was doing. How could he leave his best friend alone with that bitch? The smoke smell grew stronger as she came close, but there was another smell she recognized as well. She rolled her eyes and stopped a metre from the group.

"You abandoned your best friend to go smoke a joint?"

Keith smiled when he saw her. "Hey, Skye. Wanna toke?"

She crossed her arms. "No, I don't. How could you leave Brad alone with Tina? You know she's after him again."

"Hey, when DevDude asked if I wanted to go smoke one, how could I say no?"

The group chuckled and agreed, and that's when Skye noticed him in the shadows. Leaning against the brick entranceway. His brown hair was long except for some bangs in the front. He was just a few inches taller than her, with dark eyes and she always thought he had a nice smile. His eyes seemed to light up when he did. He was handsome and really popular, and she'd had a crush on him since the fourth grade but he was a few grades ahead so he never noticed her. He was so cool. Everyone wanted to be like him. A cigarette hung from the corner of his mouth, and when he took a drag, the tip lit up orange. He worked a rolling paper with weed between his fingers, then exhaled the smoke through his nose. Doing all of this in the dim light of the side parking lot was the coolest thing she ever saw.

"That Tina's a real bitch," DevDude said, and handed the newly rolled joint to Keith. "But she's cute. I'd fuck her."

She felt uncomfortable with the loud raucous laughter and smiled awkwardly.

"Just go back inside and hang with him. Get him away from Tina."

DevDude mimicked her in a high pitch voice. Everyone laughter and Skye's face went hot with embarrassment.

He took the joint from Keith, lit it and held it out to her. "Come on, take a toke and chill."

She looked at the joint between his fingers. Her parents told her to stay away from drugs all the time, but why? What was it like? She reached for the joint. One little puff couldn't hurt and then she could say that she tried it, and nothing happened. She put the paper tip to her lips and sucked in. The smoke filled her mouth and tasted like ash. She pulled the joint back and took a small breath in. Instantly, her lungs hurt, and she coughed out the rest of the smoke.

Keith took the joint from her. "Yeah, first time is always a killer."

"Now will you go and get him away from her?"

He nodded and took a drag before handing it back to DevDude.

Skye coughed a few more times before she got to the far entrance. Her lungs hurt and her throat felt raw, but he spoke to her! That was the first time he'd ever noticed her, and maybe, since she took a puff, he'd talk to her now? She could go and hang out with him and Keith in the Grotto. He'd get to know her better and maybe he'd ask her out? Yeah, this was a great night.

She hurried back inside with Keith somewhat behind her. There was a break in the music, and she hurried into the gym. Brad was still sitting with Tina and her friends, but when she looked over at the refreshment table, Eva was gone.

"Oh shit. Where did she go?"

Keith came up behind her. "Where'd who go?"

"Eva. She's gone."

"Maybe she went home?"

"No, we're taking her after the dance." She hurried to Brad. "Have you seen Eva?"

He looked concerned. "No. I thought she was with you."

She pursed her lips. "She was, but I went out to get stoner here, and now she's gone."

Tina scrunched up her face. "Who cares. She's a loser anyway."

Skye's anger from the change room boiled over. "You're such a fucking bitch!"

She stormed across the dance floor toward her cousin. She was so done with Tina. She stood in front of Carla. Her arms crossed. Carla stopped laughing with her friends and glared up at her, but before she could get out a snarly comment, Skye cut her off.

"Tina's wearing her cheerleading outfit as a Halloween costume."

She looked past Skye and across the floor to the small group of first year students. "What the fuck?"

"Yeah, I thought you'd like to know."

Carla stood so fast her chair fell back. "That bitch." She shoved Skye out of the way and stormed across the floor, with Shelly right behind her. Skye gave an evil grin as Brad and Keith came toward her.

"What did you do?" Brad asked, looking back at the girls.

"See how she likes being bullied."

Keith looked confused. "I don't get it."

"Well if you'd stayed with Brad instead of going off and getting high, you'd know."

He shook his head disappointed. "You're nasty when you smoke dope."

Brad was shocked. "You smoked dope?"

Skye huffed in frustration. "Doesn't matter. Now we have to find Eva."

Eva felt uncomfortable the moment Skye walked away, especially now that she knew about a possible confrontation. She wanted to go and sit with Brad, but he looked like he was having a good time with Tina, and she needed to avoid her at any cost, which was hard when she sat next to the guy she liked.

There were a group of empty chairs on the far side of the gym, but Carla, Shelly, and several seniors sat together close to the DJ and a scowl from her nemesis meant she had to stay where she was. She sipped the last of her drink and tried to listen to the music. Nothing was fun anymore. She should have gone to Wynden with her family for the Sow'een celebration. Anything would have been better than standing here all by herself. Her gaze fell on Brad. He was still having a good time talking to Tina. He even laughed. Tina looked her way, with a smug smile all over her face.

Eva scurried across the dance floor and to the cement bleachers at the back of the gym. The top tier was dark. A perfect place to hide from everyone, and it gave her a good view of the whole gym. The right side corner was completely hidden by shadows. It was perfect. She could keep an eye on Tina and Carla at the same time.

She brought her knees close to her chest and looked out over the floor. It was fun when they first got there, so the whole night wasn't a disaster, but no one would have threatened her in Wynden and right now she really wanted to talk to her mother, but she couldn't even do that. At least not without casting a spell. Hopefully, Skye would be back soon. She lowered her head to her knees and closed her eyes. She thought back the last Sow'een celebration. She'd been excited to tell her grandparents about coming to the high school and they wanted to know all about it, but she doubted they wanted to know about this. She remembered the burial cake they bought and brought to the crypt. It was her Greatnana's favourite. It was gooey and sticky and she could taste some of the sweetness on her tongue. That was the point. It was a way to remember the person who passed.

Several more songs played, but no sign of Skye. Maybe she thought Eva went home? She checked over to where Brad was sitting, but he was gone. Only Tina's friends, Beth and Vikki were there. She frantically searched the dance floor. Carla was gone too. She searched the bleachers to see if they found her, but no one else was around. Eva put her head down again on her knees. She just wanted to go home.

"Where have you been?" Skye's voice was barely audible over the music as she hurried up the far set of stairs. "I've been looking all over for you."

Eva raised her head and smiled wide. "You're back!"

Skye stood in front of her. "I said I would be."

"What took you so long?"

Her friend shook her head. "It was just dumb." She sat next to her. "Guess who I was talking to?"

"Who?"

"Dev Rogers."

Eva had a faint image that went with the name, but nothing clear. It must have shown on her face because Skye had a look of disbelief.

"Keiths' friend? DevDude?" Her smile went from ear to ear. "He told me to hang out with them for a bit, so I did."

Eva sat up. "That's cool."

"Yeah. So why are you here?"

"I wanted to be by myself."

Skye sat next to her. "Brad's looking for you."

Eva's heart skipped. "Really?"

"Yeah." She looked out onto the dance floor. "You want me to tell him you're here?"

She *wanted* to go home and tell Dom about the Carla thing, but she wanted to be with Brad more. "No. I'll go see him, in a bit."

"Okay." Skye stood. "I'm gonna go dance."

Eva shook her head and Skye left her alone. After a few moments, she took the stairs to the floor and walked out of the gym. A small group of people stood at the far end of the corridor, smoking, and she waved the smoke away as she walked past and outside.

The cool air felt good, and she leaned against the brick wall of the school and let it clear her mind. Maybe she should have gone to Sow'een. At least no one wanted to beat her up there.

Another small group of kids stood several meters away from the school. Keith stood in with the group and held out a small joint to her. "Hey, Eva. Wanna puff?"

She shook her head. "No thanks."

"You sure? Y'look a little bummed."

"I'm good." She walked back inside and down the adjacent corridor. There were a couple of benches along the wall with more people smoking. She headed to the far end and opened a window before sitting on the last bench.

The door to the boys' change room opened, and Brad walked out. "Hey, where'd you take off to?"

"No where special."

He glanced down the corridor at the small group of smokers puffing away. "Well, you found it."

Brad sat on the bench next to her. "What's wrong?"

"Nothing."

"Come on. I know there's something wrong."

"No. Really."

"You're not having a good time?"

"No, the dance is fun."

"So, what's going on?"

Eva examined his face. The small wisps of stubble were just noticeable in patches on his chin and cheek.

"You and Tina used to go out?"

"Yeah, a while ago. Why? Wait, is that what's bugging you?"

"No, I don't care about that, but she doesn't like you hanging with other girls."

"How do you know that?"

"I heard her, Vikki, and Beth talking about me in the change room."

He frowned. "What'd she say?"

"Not much, just that she couldn't believe you danced with me." She sat forward. "She wants to go back out with you."

"I know," he said and faced forward. "She's been trying to get back together since school started."

Eva looked away. "Do you want to?"

He looked insulted. "No."

She faced him. "Well, tell her that."

He took her chin in his hand and moved it closer to him. "I'd rather go out with you."

Eva stared into his eyes. She didn't think they'd be so blue. "Really?"

"Yeah." He looked away. "If you want to."

Her heart raced and her mouth went dry. She just had to say one word, but her body made it difficult. She swallowed a few times. "Sure."

He looked up at her and smiled. "Cool."

The door at the far end burst open again and Keith rushed through the exit. He stopped short when he saw Eva and Brad. "What're you doing here? Y'don't smoke."

Brad took Eva's hand in his. "We just wanted some time alone."

A wide smile filled Keith's face. "Well, it's about time, dude."

Eva smiled as she tightened her fingers around his. She wanted to scream, cry, and laugh all at the same time.

"Hey." Skye walked up to them. "Why is everyone hanging out here?"

Keith pointed at Eva and Brad. "Just congratulating the happy couple."

Skye's face lit up. "Really? That's so totally awesome!"

A loud crash of glass came from farther down the hall. Everyone in the corridor turned toward the noise and after a moment, headed toward the far end. Keith pushed open the double doors and led them into a corridor that connected to the main foyer.

The glass in the trophy display was smashed and several of the award plaques were ripped from their holdings on the back of the wall. Skye's posters covered the destroyed case, with the words SAVE THE PLANET spray painted in dark blue on the wall above, and ACID RAIN KILLS LAKES in green.

Keith looked over the damage. "Skye, aren't those your posters?"

She walked closer to the case, stunned. "Yeah, but—" She turned to Eva. "They're supposed to be in your locker."

Eva stared at the damage. They were in her locker, and she was positive it was locked.

Mrs. Craine, the English teacher, hurried into the foyer from a side corridor. She had a look of anger when she saw all the kids standing in the foyer, but it turned to shock when she saw the damaged trophy case.

She turned to the group. "What happened?" No one said a word. "Did any of you see who did this?"

"No, ma'am," Skye said.

She looked at the boys as well. "None of you?"

Keith shrugged. "We were just all hangin' out and heard a loud crash."

"And you saw *nothing*?"

They shook their heads vigorously.

"I recognize these." She examined the posters and turned to Skye. "They belong to you, don't they?"

Skye nodded quickly. "Yes, ma'am.

"So why are they here?"

Skye looked at Eva. "I don't know. Last I saw the posters were in her locker."

Mrs. Craine focused on Eva. "Well, it seems they're not in your locker anymore."

The door opened. Tina and her small group came and stood just by the main doors to the school and were followed by a dozen other students. A male teacher came from the opposite direction and became quite upset at the scene. More students wandered in from the gym until half the foyer was full. A few more teachers arrived and began herding students out of the foyer, while Mrs. Craine kept Eva and Skye at her side.

"The damage to the trophy case aside, do you have any idea how your protest posters got from Miss Shade's locker to here?"

Both girls shook their heads.

"You do realize that this is a serious matter. Whether or not you admit guilt in this, the evidence is clear that you had some part in it."

Skye pointed at the wall. "Why would we vandalize the trophy display?"

"To bring more attention to your protests."

"Why—"

"We made a promise to the principal, Mrs. Craine," Eva said. "We weren't going to do any more protests until the new year."

"Yeah, he said he'd talk to the school board for us. Why would we go and ruin that?"

"I don't know, Miss Daniels, but you're going to have a lot of explaining to do to the principal."

Stifled snickers caught Eva's attention, as Tina and her friends tried to hide their amusement. She took another look at the damage. They didn't do this, but she had a good idea of who could have. The problem would be trying to prove it.

Chapter Seven

Eight-forty-five in the morning seemed a little early to be in the principal's office on a Monday, but there Eva and Skye were, seated in the row of chairs in the waiting area outside the vice principal's office. They tried to ignore the commotion from the secretaries in the next room, but it was hard when you were the topic. The destroyed trophy case was on everyone's lips; what should be done with the vandals, and who was going to pay for it, namely, the vandals. A few looks of contempt were sent their way, and Eva was sure she heard the words' criminals' and 'expulsion'

"Those were the posters from your locker." Skye's arms were crossed, and she had a quizzical look on her face. It still didn't seem real to Eva. The whole weekend, she sat in her room and tried to figure out why someone would destroy school property and make it look like they did it. She had a few ideas of who; Carla was at the top of her list. Making good on her threat, but how did she get the posters? Her parents weren't so angry as much as they were confused. They believed her when she said they didn't do it. There was no reason for her to damage school property, but what they couldn't understand is why someone would make it look like they had. Her father was quick to suspect that it had something to do with this new friend she'd made, and that his daughter had somehow been accused by association. Who was this girl? Who were her family? She seemed a little young to be so concerned about the world around her. Her mother was calmer about it, but that being said, she still felt uncomfortable that Eva had been blamed for something she didn't do and readily agreed to meet with the principal when he called their home the next day.

"I bet Tina had something to do with this," Eva said. "She's the only one who can get into the locker, and she's on the squad." She looked down at her lap. "She hates me because Brad likes me."

Skye frowned. "I hate a lot of people, but I don't go breaking things and making it look like they did it." She paused. "I bet Carla threatened to kick her off the squad if she didn't help. That's probably how she got our stuff."

Eva relaxed into her chair. "She really doesn't want me to go out with Brad."

A sarcastic look replaced Skye's concerned one. "No duh. She's been hanging on him a lot more since school started." She paused. "We need to tell the principal. We could say that she did it for revenge against you."

"But would he believe us?"

Skye shrugged in response. "I was gonna say you could do a spell to make them believe us, but you can't do magic anymore."

Eva glanced through the main office as her parents walked in at the far end. "And it's not the magic I'd want to do."

Five minutes later Principal Jerrod appeared in the doorway. He was tall and round and nearly took up the entire entranceway. "Ladies, your parents are here. We can get started." He was calm as he motioned the girls to follow him through the main office.

Eva felt the glare of eyes on them. She wanted to scream and shout that it wasn't them, but it was all she could do to keep from openly crying.

The principal's office was located on the far side of the main office. It was larger than the vice principal's and had the same wood panelling and large desk. Six chairs sat in a semi-circle at the back of the room. Four were already occupied.

He held out his hand to the two empty seats. "Sit with your families, please."

Egori kept his focus straight ahead; his jaw clenched, while her mother examined the wall full of plaques and degrees next to her. Skye's father looked more bored than angry, and her mother's concerned gaze and gentle smile fell on both of them.

Principal Jarrod walked behind his desk. "I'm sorry that this has to be the first time we meet." He took two files from a small pile on the edge and sat down. "But under the circumstances, I felt it was appropriate." He opened the top file. "Your daughters have already been in to see Mr. Banta over a protest in the cafeteria a few weeks back, but this new incident has me very concerned."

"We figured out who could have done this," Eva said, and turned to her father. "We know it was Carla and Tina."

Egori held up his hand. "We will discuss this later."

Skye turned to her parents. "You know I believe in peaceful protests, just like you guys did in the sixties. There's no way I'd do this."

Mrs. Daniels took her daughter's hand. "We know that sweetie."

Mr. Daniels sat straight in his chair. "So, what are we talking about here? Detention? Suspension?" He paused. "Expulsion?"

Principal Jarrod took a deep breath. "The girls will be suspended from school for two weeks on the grounds that the school is reimbursed for the damage."

"And what if they don't get their money?"

"Considering both girls have a prior history with protests, they will be expelled."

"What?" Skye said, in complete disgust.

"That's not fair," Mrs. Daniels said. "They didn't do anything."

"We have witnesses," Skye said. "We were with Keith and Brad in the smoking area when it happened. *They* heard the glass break when we were there."

"Have you spoken to these other children?" Venera spoke softly. "If they are witnesses—"

"Which is the reason I am only suspending them." He leaned back in his chair. "If there are other people behind this—"

Sky blurted out. "If?"

Mr. Daniels held up his hand. "Let's get back to this reimbursement. I'm assuming you want us to pay the school back?"

"That would be the appropriate course of action."

He shook his head. "But what does that teach them? That they can do whatever they want and someone else will pick up the tab?"

Egori turned to his wife. "What is a tab?"

Mrs. Daniels placed her hand on her husband's arm. "Lennon, don't start."

He faced her, very annoyed. "What d'you mean don't start. My daughter is being accused of something that she may not have done, but we have to pay for it." He turned back to the principal. "How much does a trophy case cost? A couple thousand? Why don't you find out who actually did it, and charge them?"

"Right now, all evidence points to the girls. I've already talked to the board trustees, and they insist on immediate reimbursement."

Lennon let out a sarcastic chuckle. "I'm not paying a dime."

"Then I'm afraid I'll have to expel them."

The room erupted into chaos.

Lennon put up his hand. "Whoa, hang on a minute. Don't you think that's a bit much?"

"It's not my call, Mr. Daniels. It's what the school board has deemed the proper punishment considering their past behavior."

Melanie was openly upset. "But to expel them?"

Lennon shook his head.

"What if the girls reimburse the school?" He turned to Egori. "You know, they could get a job."

Skye's eyes went wide. "Dad!"

Egori's voice was low. "And what exactly would two fourteen-year-old girls do for employment?"

"How the hell should I know, but I don't have that kind of money to fork over."

"What if I put the money given to the school in a trust fund until the investigation is over," Mr. Jarrod said. "If they're proven innocent, the money will be returned to you."

Lennon nodded. "Sounds reasonable." He turned to his daughter. "You can get a job and pay the school back."

"But dad—"

He held up his hand. "I'm not saying you're guilty, but your little drawings were all over the place."

"Because they broke into Eva's locker!"

"And what have I told you about being responsible for your things?" His stern look softened. "Maybe you shouldn't have had your things in her locker in the first place."

"If it turns out someone else is to blame," Mr. Jarrod said, "I will make sure the girls are vindicated, and they'll have a nice pile of money to spend over the summer."

Eva slumped in her chair as Skye went on about locker combinations, conspiracies by other students, how they were being framed, and how no one else saw that, but in the end, Eva and Skye were still suspended for two weeks.

Principal Jarrod stood. "Suspension starts immediately. The girls have until nine-thirty to be off school property."

Eva's father stood and was the first one out the door. He mumbled something in Russian to her mother in the hall and quickly left the building. Eva wished she knew more Russian, but she was pretty sure she didn't want to know what he said today.

The group paused for a moment outside the office. Mrs. Daniels exhaled and gave an exasperated look at Eva's mother. "At least they're not expelled."

"Come on." Mr. Daniels turned her daughter's shoulders down the hall. "Let's collect your things and go."

Melanie held out her hand. "It was nice to meet you. I just wish it was under better circumstances."

Venera took her hand. "I agree."

Skye protested all the way down the hall and Eva held back her tears as her only friend disappeared down another corridor.

"Don't worry." Venera put her arm around her daughter and led her away from the office. "This will work itself out. Now, where is your locker?"

Eva led her through the main foyer and stared at the boarded-up trophy case. The spray-painted words were still visible across the painted brick. A few students were hanging out and they gave her dirty looks and whispered to each other as they walked by. In front of her locker, Eva stared at the combination lock.

Her mother's soft voice came from behind. "What's wrong?"

"What did dad say to you?"

"When?"

"Back there, before he left."

Venera placed her hands gently on her daughter's shoulders and leaned into her left ear. " Your father isn't mad at you if that's what you think, but he is concerned about all of this, and he knows the Council of Ministers will be as well."

Eva opened her locker. Posters and craft items tumbled onto the floor, along with binders that belonged to one of Tina's friends. She bent down and quickly scooped them up.

Venera lifted some of the school items on the top shelf. "You're taking French?"

"No. That belongs to Vikki."

"I thought you said your locker partner's name was Tina?"

"It is."

Venera placed the book on the top shelf. "Who else shares this locker with you?"

"A few of Tina's friends dump their stuff in here." Eva grabbed her Adidas bag and stuffed a few things inside.

"Maybe they had something to do with the vandalism?" She gently moved Eva away from the locker. "Let's see who else has opened this door recently." She went through her small black velvet bag and removed a smaller velvet bag.

"Mom! You can't Spellcast in the school. What if someone sees?"

"Then go make sure no one's around."

Eva hurried to the branching corridor, checked and shook her head. "All clear."

Venera poured some of the contents of the smaller bag into the palm of her hand. It was a light-yellow powder that shifted to white in the light. She sprinkled the powder on the floor, raised her hands to shoulder height, and made small, clockwise rotations with her right hand, and counter-clockwise with her left. "Mist and smoke, dust and air, reveal to me those who opened the locker there." She gave her daughter an indifferent look. "I like to make my incantations rhyme."

A gentle breeze blew down the hall and gathered the powder up into a vortex. It swirled in front of the locker until a shape appeared that resembled Eva.

"That's from this morning," Eva said.

Venera waved her left hand counter-clockwise. The powder quickly disappeared and reformed into Tina, Beth, and Vikki.

"Who are these girls?"

"That's Tina and her friends. Tina's the one with long brown hair." She sighed. "Probably from this morning."

Venera stared at the image for a few moments, and then did a quick counter-clockwise motion. The powder reformed for a third time into the shape of Carla and Tina. They stood in a position that depicted them taking things from the locker.

Eva glared at the face. "That's Carla."

"The one your brother is dating?"

"*Was* dating. He dumped her." The threats from the dance filled her mind. She knew Carla was nasty, and for a brief moment she felt bad for Tina. It was funny that they now had something in common.

Venera made a clockwise motion with her right and the image returned to the previous one with all three girls. "Her clothing is different from the other image."

"That other one was from the night of the dance. Tina was wearing her cheer-leading outfit."

"To a Halloween party?"

"Dance," Eva corrected, "And yeah, Skye said she'd get in trouble from Carla for using it as a costume."

Venera nodded, slowly. "Disrespecting the uniform. That could entail serious consequences."

"She could be kicked off the squad."

"So, she would be at the mercy of this Carla?"

Laughter echoed from somewhere down the hall and Venera snapped her fingers. The powder fell to the ground and turned brown. She dispersed the remains with her foot before they walked away.

"But why would Skye's cousin want into your locker?"

"Carla's a bully and she's just heinous and has had it in for me since the first day of school."

Venera stopped her daughter right before the main exit. "Is this the girl you mentioned about when you came home that day?"

"It is, but don't worry about it."

"You keep saying that, and then something happens to make me worry about it."

Eva kept quiet as she pushed open the door and went outside.

Her mother followed. "Did she see you Spellcast? Is all of this the result of a spell?"

"No!"

Venera took her by the arm. "Eva, tell me what's going on."

A car horn beeped as the station wagon with the Daniels' family drove slowly past, and Skye waved from the backseat as they pulled onto the main road.

"Eva, please."

She turned to her mother. "I told you. It's nothing."

The ride home was unbearably quiet. Skye's heart raced, not because of her punishment, but what would probably come afterward. Her dad had taken the day off to go to the meeting, which meant he'd be in a lousy mood for the rest of the day. Her mom looked like she was about to burst into tears at any moment, but all Skye could think about was how to prove that it wasn't her or Eva that destroyed the trophy case.

"Well, young lady, I hope all of this has taught you a lesson," Mr. Daniels said as they turned into their gravel driveway. "You need to be responsible with your things all the time. If someone has a grudge against you, they'll find a way to bring you down."

Her mother frowned. "What are you talking about? Your daughter was unjustly accused of ruining school property, and you're making it sound like she was partly to blame."

"The principal said it was her stuff displayed all over the foyer?"

"But it doesn't mean she did it. There has to be another explanation."

He glanced back at Skye through the rear-view mirror. "What do you have to say for yourself?"

"I told you, it was Carla and Tina."

The car came to an abrupt stop just short of the regular parking spot. Mrs. Daniels opened her door and climbed out, but her father stayed in the car.

"Aren't you coming, Lennon?"

"I'm going back to work and try to salvage what's left of the day." He turned to Skye. "Do you want to get out please?"

Skye grabbed her backpack and opened the car door. She'd barely closed it when the car sped off and turned back toward the main road. She let her backpack fall to the ground.

"He hates me."

Mrs. Daniels put her arm around Skye's shoulder. "No, he doesn't hate you, but he is concerned about how this suspension could affect your grades."

She frowned. "There's more to life than grades, Mom."

"Not where your dad is concerned."

She led Skye up to the house and inside. It felt different to be home in the morning on a weekday, and she stood in the kitchen and just looked around. There was a calming silence that permeated the whole house. No brothers and sisters yelling. No parents fighting. Just peaceful silence.

She went up to her room and dropped her backpack near the bed. The sun was bright, and she opened a window and let the breeze play with the curtains. She leaned against the frame and stared at her reflection in the glass. Even if she could prove Carla destroyed the trophy case, her aunt and uncle had money and would make some grand gesture to the school to keep her from getting into any real trouble. That's what they did when Carla broke a window in grade school. Her father donated a pile of money to the school board, and they put in a new tetherball pole in the playground. She got away with it then, and Skye was convinced she'd get away with it now.

A soft knock echoed in the quietness of her room before her mother opened the door. Mrs. Daniels had a tray with milk and cookies on it. Skye watched her mother in the reflection of the glass as she put the tray carefully on her bed.

"I thought you'd want something to eat."

Skye rolled her eyes and faced her. "Mom, I had breakfast, like, an hour ago."

Mrs. Daniels gave a quick nod and glanced down at the floor before turning way. "Well, then, I'll just leave you alone."

A wave of guilt washed over Skye. "Mom, wait." She walked to the bed and took one of the cookies off the plate. "Why does Carla hate me so much?"

The personal question seemed to perk her mother up.

"I don't think she hates you dear."

Skye sat on the bed. "Oh, she hates my guts, *fer sure*. She always has."

Mrs. Daniels came toward the bed. "I think Carla's attitude toward you has been greatly influenced by her mother."

Skye's brow rose. "Aunt Shelia hates me?"

Her mother chuckled softly. "No, Aunt Shelia doesn't hate you, but your aunt is hanging on to things that happened in our past and allowing it to influence things that are happening now."

"What'd you mean?"

Melanie sat carefully on the other side of the bed. "Your Aunt is a—" She took a cookie from the plate and brought it to her lips. Taking a bit before she spoke again. "—complicated person. Being younger than myself, she was treated differently by our parents."

"You mean spoiled." Skye picked up another cookie. "I know Grandma and Poppy spoil Carla all the time."

"That's because my grandparents spoiled me when we were children."

"Your grandparents?"

She nodded. "My maternal grandmother." Melanie looked around her room. "This was her home for all of her life. Anyway, she said that I reminded her of her own mother, and that's why she doted on me."

"And not Aunt Shelia?"

"She figured our parents spoiled her enough for the both of them."

Skye smiled. "You mean doted."

Melanie gave a sly smile. "Yes."

"So, what happened?"

A softness washed over her mother as she stared off toward the window. "The summer before my sophomore year of college, she sent me to Europe for a couple of months. She said I needed a good break away to explore and relax from such a hard year of school."

"Wow, that was nice of her."

"It was, but your Aunt Shelia moaned and complained that she should be allowed to go to. After all, she'd just spent her last year in high school preparing for college and she convinced my parents that she deserved a trip through Europe as well."

Skye balked. "I hope your grandmother didn't pay for it."

"She didn't. My parents did. As a matter of fact, we all ended up going together."

"So, she scammed her way into your trip? That totally sucks."

Melanie brushed off the comment. "Oh, I didn't mind that so much. It was nice having everyone with me."

"What happened?"

Melanie took another cookie and turned to her daughter. "We were in Greece having the time of our lives, and one night, I went out, just to have some time to myself, but your aunt had to follow. She didn't want to be stuck in a hotel all night with our parents. Well, as it happens, we ran into a group of young men. Very dashing, and your aunt took a liking to one of them, but as it turned out, he wasn't interested in her." A look of pride came over her. "He was more interested in me."

Skye's eyes were wide. "I bet she didn't like that."

"Not one bit. We travelled around the city together for a few weeks. The entire time, your Aunt Shelia was green with jealousy."

"I bet!"

"When it was time to leave, we said farewell and parted ways, but she never got over the fact that he liked me more than her."

"Did you ever talk to him again? Like write to him?"

"Oh no. By the time our vacation was over, I was too busy getting ready for college."

"So, you never saw him again?"

Melanie was quiet, a faraway look of sorrow on her face. "No."

Skye picked up her glass of milk. "That's, like, totally heartbreaking."

Her mother smiled weakly. "It was a long time ago. Your aunt did get her revenge by stealing a beau I had in my third year. She married him right out of college and his job in banking made him quite wealthy, and she seems to think that she bested me."

"But she didn't, right?"

Melanie shook her head. "No, she didn't. The following year I met your father at a protest and—" She held her hands up. "—here we are."

There was a smile on her face, but Skye could see it in her mother's eyes that she was just putting on a brave face.

Melanie gently touched the corner of her left eye and stood. "Well, I think I've said enough for one day." She picked up the plate of cookies and set them on the end table next to the bed. "I have work to do and it won't get done if I'm up here jabbering on."

She left before Skye could reply, leaving her alone in her room and wondering if her life would ever just be normal.

Time moved slowly. The days dragged on for longer than Eva thought they could, and at one point she was sure Dom had spell-cast all the clocks in the house to move slow just to mess with her. What was worse, her parents refused to let her call anyone. Eva sat and stared out the window, remembering when Skye was there and how well she took the news that Eva's family could do magic, but that was Skye; open-minded and understanding, and people like that don't break trophy cases. Why didn't the principal see that?

By Wednesday of the first week, Eva thought she would die from being cooped up for so long and decided to set up a routine for herself.

It was breakfast, followed by an hour of reading, then some light calisthenics, and then lunch. The afternoon consisted of reading and spell-work; sometimes she combined the two and read about spell-work. With her parents gone for the whole day and sometimes into the evening, she would prepare dinner for them when they got home, and for a little while, it was like it used to be before everyone's lives got so hectic. Dom was mysteriously absent throughout the day. He'd leave early in the morning and wouldn't be home until late afternoon, and then would lock himself in his room for the night, and only come out for dinner. Some nights her mother would bring a plate of food up to him.

Eva couldn't even sneak out. Sem'ya kept all exits locked once everyone was gone. Friday morning, after everyone left early, she burnt her pancake breakfast, and when she tried to open the kitchen window to get rid of the smoke, it wouldn't budge.

By the end of the second week, she'd grown accustomed to the quietness and realized the time alone was a good thing. Her spell-work had improved, and she'd mastered a few advanced elemental spells. This was the first time since they moved that she'd had the time to be *in* the house. On Wednesday of the second week, she found herself staring at the stone archway in the foyer. She rested her hand against the cold stone of the frame and examined it closely. The grey rock was smooth to the touch, and she examined a groove that split one of the stones. She followed it to the side to a small crack in the plaster near the base. She picked at the crack with her fingernail, and a small chunk broke away. She dug at the plaster a bit more until she'd picked open a small hole. Behind the plaster, a rune lay exposed, embedded into a light-coloured wood.

The front door creaked and groaned as Dom walked in. "What are you doing?"

Eva quickly turned. "Nothing. Just looking at the archway."

He held out a file toward her. "This is for you."

"What is it?" She took the file and leafed through the contents.

"Homework," Dom said and headed to the kitchen. "Mom was worried you'd fall behind, so she called the school and asked if you could keep up on your studies and asked me to pick it up."

Eva followed him and examined the sheets of paper. "Wow. There's a lot of stuff here."

He opened the fridge door. "Good. Should keep you busy."

She sat at the kitchen table. "Where were you?"

He scanned the contents of the fridge. "Out."

"I know that, but where did you go?"

He took a plate of leftovers wrapped in cling wrap from the fridge and leaned on the door. "What's it to you?"

Eva shrugged. "Just curious."

"Well, you're the one who says I need to get out, so I'm getting out." He walked to the hall. "Oh, I ran into one of your little friends, Shelly's cousin. Brad? Anyway, he wanted me to tell you something about him and some girl named Tina?"

Eva's heart skipped a beat. "What about them?"

"I dunno, something about doing something together?"

"Going out?"

He shrugged. "Maybe. Wasn't really paying attention."

Eva's heart sank. This topped the worse week of her life. She couldn't talk to her best friend, and now her brand-new boyfriend was going out with his old girlfriend. Her emotions overwhelmed her and she ran up to her room. She slammed her bedroom door. She wanted to scream but instead, flopped onto her bed, buried her face in her pillow and cried.

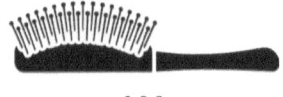

Light snow fell outside the next morning. Eva's room was cold, and she snuggled deeper under the blankets to keep warm. She stared at the wall. Her eyes were still puffy from crying all night. Maybe it was a good thing she wasn't at school. Seeing Brad with Tina would be impossible to handle. At least she had a week to get over him before going back.

She got out of bed and went to the window. Frost lines etched across the glass, and she traced one with her finger. Outside, enough snow had fallen to make the ground white, but a few patches of grass still managed to poke through. The island across the channel was lost in a fog of snow, and the water took on a particularly grey hue. She sat on the bench seat and brought her knees to her chest.

A quick knock on her door was followed by the sudden entrance of her mother. "Egori, it's cold in here too." She walked over to Eva and hugged her. "How are you doing sweetie? Dom told us what happened."

Eva tried to smile. "I'm fine."

Venera gently kissed the crown of her head. "I'm sorry."

Her father entered the room. "This is not cold, *moya lyubov*. Live in Siberia for a time. Then you will know cold."

Venera glared at her husband. "With the winds right off the lake, this room is colder than the others." She crossed her arms. "Do you want your daughter to get sick?"

Egori went to Eva's side. "Your mother wishes for fireplaces to be installed in each room, so where would you like yours?"

Eva rested her head on her knees. "I don't care."

He placed his hand gently on her head. "I know you are in pain, but you know where you stand with this person." He bent down and kissed her forehead. "A lesson learned for the future."

Her parents examined her room closely, trying to find a suitable place for a hearth. Her mother showed her several sketches; some brick, some stone, but Eva's attention was still on her heartbreak. Her first boyfriend and she only kissed him once. How was she going to face everyone when she went back to school? Did anyone know? Tina would probably tell everyone what happened, but what about Keith? It was totally humiliating.

"Do I have to go back?"

"To school?" Her father held up a sketch against the far wall. "Of course you do."

"Really? Because I've been thinking of maybe getting an apprenticeship at the Crypt? Or maybe the alchemy fields?"

Egori lowered the sketches. "You want to be a farmer?"

Her mother shook her head. "All the placements have been filled for this year." She tilted her head to one side. "What about the Italian Renaissance?" Egori flipped through the sketches and held up one sketched out in dark materials. Venera waved it away. "No, that's too dark."

"They can't *all* be filled," Eva said. "There has to be something left."

Venera pointed to the wall next to the window. "Hold up the French Provincial on the outer wall." She glanced at Eva. "Sweetheart, we discussed this. The Autumn Equinox was the deadline."

"But—"

"If you want an apprenticeship, you're just going to have to wait and apply next Summer."

"Who wants to apply where now?" Dom said as he leaned against the door frame.

Egori held up another sketch. "Your sister does not wish to return to the high school."

A devilish smile crept across Dom's lips as he stepped inside her room. "Does she now?"

Eva sat up straight. She forgot all about the bet she made with him, and now felt even more humiliated. "I didn't say I *wasn't* going back. I was just asking if I had to."

Dom nodded. "Sure, sure. So, when do you want to start doing my chores? Tonight, or tomorrow?"

Egori frowned. "Why would she do that?"

"We had—"

"I said, I wasn't quitting!"

Venera's gaze drifted from Dom to Eva. "What's going on with you two?"

Eva and Dom exchanged warning looks until Dom spoke.

"Nothing. I'm just teasing her."

Egori held up another sketch. "Stop teasing your sister." He focused on Eva. "These people who hurt you, these so-called friends, when you see them next, tell them you no longer care for their friendship."

Eva sank back into her seat. "They weren't my friends, just dumb kids at school."

"Either way, you do not need people like this in your life."

In the end, her parents settled on a small Baroque-style fireplace that would fit nicely on the wall that faced the right side of her bed, and Eva decided no matter what happened, she would go back to school when her suspension was finished, and make sure Brad knew what kind of boyfriend he really was.

It wasn't often that something caught Eva's parents off-guard, but two days later, right before supper, the ringing of the phone in the front hall did just that. Venera and Egori stood by the small wood table and stared at the antique French phone. The ring echoed in the partially empty room, and they took turns giving it odd glances.

"Why is it doing that?" Egori asked.

Dom walked past and gave the phone a quick side glance. "Someone's calling."

Venera placed her hands over her ears. "Can you make it stop?"

Egori followed his son out of the room. "Who? Who would call us?"

Eva ran down the stairs. "Don't answer it! It's for me!"

She sprinted to the table and picked up the receiver. "Hello?" Her face lit up. "Hey, Skye! What's up?" She put her hand over the receiver.

"I was right! It's Skye. Can I talk to her? Please?"

Venera nodded with a smile and left.

Eva removed her hand and flopped herself down in the old chair next to the table. "Yeah, I'm totally bored at home too. What have you been doing?"

"Not much," Skye said, on the other end. "I have to do everyone's chores now."

"That sucks."

"Totally, but at least it kills time."

"I thought you'd be working out new ideas for protests."

"Nope. Mom 'n Dad said I'm not allowed to do any protest stuff for the rest of the year."

"So, for two more months?"

"Yeah, 'bout that. What about you?"

Eva paused. "My parents put a fireplace in my room, cos it's too cold."

"That's cool. Like a magical one?"

"No, Baroque."

"Why'd they put a broken fireplace in your room?"

Eva giggled. "No *Bar*-oak. It's a style my mom likes."

"Oh. My mom likes cows. She says she's going to redo the whole kitchen in a cow pattern."

"That's really weird."

"I know. Dad keeps talking her out of it."

There was a long, awkward silence.

"So," Eva said and twirled the phone cord between her fingers. "Have you seen Keith or anyone?"

"No. Have you talked to Brad?"

"No. He hasn't called." Eva's heart skipped a beat. "I think we broke up."

"What? When?"

"I don't know. Dom said he ran into Brad, and he said he was going out with Tina now."

"That's bullshit! Brad *hates* Tina. Your brother must have got it wrong. There's *no way* he'd dump you for her."

"You sure?"

"Positive." She paused. "Did you call him?"

"No, I was so upset I didn't want to."

"Then I will."

"No. He'll think I made you call him, and if he is going out with Tina—"

"He's not going out with Tina!"

"But he might be, and I don't want him to think I'm upset about it."

There was a pause on the other end.

"I'll call Keith. He'd know for sure."

Eva cupped the mouthpiece. "Okay and call me right back."

She dropped the receiver on the hook. The Grandfather clock said five forty-five. It felt good that Brad hated Tina, and Keith would know if Brad was going out with Tina again. She glanced at the clock; five forty-seven. How long did it take to make a call? Would he even be home?

"Evie!" Dom's voice bellowed from the kitchen. "Food!"

She glanced over her shoulder at the phone, hoping it would ring before she got up. Her mother's voice echoed down the narrow corridor, reprimanding Dom for yelling, to which he noted that she never said he *couldn't* yell, and then there was something about 'splitting hairs'. She sat at the small kitchen table and stared at her empty plate.

"Can I eat by the phone?"

"Why?"

"Skye's going to call me back."

Her mother handed her a bowl of *vareniki*. "No. You can sit at the table and eat like a civilized person."

She slopped a few pieces from the bowl onto her plate. "It was really good talking to her."

"Your conversation did not last long," her father said. "I would have thought there would be more to discuss."

"There is. That's why I want to eat by the phone. For when she calls back." The phone rang and Eva jumped out of her chair. "I'll get it!" She raced back out into the foyer and grabbed the receiver before the third ring. "Skye?"

"Yeah, so Keith said that Brad said he isn't going out with Tina."

"Is he sure?"

"Pretty sure."

"So why would Dom say that he said they were going out?"

"Did Brad really say that?"

"Dom said he ran into Brad at school and Brad told him that him and Tina were going out."

"Well Keith said he's not, so I don't know what your brother's talking about."

Eva moved the mouthpiece from her face. "Dom, did Brad tell you him and Tina were going out?"

"I don't know."

Eva rolled her eyes. "Now he says he doesn't know."

"I'll call Keith and get him to find out from Brad what he said."

"Okay." Eva hung up and headed back to the kitchen. She glared at her brother as she sat down. "Brad and Tina *aren't* going out."

He scrunched up his face. "So?"

"So, you said they were!"

Dom shook his head. "Whatever."

"Is this what you are so upset about?" her father asked, "Brad dating this Tina?"

"Yes, but they're not, so I'm not upset anymore."

"Good."

The phone rang again, and Eva quickly left the table.

Egori slammed his hands on the table and his cutlery clanged against the plate. "*Chto s ney tvoritsya?*"

Venera patted her husband on the arm. "It's all right."

"Dominik did not act this way."

Dom stuffed a forkful of food into his mouth. "I didn't go to a high school."

Eva grabbed the receiver again. "Skye?"

"Yeah, so Keith said that Brad said that he *did* talk to your brother but didn't say he was going out with Tina."

"So what did he say?"

"Keith said that Brad said he was *going* to find out if Tina had anything to do with what happened at the dance."

Eva's eyes narrowed. "She had something to do with it, I know it."

"Oh, totally, and Brad asked Keith to ask me to ask you if you wanted to go to the movies. If you're allowed."

"Are you going?"

"Yeah, Mom said I learned my lesson, or whatever."

"I'll ask if I can too. What time?"

"Dunno, I'll call Keith and find out."

"Okay."

She did a little skip as she headed back down the hall. Brad wasn't going out with Tina, and he was on her side on this, but that's what boyfriends were supposed to do; be supportive of their girlfriends. She sat back at the table and dug into her food.

"I know I'm grounded, but is it okay if I go to the movies?"

"You're still grounded," her mother said.

"But I really wanna go, and I haven't bugged you about anything the whole time."

Egori clasped his hands over his plate. "Who will you be with?"

Eva paused for just a moment. They might not let her go if they knew Skye was going too. Even though they liked her and thought she was mature, they hadn't talked about their friendship since the whole thing with the trophy case. She could just say she was meeting Brad, but she hated the idea of lying to them. Especially her father.

She lowered her gaze. "Brad, and Keith."

"Is Skye going?" Her father's voice was low.

Eva shrugged. "Maybe."

The phone rang again, and she jumped up from the table and raced into the hall.

Her father's voice boomed from the table. "Evandra!"

Eva froze just at the entrance to the foyer. She'd never heard her father's voice so angry. She turned to see him standing up from the table.

Egori stood and glared at her, his arms crossed.

The phone rang a third time.

Eva slumped. It wasn't often that he called her by her full name, and his piercing look made her feel bad for asking to go out.

The phone rang a fourth time.

Her mother reached up and gently placed her hand on her husband's arm. His gaze fell on her and softened.

The phone rang a fifth time.

Egori exhaled. "Tell your friends that from now on, they are not to call between five and seven, understand?"

Eva smiled. "*Da, otets*. So can I go?"

Her mother smiled and nodded.

Eva ran and picked up the receiver. "So, what movie are they seeing?"

An hour later, Eva met Skye at the main entrance to the Odeon movie theatre downtown. The bus took her close and she didn't mind walking the rest of the way, even on the chilly November night. If anything, she was just glad to get out. Their conversation went at a rapid pace as they tried to catch up on each other's life over the last week and a half.

"I didn't think my parents would let me come," Eva said, as they stood by the glass front doors.

"Same," Skye said. "But they've been, like, totally cool 'bout all of this." She gave a quick look back at the marquis. "So, is this, like, you're first time at a movie theatre?"

"Yeah."

Skye nodded. "Okay, so we gotta figure out what movie we wanna see." She led her to a row of posters on the far wall. "What d'ya think?"

Eva looked over the half dozen posters. "I don't know. You pick one."

Skye looked them over, but her gaze stayed on one in particular. "I like Cher, so I'd see the Jimmy Dean one."

Eva pointed to a poster of *The Scarlet Pimpernel*. "I like the clothes they're wearing."

Skye nodded. "Yeah, that one looks cool too."

"Hey, hey," Keith's voice said from behind. "If it isn't the leader of the juvenile delinquents!"

The girls turned to him and Brad. Skye gave them both a dirty look.

"What?"

Brad walked up to Eva. "Yeah, that's what Mrs. Craine was calling you two."

Eva panicked. "Why?"

"Cause of what happened. It's all over school that you two busted up the trophy case 'cause Mr. Banta busted up your protest."

"That's not true!"

"Doesn't matter," Keith said, with a slight grin. "That's what's goin' 'round."

Skye rolled her eyes and turned back to the posters. "Great. I wanted people to talk about it, but not like this."

Brad took Eva's hand. "Why'd you think I was going back out with Tina?"

She shook her head. "Because of my dumb brother."

"Why? What'd he say?"

"Nothing. It's stupid."

Skye turned to them. "So, what movie are we gonna see?"

Keith motioned to one poster. "Well, I wanna see Halloween 3."

Skye scrunched up her face. "Ew. No thanks. I wanna sleep tonight."

Brad turned to Eva. "What do you wanna see?"

"I don't know. You pick."

He glanced at the posters. "What kind of movies do you like?"

She shrugged. "What kind do you like?"

"Oh fer shit's sakes," Keith said, frustrated. "Just pick one, already. I'm freezing!"

Brad turned to Eva. "Class Reunion?"

She nodded and smiled.

He turned to Keith and Skye. "You guys good with that one?"

"Sure," Keith said. "It's from National Lampoon. It'll be awesome!"

An hour and twenty minutes later they left the theatre.

Keith gave the middle finger to the movie poster as they walked by. "That movie sucked, big time."

Eva and Brad were holding hands and walked behind him. Eva shook her head. "How can anyone think killing people would be funny?"

Brad shrugged. "I dunno. Some people have weird ideas."

Skye followed behind them. "Wait'll I tell my dad how bad it was. He really liked Animal House."

Keith turned and walked backward, facing them. "So, it's still early. What d'ya wanna do now?"

"I'm hungry," Eva said. "I didn't care for the popcorn."

"The Sarcoma's open twenty-four hours. Wanna go there?"

The corner restaurant was busy for it being past nine at night. The decor was straight out of the early sixties, with a mixture of university students, a few homeless, shift workers and other movie patrons. The guys headed down one aisle to a corner booth as Eva pulled Skye to fall back.

"My mom and dad know we didn't break the trophy case."

"How do they know?"

"Mom did a spell before we left the school to find out who could have gotten into my locker."

Skye's eyes went wide. "And?"

"It was Carla. With help from Tina."

Skye stopped in the middle of the aisle. "Those bitches!" Her voice carried all through the restaurant. "I knew she was up to something, but shit!" A wide grin creased her face. "Wait'll my mom finds out. She knows Carla's bad news. I bet she'll call Aunt Sheila and tell her."

Eva grabbed her by the arm. "No, you can't say anything to your parents."

"Why not?"

"Because they're going to ask you how you know. You can't tell them it was by magic."

"But this could get us out of trouble!"

"Not if we don't have any real proof."

A look of disappointment replaced Skye's grin. "Yeah, I know. I just wanna see her get in shit for once." They headed toward the guys. "Did you see Shelly too?"

"No. Just her and Tina."

They joined the guys at the booth near a corner window. Skye and Keith on one side, and Brad and Eva on the other.

Eva sat close to Brad. "Even though the movie was horrible, I had a fun time." She looked down at her hand. "I missed you."

"Yeah, me too." He leaned in and kissed her on the lips. He smelled of aftershave and his lips felt rough.

A waitress came up to them they all ordered pop with fries with gravy.

"So," Keith said, as he looked over a cocktail menu. "Any idea how your stuff got all over the foyer?"

Skye took a quick look at Eva. "Well, all of that was in Eva's locker, so it had to be someone who knew the combination."

Brad nodded. "Tina."

Eva shrugged. "That's one possibility."

"Who else knows the combo?" Keith asked.

"Vikki, Beth. Maybe Janice and Mel?"

Brad frowned. "I could totally see them helping her."

Keith nodded. "I definitely think Carla was in on it."

Skye frowned. "Why?"

"Shell's pissed at her for something."

Eva snorted. "With Carla, that could be just about anything."

The waitress brought over the drinks.

Keith reached for a drink. "Maybe she found out about her and Donnie?"

Eva's eyes went wide, and she shot a shocked look at Skye.

"Yeah." Brad nodded. "I told him."

Skye shot Eva a knowing look. "You really think it was her?"

"Could be," Keith said. "All I know is that I haven't seen her ugly mug around our house in about a week."

"Whatever." Skye shifted in her seat. "I don't wanna talk about her anymore."

There was silence at the table until the waitress brought over their food.

Keith shoved some fries into his mouth. "So, it's all over school that you guys have to pay for the damage."

"Yeah, but I don't know how," Eva said. "Unless we get jobs."

Skye's face lit up. "Maybe we can get jobs in the mall!"

Brad scrunched up his face. "Where? You gotta be sixteen to get a job there."

Eva's shoulders slumped. "Seriously?"

"Yeah. That's the law."

Keith took a long sip from his drink and belched before he spoke. "Fast-food places you don't. I worked at McDonald's during the summer."

Skye exhaled in disgust. "I don't wanna work at McDonald's."

"You don't have a lot of options, Skye," Brad said. "And it's not like it's forever. Just do it until you get the trophy case paid off, and then quit."

She mulled it around. "Yeah, maybe."

A wide grin appeared on Keith's face. "Yeah, and you get a discount on food."

She made a face. "I don't like their food. I'd rather eat at Burger King."

"Maybe you could work at Burger King?" Brad said. He turned to Eva. "Where'd you like to work?"

She shrugged. "I don't know, but I might be able to get a job in the same place my mom works."

Skye scrunched up her nose. "Ew. She works in a morgue, right?"

"Yeah, but at least it's a job." Brad smiled at Eva. "It's kinda cool too. Working in a mortuary."

"Yeah, she likes it. She comes home with all kinds of interesting stories."

Keith laughed. "I bet! Any of the dead bodies try to get out?" He held up his arms and pretended to walk like a zombie. "You know, like Night of the Living Dead."

They laughed and changed the subject to school and the exams coming up. She could ask if they needed some help at the Crypt. Unimportant stuff like cleaning or running errands. She didn't want to work with dead people, but she had to find something. Spellcasting for a large amount would have serious consequences, and the last thing she needed was more problems. There had to be a way out of this.

It was close to ten o'clock when Skye's father came to pick them up. Shelly pulled in behind Mr. Daniels car and the boys got inside. Skye told her father how horrible the movie was, how bland the popcorn was and how flat the sodas were. He, in return, scolded her for being at The Sarcoma.

"It's not a decent place to hang out," he said, looking back at the girls from the rear-view mirror. "All kinds of weirdos hang out at that place, and I don't want you getting mixed up with them."

Skye frowned. "We just had some food."

"Doesn't matter. One minute you're having a nice meal with your friends, the next you're all hopped up on drugs wandering around downtown." He pulled up next to Eva's house and turned to them. "You two were lucky with this whole school thing. You got a second chance. Don't blow it."

The girls said goodbye and Eva strolled up to the house as the car pulled away. This had to be the best night ever! Brad was still her boyfriend, and it was awesome to see Keith and Skye again. Even the gargoyles seemed to be in a good mood as they raced around the roof in the shadows, and she stopped and watched a few.

The front door to the house opened, but no one stepped through the entrance. Eva slowly walked up to the door and went inside. The house was quiet and dark. Only the light from a few black pillar candles on the hall table illuminated the room. Her heart pounded. She recognized those candles. They were special ones her father used, and he kept them locked up with the scepter. She hated them. They gave off no light but swallowed everything in distorted shadows. The door closed behind her and the shadows overtook the entrance and enveloped it into the darkness.

"How was your movie?"

Egori was completely hidden within the shadows. She didn't

know what spell he cast to make himself so invisible, but a chill raced through her as he stepped from the archway into the dim light.

"Da? What's going on?"

"I was called to a special council meeting about your incident at the school."

Eva's heart leapt into her throat. "But you know we didn't do it."

"That is not the one I am talking about." Egori stepped out from the shadows. In the disconcerting light he looked different. Angry, but not. "I am speaking of the incident that took place on the night of Sow'een."

She thought back to that night. A lot had happened, good and bad, but it wasn't until her mind rested on the incident in the girls change room that it dawned on her.

"You know what happened?"

He nodded. "You almost cast a spell."

"Carla threw me up against the sink. I was angry and—"

"And you friend had to stop you, because you had no self-control." He walked over to the table with the candles. "There are some on the council who feel that you are incapable of keeping your word."

"But I haven't even tried to spellcast since that night." She ran to him. "*Otets*, I'm sorry. I was angry. She threatened me an-and it happened so fast!"

"Nonetheless, your first instinct was to attack her with magic. This is far more serious than doing a spell for food."

Eva stood nervously and hung on every word her father spoke. If a council meeting was called, and given his sombre demeanor, she wasn't going to like the outcome from it.

"What's going to happen?"

"The council has decided that a binding spell is in order."

"What?" Her eyes went wide as tears formed. "But she forced me—"

He turned to her and cupped her face. His hands were cold and there was fear in his eyes.

"*Moy dorogoy rebenok,* there were those on the council who feel you are a grave threat to our world and should be sent to a penal institution for even thinking about attacking that girl."

She trembled. "Prison! I'm going to prison?"

He gently kissed her forehead. "*Net, malyshka,* Councilor Kaige argued that while this could have been serious, you did not follow through and therefore did not warrant such a harsh penalty, but if you do not watch yourself, and you spellcast out of anger again, they will enact a harsher penalty."

He removed his hands. The air felt warm where he'd touched her. He reached into his pocket and removed a black stone pendant on a silver chain. "The council has issued that a binding spell be immediately placed on you to prevent you from breaching your contract any farther."

Her lip trembled. "So, I can't spellcast ever?'

"Only within our realm."

The stone was as black as the skull on the scepter, and she felt the energy from the stone tug at her body.

"This binding pendant, will create a magical barrier around you, and prevent any spells from manifesting." A small electrical charge emanated from the chain as he separated the link. "You are required to wear it at all times."

Tears ran down her cheeks as he leaned close to her. He clasped the chain back together behind her head. It felt heavy and cold against her skin. She touched it and a small charge leapt from the stone.

"How long do I have to wear this?"

"Until you no longer attend your school."

More tears trickled down her cheek and her father opened his arms.

"I am so sorry."

She fell into his embrace and openly sobbed. "Why is this happening to me?"

He rubbed her back. "I don't know, *dochka*, but we learn the most from the hardest lessons."

She sniffed and stepped back as her father walked over to the hall table and snuffed out the pillar candles. Light from the lamps returned the hall to normal, and the black candles no longer burned.

Egori smiled at his daughter. "Now tell me, was your outing to your satisfaction?"

She shrugged and touched the pendant against her chest. "I guess."

He held out his arm as he walked toward the kitchen. "Come, tell me all about it."

Chapter Eight

The first few days back at school were a little surreal. No one bothered them about their suspension. A few kids in their classes were curious, and there was the odd, nasty look from a teacher or two, but by the end of the first week, things had pretty much returned to normal.

"Do you think Carla feels bad about what she said to me in the change room?" Eva asked Skye that Friday at the end of the day.

Skye shook her head. "I doubt it. I overheard Mom talking to Aunt Sheila. She was *so* drunk she doesn't even remember how she got home. Did you tell your brother?"

"I was going to, but I don't think he likes her anymore."

"Yeah? Good for him. He doesn't need that kind of grief, and I am so sick of her always getting her own way."

They turned into the corridor that headed toward the cafeteria and stopped in front of Eva's locker.

"Has Tina said anything to you?" Skye asked.

"Nope, and I want to know why she let Carla into our locker."

"Yeah, but then you'd have to tell her how you know it was her." Her gaze fell on the pendant. "I still can't believe you can't do magic anymore. That's so heinous."

Eva touched the stone. It was cold. It was always cold. "I hate wearing it. I tried to pull the chain apart but it's too strong."

Skye put her open hands up in front of her friend. "Funny, I can't feel any barrier. Are you sure it's there?"

"Its there. I tried to cast a spell last night with my mom, but nothing happened."

"That totally sucks."

Eva sighed. "Yeah, totally."

She leaned against the adjacent locker as Eva fiddled with the lock. "Mid-term exams are coming up and we need to study. Can you come over this weekend? Mom is going to Toronto to see my Nanny, and she's taking the twins and my brothers as well."

Eva winced. "I already made plans with Brad. Sorry."

Skye shrugged. "No big deal. Maybe another time."

Eva nodded. "Definitely."

Brad walked up to them and smiled. "Hey. Ready to go?"

"Yup." Eva grabbed her Adidas bag from the bottom of the locker as she forced two binders onto the top shelf.

"Cool, Shelly said she'd drive us to your place." He turned to Skye. "You want a ride home?"

Eva's heart raced. "What?"

He frowned. "Yeah, that's okay right? I mean, I know she's a pain in the ass sometimes, but it beats taking the bus."

Eva's gaze jumped between him and Skye. "Yeah, I guess."

"She's a different person when she's not around Carla," he said.

Skye snorted. "I doubt that."

"No, she is, really."

Eva didn't know what to say.

Skye gave him a weak smile. "Thanks, but my dad's picking me up at the donut shop."

Brad became concerned. "You sure? I can ask her—"

"Naw, that's okay. I'm good."

Skye swung her backpack over her shoulder and waved as she walked off. "Have a nice ride home."

The final bell rang out and the halls filled with students. Skye quickly disappeared into a sea of bodies and the corridor filled. This was the first time she didn't go over to her friends' house when asked, and a part of her felt guilty about not going.

Brad put his arm around her waist. "Come on."

They walked toward the main foyer arm in arm, smiling and chatting. Brad talked about his grade ten academic English class, and the only way he was allowed to do it was because of his grades in public school. Brad was smart. Smarter than anyone she knew, and she loved to just listen to him talk about things and watch his face. His eyes would grow wide when he mentioned something he was very interested in, and how the tone of his voice changed as well.

"I mean, it's all a bunch of reading," he said as they walked out the front doors of the school. "That's all most of the English classes are, but it'll get me ready for university 'cause I know I'll have a pile of reading to do then."

They stopped at the edge of the parking lot.

"I can't believe you already know what you want to do after high school."

"Oh yeah, I want to be a lawyer."

Her brow rose. "Really?"

"Yeah, my grandpa was a lawyer and he used to tell me all these stories about cases he represented in court." He leaned close to her. "Some of them were pretty gnarly."

Keith ran up behind Brad and punched him on the arm. "Dude!"

Brad immediately threw his own punch back. "Dude!"

Shelly walked past them. "Fer fuck sakes."

They followed her through the parking lot to her small red Honda at the far end. Eva and Brad climbed into the backseat as Keith got into the passenger seat up front.

The back was clean with a few cigarette butts in the ashtray. Eva looked unsure at Brad before she looked forward.

"This is a nice car you have." She turned to Brad and shrugged.

"Thanks!" Keith said, "Our parents bought a new one, so we get to drive the old one."

"I get to drive," Shelly said. She looked into the backseat through the rear-view mirror. "Where am I going? Your place or his?"

"Mine," Eva's voice cracked. She couldn't believe she was in her tormentor's car.

Shelly turned the ignition, and they headed out of the parking lot and onto the main road. At the first intersection she turned on the radio. Keith looked back at Eva.

"I hear your place is cool."

Eva was surprised. "Where'd you hear that?"

He thumbed in his sister's direction. "She said it was pretty sweet."

Shelly rolled her eyes. "I said it was in a sweet neighbourhood, dork."

He snorted. "Whatever. How long you been there?"

Eva's gaze shifted between the three other passengers. "Since July."

There was an awkward silence as the radio blasted a tune.

"So," Keith spoke again. "I heard your brother dumped Carla."

Eva's eyes went wide. "Yeah, I guess." Her gaze went straight to the rear-view mirror where Shelly was already watching her.

"You think they're gonna get back together?" Keith asked.

She shrugged. "I don't know."

Brad tilted his head thoughtfully. "Didn't you say he broke up with his last girlfriend just before he started going out with Carla?"

Eva swallowed. "She dumped him, but, uh, yeah."

Keith nodded slowly. "He was on the rebound."

"I guess?"

The light changed and the car shot through the intersection. The guys didn't seem bothered by the fact Shelly was driving faster than the speed limit, so Eva slouched down and kept quiet. Keith and Brad joked with each other, as their driver dodged in and out of traffic. At one point Eva tightly gripped the arm rest on the door.

"Don't worry," Brad said, "Shelly's a good driver."

"A bit of a maniac," Keith laughed, "but that's what you get when you watch too many Nascar races."

Shelly gave a grin as she quickly switched to the right-hand lane.

"Hey, remember when Carla tried to do that thing were you zig-zag between the cars?"

Shelly snorted with a grin. "Carla can't drive worth shit."

They made it to Eva's home sooner than she expected and she jumped out of the car the moment it came to a stop.

"Hey," Shelly motioned her to come to the driver's side. "Your brother's a good guy. Tell him I said hi, will ya."

Eva nodded. "Okay."

She joined Brad on the side of the road as the Honda pulled away. Keith hung out the window shouting his goodbyes as loud as he could, along with a few other things that Eva couldn't understand.

Brad shook his head. "He's such a dork."

Eva turned to him with a wide grin. "Are you ready?"

He nodded.

She took him by the hand, and they walked up the path. As they got to the top step the door swung open and Dom stood in the entranceway with his arms crossed, a serious look on his face.

He glared at Brad. "So, you're the guy who made my sister cry." Brad squeezed Eva's hand.

She rolled her eyes. "Dom, leave him alone."

Her brother moved and filled up the whole doorway. "I thought you were dating some girl named Tina?"

"Dom!"

"*Ostav' ikh.*"

Her father's voice echoed from inside the house and was more menacing. Dom's posture deflated and he slunk back into the front hall. A moment later both her parents appeared.

Venera smiled wide. "Welcome to our home." She stepped back as they walked inside.

Eva nervously looked around the room, waiting for Sem'ya to do something, but the house stayed quiet. Dom leaned against the stone archway with his arms crossed and glared at the young man.

Brad pulled off his backpack and placed it on the floor near the front door, as Venera closed it behind them. He held out his hand and took a few steps toward Egori.

"*YA rad vstretit' tebya.*"

Egori's brow rose as he took Brads hand.

Dom frowned. "You speak Russian?"

"No, I just learned that phrase from language program at the library."

Egori nodded. "And we are pleased to meet you."

Eva grabbed his backpack in one hand and Brad's free hand with the other. "Okay, we're gonna do our homework now." She dragged him into the study. "Call us when dinner's ready."

She closed the sliding doors to the study and rested her forehead. That went better than she thought.

Now if they could get through the rest of the night without anything magical happening, it would be perfect.

Skye's schoolbooks took up two spots on the counter at the coffee shop. She knew her dad wouldn't be there right when she was finished class and didn't mind the extra time to do her homework. That just meant she didn't have to do it over the weekend, but the stool was getting uncomfortable and twice she had to stand up to keep her butt from getting all tingly.

She looked up from her geography notebook to the counter next to her. She had half a cup of coffee, a half-eaten donut and some change sitting neatly in a pile. She took the donut and shoved the rest of it in her mouth. She probably didn't need to eat dinner tonight.

The middle-aged waitress walked up with the coffee pot. "Need a touch up?"

Skye nodded. "If you don't mind."

Her smile was warm and friendly as she dropped a few creamers next to Skye's mug. "Not at all, sweetie, but isn't it getting late? Shouldn't you be going home?"

"I wish. I'm just waiting for my dad."

The waitress looked worried. "It's almost six pm. Shouldn't you call him? Find out where he is?"

"Thanks, but I'm good. He's just working late."

The woman nodded and walked off. Skye looked up at the clock. It was almost 6 pm. He'd never been this late before. Maybe he got stuck doing something important and couldn't get away on time? She glanced out the large picture window to the few cars in the parking lot. The sunlight was just an orange sliver in the west now, and she could see a few stars blinking in the twilight. She clenched her jaw to hold back the tears. She wanted to be home. In her room or having dinner. Anything other than being in this place.

A group of older teenage boys boisterously piled into the coffee shop. Their raunchy laughter forced Skye out of her emotional slump, especially when she saw DevDude in the crowd. She watched him as he joked around with his friends. The way his mouth moved when he spoke, and his stance when he leaned against the counter. His jean jacket was full of patches of rock bands and pins. Even his ratty Nike sneakers were cool. She imagined what it would be like to be around him all the time. He was popular and everyone wanted to be his friend. At least, everyone she knew did. She was so wrapped up in her daydream that she didn't notice him staring right at her.

"Hey, you're Keith's friend," he said, and took a few steps toward her. "What's with him anyway?"

Skye blinked. Was he actually talking to her?

"What about him?"

"Y'know, what's his deal?"

She had no idea what he was talking about but didn't want to look stupid in front of him and his friends.

She shrugged. "Don't know. I just got off suspension."

His brow rose. "For what?"

"They think me and a friend of mine trashed the trophy case."

There was a round of approval from the other guys as Dev smiled and nodded.

"I heard about that. Pretty gnarly thing to do."

She opened her lips slightly, wanting to tell him that she didn't do it, but he was looking at her and smiling. He was genuinely looking at her!

He motioned in her direction. "Skye, right?"

He knew her name! "Yeah."

"Keith said you're related to that bitch, Carla?"

Skye rolled her eyes "Don't remind me."

A few in the group laughed and she tried hard to not to show her approval. Excitement took hold. These were way older students. Some looked like they were too old for high school, and she was sitting with them. Talking!

"Yeah, but I'd do her," one of the older teens said.

Skye balked. "Good luck with that. You're too broke for her to even look at."

Another round of raunchy laughter.

He glared at her. "What the fuck do you know?"

Dev snorted. "Hey. She's her fucking cousin, moron."

Dejected, the teen turned away from them. "Whatever."

They calmed down quickly as the conversation turned to the selling of pot. They leaned closer to one another, and their voices lowered. They didn't seem to care that Skye was right there, overhearing everything being said, and she rotated on her stool and looked out the window. She pretended not to care about their conversation, which wasn't that hard to do. She could see Dev's reflection in the glass and watched him as they quietly talked. A few times she noticed he glanced her way, and her heart skipped a beat each time.

She closed her textbooks and stared out into the parking lot. A few of her classmates from her English class strolled past and she immediately swivelled back around to face the group. She glanced out the window a few times, hoping they'd see her, but the lights from inside reflected too much in the window and it was too dark out to really get a good look at what they were doing. She picked up her coffee mug and sat facing them, but not really looking at any of them, and not paying attention to what they were saying, but hopefully it would look like she was with them. They talked a bit more about the hows and wheres of their pot distribution. She didn't understand Keith's obsession with selling dope, but he'd been going on about it for about a year.

Several from the group got up, Dev included. He turned to her. "We're gonna smoke one. Wanna come?"

Skye didn't know how to answer. If she turned him down, would he think she was a loser? She shrugged. "Sure. Whatever."

She followed them out and around to the side of the building. They hid from the lights from the parking lot with just the lit tip of the joint glowing in the dark. One by one, they each took a drag from the joint, and Skye felt awkward when they handed it to her. She tried to look cool as she held it between her index and middle finger and brought it up to her lips. The smoke smelled like skunk as she cautiously brought it to her lips.

Her heart raced. Would she get stoned from one haul? She didn't last time, but what about a second time? What if her father showed up, like right now? Would he be able to tell? The ash taste filled her mouth as she took a drag and opened her lips slightly to inhale. Her lungs stung with her inhalation, and she coughed hard and passed the joint on to the next person.

"First time?" Dev asked, from the shadows.

Skye coughed. "No. I smoked some at the Halloween dance."

A goofy smile lit up his face. "Oh yeah. I remember that." He held out a second joint in front of her. "Gets better each time you inhale."

She took it between her fingers. The second time was easier, but her lungs still burned and now her stomach felt queasy. She coughed a few more times as the first joint came back her way, but this time she passed.

She stood with the group until the last of the joint was gone and followed behind back inside the building. Her head felt funny, like it was full of fluff, and she just wanted to stare at the coffee in her mug. She shook her head a few times, but the off feeling didn't go away.

Was this what it was like to be stoned?

A car horn beeped from outside. When she looked up, the familiar wagon sat in the parking spot right in front of her. She stared at her father, happy to see him, but why was he so late? She drank the rest of her coffee and slowly put her books back in her backpack. The fuzziness made it difficult to focus on what she was doing and moving slowly seemed to be the only way to do things. She got up and walked to the glass doors, ignoring everyone on her way by. She thought she heard someone say something to her, but she just wanted to get out of there and back home.

She climbed into the back seat and shut the door.

Her father turned around. "Aren't you going to sit up here with me?"

His face was hidden in shadows as she quickly shook her head.

He turned forward and put the car in reverse. "I'm sorry I'm late. I'm used to working late when you all go out of town. I forgot you didn't go to Toronto with your mother." He paused. "I ate at the office. Did you want me to stop at McDonald's and grab you something?"

Skye turned her head and looked out the window. "Sure."

He turned left at the intersection. "You smell like smoke."

Her heart leapt into her throat. He knew she'd been smoking pot! That's it. She's grounded for sure.

He pulled into the drive-thru at the side of the restaurant and ordered a burger meal. "They really shouldn't let people smoke around children. That stuff is nasty. You'll have to wash your clothes when you get home or it'll just stink up the whole house."

Skye sat quietly in the backseat with his words rolling around in her head.

He forgot she wasn't with her mother.

He forgot about her.

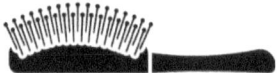

Eva's cheeks hurt from smiling. Dinner went better than she imagined, and even Dom was behaving graciously. He stopped glaring at Brad when they entered the dining room, something she was sure her parents made him do. Her parents were interested in his life, and his family and asked so many questions Eva started to feel a little embarrassed. Brad said he didn't mind and told her he was expecting this. It happened when he met Tina's family for the first time too.

"I'm sorry," he said as they sat on the front porch. "I didn't mean to bring up her name."

The night air was really cold, and Eva shivered standing next to him. "It's okay. I can't pretend she doesn't exist, even though I want to."

"I think she's learned her lesson. From what I've heard, Carla really laid into her."

"Yeah, Skye said Carla will do what she needs to, to protect her spot."

"To be honest, she's earned it."

Eva was dumbstruck. "Are you taking her side?"

"No, I'm just saying, Carla worked hard to become captain and she might be a nightmare at school, but she's really good at leading the team."

She shook her head. "She's still nasty."

He pulled her close to him. "She's only going to be around for a few more months, then she graduates, and we never have to deal with her again."

Eva smiled. That was something to look forward to.

He took her hand. "I had a really nice time."

"So did I, and now that you've met my parents, you can come over anytime."

"I'd like that, but it probably won't be until after exams. I really have to ace them."

"But university isn't for another five years."

"Yeah, but they'll look at my grades all through high school and my grade point average for each year."

"That's not fair. They should just take you because you're smart."

"And there are a lot of other smart people out there too."

Eva slumped. "I guess."

"Don't be mad. I really want to do this." He gave her a kiss on the cheek. "You understand that, right?"

"I do, but if you're studying all the time and I am too, we're never going to see each other."

"We have school. We can spend time together there."

It wasn't what she wanted to hear, but it was better than nothing.

"I guess."

"After exams, the weather will start getting nicer and we can do more things together."

"Until finals."

"Yeah, but then we'll have the whole summer to ourselves."

She perked up. "I'd like that."

A car pulled up alongside the curb and honked. Brad and Eva stood.

"That's my ride."

He leaned in and gave her a long kiss. The softness of his lips as well as the warmth sent a spark of excitement through her. With a second honk, the two separated and Brad hurried down the steps and along the front walk. She waved to him as the car pulled away and stood for a few moments longer, remembering his soft kiss. She smiled again and turned to the house. Her cheeks were sore, but she didn't care.

She walked toward the staircase, still feeling his kiss on her lips, the way he smelled, his smile, his words. He was right. University was important and she'd do whatever she could to help him.

"*Dochka?*" her father's voice was soft as he called out from the parlour. "I believe everything went smoothly tonight?"

She turned from the stairs and walked to the parlour entrance. A small fire burned in the hearth as her father sat in high back chairs, reading as her mother sat on the sofa and knitted.

"Everything went perfectly."

"Good. He is a very nice young man. Very good manners."

Her mother chuckled. "You're just saying that because he greeted you in Russian."

Egori turned to her with a wicked smile. "To take the time to learn shows his respect." He turned back to his daughter. "His parents brought him up well."

Eva beamed with pride. "I'm going to bed."

"Pleasant dreams," her mother said.

Eva turned and ran up the stairs. She was so happy she doubted if she could or would sleep, but if she did, then she'd dream about Brad.

The Daniels house was dark, with only the light from the back hall near the stairs illuminating the kitchen. Skye sat at the kitchen table with the remains of her burger meal spread out in front of her. She ate it too fast and now she felt sick. She stared at the wrapper the burger came in, her mind slowly clearing up from the fog that smoking that joint gave her. It wasn't a bad feeling, just different, and nowhere near the wonderfulness that Keith made it out to be.

The dryer buzzed the end of its cycle from the little enclosed laundry space in the wall. Her father made her wash them the minute they got home. Said he didn't want it stinking up the house and then rambled some more about how they shouldn't let people smoke around children.

She glanced up at the Kit Cat clock on the wall next to the door frame. The bulging eyes and tail darted back and forth in rhythm with the second hand and from the table she could just make out the time. Ten minutes to nine. She itched to call Eva and tell her how miserable her night was, but Brad was probably still there, and she didn't want to interrupt.

She got up and went to the dryer. She felt like a third wheel now that Eva was going out with Brad. He was her friend too, but there was something different about their group now. Like they were part of a secret club she wasn't allowed in. She was happy for them, but part of her wished that it would go back to the way it used to be.

She pulled out her clothes and tossed them on top of the machine. The house felt different too. This was the first time she didn't go with her mother to Toronto to see her grandparents and now she wished she had. Being here with no one to talk to just made her feel miserable.

Heavy footsteps pounded on the stairs and her father appeared a few moments later. He was out of his work uniform and wearing a pair of plaid pyjamas the twins got him last year for Christmas. He looked tired as he strolled through the kitchen toward the fridge, like he just got up from a short nap.

"How was your burger?"

She leaned against the dryer. "Good."

The light from inside the fridge lit up the far end of the kitchen. "Don't tell your mother I forgot to pick you up, all right?" He grabbed a beer from the fridge door. "You know how she goes on about stuff like that."

Skye nodded. "I won't say anything."

He let the door close by itself. "Good." He opened a drawer next to the fridge and brought out a bottle opener. "Did you take a shower like I told you to?"

"No, not yet. You said to wash my clothes first."

The beer fizzed as he bent off the cap with the opener. "Oh yeah. Well, your laundry's done now so go take one."

She scooped up her warm clothing and headed for the stairs.

"Hey, come back here and clean up your mess."

Skye turned and walked back. Her father was pointing at the wrappers on the table.

"Don't just leave them there."

She dropped her clothes on the table and grabbed the fast-food wrappers.

He took a large sip from the bottle. "Your mother's always cleaning up after you kids. You need to just start doing it yourself. Show a little responsibility."

She kept silent as she stuffed the wrappers into the garbage. She didn't like talking to him when he drank, because she knew there'd be more than one beer and he'd yell at her if she tried to talk to him. About anything.

Skye quickly grabbed her clothing and ran up the stairs. She hurried down the dark hall to her room and flipped the light switch with her elbow. Her room was cold, and she shivered when she dropped the clothing onto her bed. She went back out into the hall and down in front of two large bi-fold doors. As she opened one, she heard the television from downstairs and the familiar opening music to The Dukes of Hazzard. It was her father's favourite show. Her's too and she hurried down the stairs and peeked around the corner into the living room.

Lennon sat in the dark with just the light from the television. He glanced at her out of the corner of his eye. "Thought I told you to clean up?"

"Yeah, but I like this show, and my rooms cold so I got the door open to warm up a bit."

He was quiet for a moment and then he put his beer on the table next to his recliner and moved to sit up. "Go take a shower. I'll start a fire, make some popcorn and you can warm up here and watch the show."

Skye smiled. "Cool."

She hurried back upstairs and grabbed a towel from the closet. Maybe this night wouldn't be so bad after all.

By the end of November, things were back to normal, and everyone had forgotten about what happened in the cafeteria, but the school gossip hadn't forgotten about the trophy case. Neither had Eva and Skye. Eva stared at it when she passed through the main foyer to get to her locker and it brought back all the bad memories of the Halloween dance, and she had to remind herself that the night wasn't all bad. After all, it was the night Brad asked her out.

Skye dropped her brown-bag lunch on the table across from Eva in the cafeteria, before flopping down in a chair. Eva noted the concerned look on her friend's face and lowered her fork.

"What happened?"

Skye's shoulders slumped. "My geography teacher handed out a worksheet for exams." She opened her lunch and pulled out a sandwich. "It's everything we've done since September. How am I supposed to study all that, and everything else from my other classes?"

A pang of fear raced through Eva. "Everything?'

"Everything." Skye bit into her food. "Math and science are gonna be killers too, and I have a project for my art class due before the holidays."

Curious, Eva tilted her head to one side. "What holidays?"

Skye motioned to the entrance to the kitchen, where two students were putting up a string of Christmas decorations.

"We have the last two weeks of the month off for the Christmas break. I guess I can use that time to study, but we're going away for the first week to Toronto to see my grandparents and stuff." She paused as she chewed her food. "There's gonna be too much going on. How am I supposed to study?"

"You're going away?"

"Yeah, we do every year." Skye frowned. "Why?"

"We have our Winter Solstice celebration on the 20th. I was going to ask if you could come."

Skye smiled weakly. "Yeah, thanks, but we're leaving for Toronto on the 18th. Mom has a lot of family, and we have to stop and see *everyone*." She dropped her food on the paper bag. "I don't even know most of them."

Eva stared at the decorations. None of her teachers had mentioned anything about exams, but then, a few of Skye's classes were a level above hers, so it made sense they'd want her to start early.

Skye looked around before she leaned forward. "I know you're not supposed to do any spells, but is there a way we could use magic to, like, help study?"

Eva shook her head. "I don't know. All the magic I know isn't that strong, and I only learn new spells with an apprenticeship." She turned to her friend. "We learn what we need to. That's it."

Skye slumped in her chair. "Can you ask your parents?"

Eva shot her a sarcastic look.

"Yeah, I know. Just thought I'd ask."

Brad appeared next to Eva and quickly sat down. Eva gave him a small kiss on the cheek, but Brad was only focused on Skye.

"Keith said you were hanging out with DevDude last week?"

Skye shrugged as she pulled out the rest of her lunch. "Yeah, so what?"

"Skye, the guy's bad news. You know that."

Skye rolled her eyes. "I know, but it's not like I hang with him all the time now." She glared at him. "Besides, Keith hangs with him."

"Yeah, and I tell him the same thing all the time, too."

She bit into her sandwich. "Why are you making such a big deal?"

"Because I know you like him."

Skye shot Eva a glare, who just shrugged and looked away.

"What? We were talking and it kinda popped out."

Brad relaxed. "You're my friend, Skye. I just don't want to see you get hurt, is all."

"I won't, besides, he doesn't even know I exist."

"And he has a girlfriend."

Skye looked sorrowfully at him before looking away. "Okay, fine. I get it."

A boisterous group of older teens stormed the cafeteria with Carla in the lead. While she was glad her brother and her weren't going out anymore, she couldn't see what Dom saw in her to begin with.

Carla sauntered her way over to their table. "Well, if it isn't the nerd squad." She tilted her head to one side. "I hear you still haven't paid the school for the new trophy case." She turned to her cousin. "My mom said your parents are too poor and can't pay for it, so they're making you do it."

"Fuck off, Carla."

She feigned an innocent look. "What? That's what I heard."

She gave a smug grin as she walked away. Yeah, Eva couldn't see any reason why he'd date her.

Brad gave Eva a quick kiss. "Sorry, I still have a class before lunch." He hurried off into the crowd of exiting students.

Skye exhaled. "She's right. My parents can't afford to pay for it." She glanced at Eva. "Are yours?"

Eva shrugged. "They don't want to because we know who really did it, but we can't prove it without involving magic."

"Then we gotta figure something out."

"We could get jobs?"

"We're fourteen. Who's going to hire us?"

Eva thought for a moment. "Maybe we could make something and sell it?"

"Like what?"

"Your paintings?"

"Eva, I've got enough to do without adding that to it. Can you make something we can sell?"

She sighed. "No." She smiled weakly at her friend. "Don't worry. We'll think of something."

Chapter Nine

December roared in with a snowstorm that shut the school down for a couple of days, but when it was over, the world was transformed into a winter paradise of white and cold. The days were shorter now and by the time Eva got home from school, the final rays of twilight were on the horizon. She liked the snow and cold weather. It meant that she could have a fire in her bedroom hearth and read by its light before she went to bed. She used to do that at their old home in Wynden. There was nothing like snuggling under the blanket with a good book and reading by firelight.

Shelly drove her home after school most days, as she was now Brad's girlfriend. It was nice to get home early and not to take the bus, especially now that it was so cold out. Every Friday they stopped at the coffee shop first and grabbed some drinks and donuts. The last Friday before Christmas break was Brad's turn to pay, and Keith went inside with him.

It felt awkward being alone with Shelly, considering what happened. Eva kept her gaze out the back window. She didn't even know why Shelly would drive her home if she hated her so much. She should have gone inside with the guys.

After what felt like an eternity, they returned with hot chocolates for them, a coffee for Shelly, and a bag of donuts for the ride home. Keith turned on the radio as he handed out the food. After a holiday ad, a familiar song came on and Eva quietly sang along.

Brad frowned. "I didn't think you liked this kind of music?"

"Dom plays this record a lot. I know all the words whether I want to or not."

Keith nodded. "They're a cool band."

She nodded. "Yeah, he got into them after him and Alisha split up." She took a sip of her drink. "She really hurt him too, and when he didn't get the job with her dad, he totally spiralled."

"Shit," Keith said, "I would too." He looked into the bag. "Be doubting I'd go out with anyone after that."

Eva's gaze fell on the rear-view mirror and Shelly looking back at her but there wasn't anger or hate in her eyes. More of a sadness.

"What's he doing now?" Brad asked.

"Mom got him a job doing some errands for where she works."

He scrunched up his face. "At the funeral home?"

"Yeah, it's not much, but it keeps him busy."

"Hey, maybe you could get a job there too? Start paying back your parents for the trophy case?"

Again, her gaze shifted to the rear-view mirror and Shelly's sorrowful look.

Eva shook her head. "I'm too young, and there's not really that much for him to do."

She turned to Brad. "Speaking of things to do, maybe we can get together after the holidays and do some studying?"

He glanced down at his drink for a moment. "I can't. Christmas break is the only time we visit my grandparents."

Keith nodded. "Yeah, we gotta go visit our them up north, but at least we don't have to ride with our parents this year." He motioned to Shelly. "Dad's letting her drive up, so Brad and I are going with her."

Eva was crestfallen. "When do you leave?"

"Not until the twenty-third and we're coming back until after the New Year." He looked at her strangely. "I thought you were going away too?"

"Yeah but—" She stopped before she said anything about the portal to Wynden. "It's not gonna be for very long."

Keith nodded. "Yeah, my dad hates to travel too."

She sat closer to Brad as they drove into the city. Shelly had to stop at a few places, so it was late when they finally drove along the waterfront toward the Eva's home.

Her red car slowly drove along the main street in Eva's neighbourhood. Almost all the homes were lit with strings of bright lights of red, blue, green, yellow and white around the roof edges of the houses. Large pine trees stood in front windows, covered in more lights, ornaments and silver tinsel with displays of reindeer, Santa, snowmen and candy-canes all lit up bright.

"Jesus," Keith said as they passed one house that had a multitude of lights on display, his eyes wide with awe.

Brad beamed. "I love this neighbourhood."

Eva smiled proudly and gave his hand a squeeze. "It's so pretty."

Shelly shook her head as they passed another heavily lit house. "Leave it to the rich to gaudy things up."

Keith turned to her. "You don't like it?"

"I guess, but some of these places are going way over the top."

He turned to Eva in the back seat. "Did you guys put up lights?"

"No."

Shelly chuckled as they pulled up beside Eva's house. "Oh really?"

Eva got out of the car, mouth open, followed by Brad, and slowly walked toward her home. Outside, on the snow-covered front lawn, her brother stood and watched as her father, on a ladder, placed a string of Christmas lights along the edge of the porch roof. Dom stood a few feet from the bottom of the ladder, a flashlight in one hand; the beam pointed at where his father was working, and a second string of lights in the other. There were no lights on, except for the ones they were putting up, and every now and then, a small section of the lights would detach from the roof. This was followed by muffled Russian that Eva was sure were swear words.

Eva walked up to her brother. "What are you doing?"

He turned to her and chuckled sarcastically. "What d'you think we're doing?"

Egori noticed her and climbed down the ladder. "I had hoped to have these up before you returned." He turned to Brad. "Good evening, Brad."

The young man gave a curt nod. "Hello, Mr. Shade."

"Here." Dom handed Eva the string of lights as he headed to Shelly's car. "You deal with it."

Another small section dropped from the roof. Egori muttered something in Russian and moved the ladder to re-hook the two small sections of lights.

Brad walked up to the ladder. "Do you need some help, Mr. Shade?"

Egori reattached the section and looked down and nodded. Brad took the lights from Eva and waited by the ladder for instructions.

She grinned uncontrollably as her boyfriend helped her father put up decorations. What more could she ask for?

She turned to the road. Dom was joking around with Shelly on the driver's side. She hadn't seen him in a good mood in a while. Joking? Never.

Brad handed up the end of the string of lights and stepped away from the ladder. He reached into the front pocket of his coat and pulled out a small box. "I wanted to give you this today, but it was just too hectic." He handed her a small, gift-wrapped box.

Eva's eyes went wide. "You bought me something?"

He shrugged. "It's not much, but I thought you could use it."

She quickly tore the colourful paper off and opened the box. Inside was a small, red, heart-shaped key chain with the words KISS ME, I'M YOURS etched in calligraphy to the plastic.

"I thought you could use this for your house key."

She reached inside her pocket and brought out the metal key. He helped her put it on the keyring, and she gave him a kiss when it was secure.

"I love it. Thank you!"

He shrugged. "It's just something I thought you could use."

"Come on, Brad," Keith yelled from his seat. "I wanna go home!"

Dom came around the car and stood next to the curb as Brad returned to the car with Eva.

"I think there's something wrong with your roof," he said, as they walked. "The lights don't stay up." He looked back at the house. "They keep dropping off." He gave her a kiss and got into the back seat.

"Call me later," Eva said, and stopped next to Dom.

As the car pulled away, Eva turned back to the house. "What's with the lights?"

"Take a guess," Dom said.

"The gargoyles?"

"Yeah. Mom thinks they see it as an intrusion into their territory."

"They're just Christmas lights."

He shrugged. "They don't know that. Dad seems to think he can convince them to leave them alone, but it hasn't worked yet."

Eva shook her head and headed toward the house. She glanced up at her father and his struggle with the lights and giggled as a gnarled claw reached from the shadows and plucked off a portion of lights.

Egori swore in Russian and called for his son.

Eva hid her laughter and went inside. The front room was decorated with long pine branches dotted with sprigs of holly and ivy. Tall, coloured pillar candles lay in the centre of rings of laurel sprigs and a sweet and savoury aroma came from the kitchen. Eva dropped her Adidas bag near the stairs and walked into the kitchen.

Venera stood near the stove stirring a large black pot and smiled as her daughter sat at the kitchen table. "How was your last day?"

"Fine. We didn't really do anything."

"That must have been a nice relief."

"Yes, but they gave us study material to go over for the break."

Her mother put the wooden spoon down next to the stove. "Well, we'll have to make sure we don't spend your entire winter vacation in Wynden."

"I wish Skye could come with us."

"Maybe next year," Venera said, as she dropped some herbs into the pot. "She's been very good at keeping our secret, but she's still new to all of this and she's still quite young."

"She's the same age as me."

"And look how well did you kept your promise to not do magic."

Eva shrugged. "It wasn't all my fault."

"That's not the point. Go put your school things away. Dinner won't be ready for a while."

Eva nodded and slowly walked back out to the main hall and up the stairs with her Adidas bag in tow. Her room was dark with only the glow of embers in her bedroom hearth for light. The walls of her room were decorated with boughs of evergreen and red bows, and frost lined the windowpanes. She flopped down on her bed and stared at the ceiling, but some how, it didn't feel special.

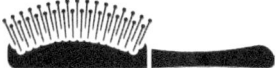

The day of the Winter Solstice, the Shade family gathered up some fancy clothing and crossed the portal threshold into the realm of Wynden. Eva was too excited and ran through the archway first with a large garment bag in her arms.

Their house here felt empty and cold, now that all their furniture and belongings were in Kingston. The parlor was empty except for a lone table with a red pillar candle burning inside a large round, glass dome.

Eva walked to the large window that overlooked the back yard. The gardens were overgrown with weeds and the remains of wildflowers, and a carpet of multicoloured leaves from the surrounding trees blanketed the ground. There was a light dusting of snow on the leaves, with small amounts gathered in the corners of the yard. Wynden didn't get much snow, not like Kingston, but what little did fall always made the town look magical.

A strong gust of air blew through the room as her parents and brother arrived through the portal. "Did you put your things away?" her mother called out from the hall.

Eva kept her gaze out the window. "Not yet."

Venera walked into the parlour. "Get it done now, before our guests arrive."

Eva raced up stairs and into the first room to her right. It was just as bare as the rest of the house, and a small fire burst alive in the cold stone hearth. She carefully hung a garment bag on a hook and untied the strings of the bag. A long, dark green dress and white cape with fur around the hem hung neatly inside. Eva's excitement grew as she quickly undressed. The chill in the room sent goosebumps racing across her body, but the dress and cape quickly warmed her back up. Music played from somewhere outside, and she left her clothes on the floor and went to the window. Her room overlooked the front yard, and through the bare branches, she saw a small group of musicians playing for a group of bystanders. Candles in the streetlamps flickered to life as the last rays of light ebbed on the horizon.

Everyone gathered in the living room around the lone piece of furniture. Both her father and brother wore suits of a dark colour with dark coloured capes and her mother wore a long dress of purple with gold embroidery along the hem.

The table was old, very old, crafted from branches tied together for the legs and small flat pieces of wood for the surface. A glass dome sat in the center of the table, and Eva walked up to it and peered inside. Small multi-coloured twinkling orbs of lights fluttered clockwise around a flame and their glow intensified with her presence.

Her mother walked up to the table. "Are we ready?"

"Quickly, *moya lyubov'*. Our guests will be here soon."

She carefully lifted the glass bulb from the candle and the orbs few out and hovered over the table. Egori took one in his hand and flung it against the far wall. It burst into shards of sparkles that dissipated quickly and revealed intricately carved wood table. Venera came behind him with several more orbs and tossed them toward the wall next to the table. A dozen chairs with brightly coloured cushions, burst from the sparkling shards and lined the far wall, while a few more burst over the table and formed into red, green, and white pillar candles.

Venera smiled at her husband. "You do the furniture. I'll do the decorations."

Egori gave her a stern look. "Not as many candles this year, please. We do not want another episode like last year."

Venera shot her husband a frustrated look, but then smiled and scooped up more orbs before walking off.

Another table appeared with a burst of sparkling radiance, and held silverware, porcelain plates depicting the front of the house during the holidays, along with gold goblets. Other orbs burst close to the doorway and windows, revealing heavy drapes with thick cord tiebacks, and decorations of branches of pine, bay and ivy twigs, intertwined with red bows and berries. A fire burst in the large hearth and crackled as the room quickly warmed.

Once the last of the orbs had extinguished, Venera turned to her children. "Dom, Eva. The food should be ready. I put the order in last week. Go and get it while we finish the house."

Eva nodded and hurried toward the front door. It swung open as she approached, and the sound of festive music and conversation echoed from the street. The air held a chill from the light snow that covered the ground, but at the same time, it was warm enough that it didn't feel uncomfortable.

Trees of pine, spruce, and fir dotted the front yard with their tips lightly coated in snow. Out past the stone wall, juniper and yew lined the pedestrian paths, with small red bows as decorations. Small evergreens of purple, silver, and gold were everywhere and decorated with ornaments made of natural materials. The wrought-iron lamp posts held bows of evergreen, holly and ivy, and a few sprigs of mistletoe. White candles burned atop the posts in coloured glass lanterns of green, red, blue, and yellow. Groups of people passed by many dressed in outfits of seasonal colour. Most didn't pay them any attention, but those who did nodded politely.

They crossed a bridge and listened to a trio of musicians play a lively tune. The promenade hosted small food stalls decorated with natural garlands of evergreen, holly and mistletoe. Eva eyed a couple of sugar-coated fruits on sticks and hot chocolate warming in a cauldron. A bonfire of light blue burned brightly in the centre of a large courtyard nearby. Several stalls surrounding the bonfire had people busy putting together and decorating small logs.

Eva watched the patrons in the yard. "Maybe I should burn a Yule log this year."

Dom frowned. "Why?"

"To make sure I pass my exams."

"Wouldn't that go against your contract with the council?"

"Technically, no."

He frowned. "Technically, you're doing magic."

"Yeah, but I'm doing it here."

"But it's to influence what you do over there."

She rolled her eyes. "But everyone burns Yule logs for something."

"Yeah, but how many of the other students at the high school are doing it?"

She paused, disappointed. "You really think it would be cheating?"

"I think it would be close to it." He tugged on her cloak. "Come on, we have to get back before the guests arrive."

She followed him down a cobblestone lane to the front of a restaurant. The double doors were wide open with people passing through and the smell of cooking meat wafting in the air. Inside, the savoury aroma of cooking meat filled the room as patrons waited patiently chatting with each other or the staff. Dom walked up to the hostess and nodded.

"We're here to pick up the order for Shade."

She nodded and walked off.

Eva watched the customers in the dining area. "I'd love to bring Skye here next year."

"The council isn't going to give you permission."

"You don't know that."

"Ask Mr. Allard then. See what he says."

The young woman came back a few moments later with a wooden serving tray in her hands. The lid had their family name burned into the surface, and she handed it to him.

Eva watched the bonfire again as they passed by. Everyone burned a Yule log over the Solstice celebration. It was tradition, but the idea of her burning one for her exams did sound like cheating the more she thought about it.

When they arrived back at the house, the door was still open, and their father anxiously stood in the doorway motioning them to hurry.

Egori took the serving tray from Dom. "What took you so long?"

"Eva had to stop and watch the Yule bonfires," he said, as he took his cloak off and hung it on a hook. "She wants to burn one."

He nodded and hurried into the parlour. "That is good. Wish for a fresh start."

Eva hung her cloak next to her brother's. The house was warm now, and the smell of cooked food and spices filled the air. An old woman sat on one of the more comfortable chairs near the hearth, and Eva's eyes went wide with joy.

"Granny!" She hurried to the old woman and gave her a hug. "I'm so happy you could make it this year."

"*Ye didne hink eh'd miss thes day, did ye?*"

Eva paused for a moment. It had been a long while since she last spoke to her grandmother, and she forgot just how thick her Scottish accent was and had to mentally translate what the woman said.

"You were busy last year," Eva said. "I hoped you wouldn't be busy again this year."

Esadora Shade was a small woman and as thin as a pencil. Her salt and pepper hair was more salt than pepper and there were as many wrinkles on her face as there were in her dress, but it was her eyes that everyone noticed. Even Eva. They were a bright blue and full of life and smiled when she looked at the teen.

Venera came and stood next to her mother. "Granny will always be an active member of her council." She placed her hands on the old woman's shoulders. "But one of these days she's going to have to retire."

Esadora pouted. "Nae if ah can help it."

"But you should." Her daughter said. "There are others who are just as competent as you. They need to have their chance."

"Mah years ay knowledge weel ootweighs their need. I'll dae thes job until they pit me in th' grin."

Venera shook her head. "No. We're not having this argument. Not today." She walked away before her mother could reply.

The old woman patted the seat next to her. "Come sit an' teel me abit thes skale ye gang tae."

Eva sat and was about to tell her everything, when a loud shout came from the front of the house, followed by a lot of loud Russian. The Allards entered the home with as much boisterous energy as possible and brought a small band of musicians with them. Immediately, Delano and Dom met up and started a conversation that took them to another part of the house.

Luca Allard was a tall man who resembled an older version of his son. His clothing was of much finer material than her father's, and he held an air of distinction in his posture. He and her father had been friends for a long as Eva could remember, and Eva truly believed, it was because of him that her family prospered.

Luca and Egori embraced with pats on the back before they entered the parlour. Their guest made his way to a table with drinks and took one of the goblets.

"Well, Lady Esadora. It's nice to see you again."

The old woman gave a curt nod. "Ye an aw."

He focused on Eva. "And I hear things are going well for you at your new school."

Eva was silent. He didn't know about the trophy case or the restrictions she had on spell casting. Should she tell him?

"Eva has been doing well," Egori said, picking up a goblet. "It's been a challenge for her, but I feel she is doing her best."

Luca smiled and nodded. "Good to hear. I look forward to hearing more about your experiences." He turned to her father. "If things bode well, it might be a good start to exploring more options outside our realm." He focused on her. "There was a lot of negative chatter on the council about your request. I'm glad to see things are working out in your favour."

Eva gave a weak smile and glanced at her father. He stood tall and proud next to his friend. She had to do better.

Another loud commotion came from the front hall as Mr. Nithercott entered the home. His clothing was old fashioned and all the same colour of dark plum with some gold embroidery of rune symbols that morphed into Greek letters and then into Latin. She only knew that because she asked her mother several years ago why his solstice clothing did that, and it had something to do with his lineage.

Eva turned to her grandmother. "I'll be right back."

She hurried to Mr. Nithercott and waited for her turn to talk to him. He would know for sure if burning a Yule log was against the rules.

He looked at her proudly. "Blessed Yule, Evandra."

She nodded. "Blessed Yule." She stayed silent, unsure of how to word her question.

"What's on your mind?"

"Would I get into trouble if I burned a Yule log for my exams? They're really hard and I need all the help I can get." She turned back and looked at her father still chatting with Luca Allard. "I don't want to let my parents down."

The old man exhaled, staring past her as he thought. "I don't see why not. Providing that you're not using the spell to extract the answers, and that it's created here."

Excitement raced through Eva. "So, I wouldn't be going against my agreement?"

His lips pouted as he shook his head. "No, I think you will be well within the boundaries of your contract."

She let out a small squeal of excitement, thanked him and hurried out the front door. Maybe she could make one for Skye too. She would need some help with a few of her exams as well. Her mind raced as she hurried across the bridge and to the bonfire.

Skye sat on the far side of the flowered sofa and watched the Christmas cartoons on the small, black and white television screen. They'd been at her maternal grandparents' house for a little over a day, and already she wanted to go home. Her grandparents, Dorthy and Walt Wilson, still lived in the small wartime house her mother grew up in. There were two bedrooms and a bath upstairs, a small kitchen and dining area and an even smaller living room on the main floor. It was crammed with old, dusty furniture and the decorations were right out of the forties, including the silver Christmas Tree and the large lights with tin flower petals to amplify the light. A row of wax choir boys and other candles on the mantle barely had any colour, and whole place smelled funny. Worse yet, she had to sleep in a musty sleeping bag on the living room floor with her brothers. This had to be the worst Christmas ever.

The doorbell rang and a moment later, her aunt and uncle burst through the front door. There was a lot of welcoming commotion in the small entranceway that quickly moved to the hall, but Skye kept her focus on the television screen. When a long shadow fell over her, she knew exactly who it belonged to.

"Aren't you going to wish us a merry Christmas?" Carla's condescending tone cut into her like a knife.

Skye's anger rose as she slowly looked up at her cousin. "Don't talk to me."

Carla wore an expensive outfit under her long winter coat, and she played with a gold necklace between her fingers. "Not very festive, are you?"

Skye focused back on the television. "Leave me alone."

The older teen snorted. "Whatever."

She walked off and was fawned over by their grandparents.

"Gawd," Stoney said next to her, as he stuffed a small chocolate Santa into his mouth. "She's such a douchebag."

Skye snorted a laugh and sank deeper into her spot. There was one good thing about her grandparents' place. There wasn't enough room to have Carla and her aunt and uncle stay the night, so all she had to do was get through a few hours tonight and tomorrow and she'd be good.

The phone rang several times from the front hall. With all the loud commotion going on, it was several more rings before someone answered it.

Her grandfather walked peered around the corner from the hall. "Skye? Someone named Eva is calling for you."

"Oh, that's right," Melanie said. "I said it was okay if Skye gave this number to her friend."

Her grandfather held his hand over the receiver and motioned to the stairs. "You can talk to her up in the spare room. A lot quieter up there."

"Thanks, Grandpa."

Skye leapt off the couch and ran up the stairs to the bedroom on the right. She flicked on the light. Two single beds sat on opposite sides of the room with an end table between them. The walls were decorated with award certificates and other memorabilia from when her mother and aunt were in school, and the phone sat on the end table right in the middle.

Skye picked up the extension. "Oh, my, gawd I'm so glad you called. This place is totally heinous."

"You're not having fun with your family?" Eva asked on the other end.

Skye frowned. "Who has fun with their family during the holidays? I totally want to be back home right now." She sat down on one of the beds and leaned back on the headboard. "How's your vacation going?"

"Not bad. We came back this afternoon." There was a long pause on the other end. "I really miss my old house."

"But you can go back and see it anytime, right?"

"Yeah, but all our stuff is here. It just doesn't feel the same."

"I guess. So how was your celebration?"

"Great. We had so many people show up at our home. Mom had to order more food."

"Wow. Sounds like an awesome party."

"It was. There were a lot of people there I didn't know, but I think that's because of Dad's new position. When Mom started at the crypt, we had all her coworkers show up for the Solstice that winter." She paused. "How was your holiday?"

"Doesn't really start until tomorrow."

"Oh, but it must be nice to see your grandparents again?"

"Yeah, but—"

"But?"

Skye inhaled slowly. "Dad got on my case about grades right in front of them and the whole trophy thing."

"Again?"

"Yeah." Skye blinked back a few tears and swallowed a few times to keep her lip from trembling. "Eva, he's so disappointed in me, and now my grandparents are too. I just gotta get my grades up. I gotta show them I'm not a flake."

"We can do that."

"Its going to take a lot of studying. I've got so many classes."

"I think a little magic might help."

Skye sat up. She couldn't have heard that right. "Magic? You're not going to cast a spell to cheat on your exams?"

"No, nothing like that, but I can do a spell to help us study."

Giddiness swept through Skye. "What kind of spell?"

"Wish magic using Yule logs."

Skye frowned. "What's a Yule log?"

"It's a piece of wood that is adorned with items that represent what you want to wish for in your life."

"So, we decorate this log and burn it?"

"In a special fire. We've got one burning now in the house in Wynden, so we can do it in privacy."

She frowned. "We won't be back until the twenty-seventh."

"The Solstice celebration goes on until the end of the first week of January. I'll get all the stuff we need, and we can put it together in Wynden."

"But that's in your realm? How am I gonna get there?"

Eva was quiet for a moment. "I'll think of something."

"Are you sure? I don't want you getting into trouble again."

Eva exhaled. "Maybe I should double-check."

"Yeah, and if it's cool, we can get together."

"And I won't be breaking any more of my contract because I'll be doing the spells in our realm."

Skye's grandmother called to her from the bottom of the stairs.

"I have to go," she said.

"Okay, call me when you get back to town."

Skye hung up and headed back downstairs. If Eva was right about this and she did well on her exams, it might be enough to keep her father off her case about everything else. By the time she reached the bottom of the stairs, she was in a more festive mood.

Chapter Ten

Eva sat at the breakfast table, arms folded in front of her. The steam from her bowl of oatmeal smelled of brown sugar, but she ignored it and stared at her brother. Skye was back from her holidays, and she still hadn't been able to figure out a way to get her best friend into Wynden. Not to mention getting herself there. Her father said the portal was still too unstable and the extra incantation to stabilize it was way beyond her magical knowledge, but it wasn't a problem for her brother.

Dom kept his gaze low as he slurped his food. "You can stare at me all you want. I'm not doing it."

"It's just one time."

"Mom 'n Dad will disown me if I take you both over."

"We don't have to tell them."

He stared into her eyes. "What are you planning?"

She turned from his gaze. "Nothing."

"No, you're planning something."

She exhaled loudly. "I want to burn a Yule log with Skye so she can pass her exams."

He frowned. "Why?"

"Because her parents are all over her about grades, especially since the whole trophy case thing." Her eyes narrowed. "Which was partly your fault."

"How?"

"You dumped Carla, and she got even for that by destroying the case and we got the blame."

He went to open his mouth, but she cut him off.

"You never should have gone out with her right after Alisha. Keith said it was a rebound, and I think she might not have done it if you didn't dump her."

He pursed his lips. "Fine. I'll open it for you, but Skye still can't come through. She'll need a travel cloak, and we don't have any spares."

Eva slumped in her chair. "I told her she could come."

"Can't you put them together and burn it yourself."

She rolled her eyes. "I can't manifest *her* wish spell."

He shrugged and picked up his bowl. "Then you're out of luck."

He put everything in the sink and walked out of the kitchen without saying another word, leaving Eva to sit and fume at the table. The Yule Log was only going to work if Skye created it herself, otherwise, what was the point?

She dipped her spoon in to her oatmeal. This was the perfect solution for both of them. They'd pass their exams and that would ease both sets of parents, but they still had to come up with a plan to pay back the school for the trophy case. She had to convince him to bring Skye too. There was no other way.

She got up from the table and hurried out of the kitchen and to the parlour. "You know, Carla's giving Skye a hard time too about all of this."

"Knock it off, Evie."

"Carla destroyed the trophy case, and then made it look like we did it." Dom went to reply but she cut him off. "Because *you* dumped her."

"Eva—"

"She threatened me at the dance, Dom. Said I had to make you go out with her again or else. She framed us just to make good on her threat!"

It was clear from the look on his face that he didn't realize just how badly Carla had made Eva's life miserable.

He looked down at the book. "I can't handle her anymore. She's an ugly person with an ugly soul."

"Did you tell her that when you ended it?"

"No. I just told her I didn't want to see her anymore."

She stormed toward him and swatted the book from his hands. "I told you what she was like, and you still went out with her. Why? Because she was paying you some attention? Did you know she torments Skye? Or the names she calls me, or the looks?" She blinked back her tears. "She makes school a living nightmare and because of her, me and my best friend were suspended." She sniffed and wiped her eyes. "All because you dumped her, and you didn't even have the *balls* to tell her why!" She stormed out of the room and back into the kitchen, trying to keep her tears and her temper from getting the better part of her.

She picked up her spoon and dug into her breakfast, but she was still too upset and after a couple of mouthfuls, she stopped eating.

Dom came up and stood in the entranceway to the kitchen. The book he was reading was tucked under his arm.

"I'm sorry all that unpleasantness fell on you."

Eva kept silent and didn't look at him.

"And I'm sorry you and your friend got caught in the middle." He walked to the table and sat down. "I don't know why I went out with her. She was nice, and maybe you're right? After what happened with Alisha and the way she ended our relationship, it was nice to be around a girl who wanted to be with me." He shook his head. "I thought I could handle it, but after a while I began to see the real Carla, and honestly she's a nasty piece of work." He sat back in his chair and stared at the table. "She treats people like dirt, even her best friend."

Eva looked his way. "We have to pay back the school. They might expel us if we don't, and the council will revoke my privilege if that happens."

Dom nodded and placed the book on the table. "I know, and I think I've found a way to help."

Eva's gaze fell on the book. It was an old family spell book. One of the ones her father kept locked up.

"You found it in there?"

He nodded and opened the thick leather cover. "You can do an Infusion Spell. It's easier to put together, and it's a lot stronger." He flipped through the pages. "The results from a Wish Magic spell can be pretty vague, but Infusion spells are more potent, so you'll have to be precise on what you want."

Eva pulled the book closer. "Precise how?"

"An Infusion Spell is more intent driven, so you don't have to keep manifesting your intent like you do with Wish Magic. You just manifest once, while you're creating it."

He reached across and flipped through the pages until he came to a certain page and pointed to a spell. Eva excitedly read it over.

"You need a few more ingredients than a Wish Spell, but you can buy those along the promenade."

She read from the book. "Depending on the abilities and intent, the Spellcaster can achieve anywhere from mild fulfillment to complete success." She paused. "Impact is weak with little to no permanent consequences." Her mood lightened. "That's not too bad."

"You just have to figure out a method of delivery."

She frowned. "What would be the easiest way?"

"I don't know, maybe something small, but what ever it is, Mom 'n Dad can't find out about it."

Eva rested her chin on her hands. What could she infuse that was small enough that she could hide it from her parents?

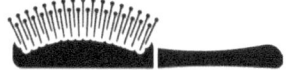

Skye stared, dumbstruck, at the light blue Dodge Omni that sat in the driveway at her grandparents' house. Outside, Carla squealed and jumped up and down before hugging her grandfather.

Skye scoffed. "Are you fucking kidding me?"

Her younger brother Ash stood next to her, nibbling on a large chocolate Santa. "She's the favourite. What'd you expect?"

"But a car?"

Grandma Dorthy came up behind them. "We didn't need it anymore since your grandfather purchased the new Oldsmobile. This way, she has some independence and won't need to rely on her parents or friends to drive her around." She nudged Skye. "Maybe, if you ask nice, she'll drive you to school. Wouldn't that be something?"

"I'd rather die than be in the same car as her."

"Come now," her grandmother put her arm around her. "She can't be all that bad."

"You have no idea."

She looked out the window. "Carla's under a lot of stress. She's going to university in the fall. That's a lot of pressure on a young lady."

Skye rolled her eyes. "Whatever."

She pulled her close. "Oh, I'm sure whatever it is that you two are fighting about, it'll blow over." She turned and walked toward the front door. "You'll see."

Several hours later, everyone was saying their goodbyes in front of the house. Skye lugged her suitcase and an over-flowing tote bag out to her family's station wagon and handed them to her father.

Lennon motioned to Carla's car. "Why don't you ride back to Kingston with your cousin?"

She frowned. "Why?"

"Because your aunt and uncle don't want her driving on the four-oh-one by herself."

"But she's, like, my worst enemy!"

He gave her a sarcastic look. "Knock it off with the melodramatics, Skye."

"But it's true!"

Her mother came and stood next to her. "Did your father ask you about going back with Carla?"

Skye's posture slumped. Usually, she could get her mother on her side when it came to her cousin, but from the sounds of it, this wasn't going to be one of those times.

"Do I have to?"

"You'd be doing your aunt and uncle a favour, sweetie." Her mother leaned close to her head and placed a gentle kiss along her hairline. "Do this for me, please?"

Skye could feel tears building in her eyes and she tried to keep her lip from trembling. "Fine."

Everyone said their final goodbyes and got into their respective cars. Skye slumped in the passenger seat of Carla's Christmas present and stared straight ahead. She didn't want to know anything about this car, because, as usual, it was Carla getting what she wanted.

Her cousin let out a tiny squeal as she got into the drivers' seat. It was a three-hour trip back to Kingston, and Skye wondered if she could keep calm the whole time.

"Just so you know," Carla's tone dripped with detest. "I don't need you to drive back, but Grampy didn't think it was right for a lady to drive the highway alone."

"Whatever."

She put the key in the ignition. "Unless you wanna ride back with your siblings screaming all the way."

Skye frowned. "They're not that bad."

The Daniels station wagon pulled out onto the street followed by Carla's parents' car. Carla squealed again, waved to her grandparents and followed behind her parents.

"Oh, spare me," she said, as they turned onto the main road. "They're brats. I don't know how you can stand to be around them."

"They're not always like that."

"Sure."

The four-oh-one was busy, and traffic was thick. Skye spent most of the time staring ahead while Carla sung along to her favourite songs on the radio, which was about every other tune.

"You know," she began, as a romantic song played. "This is Dom and mine's song."

Skye stayed quiet.

"I think we'll get back together in the new year."

"I'd be doubting it," Skye blurted out with a chuckle.

Carla huffed with confidence as she hastily merged into the left-hand lane. "He's mesmerized by me, you know. Shelly and I saw him in the mall a while back and he couldn't stop staring at me."

Skye straightened up in her seat and gripped the handle on the door when she made the lane change.

They sped past a car, pulled into the right-hand lane and accelerated.

"He's going to ask me back out. I know it."

"You don't know that for sure."

"Oh please." Her gaze shifted quickly between the road and Skye. "Who do you think he was staring at? Shells?"

Skye smirked. "Maybe?"

"Maybe?" Carla jerked the wheel, and the car veered quickly again into the passing lane. She kept her foot on the accelerator as they raced past a line of cars. "I'm the one he went out with. What could he see in her?"

Skye gripped the side of her seat and kept her other hand on the arm rest as Carla darted in between traffic.

"I saw him first." Carla continued. "He doesn't have any interest in her. I'd know it if he did."

Skye braced herself against her seat. "Okay, if you say so."

She eyed her cousin suspiciously "Did Eva say something?"

"No."

"She did, didn't she?"

The car pulled out in front of a transport.

"No, I swear!"

"Then why would you say that?"

"I didn't. I just said—"

"You know something!"

"No I don't!"

"She's my best friend. How could she do that to me?"

Skye's fear took over as the car raced down the highway. "What? Like how you went out with Donnie behind her back?"

Carla glared at Skye. "Who told you?"

"No one. Eva and I saw you two at the donut shop."

She swerved into the passing lane. "And Eva told Dom. That's why he dumped me."

"She didn't say anything to him."

Carla darted into the right lane. "Oh right, and I'm supposed to believe you?"

"It's true!"

Carla was silent as she drove. Skye's heart raced from her cousin's erratic driving, but as the car slowed to a normal speed, she relaxed a bit.

The right-turn blinker went on. "You hungry?"

"Not really."

"Whatever." She pulled off the highway and into a large rest stop. "I need something to eat." She glanced at Skye with a sickening sweet smile. "My treat."

Skye blinked a few times "Uh, sure. Just a bag of chips and a coke."

"What kind?"

"Dill pickle."

Carla grabbed her purse and opened the door. "Don't change the station. I'll be right back."

Skye sunk into her seat as her cousin walked away. They still had another hour and a half to go, and if this was the way Carla drove, she wondered if she'd make it home alive.

A few days later, Eva and Skye met up at the food court at the mall. Skye was so happy to see Eva, she gave her a hug. The whole ride back to Kingston was a nightmare, and she spilled over her words trying to tell her best friend what happened.

"I was terrified," Skye said, as they walked up to one of the food kiosks. "I totally thought we were gonna crash or something."

Eva nodded. "Shelly said she wasn't a good driver."

Skye frowned. "When were you talking to her?"

"One time when Brad and I got a ride home."

For a brief moment, Skye was upset. She got that Brad and Eva were a couple, but it seemed like her and Eva were drifting.

They paid for their food and found a table close by. She looked around at the patrons as she nibbled on a few French fries. The mall was crazy busy with shoppers. Almost as many now as there was before Christmas.

"So, I've been thinking," Eva said. "Dom says that the wish spell won't work very well and gave me the instructions for an Infusion Spell."

Skye nodded. "Cool. What's the difference?"

"Infusion spell is stronger, but it's more precise, so instead of wishing to pass our exams, our intent would be that we'd have to pass English or Math."

"Sounds easy enough, but you'll have to show me how to do it."

Eva made a sorrowful face. "That's going to be a problem. Dom can't take us both into Wynden."

"Why not?"

"We don't have extra travelling capes."

That sounded absurd to Skye. "Why do I need that?"

"The capes are the only thing that protect people when they go into the Void. You need one to pass through, otherwise you could end up in another place." She took a sip from her drink. "Or worse, another dimension and then you'd never get back."

"There are other dimensions?"

Eva nodded. "Oh yeah."

"Can you bring the stuff here?"

"No. I can't bring the Yule Fire through the portal."

"So how am I supposed to do this?"

"That's what we need to figure out. I can bring stuff over and make the Infusion Spell there and bring it back. It just has to be small enough that I can hide it from my parents."

"Like what?"

Eva shrugged. "Don't know. I thought we could brainstorm on it."

"How big does it have to be?"

"Not that big, and we have to be able to carry it with us."

Skye thought for a moment. "What about a painting?"

"How big?"

Skye held up her hands and made a circle with her thumb and index finger. "Like, that big?"

"So, we'd wear it?"

"Yeah."

Eva shook her head. "No. Besides, who carries around a picture with them?"

"What about a stone or pebble?"

"That's even stranger than a picture."

"I dunno. My mom has a necklace with a stone on it. She wears it all the time."

"Okay but let's keep thinking."

They sat in silence eating their food. There had to be something that they could use. Skye looked up and saw Keith across the food court and her heart skipped a beat when she saw Dev was with him. He was wearing a new jean jacket under his winter coat and a nice pair of pants. It made him look a lot older.

Eva turned in her seat. "Who are you looking at?"

She glanced down at her food. "No one." She paused. "You know, it'd be cool if we could do this for other people too."

"Like Brad and Keith?"

"Yeah. They've got exams too and Keith said he was having a hard time with his chemistry class."

Eva nodded. "Brad wants to go to university to become a lawyer and need really good grades all through high school."

"Maybe we can infuse a stone for them?"

"I doubt Brad would carry a stone."

"But if you made it, I bet he would."

She shook her head. "I doubt anyone but us would carry a stone." Eva's eyes went wide. "What about hair dye?"

"What about it?"

"What if we made infused hair dye?"

"Would that work?"

"It should. It's just powder, right?"

"Yeah, but how much would we need?" Skye slumped. "And we still haven't figured out a way to get me to Wynden, unless you want to make it?"

Eva shook her head. "I'll be too busy putting together the spell."

"Do you know anyone who has an extra cloak?"

"No one. Cloaks are made by family members. Any extras are contracted out by the Council."

"All of them?"

"There are a few that are used for special occasions, and I don't know anyone else who would have one that we could borrow." A look of realization washed across Eva's face. "Delano. Dom's friend. His sister is out of town for a while. Maybe we could use hers?"

Giddiness swept through Skye. "Only one way to find out, right?"

Eva raced through the house when the doorbell rang. Skye stood on the other side, and they both waved at the station wagon as Mr. Daniels drove off. Eva grabbed her and quickly pulled her inside.

"Did you bring the stuff?"

Skye let her backpack drop from her shoulder.

"Everything we need is right here."

"Good. Mom 'n Dad are at work. I told them you were coming over and we were going to study."

"So did you get the cloak?"

She led her into the parlor where Delano sat on the sofa reading one of the leather-bound books. He glanced up and gave the girls a polite nod.

Skye frowned. "Why's he here?"

Delano closed the book. "If you're going to use my younger sister's cloak then I need to accompany you."

Eva leaned close. "Little kids aren't supposed to cross the barrier on their own. Age restriction."

Skye nodded. "Makes sense."

Dom walked into the hall from the kitchen. "Also, it's his family's property."

Skye shook her head. "Whatever. As long as I can go, I don't care."

Delano turned to Eva. "She has to stay inside the lodgings. If she steps out into our world without the cloak on, she will be detected, and you'll have unpleasant company show up."

Eva nodded. "Understood."

"And you'll have to do whatever it is you're planning within thirty minutes of arrival."

Dom carefully placed the book back into the hidden bookcase in the wall. "Delano and I have some things to do, so make sure everything is cleaned up and you're ready to go by the time we get back."

They all walked to the stone archway. Delano removed a child-size silver cloak from his bag and draped it over Skye's shoulders.

Dom drew a sigil on the stone archway. "You have an idea of what to tell Mom 'n Dad if they find out?"

"I'll just tell them I made blue hair dye." She smiled at Skye. "I'm not lying."

The centre of the archway glowed and crackled like the embers of a dying fire and slowly swirled into a pinwheel pattern. It was a matter of seconds before the orange glow turned to black mist and bubbled outward.

Delano placed his arm across Skye's shoulders, as he pulled the hood of his cloak over his head. "Take my hand and don't let go. Just keep walking straight."

Eva turned to her. A look of apprehension was all over her friend's face. "You can close your eyes. I do."

Dom stood in front of the group and focused on his sister. "Remember. Thirty minutes. That's it."

Eva closed her eyes and stepped through the portal. When she opened them again, she stood in the hall in the stone house, and she quickly got out of the way so the others could come through. Dom was next and was followed a few moments later by Delano still holding on to Skye. Once they were through, the portal quickly returned to stone.

"We're here!"

Skye slowly opened her eyes and looked around. Her mouth dropped open as she examined the walls and the nearby room.

"This is totally awesome!"

Dom and Delano headed for the front room. "Thirty minutes."

Eva grabbed Skye by the hand and pulled her down the hall. "We can make it in my room."

Skye stumbled behind her, but Eva didn't let go. Inside the bedroom, a table with some mixing bowls, stood next to the fireplace. Three white logs glowed in the hearth as a blue fire with silver flames burned and crackled.

Skye stopped and stared at the fire. "That doesn't look real."

"Yule logs were created specifically for this season. They burn longer, are warmer, and give off a brighter light."

Skye held out her hands to the flames. "That is so cool." She turned her attention to the table and dropped her backpack. "This should do. I don't need a whole lotta room to make the stuff."

Eva picked up a black bag from the side of the hearth. She unzipped the sack and pulled out several cloth bags. "Yule logs are burned with items that are associated with a specific intent."

Skye nodded and brought out some of her hair dye items. "So, we want to get all the right answers on our exams."

"That's cheating, but we can do a spell that will help us remember better when we study."

Skye exhaled. "I didn't wanna study."

"You have to put some effort into it." Eva opened the one cloth bag. "We'll make one for wisdom. This has cornflower, sweet pea, amethyst and labradorlite powder." She glanced at Skye. "I thought if this worked, maybe we could sell the hair dye to the students."

Skye frowned. "Why?" Her eyes went wide. "We could make money off this and pay the school!"

"Exactly, but it has to work. I've never done this type of spell before, so we'll need to try it out first."

Skye opened her containers of ingredients and carefully measured some out. "How much of your stuff do we need?"

Eva poured the contents of her bags into a large bowl. "A tablespoon should be good enough."

Eva carefully blended the magical ingredients. Eva's mind raced. Everyone wants to do well on their exams. If this did work, they could easily pay back the school in no time.

"You know, Carla thinks her and your brother are going to get back together."

Eva chuckled as she lit a beeswax candle. "No, they won't."

"I hope not." Skye leaned against the table. "That's all she talked about coming home. How her and Dom were meant to be together."

A spark of anger flickered. "Trust me, that's not happening. He can't stand to be around her."

"What if it does?"

Eva didn't answer. She wanted to think that she was positive that her brother wouldn't be that desperate to back out with her worse enemy, but she couldn't say that for sure. He would take Alisha back if she dumped her new boyfriend, so there was a chance he'd go back out with Carla.

"I don't wanna talk about this anymore."

Eva worked until the ingredients were ground into powder and ready to be added the hair dye. Skye had a large metal bowl almost full of a light blue powder, and a small stack of little paper bags. She'd managed to keep most of it off her and wore garden gloves to keep the powder off her hands.

"Okay, I think I'm ready." She gave the powder a few more stirs with a wooden spoon. "I'll start writing out the instructions on the bags, if you wanna start, you know, like, doing what you're gonna do."

Eva brought up a small cauldron and placed it on the table. She added the magical ingredients and stood back so Skye could add hers. The cauldron was heavy, and it took both of them to place it on the hook over the flames.

"I think I've got the words right."

"Do we need to do, like, keep some kind of image in our heads?"

"No, not this time."

Skye went back to the table and picked up one of the paper bags. "Should they put it in with shampoo?"

"How do you do it?"

"With a cream rinse."

"As long as it stays on them for at *least* five minutes." She dipped her large spoon into the cauldron and began to stir. Sparkles twinkled evenly and looked like a dusting of diamonds.

"Okay, this is going to work." She stood back and picked up the spell-book before stepping on a bellows near the foot of the hearth. "I just have to keep chanting until—" She took a quick glance at the book. "—the effect is achieved."

"How are you going to know that?"

She shrugged. "I guess I'll know when I see it." She picked up a long ash branch and began to stir. "Knowledge found and knowledge gained. Wisdom learned and wisdom named. Knowledge found and wisdom gained. Wisdom here and Knowledge reigns."

The blue/silver fire grew and engulfed half the cauldron, but the heat remained the same. She repeated the incantation again and the flames intensified. After the seventh time, she stood back and watched.

Skye came up next to her. "Is it ready?"

"I don't know."

They watched in silence together. After a few moments, the fire began to recede, but they stood in place until it had returned to its original size.

"Oh my God," Skye said with a wide grin. "It so, totally worked."

They took the cauldron off the flames and carefully put it on the table. The powder was a deep Egyptian blue with small flecks that twinkled throughout.

"That is so beautiful," Skye said, "I so wanna dye my hair with this."

"I think we both should."

Skye's smile grew wider. "We have to test it right?"

"Right. We can't sell something to the public that doesn't work."

Skye carefully spooned the concoction into one of the bags. "This is so awesome!"

Eva's bedroom in Kingston was warm with the fireplace going. It was a last-minute decision for Skye to sleep over, this way they could test the hair dye. Skye loved the feel of her bedroom. It felt grand even though it wasn't as big as hers. She picked up a small hand mirror and looked at her reflection. Her blonde hair was down a deep blue with a sheen that reflected some of the light from the hearth.

"I wish I could have a fireplace in my bedroom," she said, staring at her reflection. "It makes it feel so cozy in here."

Eva came out from her bathroom with a towel over her head. "It's great for drying hair fast too." She pulled the towel away from her head and her wet hair fell around her shoulders. It was still black, but in the light, there was a blue hue, with a sheen that sparkled.

Skye's eye went wide. "How come your hair is sparkling?"

Eva held some strands up where she could see. "I don't know?"

Skye held up the mirror again. The dark blue dye evenly coated her hair, but no sparkle. "It doesn't look the same on my hair."

"Maybe because I have magic in my blood?"

"That whole magic begat magic, thing?"

"Maybe?"

Skye lowered the mirror. Eva's hair looked awesome with the sparkles, but it was a problem if it only did that with magical people.

"The kids at school won't have sparkly hair."

Eva sat on the floor next to her. "Maybe I shouldn't have used it."

Skye pursed her lips. "Let's see if it works first."

She grabbed one of Eva's textbooks and opened it to the back. "I'm not good at science, so I'll study that."

Eva nodded. "I'll do math."

Skye flipped through the pages to the very last chapter. "So, we just read all this?"

"Yeah, and then ask each other questions."

"That's easy enough. I think there's a test at the very back of this."

They sat in silence and read. Skye skimmed over the text, but she forced herself to go back and read what she missed. This text was stupid hard, with big words she could barely read let alone pronounce. She sighed. All her classes were level five. Just high enough to get her into college. No wonder Carla was stressed. Her classes must have been murder. She pushed the thought from her mind and kept reading. When her eyes drifted, she forced herself to focus. Maybe it was a good idea she wasn't going to college. There was no way she could study stuff like this. It was too hard.

"Okay," Eva's voice broke into her thoughts. "That should do it."

Skye closed the book and stared at the cover. She couldn't remember any of what she read.

"I don't think it worked."

Eva took the science book and flipped through to the back. "You can't say that yet."

Skye sat patiently and waited. All she could remember from the book was how she couldn't pronounce some of the large words.

Eva straightened up. "Mass and weight measure different quantities, but why is one scalar and one vector?"

Skye blinked a few times. "Because mass is a scalar quantity and weight is a vector quantity?"

"But why are they different?"

Skye thought. "When an object is moved from one location to another, its mass will remain the same, but its weight may change due to the force of gravity."

Eva smile was wide. "That's right!"

"Are you fucking serious!"

"It works!"

Skye was stunned. "It just came out. Like it was buried deep in my brain."

Eva handed the math book over. "Now, read me a question."

Skye flipped through the quiz until one stood out. "Okay, so Aaron drank 2 1/2 bottles of soda and Sam drank 3/4 of a bottle. How much more soda did Aaron drink than Sam?"

Eva groaned. "I hate these questions."

"That's why I chose it."

She inhaled and thought. Her lips moved slightly as she figured out the equation. "Aaron drank 1 3/4 bottles more soda than Sam."

"That's right!"

The girls squealed and Sem'ya shifted the wallpaper in the room from its normal dull pattern into a celebratory one.

Eva grabbed Skye's hands "Oh my gawd. It worked!"

"We can totally sell this to the kids at school."

Eva sat back. "Nobody's going to believe us."

"Sure, they will."

Eva nodded with confidence and headed back into the bathroom. Skye stared at the flames. What if no one bought their dye? Or worse, it didn't work. Just because it worked on them didn't mean it would work for everyone. She pushed the negative thoughts from her mind. This had to work. It just had to.

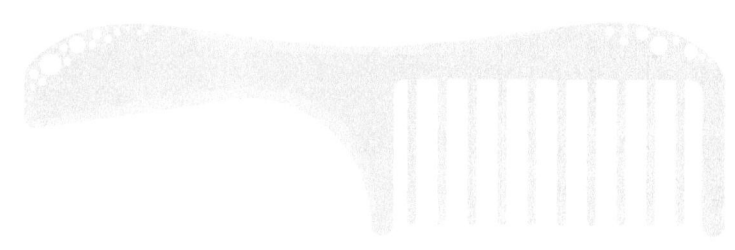

Chapter Eleven

Keith picked up one of the paper bags of hair dye and turned it around.

"Eva and Skye's Magical Hair Solution." He gave them a cockeyed look. "What the hell does that mean?"

Skye grabbed the bag from him. Her hair was still blue, but the richness of the colour had faded. "It means just what it says."

Eva and Skye had spent the last weekend of the winter break preparing the hair dye for sale. Each bag had a handwritten sticker on the front and instructions on the back. Eva came up with the name as a play on words, and they settled on a price of one dollar. With the amount they had, they could repay the school a nice sum.

He looked warily at them. "And Principal Jerrod said it was okay to sell this here?"

"He said it was fine," Eva said, placing more bags on one of the wooden school tables.

They'd set up in the main foyer right by the new trophy case. Skye made a large banner that hung on the wall behind them, and one for the table. There was a half dozen little brown paper bags sitting on Skye's grandmother's silver hors d'oeuvre tray in the centre, with the rest still in Eva's Adidas bag on a chair behind them.

Brad frowned. "But isn't that false advertising?"

"It's a gimmick." Eva shot a concerned look at Skye. "Cause there's no such thing as magic."

Brad picked up a bag. "Okay, so what's so magical about it?"

"Well, it's sparkly."

Brad went to break the seal on the bag. "How sparkly?"

Skye grabbed it from him. "You wanna see? You have to buy one first."

Brad stared at her, unamused.

"Fine." He reached into his back pocket and brought out his wallet. "I guess I can buy a bag, for the cause." He handed Eva the money, and opened the bag when Skye handed it back. His brow rose. "Wow. That's sparkly."

Keith took the bag from him and peeked inside. "So how many have you sold?"

Both girls looked dejected.

"Other than that one, none," Eva said. "But we've only been here for almost an hour."

Brad glanced around the foyer. "I don't think you're going to sell any. Everyone's in class, at the grotto or over at the coffee shop."

"That's why we set up here," Skye said. "So, we'll get them between classes."

"But we both have class next period," Eva said, "And Principal Jarrod said we can't leave the table unattended."

"I'll stay," Brad said, with a smile, "I've got a spare and I was going to study at my locker, but that chair looks a lot more comfortable than sitting on the floor."

Keith blinked a few times and looked up. "Whoa. The sparkly stuff is moving." A wide smile lit up his face. "How'd you do that?"

Brad took the bag back. "Dude, it's not moving. You're stoned."

Keith became defensive. "No, I'm not. I swear!"

The bell rang out just above them. Eva covered her ears against the noise. "Okay, we gotta go." She walked out from behind the table and kissed Brad gently on the lips. "Thanks for staying."

He smiled. "That's what boyfriends do."

She turned to head away from the table and saw Tina and the Trio standing at the entrance to the corridor she needed to walk. Her locker partner glared at her with a look that renewed Eva's belief that she definitely had something to do with the trophy incident.

All through class, Eva's mind wandered. She felt bad telling the lie to Brad, but he didn't have to know the truth. At least, not yet. She wondered if he sold one to Tina. She was standing right there and would probably buy one if he asked. Eva frowned. No, out of all the kids in the school, Tina and The Trio were the last people she wanted using their hair dye. She'd sell some to Carla and Shelly before she'd sell to her.

When the bell rang, Eva couldn't get out of the room fast enough. Excitement raced through her as she headed down to the display. She imagined that all the bags had been sold, and the principal was so impressed that he would let them set up the table again. That meant they'd have to go out for supplies. Brad would come along, of course, and they'd shop and maybe get something to eat before going back to Eva's place and making more. It would be the perfect ending to the day.

As she pushed through the crowd and entered the foyer, her heart sank. Brad was still there, but so were all the bags. Not one had been sold. Worse, no one was even looking at their stand.

She walked up to the table.

"Did you sell any?"

Brad looked up from his chemistry book. "Not one."

"Did anyone even come over and look?"

There was a sympathetic look as he shook his head.

Eva exhaled. "I don't get it. Why isn't anyone interested?"

Skye ran up to the table. "Did you sell any?"

"No," Eva said.

She picked up one of the bags. "Not even one?"

Eva sat on the corner of the table. "No one's interested."

Brad leaned over and gave Eva a kiss. "I have to get to class."

She nodded with a smile. "We'll meet up for lunch?"

"Sure."

Keith ran up to the table. "Dude, can I borrow your notes for chemistry?"

Brad frowned. "Where are yours?"

"Mine are okay, but not as good as yours."

Skye's brow creased. "You take chemistry?"

"Yeah, why not?" He stood back with a large smile. "If I'm gonna be a big-time pot grower, I gotta know how the chemicals work, right?" He faced his cousin. "So, can I?" There was an almost pleading tone to his tone.

Brad pulled off his backpack with a sigh. "I guess, but you've skipped the last two prep classes. I don't know how much these notes are going to help you."

Skye turned to Eva with a wide smile. "Bet we could help you."

Keith frowned. "You don't take chemistry."

"But our hair dye will give you the confidence you need to tackle that test." She grabbed a bag and turned it. "See, it says right here that blue is the colour of knowledge and wisdom. Use this and you'll pass your test."

Eva leaned toward Brad. "That's the magical part."

Keith looked skeptic. "I dunno."

"Come on," Skye pleaded, "It's just a buck. For fun."

He stared at the table and the brown bag for a few moments. "Fine, but just this once." He turned and almost hit DevDude. "Dude. What's up?"

Skye perked up. "Hey Dev."

Dev gave her a curt nod before answering. "I'm skipping next class. Let's head to the grotto."

"Sounds cool, but no can do."

Dev frowned. "Why not?"

The smile on Keith's face was wide. "Gotta study. Chem test today, and it's Mr. Harding's class so it's gonna be harsh."

"Blow it off."

"Can't. It's part of my final mark."

Dev wasn't impressed. "Who fucking cares? Blow it off and we'll go get high."

The adventurous smile on Keith's face disappeared. "Dude, I told you. I can't."

Dev rolled his eyes. "Whatever. Fuck you."

They kept quiet as the older teen walked away. Eva saw the look on Skye's face as he forced his way through the crowd. She liked him, but Eva wasn't so sure DevDude was boyfriend material.

"Did I just hear you right, little bro?" Shelly's voice held a hint of surprise as she walked toward them. "That you're actually gonna study for a test?"

He stood proudly. "Well, I'm gonna do my best."

She looked over the table. "What the hell is this?"

"It's the girls' venture to pay back the school," Brad said, and stared at her, "You know, for the damage that they got blamed for, that we all know they didn't do."

She ignored him and picked up one of the bags to read the back. "Blue is the colour of wisdom. It lets people know you under-stand how the world works, and Eva and Skye's Magical Blue Hair

Solution will help you show the world how smart you really are."
She looked at the girls. "This is a joke, right?"

"Nope," Eva said.

Shelly scrunched up her nose. "Jesus, you sound just like her."
She dropped the bag on the table and reached into her purse and
brought out a dollar bill. "Here you go, little bro, on me, cos you
need all the help you can get."

Keith picked up the newly purchased item. "But they said—"

"Thanks!" Skye cut him off with a dirty look as she took Shelly's
money, "We appreciate you helping out the cause."

The older teen snorted. "Whatever."

When she was out of ear shot, Keith glared at the girls.

"Why'd you take her money when you were gonna give it to me
for free?"

"Like your sister didn't help Carla set us up," Skye snapped.

"She didn't," Keith said, angrily, "I asked her, and she said she
didn't know anything about it."

Skye's eyes narrowed. "And you believe her?"

"Hey, my sister might be a heinous bitch, but she's not a liar."

"You can't blame them for thinking she was in on it," Brad said,
"They're best friends!"

He glared at Brad. "Doesn't mean she does everything that bitch
tells her to do."

Skye put her hands on her hips. "Why are you sticking up for her
all of a sudden?"

" 'Cause she's my sister. Why wouldn't I?"

" 'Cause she's nasty to you all the time."

Keith pulled back. "Yeah, well, she's going through some shit
and I'm trying to be supportive." He turned to Eva. "Look, are we
gonna do this hair thing or not?"

"Sure. When?"

"We can do it now in the girls change room," Skye said. "There's no class this period."

"Yeah, but I have class."

Skye scoffed. "You wanna pass your test or not?"

Keith exhaled and followed behind her."

"You know, that stings a little," Keith said, as the girls slathered his head and hair in a sloppy combination of blue powder and shampoo. He stood, bent at the waist, in one of the shower stalls, as they plastered the goop on him from either side. The more solution they put on his hair, the bluer it became.

"Really bad?" Eva asked, plastering more on.

"No, just uncomfortable. What's in it?"

"All natural ingredients," Skye said, "There's nothing that'll hurt you."

"So why is it hurting?"

Eva washed off the goo under a warm stream of water.

"Okay, so we'll leave that on for ten minutes and then wash it out."

Brad stood behind his cousin reading the back of the bottle.

"The dye could be reacting with the ingredients in the shampoo." He handed it to her. "Maybe put a warning that it could cause a mild reaction."

"Then no one would buy it." She looked at the ingredients. "This is medicated stuff. That could be why."

Eva headed to her Adidas bag on the far side of the room. "I'll write on the bags to be used with regular conditioner."

Keith was frantic. "So, what do I do now?"

"Stay there," Skye said.

"Bent over?"

"Yeah, unless you want it to run all down your back."

Keith grumbled something under his breath and got down on all fours in the stall.

Eva took one of the dye bags and wrote down a warning under the description.

Brad wandered around the room. "This is almost the same as the boys change room."

"Almost?" Eva said.

He shrugged with a grin. "No urinals." He walked to Eva. "You know, I believe Keith when he says Shelly wasn't with Carla."

"Yeah, me too." Eva glanced at Keith before answering. "What's going on with Shelly?"

Brad motioned her to sit on the wood bench next to him. He leaned close to her.

"She thinks she's pregnant."

Eva's eyes went wide. "You're kidding."

"Nope. I heard my mom talking to Keith's mom about it." He looked at his cousin. "They did one of those home pregnancy tests and it came back positive. So now they have to wait for the doctor to confirm." He looked down at the floor. "The whole family is freaked out right now."

"I bet." She paused. "I bet Donnie's freaking out too."

Brad scoffed. "I don't really give a fuck about that asshole." He looked into her eyes. "Ever since you guys told me he was cheating on her with Carla, he can go to hell."

"Does Shelly know yet?"

He shrugged. "Not sure, but that would really suck if she was pregnant with his kid."

"What's she going to do?"

"Don't know."

They sat quietly on the bench and watched Skye and Keith inter-act. Eva felt sad for Shelly. No wonder he was so protective of her.

The ten minutes went by quickly. Eva was nervous about the results. The entire shower stall sparkled dark blue as the girls helped Keith wash the remaining dye from his hair. They dropped his gym towel over his head, and he frantically rubbed at his skull.

"Now my head itches!"

Skye rubbed furiously. "At least it stopped hurting."

With the towel still over his head, they led him to the mirror. Eva's heart pounded in her chest. What if it didn't take?

"Okay." Skye's voice boomed through the change room. "Are you ready to see the new you?

"Yeah. Hey, are you sure this colour stuff is gonna help me? I could really do with knowing the answers to the chem test."

"It won't give you the answers," Eva turned to Brad. "But it'll help you to remember."

"So, I still have to study?"

"Yeah," Skye said. "But you just have to read it. You don't have to make notes or anything."

His head bobbed under the towel. "That's cool. I'm gonna ace the chem test 'cause I know the whole book." He pulled the towel off his head. The blue sparkled for a bit and then faded into a shimmer. Every strand of his hair was blue, so much that it looked artificial. A wide smile creased his face as he spoke the words. "I'm so going to ace my chem test." He turned to his cousin. "Once I read over your notes."

Brad frowned. "Do it quick."

He glanced down at the towel. "Didn't come off on the towel. Cool."

285

Skye walked to the Adidas bag. "We can put that as a selling point too. Won't transfer to clothing."

"Is that a big thing?"

"For hair dye, yeah."

Brad handed his cousin a black binder. "Here are my notes, but I condensed everything into study notes at the back."

Keith nodded. Small flecks of blue fell from his hair but evaporated before they landed on anything.

"Thanks, dude, but I'm going to read the whole thing." He opened the binder. "Wow, there's a lot of stuff here."

"A whole term's worth."

Keith closed the binder. "Maybe I'll just skim through."

Skye pulled Eva away from them. "How is it gonna affect him?"

"It shouldn't." Eva watched Keith carefully and wondered the same thing. "I don't think."

Keith held up the binder and smiled. "Well, here goes nothing."

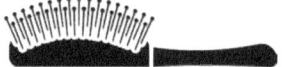

At the end of school a few days later, the girls sat on a broken cement wall in the Grotto. Last class had been over for almost ten minutes and the school buses had pulled in and were waiting. Keith said the chemistry teacher was giving back the tests today. Eva picked at her cuticles out of nervousness, and Skye paced in front of her.

"What's taking them so long?" Skye stared at the glass doors to the grotto. "They should be here by now."

"The class is on the far side of the school." Eva tried to sound nonchalant, but their lateness was making her impatient too. "Probably went back to their locker, or something."

Skye let out a burst of disgust. "They know we're waiting for them."

The glass doors opened, and a crowd of kids poured into the

Grotto. In the centre of the group was Keith talking a mile a minute to everyone around him. A sheet of paper passed between student to student, and he took it from a kid before he and Brad walked up to the girls. A wide grin on Keith's face meant he was stoned or...

"I aced the test!" He handed the paper to Skye. "Ninety-nine out of a hundred."

Eva grabbed the paper from him. "Why not a hundred?" She frowned as she looked over the test. "What's with all the red exes and scribble marks?"

"The teacher thought he cheated," Brad said, "And grilled him with other questions that weren't on the test." He gave his cousin a gentle punch. "But the dude got everyone right."

"And once he realized I wasn't cheating, he changed the mark." His smile lessened. "Never seen a teacher speechless before."

Eva eyed Keith. "So, you aced the test and the stuff he asked you today?"

"Yup." Keith turned to the growing crowd in the Grotto. "I aced Mr. Harding's Chem test!"

Tina and the Trio pushed through the crowd. Tina took the test from him.

"Are you kidding me? I studied for weeks, and I barely got eighty percent." There was an eagerness in her eyes. "What did you do?"

He shot her a condescending look. "I studied."

She balked. "Oh please. You were stoned in class, and we all know it."

"No, I wasn't!"

Shelly pushed past Tina. "I heard you humiliated Harding." There was a smirk on her face. "Way to go, little bro." She touched a strand of his blue hair. "The colour of wisdom, eh?" She looked past him to the girls. "Maybe your hair dye isn't shit after all."

Tina's eyes went wide. "What hair dye?"

"The hair dye we made," Skye said, "Blue, for the colour of wisdom, and it helped him pass his test."

Tina gave her a quick once over. "Bullshit."

Vikki pushed past Tina. "How much?"

"One dollar."

She and Beth scrounged through their purses.

Tina frowned. "You don't believe their crap, do you?" She turned a hopeful look to Shelly. "Do you?"

The older teen shrugged. "I know my brother. He's a shit student but something helped him ace that test."

Vikki, and Beth both wave their money at Skye.

Tina looked mortified. "What are you doing?"

"I have a science test I need to pass," Beth said.

"Their little stunt isn't going to help."

"Helped me," Keith jiggled his test in front of Tina's face.

"The instructions are on the back," Eva said, as Skye took the money, "Read them over carefully, and do exactly what it says."

A few more fists handed them money. Brad moved to the far side and helped Eva distribute the dye.

"I'm not joking, folks." Keith stood a few feet in front of the girls. "Harding is a hard-ass, and I still aced his test."

Soon a large crowd stood around them, all eagerly wanting to purchase a package of Eva and Skye's Magical Hair Solution.

Skye leaned close to Eva. "I think we need to make more dye."

Chapter Twelve

Eva sat in the chair behind their stall in the main foyer and wrote out labels for the two dozen packages of hair dye that sat in front of her. In the month since they sold the first package to Keith, their business had boomed, so much so that with the ebbing flames of the Yule fire, they decided to add two new colours; red and yellow. Yellow would make you more creative and was aptly named The Radiant Yellow, while red would make you more attractive and was given the teasing name R U Red-ee? They were weird names, but Keith read in Shelly's marketing textbook that the name of the product should reflect what it does in some way, which is why they named their first creation A Blu-Brainer.

Eva leaned back in her chair and took a quick look around the foyer. A few small groups of kids were gathered near the entrances, and she smiled as she noted their blue, red, and yellow hair. So far, they'd managed to pay back the school almost half of what they owed, and were very optimistic that with the new colours, they could have the entire debt paid off by the end of the school year.

Skye dropped her backpack on the edge of the table. A lemon-yellow ponytail bounced behind her.

"I hate math. I already know how to add, subtract, multiply, and divide, why do I need to learn algebra?"

"Because it's probably needed if you want to go to college."

She flopped down on the floor.

"That's not gonna happen. The only way I can get good grades is if I keep using the dye." She tilted her head to one side. "Can I keep using it?"

"You shouldn't. Probably not good for your hair."

"No, I mean for the magical part."

Eva thought for a moment. "Magical buildup is possible. The spell-book said there would be nominal after-effects, but the spell was meant to be used once, not over and over."

Skye picked up one of the bags. "We should put a warning on the back. No repeat uses, or something like that."

"Good idea."

Skye pulled out a sheet of paper from her backpack. "I was thinking we could expand our colour range." She handed a list to Eva. "I know we agreed on just the three, but this stuff is popular. We could add more colours and make more money."

Eva read over the list. "Orange, purple, and green?"

"Yeah, secondary colours."

"Sounds good."

"Okay, why don't we work on it this weekend? Say, at my place? Mom is going to Brampton for the weekend and she's taking my brothers and sisters with her. We'll have the whole place to ourselves."

"What about your dad?"

"He said with mom gone, he's gonna use the time to catch up on some work."

Eva nodded. "Cool."

The cab pulled up in front of Skye's home and the girls jumped out before Skye handed the driver some money. The snow was still deep on the property, and someone had shovelled a small path bare-ly the width of the stone walkway up to the front porch. There were a half dozen slightly desecrated snowmen scattered around the front of the house, along with the worn indentations of snow angels. A pair of snow walls sat on the far side of the house that looked as though they'd taken a good beating.

They hurried up to the house and Skye unlocked the door with a key she had on a thin, crochet rope that hung around her neck. The house was cool, and Skye dropped her things and hurried through the living room.

"Fire's out," she said, and ran into the living room, "But I can have it going in a sec."

Eva took off her boots but kept her coat on and dropped her Adidas bag near the front door. It felt good to be back at Skye's home. She missed it; the way it smelled, the way it felt, and she didn't have to worry about offending it either. She wandered to the large kitchen table. There was a plate of cookies and other goodies in a container in the center.

Skye came into the kitchen rubbing her hands together as she walked into the kitchen. "Won't be long to warm up the house."

Eva pointed to the table. "Your mom left us something to eat."

Skye nodded. "Cool. You hungry?"

"Not really."

"Me neither." Her eyes went wide. "Shit. I almost forgot. I gotta do the animals."

They put their boots back on and headed out the back door. The old barn doors were closed and creaked as Skye pulled them open. Inside, the goats wandered around their indoor pen, and the mule just ignored them. The chickens clucked and pecked at the ground, and Skye was quick to throw some feed into their indoor coop.

"I promised Mom I'd feed the animals after school," Skye said, and tossed some hay in with the goats.

"Need some help?"

"Naw, I'm good."

Eva strolled through the barn and looked out a side window that overlooked the woods. Most of the trees had lost their leaves, and she could see clearly to the lake.

"It's funny," Skye said, from the far side, "But ever since I learned about you and your family, this place feels different."

Eva stared at the treetops. "Really?"

"Yeah, like maybe a little bit of your world came back with me." She picked up a small bale of hay. "Can that happen?"

Eva shrugged. "Don't know. Maybe it's been here all along, but you didn't notice it until after you met us?"

Skye nodded. "So, like there's magic here?"

Eva turned to her. "There's magic everywhere. You just gotta know how to find it."

Skye stood in front of the mule's pen. The hay balanced on the edge of the gate.

"That's so deep."

The mule let out a loud bray and Skye dropped the bale. "Sorry, Francis."

They walked back out of the barn and Skye closed up the door behind them. The small path back to the house took them past where the fire pit had been, now buried under the snow. She stopped and glanced at the trees, remembering the strange breeze that swept through the property the night of their bonfire.

"What is it?" Skye asked.

Eva paused. Should she mention what she thought she saw? Skye was cool with knowing about magic and her world, but would she be the same if she knew there was something supernatural on her property?

"Eva?"

Eva smiled. "It's nothing." She continued on to the house, but now Skye was still.

"I was right. Something from your world followed me home."

"I don't think it followed you." Eva opened the back door. "I think it was already here."

Skye hurried to the house. "Really? What is it?"

Eva turned to the back yard. "I don't know, but it's harmless."

"So it's, like, magical?"

Eva shrugged and went inside. "I didn't really see what it was."

Skye followed. "So how do you know something's there?"

They took off their boots and put them on a rubber mat by the door.

"It was the way the trees moved in the wind. I'd have to ask my mom about it. That's if you're interested."

Skye's eyes went wide. "Hell yes!"

Eva grinned. She loved the fact her best friend was so accepting. They grabbed their stuff and went into the living room. The fire had warmed the room enough to make it comfortable, and they sat on the floor in front of the hearth. Skye went back into the kitchen and brought out the large plate of goodies. They spread out their schoolbooks in front of them and did their homework and nibbled on the treats. They were about fifteen minutes into their homework, when Skye leaned back against the couch.

"Are you and Brad going to the Badman Rays concert?"

Eva shrugged. "I don't know. We really haven't talked about it." She looked up at her friend. "Are you going?"

She shrugged. "I like their music, but I don't want to go by myself."

"Why don't you ask someone?"

Skye gave her a strange look. "Who am I gonna ask?" She let out a disappointed sigh and slammed her book shut. "I really thought you and I could go together."

"If we do go, you can come with us."

"And be a third wheel? No thanks."

"What if you invite Keith?"

She scrunched up her face. "No, besides, he doesn't like them."

"Is there someone you'd like to ask?" Eva knew the answer before she even asked.

"Yeah, Keith's friend DevDude, but fat chance he'll go with me." Her eyes went wide. "We could make a hair dye that would guarantee he'd go with me."

Eva frowned, a little concerned. "The Yule fire is almost gone. It'd have to be a powerful colour."

"Are there any?"

Eva exhaled. "Well, there are two that are very powerful." Eva closed her textbook. "Silver and gold. Silver covers communications, you know, like that saying, silver-tongued devil, and gold is used for luck."

"I'd need the gold," Skye said, "Silver would be good if I had a problem talking to him, but I can do that. I think gold would be better."

"We'd have to use the real thing."

"Like a necklace or something?"

"Yeah."

"Gold's expensive, though, and a lot of it is mixed with other stuff."

"So, it wouldn't work?"

"Maybe if we had some really old gold."

Skye jumped up and ran up the stairs. A few minutes later she came back down with a small jewelry box in her hand and placed it on the table. The dark wood and metal joints glistened in the fire light.

"My grandmother gave this to me before she died." Skye opened the box carefully. "It's some stuff that her mom gave her." She took out several gold rings with stones, a gold bracelet with a locket, two pairs of gold earrings and a long gold necklace. "One of the rings is broken. Dad says it would cost too much to get it repaired 'cause the gold is pure." She handed it to Eva. "Do you think you could use that?"

Eva examined the ring and the garnet stone that was set in it. "These are family heirlooms, Skye."

"But I can't wear it."

Eva shook her head and gave back the ring. "No. I can't let you destroy something that belonged to your grandmother."

"It's mine. I can do what I want with it." She rummaged through the box again and brought out an old silver coin. "I got a whole bunch of these when my grandpa on my dad's side died." She handed it to Eva. "I'm not gonna miss a few."

Eva stared at the precious metals in her hand. "You get it that if we use these, it will completely destroy them. You'll never have them again. Ever."

"Yeah, I get it." She glanced down inside the box. "But don't tell my parents, okay?"

"My lips are sealed."

Skye closed the lid and placed it on the square coffee table. "So, is there enough fire to do secondary colours, like green, orange or purple?"

"We should." Eva took out several sheets of lined paper from one of her school binders.

Skye stared at the paper. "What's that?"

Eva flipped through the pages and held one up. "I wrote this out the other night. It's colour information from our family Grimoire."

"Isn't that, like, your family's sacred book, or something?"

"Yeah, we're not suppose to show them off, cos families are very secretive of how they do their spells, so I wrote out what we needed instead."

Skye looked over the information. "Cool." She pointed to a small green square. "Use the colour green for anything related to health, orange for confidence." She scrunched up her nose. "Can't see why, and purple for popularity."

Eva sighed. "We're going to need a lot of purple."

"Can you use some of the money from what we've sold?"

She nodded. "If you want. I can get Delano to do a currency exchange for me."

Skye nodded and sat back. "Good. We still owe the school a lot of money and if we run out of supplies, we'll be out of business real quick."

By the middle of February, the Yule flame was gone, but they had a large quantity of magical powder. Along with the original three, they now had Orange U Go for confidence, Purple People Eater for popularity, and Green Machine for health. Eva sat behind their table and carefully put out the new colours. A small group of teenage girls quickly flocked around to examine the new offerings. They giggled at the funny names, but quickly bought several of the new colours.

"I knew the new colours were going to be popular," Skye said, walking up to the table. Her hair was a golden yellow and shimmered in the sunlight. "I'm glad we decided to make extra."

Eva didn't say anything for a moment and just stared at Skye's hair.

Skye frowned. "What's wrong?"

Eva's was impressed. "Your hair is gorgeous!"

A sly smiled creased her lips. "Right! And, like, nothing's gone wrong all day."

Eva tilted her head to one side. "Just remember to wash your hair a lot. It's more concentrated than the others and might stay in longer." She glanced down at her Adidas bag. There were a dozen other bags still inside. "I don't know about the price though. I still think it's too expensive."

"It's silver and gold," Skye said, "It has to be more expensive." She took one of the bags and placed it at the front of the table. "Look around. People like our product, so they'll pay a bit more for the new colours."

"A bit more? Silver and gold is a lot more."

"And people will pay it."

Carla sauntered up to the table. "Well, hello losers." She picked up one of the new colours. "Purple People Eater? What the hell is that?"

Skye grabbed the bag from her. "It helps make you more popular."

The older teen scoffed. "So why isn't your hair purple?"

She crossed her arms. "Is there something you want, Carla?"

Her cousin slowly looked over the other bags. "Yeah, I thought I'd try out your crap." She motioned to Skye's hair. "What colour is that?"

Skye held out one of the gold packages. "It's a new shade. Golden Opportunity."

Carla picked up a bag of gold dye and turned it around. "Want to ace your job interview? Get a perfect score on a test? Golden Opportunity will open the way for you to get what you want." Her gaze focused on Eva. "What kind of bullshit is this?"

"Do you want it or not?"

Carla tossed her blonde hair.

"It *would* go with my natural colour."

Eva sent a warning glare at her friend, but Skye brushed it off.

Carla pulled out a bill from her purse. "Can you break a twenty?"

"As a matter of fact, we can." Skye pulled out a small black bag from Eva's Adidas bag. "We always carry a float with us, just in case." The transaction was done in a matter of seconds. Skye gave her cousin a fake smile. "Have a nice day."

Carla was out of earshot when Eva swatted her friend. "Why did you sell one to her?"

Skye gave her a sarcastic look. "Why not. Her money is good."

"But she bought a *gold* one."

"Yeah, for fifteen dollars!"

"Skye, she's nasty to start with and that dye will let her be even more nasty and get away with it."

Skye suddenly had a flash of awareness. "Shit. I never thought of that." She shook her head, and her gold locks fell about her face in an alluring manner. "Doesn't matter anyway. With as many times as she washes her hair, I'll bet it only stays in for a few days."

Eva crossed her arms. "Yeah, well she can do a lot of damage in a few days." Eva turned to continue her conversation, but Skye was across the foyer and standing in front of DevDude. Skye did most of the talking, and it seemed like the teenager was keen on listening to her. It was the hair dye, of course, and Eva became a little concerned when he smiled and nodded. After a few moments, they gave a short wave and DevDude continued on down the hall. Skye turned and walked back with the largest smile Eva had ever seen.

"I just asked if he'd go to the concert with me," Skye said, almost busting with pride. "And he said yes!"

Eva watched him walk down the hall, troubled. "Good for you."

Skye exhaled heavily. "Like, I know you don't like him, but he can be really nice."

"I just think you can do a lot better than him," Eva said, "He's a worse pothead than Keith."

"Yeah, but he's cute and way cool, and now we can double date for the concert!"

It was freezing the night of the concert, and the cute outfit Eva wore was buried under a layer of winter outerwear and boots. The floor of the old hockey area was packed with teenagers from all the high schools, with the stands holding the overflow.

Brad and Eva sat on the top row of the cement bleachers at one side of the arena. The stage was full of instruments and roadies checking the equipment. An excited chill ran through Eva. Her first time at a concert—and with her boyfriend—made it even better.

She leaned close to him. "You look nice."

He smiled. "Thanks. You too."

"Thanks, but I'm *freezing*!"

He took a quick look around the room. "Do you see them yet?"

"No, but she said they might be a little late."

Brad shook his head. "Dev is such an asshole. I can't believe she'd go for a guy like him."

"She thinks he's really cute."

"I heard he treats his girlfriends like shit."

"Then I hope this is just one date."

He snorted. "Hopefully."

Eva scanned the crowd until a flash of deep red caught her eye. She recognized the colour: it was the red dye, and it had replaced the gold in Skye's hair. She tapped Brad on the leg and pointed to the arena entrance on their side.

"There they are."

They waved at the couple and headed down the stairs. Dev kept Skye to him with his arm draped around her neck, and when he pulled her close, it looked more like a choke hold than an affectionate embrace. Eva's eyes narrowed. With Skye's hair red, she'd gone from being lucky to being attractive, but Eva wasn't sure he'd feel the same way once the spell wore off.

"'Bout time you got here," Eva said, as she admired Skye's very tight-fitting outfit, "What took you so long?"

Skye shrugged. "Dev and his friends had a *smoke break*." She made air quotes around the last two words, and Eva knew exactly what she meant.

Dev gave a quick nod in Brad's direction. "'Sup."

The teen reciprocated. "Not much."

"I saw Dom." Skye turned to face the crowd on the ice. "I didn't think he liked non-ma—" She cut herself off. Eva's eyes went wide. "—etal music?"

"Yeah." Eva took a quick look at Brad to make sure he didn't catch her friend's almost-blunder. "I didn't think so either."

Dev nodded his head. "Metal *rocks*! I saw the Despairs in Toronto last summer. Totally awesome!"

"He's with Delano, and I saw Carla."

"Was Shelly with her?"

"No." Skye wrapped her arm around Dev. "But she was with a bunch of guys. Looks like she was wrong about Dom going out with her again."

"Good thing."

A moment later, the smiling face of Delano Allard appeared behind Skye.

"Well, Dom, look who we've run into?" His long, tan dress coat and fancy outfit stood out against the jean jacket and leather clad crowd around them. "Eva and her beau." He held out his hand. "Welcome to the family. What's your name again?"

"Brad."

Dom walked up behind him and gave a curt nod to the girls. "Hey."

Eva leaned close to him. "Carla's here."

Dom rolled his eyes. "I know."

Delano looked unamused. "We had the unfortunate pleasure of running into her out in the parking lot. Her along with a friend and a rather large group of men." He turned to his Dom. "Apparently, she was trying to make your brother jealous. Not that it worked, mind you, but you have to give her credit for trying."

Dom turned a concerned look to his sister. "She said something about buying gold hair dye from you?"

"Yeah," Skye said. "We're selling hair dye to pay back the school."

Brad looked enthusiastic. "They made different coloured hair dye imbued with traits to help people."

Dom's brow rose. "Help people?"

"Yeah, you know," Dev said, putting his arm around Skye's waist. "Make them smarter, or prettier."

He focused on Skye. "Is that what you're doing at the house?"

Eva shrugged. "Maybe."

"Evie, if you're doing what I think you're doing, you know there are consequences if they're always using it?"

"Of course I know."

"Then maybe you should stop making it?"

"When we're done paying back the school."

Delano stepped in between the siblings. "Now, I'm sure our little Evie understands what she's doing."

Dom looked away. "I hope so."

Skye turned to Brad. "I haven't seen Shelly at school for a couple weeks. She okay?"

Brad gave a quick glance to Eva. "Yeah. I guess she's just not feeling well."

Eva grabbed Brad by the hand. "Are you thirsty? I am. Anyone want a drink?" Before the others had time to answer, she dragged him away and into the main hall that circled the building. "Sorry, but I had to get away from Dom." They stopped in front of the canteen. "How is Shelly doing?"

"Good, I guess. The… procedure was hard on her. That's why she's missed so much school."

"Is she going to finish the year?"

"She wants to, so Keith and I have been bringing her homework so she can keep up."

They stepped up to the counter and ordered some sodas in cans. "What about Donnie?"

A dark look washed over Brad. "Yeah, he was good with her getting it done, and I still hate the guy."

They took their drinks and slowly walked back to the main floor. On the ramp up to the rink, they passed Runi with a bunch of kids dressed all in black. They all looked the same with black hair, thick eyeliner around their eyes and black lipstick.

"Hey." Eva stopped. "I didn't think I'd see you here."

Runi shrugged. "Nothing else to do." She motioned to the outside doors. "Carla's here."

"Yeah, we heard."

The goth tilted her head to one side. "So, like, what's the deal with that dye stuff?"

"Our hair dyes?"

"Yeah, what's with it? Girl in my art class, can't paint worth shit, got some of that yellow dye and, like, now her stuff is gorgeous."

"It's a psychological thing," Eva said, "You know, if you think you're good, you are good."

"So, she puts this stuff in her hair, and it makes her think she can paint better?"

"Something like that."

"It works too," Brad said, "You know Lester from English?"

Runi nodded. "That loser who smells like wet dog all the time?"

"He bought some of the purple, and now everyone wants to hang out with him."

Runi's eyes went wide, and she nodded. "Right! I saw him the other day hanging out with a bunch of jocks, and I'm like what the fuck?"

"Purple is the colour of popularity," Eva said, "Each colour has a certain aura to it, and when you see it, your subconscious picks up on it."

"So, it's mind over matter?"

"Yes."

She nodded as her black lips formed a smile. "That's so cool." One of her friends swatted her gently on the arm and motioned with his head. She nodded. "Concert's gonna start soon." Runi held up her hand. "Have a good one."

At the top of the ramp, Skye and Dev were still in the same spot and took two cans of pop.

"Your brother and his friend had to leave," Skye said and opened her can, "Carla showed up and started going on about all the men fawning over her." She rolled her eyes and took a sip.

The lights dimmed and a roar from the crowd was drowned out by the piercing opening notes of an electric guitar. Eva and Brad headed up the cement stairs to the wood seats, but stopped when they noticed Skye and Dev weren't behind them. Eva turned to her, and Skye pointed to the main floor and the hordes of people standing near the stage before following her date into the mass.

Brad leaned close to her ear.

"Do you wanna go down there?"

She smiled at him. "No. I'm fine here. Unless you want to?"

He shook his head. "Too packed down there."

She watched as Skye and Dev disappeared into the crowd on the main floor. First blue hair, then gold and now red. All in just over a month and she knew her friend wasn't waiting until the old colour was gone before using a new one. Hopefully, there wouldn't be any problems, but as soon as the school was paid off, they'd stop making it.

It was close to midnight by the time the concert was over, and the crowd slowly made their way to the exits and into the parking lot. Eva and Brad stood near the exit and watched for Skye and Dev. It didn't take long for the couple to emerge, and the girls quickly ran up to each other.

"Oh my god that was an awesome!" Skye's face was full of post-concert excitement. She held up a tee-shirt with the main performance band's logo on it. "Dev even got me a tee."

Dev shrugged. "Gotta have some kinda souvenir."

She gave him a kiss on the cheek. "Thanks again."

A car horn honk brought their attention to a lime green two-door car that was parked on the road just near the exit. Keith waved from the passenger seat. His hair still held a slight blue hue to it, while his sister sat behind the steering wheel and kept a close eye on the surrounding crowd.

"Hey," Skye smiled. "You missed and awesome concert."

Keith shrugged. "Yeah, I'm not really into them." His face brightened up as Dev approached. "DevDude! How's it hanging?" The boys did a fist bump through the open window.

"Six feet don't hang, dude, she drags."

Shelly rolled her eyes. "That's fucking gross, asshole."

Keith glanced over at Eva. "Need a ride home?"

Eva nodded. "Sure, if you don't mind."

He turned to his sister. Shelly shrugged. "Whatever."

He turned back and his happy-go-lucky expression went sour. "Here she comes."

Everyone saw Carla walk toward them with the half dozen older guys trailing behind her. Her hair was still gold and her very revealing outfit was more than noticeable as she walked to the driver's side of the car.

"Hey, girlfriend! Where ya been?"

The tension rose as Shelly shifted awkwardly in her seat. "Been sick."

"Yeah, I know. Your mom keeps telling me that when I call." She bent down. "You don't look sick."

"Well, I am."

Carla straightened up. "Fine. Whatever."

Shelly frowned up at her. "What'd you do to your hair?"

"I bought some of the losers' hair stuff." She played with a strand around her finger. "I think it looks pretty good, don't you?"

"Yeah, I guess."

Carla focused on Skye. "That reminds me. I wanna buy more."

"Sorry," Eva said, before Skye could answer, "But we're all out."

"So make more."

"It's not that easy."

"We have other colours," Skye said, "You wanna buy one of those instead?"

"No, I want the gold."

"If we make more, I'll let you know."

"Eva." Dom's voice called to her from a few metres away, "We're heading back to the house. Are you coming?"

"I'm getting a ride with Keith and his sister."

Dom came toward them and looked inside the car.

"Hey Shelly."

"Hi, Dom."

He motioned to the arena. "Didn't think this concert was your thing?"

She chuckled. "Could say the same about you."

Delano moved in front of his friend. "I'm afraid I forced him to go. I've never seen a rock concert and I thought it would make for an interesting evening."

Carla leaned provocatively over the hood of Shelly's car.

"Hey, Dom."

He looked at her briefly. "Hey."

"Good evening, yet again, Carla," Delano said, and stood on the opposite side of the hood.

"Can we leave now?" Shelly said impatiently from inside the car. "I'm fucking freezing!"

Keith jumped out and pulled back his seat. Eva and Brad hurried into the back.

Dom leaned down into Keith's window. "Tell Mom 'n Dad I'll be home late." He glanced at Shelly. "Good seeing you."

Shelly nodded. "Same."

Skye stuck her head in the window.

"Call me tomorrow."

Carla and her men stood back as Shelly started the car. Keith rolled up his window as she switched the heat on full blast. Eva turned and stared out the back window. Skye and Dev walked back toward the arena, as Carla moved toward Dom.

"You okay?" Brad asked.

"I shouldn't have left Skye alone."

"She's got someone coming for her, right?"

"I think so."

It took a while to drive away from the arena. There were so many cars trying to get out that the entire neighbourhood was congested. Once on the main road, Shelly headed for the far end of town and Eva's neighbourhood.

Brad leaned forward slightly.

"Do you still need me to pick up your schoolwork?"

Shelly was quiet for a moment. "Yeah, if you don't mind."

"You told mom you were going back on Monday," Keith said.

"Yeah, well I've changed my mind."

"It's 'cause of Carla, right?"

"No." Her jaw clenched as she drove. "I just don't feel like going just yet."

Everyone was silent.

Eva looked at each of the boys. "My mom always said that if you're sick and don't want to do anything, that's your body's way of saying you need more time to rest and heal."

She looked at Eva in the mirror. A weak smile creased her lips. "Yeah, I just need more time."

Brad took Eva's hand and gave it a squeeze, and she squeezed back before staring out the window. She knew her best friend was okay, but a part of her really wished she'd stayed.

Chapter Thirteen

I t was the week before March break, and Eva sat at their 'shop' and took stock of the remaining colours. They had restocked their product, especially the red as they ran out for Valentine's Day and had about a half dozen of the others. They were popular, and Eva wanted to make more, but Skye was always too busy after school now. Ever since the concert, Skye spent all her free time with Dev. Lunches too. She didn't want to complain, since her and Brad spent a lot of time together too, but she missed her best friend, and it felt like they were drifting apart.

Raucous laughter echoed from the nearby corridor as Dev and a few of his friends roughhoused in the hall. Dev had his arm around Skye's neck and let it dangle down her front. A few times he pulled her tight to him, but his choke hold wasn't what bothered her. Skye's hair was still red. She was still using the dye.

Skye broke away from Dev and came to the table.

"Hey. Did we sell any?"

"Just a few," Eva said, and gathered up her books, "You should do better this period with the gym classes."

Skye bit her lower lip.

"Yeah, about that. I can't look after the stall this period."

"Why not?"

"Dev and I are headed downtown with his friends."

Eva's posture drooped. "Again?"

Skye snorted. "Yeah, so?"

"So I have class and you said you'd watch the table."

"Yeah, and now I wanna go downtown."

Eva clenched her jaw. She picked up her Adidas bag and shoved some of the packages inside.

"We need to sell the rest of this, Skye."

"We will."

She stared at her. "No, we won't. Not if you're always going off with Dev somewhere. And did you dye your hair red *again*?"

"Look, I'll watch over the table tomorrow morning. I promise."

Dev came up to her and wrapped his arm around her neck and pulled her away from the table. "Come on. They're waiting for us." Skye didn't say goodbye.

Eva stared down at the other packages. She wanted to throw them all in the garbage and walk away, but she couldn't. It wasn't just that she had to pay back the school. They'd made something with magic and it either had to be disposed of properly or used.

"Hey," Runi said, as she and a few of her friends walked up to the table, "I was thinking about buying some of your stuff."

Eva didn't look at her as she tried to hold back her emotions. "Okay. Which one?"

"Maybe I'll get that gold one. Looks pretty cool."

She inhaled and pulled out one of the gold packages. "It'll look nice with your black, but it's more expensive than the others."

"How much more?"

"Twenty dollars."

Runi's brow rose. "Ouch, yeah, I don't have that kind of money."

Eva exhaled. "What about a yellow one? It'll make you more creative."

"Seriously?"

"Yeah, and I'll give it to you for free." She picked up one of the gold dyes and handed it to Runi. "My way of saying thanks for your support at the Halloween dance."

Runi stared at the package. "Cool, and thanks."

Eva packed up the rest of the dye and left the foyer. Two more classes and she could go home, but she couldn't stop thinking about her best friend.

The next day, Skye wasn't at school. Eva sat at their stall and waited for a long as she could, but when the first bell went off, she had to drag her Adidas bag to class. She didn't see her at lunch either or in their history class. By Friday night, Skye had missed the last three days of school, and wasn't taking her calls.

Later that evening, she got a call from Brad.

"Did Skye tell you what happened to Dev?"

"No. I haven't seen her since Tuesday. What happened to Dev?"

"He got expelled from school for selling drugs."

Eva's jaw dropped. "Seriously?"

"Yup. Keith told me."

"When?"

"Wednesday morning. Banta caught him by the portables before class. Kicked him out that day."

"Poor Skye. Maybe that's why we haven't seen her."

"Maybe. Keith said he's going to Loyalist Secondary. I hope he takes all his druggie friends with him."

She rolled over onto her side. "What are we going to do for the March Break?"

There was a long pause on the other end.

"Yeah, about that. My family is going away."

Eva sat up. "Going away?"

"Yeah, they've been talking about it with my aunt and uncle, 'cause of everything that Shelly's gone through, but they didn't really say anything until last night."

Eva's heart sank. "Oh."

"I know you wanted to hang out and stuff, but my mom thinks it's better if we all went away. You know, kinda put everything that's happened behind us and have a start fresh."

"Well, a week isn't that long."

"Yeah, we'll be gone for two."

"Two!"

"We're heading to Disney World in Florida. It's the first time in a while that my dad's taken some time off, so he wanted to go some-place special."

Eva tried to keep her emotions in check, but her chin trembled as she spoke.

"Sounds like fun."

"I'll bring you back something."

She swallowed to clear the tightness in her throat. "You'd better."

Later, at dinner, Eva pushed the food around on her plate. Ven-era tilted her head to one side as she watched her daughter.

"What's wrong, sweetie?"

Eva sighed and put her fork down. "Brad is going away for the spring break, and he's going to be gone for two weeks."

"What about school?"

"I guess he gets to miss some."

"This is good." Egori said, and lowered his cutlery, "You and this boy have spent too much time together. You need to focus more on your schoolwork."

"*Otets*, my grades are good."

"Still, you spend too much time with him. What about your little friend?"

"Skye?"

"Yes."

"I still hang out with her." Eva paused. "Well, not so much lately. She's got a boyfriend too."

"Yeah," Dom snorted from his place at the table, "What a real winner he is."

Eva sighed. "Right? But there's nothing I can do about it."

Egori's brow crinkled. "He is not a good person?"

"No, but she's so crazy over him she doesn't see what he's really like." She turned to her mother. "How can I make her see that he's a jerk?"

"I'm afraid you can't," Venera said, "Not if you want to keep her as a friend."

She pushed her plate of food away. "Brad told me that he's horrible with his girlfriends."

"Is she in love with him?"

Eva snorted. "I hope not."

Egori picked up his fork. "She is accepting of our ways. You should introduce her to a young man from our community." He turned to his son. "One of your friends, perhaps."

Dom almost choked on his food. "She's just a kid, *Otets*. None of my friends would go anywhere near her."

Eva sat at the table long after everyone else left and thought about what her father said. Maybe there was someone in her world that would be better suited for her best friend, but since she started attending school 'outside', she really hadn't talked to any of them.

Brad left a few days later. He stopped by to say goodbye, but it was short, and Eva had to keep pinching herself to keep from crying. She didn't understand why she was so upset. It wasn't like he was going away for good, but still it hurt to see him drive off. Maybe she could get Skye to come over. That would take her mind off Brad. For a while.

It was Wednesday of the March Break and Eva was so bored she took stock of the remaining hair dye, again. They had a couple of months left to sell the rest, but it had become so popular she want-ed to sell more so she could have some money for the summer, but the Yule Fire was gone so they had no way of making anymore. So much for that plan.

She put her Adidas bag on the bed, took out the packages and grouped them by colour. They had three blue, six yellow, four or-ange, three purple, six green, and one red. The more expensive gold and silver were at four and six, respectively. She needed to keep a close eye on those colours and keep them away from Carla.

She brought out a small notebook and the lock box with their money. She checked the numbers of sales and compared it with the available cash. The red dye money didn't match the sales. That couldn't be right. She recounted. They were missing two. She checked the bag again but didn't see any extra.

There was a short knock on her door. A moment later, Skye came in.

"Hey."

Eva smiled and got up. "Hey. What's up?"

"Nothing much. Just thought I'd stop by."

"Yeah, we haven't hung out in a while."

Skye shrugged. "Dev and I have been pretty busy."

Eva noticed the red in her hair was a little faded. She also noticed that her outfit was a bit more stoner-looking than normal.

"You look nice. Are you going out somewhere?"

"No. Why?" Skye took a quick look at her clothing. "Oh, Dev likes it when I dress like this."

Eva sat on the side of the bed. "Why weren't you at school?"

Skye shrugged. "Didn't feel like it."

"I heard Dev got expelled. Brad says he's going to Loyalist Secondary?"

"Yeah, he starts after the break." She looked around the room. "I'm thinking about transferring there after the break too."

"Why?"

"Cos it's got better classes than Frontenac. That's what Dev says."

"What about our stall?"

"We've almost paid off the debt. You can keep selling it, if you want."

"But I thought you liked doing this?"

"Yeah, but that was then. I'm into doing other stuff now."

Eva turned to the packages lying on the bed.

"We have a problem. A few of the dyes are missing."

"Missing? Which ones?"

"A few red and another gold was sold." Eva turned to her. "You didn't sell another one to Carla, did you?"

Skye scrunched up her face. "Hardly."

"Neither did I. So, who sold it?"

"Maybe one of the guys did?"

Eva was concerned. "I think we should take the silver and gold out."

Sky sat on the bed next to the dye bags. "Why? People are buying them."

"Yeah, but we need to make sure it's not to the wrong person."

Skye gave her a sarcastic look. "Who cares? As long as they're selling."

A pang of anger raced through Eva. "This is magic, Skye, we have to be careful who we sell to."

Her friend put her hand on her hip. "Well, if you have a problem with it, why did you come up with that colour?"

"I suggested it for you, not in general."

Skye rolled her eyes. "Whatever."

"We're also missing some of the red."

"I used them," Skye said, matter-of-fact, "Dev really likes the colour on me."

"You can't keep using them, Skye. Remember?"

"Yeah, I know, but nothing bad has happened."

"Not yet." She paused. "How many have you used?"

"Just three."

"Three!"

Skye grabbed a bag of red dye and stood. "But I think I need just one more."

Eva blocked her as her friend went for the door. "Why?"

"Dev and I are going to a party Friday night and I wanna look good for him."

"Your colour looks fine."

Skye went around her. "Maybe I want it to look better."

"Skye, don't. That's too many too soon."

"It's all right. I know what I'm doing."

Eva tried to grab the package back. "No you don't!"

Skye was out in the hall and down the stairs in a matter of moments. Eva followed, but her friend was at the front door as she got to the bottom of the stairs.

Eva's mother stood in the foyer with a tray of cookies and drinks. "Skye's not staying?"

"No, sorry, Mrs. Shade," Skye said and opened the front door, "I just popped in for a moment." She turned to Eva. "I'll call you later."

Eva went to the door and watched Skye get into a car full of kids. The only one she recognized other than her friend, was Dev.

Venera came up behind her daughter. "Is there a problem?"

"Yes," Eva said, "But I can handle it."

Friday night came fast, but it felt like all the days just melted into one another. Skye sauntered down the stairs and into the kitchen, wearing a short jean skirt and ruffled blouse. Her hair was still damp from another application of red dye, and she gave it a good shake with her hands.

"Mom, is it all right if I use some of that perfume you got for Christmas? You know, the one Grandma got you?"

Melody sat at the kitchen table with Skye's siblings and looked up from a textbook. "I don't think so. It's very expensive perfume."

"I just want a little bit."

Her father came into the kitchen carrying an empty beer bottle. "What do you want your mother's perfume for?"

"I'm going out with Dev to his friend's place and wanted to smell nice for him."

He opened the fridge. "You really think you should be going out when you've got finals coming up?"

Melody turned to him. "That's not for another two months, and she just passed all her exams from January."

Lennon angrily looked at his wife. "Yeah, and she needs to keep up this momentum. Going out every weekend to God-knows-where and coming home all hours of the night and she's going to lose those good grades."

Skye rolled her eyes. "I'm not going to lose them, Daddy."

He cracked open a new bottle of beer. "You'd better not. You worked hard for that. Don't let them slip." He walked past her and pointed his finger at her face. "Not for a boy."

Her mother got up from the table. "So, where are you and Dev headed tonight?"

Skye shrugged. "A friend of his rented a VHS and wants us to come over and watch some movies."

"That sounds exciting."

"Yeah, and Dev said he rented some pretty cool movies too."

"Which ones?"

"Dunno, so can I wear some of your perfume?"

Melody shook her head. "No."

"Just a little bit?"

"I said no." She paused. "If you want, we can go out tomorrow to the mall and I'll buy you some that's not so expensive."

Skye exhaled. "Fine. Whatever." A car horn beeped from outside, and Skye ran to the front door, grabbing her jean jacket on the way by. "Dev's here. See ya!"

The night air was cool, and she quickly put on her jacket. Dev got out from the passenger side and she kissed him before climbing into the back seat. The car smelled of pot and she let out a small cough. The driver passed a joint to Dev as they drove away. A few empty beer bottles rolled out from under the front seat as they turned onto the highway. Dev passed the joint back to Skye and she reached for it, taking a toke before handing it back.

"So, like, where's the party?"

"Down off Division."

"What movies did your friend rent?"

The guys looked at each other and then burst out laughing.

Skye frowned. "What's so funny?"

"We ain't going to that lame party," Dev said, and handed her a new joint. "We got a better one to go to."

"Where?"

"You'll see."

It was a long drive downtown, but Skye was too wrapped up in the excitement of the evening to notice. She loved going places with Dev and being his girlfriend. He took her to all the parties and all the girls fawned over the fact she was going out with him, but what she loved was that he paid attention to her. He was interested in knowing what was going on in her life; where she was, what she was doing, who she was with, and it made her feel good about herself, and they never argued, and she wasn't about to. Her parents did too much of that. Maybe if her dad took more interest in her mother's life, like Dev did, they wouldn't argue so much?

They turned down into a rough looking neighbourhood with the music blaring from the speakers. Skye became a little wary when they passed a row of townhouses and pulled into the parking lot.

"We're in the Heights," she said as she got out from the backseat.

Dev frowned. "Yeah, so?"

She'd never been here, but she'd heard a lot about the area. Low-income housing had turned the neighbourhood into a rough part of town. Even the high school here was rough, and she gripped Dev's hand tight as they walked up to the nearest townhouse. Teenagers stood outside and drank and smoked, while music blared from inside. The closer they came to the entrance, the closer she kept to Dev's side, and once inside, she took a tight hold of his hand. He led her through a kitchen and down into the basement where a group of older men sat around talking. One of them looked her over before looking away.

Dev clasped hands with a couple of the men and they were all invited to sit.

Dev leaned close to her ear. "Keep your mouth shut."

Skye nodded. She'd been around him long enough to know there were times when you just kept quiet.

After a few moments, Dev nudged her.

"Go get me a drink."

"What'd you want?"

"A beer."

She walked back upstairs, keeping her gaze focused straight ahead. At the top there were a few guys a little older than her standing around talking.

"Can I get a beer?" she asked.

One of them, a tall blonde, smiled and opened the fridge door wide. "Pick whatever you want."

She grabbed one and he shut the door. "Haven't seen you around here before." He motioned to the rock band patch on her jacket. "Cool band."

She smiled and twisted a strand around her finger. "Right! I saw them when they were in town last month."

"Yeah, I skipped that concert. So, who you here with?"

"My boyfriend. He's downstairs talking to some friends."

"Well, if you dump him, gimme a call."

She stared at him with a blank look. "Yeah, in your dreams." She turned and headed back downstairs.

There were more people in the basement now. Skye took a quick look to see where Dev was, and noticed he was talking to a blonde. Why was he talking to her? She wore a lot of makeup, did he like that? She pushed her way through the crowd and to his side, giving the girl a quick look over. Her clothes looked cooler than hers, and her hair was so big. Why couldn't she have hair like that. He looked like he really liked talking to her. Was he going to dump her and go out with this bitch? Not if she could help it.

The girl gave her a nod. "Hey."

Skye shot her a sarcastic look. "What are you doing?"

"What'd you mean?"

She crossed her arms. "Why are you talking to him?"

"He started talking to me first."

"I fucking doubt it. Dev doesn't talk to *skanks*." She handed Dev the beer. "I'm his girlfriend, so you'd better just fuck off right now." She stood closer to the girl and gave her a slight shove. "Or I'll make you."

The girl pushed back. "Fucking make me."

Skye grabbed a handful of blonde hair and yanked it back before clumsily trying to punch her. A fist hit the side of her face, and as much as it hurt, it made her even angrier than she was. If this slut thought she could take Dev away from her, she'd make sure she was so ugly that he'd never look at her again!

Shouts echoed in her ears as Skye threw another punch and followed through with a knee to the stomach. A small clearing had formed as the girls exchanged a few more punches, until strong hands wrapped around Skye's waist and pulled them apart.

The crowd calmed down as both girls were dragged up the stairs and outside. One of the older men told them both to leave the property. A small group of teens gathered around the other girl, but Skye was alone.

She turned to the townhouse and screamed at the top of her lungs. "Dev!"

She waited for him to come out, and when he didn't, she shouted his name again. Why wasn't he out here comforting her?

One of the older partiers came out and she ran up to him. "Where's Dev? Tell him I'm out here."

He pushed her away. "Get the fuck outta here."

She stumbled back and stared at the building. The anger and jealousy slowly drained away, and after a couple minutes, as she calmed down, she realized he wasn't coming. She blinked a few times as tears formed and tricked down her cheek. Her head pounded where she was hit, and tears blurred her eyes as she headed toward the street. Her head was in a fog, and she had no idea of where she was or how to get home. She saw her reflection in a car window. Hair a mess. Face blotchy with a slight swollen right eye. Her top was ripped, and the patch she'd got from the concert was half torn off. She cried harder. What the hell happened to her?

It was Friday night and Eva felt alone and miserable. She sat on her window bench and stared out over the water. The ice was completely gone now, replaced with the dark storm cloud grey of water. She knew that what Skye was doing was going to end badly, but her friend wasn't listening to her. Why was Skye taking such a risk? She couldn't tell her parents any of it. They'd be angry and she was still afraid they'd make her leave school. She wanted to talk to Brad, but he was still on holidays and wouldn't be back for another week. She couldn't even talk to Dom. He'd tell her it was a bad idea to start with, and right now, that was the last thing she needed to hear.

There was a soft knock on her bedroom door. Venera opened it a bit and stuck her head in.

"We're leaving for Wynden. Are you sure you don't want to come?"

Eve gave her a weak smile and shook her head. "No, I just don't feel like it."

Venera opened the door all the way and walked inside.

"Are you still upset about Brad being away?"

Eva turned and stared out the window. "No. I'm over that."

"Then what's wrong?"

Eva shrugged. "It's nothing."

It wasn't, but she had to fix this herself.

"Well, if you need someone to talk to, your father and I are good listeners."

She smiled meekly at her mother's reflection. "Thanks."

"Do you want me to bring you back something? Maybe a few of those Fae wings you like from the bakery?"

"Sure."

Venera planted a gentle kiss on the top of her head, before turning and leaving her daughter alone.

Eva sat by her window and waited until she knew her parents were gone. The house was eerily silent as she wandered down the hall to the stairs, and into the library. She stood in front of the bookcase that housed the family Grimoires. The six thick, leather-bound tomes sat in order on the shelf. She closed her eyes and touched the framed glass doors. The thin wrought-iron mesh felt cool to the touch. She opened one side and removed the same book. There was a slight shimmer to the wood at the back of the shelf. Eva reached up and gently touched the surface. It rippled outward and spread all along the back. She touched it again and had the same reaction.

"Sem'ya, is there a spell on this bookcase?"

The house groaned as she examined the wall.

"Don't worry, I'm not going to try." She turned and headed out of the room. "It's probably one of Dad's spells in Russian."

She put the book under her arm and headed for the kitchen. The phone rang as she passed the table.

"Hello?" There was a lot of noise in the background. Music and laughter, but the phone distorted a lot of it.

"Eva?" Skye's voice was barely audible.

"Skye? Where are you?"

"At the Sarcoma."

Eva had to think for a moment. "What are you doing there?"

Skye's voice cracked. "Can I come to your place?"

Eva's heart dropped. Something was wrong. "Yeah, sure. Are you okay?"

"No, I just need to get away." There was a long pause on Skye's end. "Do you have any money so I can get a cab?"

"Stay there. I'll come and get you."

"How?"

"I'll be there as soon as I can."

"Hurry, okay."

Eva hung up and ran to Dom's room. She pounded on the door until he swung it open.

"What the hell?"

"Skye's in trouble. Can you open the portal so I can get her?" She spoke so fast all her words meshed together into one long sentence.

He blinked a few times. "Yeah, I guess. Where is she?"

"At the Sarcoma."

He turned back to his room. "That's at the corner of Princess and Division?"

"I think so."

Dom stood in front of a full-length mirror and waved his hand in front of it.

"Sem'ya, locate Skye Daniels at the Sarcoma." The mirror rippled

323

as a foggy image of a street slowly melted into view. Skye stood just inside the entrance near a phone booth. Her clothing was torn, and she had streaks of black running down her cheeks.

"She's a mess. What happened?"

Eva stood behind him. "I don't know."

He touched the mirror with one finger and moved the image to further inside the building. The large dining area was full of people, and he maneuvered the image to a back corridor that led to a dimly lit bar area. He pointed to a restroom door that stood off to one side.

"You can get to her from there."

Eva nodded and hurried out of the room. Tears welled up as the image of her best friend stayed in her mind. Where was Dev? Maybe this had something to do with him? Did he hurt her? Is that why her clothing looked the way it did? By the time she got to the portal entrance, her fear was replaced with seething anger.

Dom came up behind her and traced a sigil on the stone.

"I can't keep the portal open long. Maybe five minutes. Go through, get her and come right back."

Eva nodded as the portal entrance turned into a black mist that bubbled within the frame. She stepped into the mist, the coldness penetrating her body, but as quickly as it came, it dissipated, and she found herself in the ladies' washroom with a long oval vortex spinning behind her. She hurried out of the bathroom and through the small back bar. A few patrons watched her as she raced through into the dining area. For eleven at night, it was pretty busy, and seeing a teen race through in her nightgown must have been an unusual sight.

She went through the first set of glass doors to a small waiting area.

"Skye!"

Her friend turned. Her face was blotchy red, and it was obvious she'd been crying.

She sputtered out a half-laugh, half-cry. "What took you so long?"

Eva shrugged. "You know, I had to find the right pair of pajamas." She grabbed Skye's hand. "Come on. Portal's not going to stay open for long."

They raced through the dining area with all eyes on them. Skye stopped just inside the bathroom door and stared at the spinning portal.

"Wait! I don't have a cloak!"

"You don't need one. We're travelling in the same realm."

The bathroom door burst open and an older woman in a waitress uniform stood in the doorway. "You kids need to—" Her words melted away as she stared at the gaping black hole in the middle of the ladies bathroom. "What the hell is that?"

"It's nothing," Eva said, and grabbed her friend by the arm. "Don't worry about it." She pulled Skye into the void and within moments they stood in the front hall of Eva's home with Dom close by. The black mist dissipated, and the doorway returned to its normal state.

Skye stood in the middle of the room. She looked meek and vulnerable.

Dom looked her over. "What the hell happened?"

"I got into a fight."

Eva stood closer and gently touched a red welt on the side of her face. "What happened?"

"I don't know. Everything seemed fine. We were at this party, and it was a blast, then I saw some girl talking to Dev and—" She looked lost as she remembered. "—and I started fighting with her, and, and I couldn't stop! Eva, I was so jealous and angry that she looked, like, so much cooler than me I was afraid Dev would dump me for her, and...I don't understand!"

Eva embraced her tight. "It's okay. You're safe now."

Skye sobbed. "This is because of the dye, right?"

"Yeah. You used a lot of it."

Dom glared at her. "How many did you use?"

"Four."

He exploded. "Evie how could you let her use so many?"

"She didn't let me," Skye said. "I just took them. They were totally working, and things were going great between Dev and me, but this last time, I just felt different."

"Magical build-up," Dom said. "And it did the opposite of what it was supposed to do."

"It made me jealous?"

Dom exhaled. "It made you ugly."

Skye wrapped her arms around her fried. "Please don't say I told you so."

"I won't."

"Good." She let go and stood back. "I'm pretty sure Dev hates me now, and I can't go home 'cause my parents'll ask me loads of questions and I just wanna *die*."

Eva put her hand on Skye's back.

"You can stay here." She turned to Dom. "And we're not going to say anything about any of this."

"They're going to find out sooner or later."

"Then I'll deal with it then."

Skye followed her up the stairs. "Can I use your shower? I wanna get this dye out."

An hour later, Eva and Skye sat on Eva's bed. Skye wore a pair of her pajamas and had a towel wrapped around her head. When she pulled it away, her hair was still red, but not as intense as it had been.

"I think we should make something that will take the dye out right away. In case stuff like this happens to someone else."

"That's why we needed to be careful."

Skye sat on the edge of the bed. "Yeah, I get that now." She brought her feet up and sat cross-legged. "It was so weird. I mean, a part of me knew what I was doing wasn't cool, but I couldn't stop myself."

"It's the buildup," Eva said, matter-of-factly. She had the spellbook open in front of her. "I reread the spell, but it looks like all you have to do is stop using the dye and things should go back to normal."

"You should write in that the negative effect happens all at once."

"I can't write anything in this one." She closed the book. "Not until I'm older." Eva put the book on her nightstand.

"Do you wanna call Dev?"

Skye shook her head. "Naw. He's probably still at the party and I don't think he'll wanna talk to me anyway." She looked down at the patchwork comforter on the bed. "He wants me to give him a package of silver."

Eva frowned. "What for?"

"I don't know. Something about getting a good deal on a purchase?"

Eva looked gravely at her friend. "I don't think we should."

Skye nodded. "Yeah, I don't wanna. He thinks it's all bullshit anyway…" She went to the Adidas bag on the floor near the window. "You know, we've made enough money and paid back the school, maybe we should just dump the rest of them."

"That's not being very environmentally friendly," Eva joked,

"Plus, throwing away magical items is dangerous. I'd ask my parents to get rid of it properly, but…"

Skye exhaled. "Yeah, you're right. I'm just worried now. I don't want anyone else to overuse the dye now."

"We can't sell the rest, as long as we're careful, and with the Yule Fire gone, we can't make anymore."

Skye nodded and picked up the small notebook from inside the bag. "And you said there's a gold one missing?"

"Not missing, Keith sold. I called him and he told me, so all the money adds up, well, except for the one you took."

Skye walked out of her room. "I have to know who sold it." They raced down the hall and to the phone in the foyer. Skye quickly dialed a number and stood next to the table. "Hey, Keith, it's me. Who did you sell that gold dye to?" There was a brief pause. Suddenly, her eyes went wide. "Seriously? Yeah, okay. Thanks." She slammed the phone down. "Carla."

"No."

"Yeah. He said she wanted to buy more than one, but she didn't have enough money and tried to weasel her way into a discount."

Eva went to her Adidas bag. "That's it. We have to keep the gold here. That way she can't buy it."

"But we won't be able to sell it if it's here."

Eva thought for a moment. "Okay, we don't sell any more to her or her friends, okay?"

Skye chuckled. "She is so *not* going to like that."

Eva looked concerned. "Are you okay?"

Skye let out a long exhale. "I think I will be."

When classes resumed, the girls focused on selling the remaining hair dye, but the higher prices on the gold and silver meant those were the only they couldn't sell right away.

"What if we discount them?" Eva suggested. "That would get rid of them quick."

"No way," Skye said, slightly angry. "I gave up those heirlooms. I want my money out of them."

The weeks passed, and the bright multicoloured hair of their classmates quickly dulled into pastel shades, and there were a few who were upset that they weren't making any more, but overall, most of the student body was content with the limited experiment.

"Hey," Carla's voice sounded behind them in the Grotto, "Where's that pathetic table of yours?"

Skye turned to her cousin. "It's over. We're not selling any more dye."

"What about the ones your depressing little friend has stashed away?"

"You've already used two of those," Eva said, "Let someone else buy them."

Carla handed them a twenty-dollar bill.

"I won't even ask for change back."

"We're not selling you any."

"Why not?"

Eva shot Skye a worried look. "Because they've already been bought up."

Carla didn't look convinced. "By who?"

"People."

She pulled out her wallet. "Well, go find them. I'll give you twice what they did." There was a thick wad of bills in her wallet.

Skye was shocked. "Where did you get all that money?"

A smug look washed over Carla. "From my dream job. I got hired on at the Boutique in the mall just before the break."

Eva sighed. "After you used the dye you bought from Keith."

"Yeah, and now I want another one." An excited look replaced the smugness. "I have entrance exams next month and this stuff is like my good luck charm."

"Sorry," Eva said, "The shop is closed."

"Whatever." Carla stuffed the money inside her purse and stormed away.

The girls watched her disappear back into the school. Carla was jacked up on gold hair dye. It was still enhancing her and from the look of the colour, it wasn't going to dissipate any time soon.

"It's affecting her, isn't it?"

"Yeah," Eva said, "We have to watch it. We can't sell her any more." Her gaze drifted off in the direction Carla went. "Any of us."

Chapter Fourteen

April came in like a lion, and for the first full week it rained almost every day. By the second week they had sold all the remaining packages, except for the expensive ones. It didn't take long, especially when they put up a big 'GOING OUT OF BUSINESS' sign over their stand. Principal Jerrod made an announcement halfway through the week congratulating the girls on a job well done. Their debt was paid in full, and he thanked the student body for being so supportive. He commented on how wonderful it was to see the multitude of colourful hairdos that graced the halls for the last three months yet was glad to have everything go back to normal.

At lunch on the same day, the girls sat in the corner of the cafeteria and talked. The red was almost gone from Skye's hair, with just a pink hue remaining. With Skye's obsession with the dye over, she was returning to her usual self, but since Dev wasn't at their school, they still saw a lot less of each other. He was still a part of her life.

"How's Dev?" Eva asked. It had been about two weeks since Skye's 'incident', and neither of them had talked about it.

Skye didn't look up from her plate of food. "He's okay."

"Is he still mad at you?"

"No. He said his buddy thought it was the funniest thing he'd ever seen."

Eva leaned forward. "And I'm glad you decided not to transfer."

Skye's friend rolled her eyes. "Oh my God, me too. Like, what was I thinking?" She then bobbed her head from side to side and smacked herself in the forehead. "Oh yeah, that there would be girls there that I could pick a fight with." There was awkward chuckle from her, and then she went serious. "To be honest, I haven't really seen much of him since the break."

"Really?"

"Yeah, just on weekends and stuff."

"Probably 'cause he's at a different school."

"Yeah, and he does call me all the time. Mom's getting mad 'cause no one else can get through." She picked up a few fries from the paper plate. "But when summer's here, he said we can spend the whole time together."

Eva didn't like the sound of that. She'd never seen him be really mean to her, but something about the way he acted didn't feel right. She promised herself she'd be supportive, but when did support end and concern begin? "Maybe the four of us can hang out together sometime?"

Skye nodded. "That'd be cool."

They picked at the remaining food on the plate, as Runi came toward their table. She stood next to Eva and smiled.

"Hey." The teen looked uncomfortable. "Got any dye left?"

"We've only got a few," Skye said, as Eva placed the Adidas bag on the table, "But it's just the expensive ones."

Eva took out one of each. "Just the silver and gold."

Runi nodded. "That's cool. Can I get one?"

"What colour?"

Runi paused. "I've got a big test coming up, and I kinda wanted the blue, but whatever will help me is good."

Eva paused before she reached into her Adidas bag. "Maybe the gold?"

Skye scrunched up her face. "The blue would have been better."

"Whatever you got. No big deal."

Eva reached down and brought out a small bag of gold dye.

"Remember. Follow the instructions on the back completely."

"And—" Skye interrupted. "—if you want it out of your hair fast, wash your hair with dish soap."

Runi frowned. "Dish soap? Really?"

Skye nodded. "Harsher chemicals."

Eva put the bag on the table. "Fifteen dollars, please."

Runi nodded and dropped a crumpled twenty-dollar bill. Eva picked it up and reached back into the bag to pull out a pair of two-dollar bills and a one-dollar bill.

"Remember, follow the instructions."

Runi picked up the bag. "Yeah, sure thing." She nodded to them and walked away.

"How many does that leave us with?" Skye asked, as Eva un-crumpled the money.

"Three of the gold, and two of the silver."

"We should be able to get rid of them in no time."

"I hope so. I'm getting tired of carrying them around."

Skye frowned. "Then leave them at home."

"And have my parents see them?"

"In your room?"

"Duh, Sem'ya!" Eva shook her head. "I store them at home and Sem'ya will sniff them out."

Skye rolled her eyes. "Fine. Give them to me."

When the last of the dye packages were in Skye's backpack, she did up the zipper and cleaned up the plate of fries and gravy. "You wanna go to the coffee shop?"

"Sure."

The rain stopped as they headed toward the small strip mall down the street from the school. They were barely off school property when Eva noticed Runi sitting alone, slumped over on the back step of one of the stores.

"Runi?"

The teen looked up. The side of her face was red. "What?"

"Oh my God," Skye said, and they hurried to her side. "What happened?"

"I got jumped by Carla and her new thug, Val Weaver." Runi leaned back on the metal steps. "The bitch sucker punched me and took the dye." Runi winced as she stood. "Who the fuck jumps someone for hair dye?"

Skye was horrified. "Val beat you up for it?"

"Yeah, with Carla was standing there, gloating."

"How did she know you had any?"

Runi shrugged. "Must have seen me buy it from you and followed me off school property." She leaned against the building. "Carla was all freaked out because you sold me some and not her."

Skye leaned against the railing. "The dye. It's making her desperate."

Runi scoffed. "How does a dye make you desperate?"

The girls ignored the question. Skye was worried. "That's her third packet."

Eva nodded. "It has to be her last."

The third week of April was full of birds, spring flowers, and buds on the trees, despite the cool temperature, and everyone was still wrapped up in their winter clothing. The girls had a dozen or so seniors come up to them on the off chance they might have more dye. Eva offered them the gold ones, but no one was willing to buy them with that hefty price.

They sat in front of Eva's locker and did homework. Skye reached into her backpack for something, and instead, brought out a piece of the old banner from the cafeteria protest. She pouted and held up the chunk in front of her.

"I completely forgot about our protests."

Eva was quiet for a moment.

"Maybe we could do one, you know? For old time's sake?"

Skye stared at the paper a few moments more, and then crinkled it up.

"Naw, not worth it."

"Why not?"

"Because no one cares, Eva. Principal Jerrod was going to talk to the school board and get back to us, and he never did." She looked away. "He was just telling us that so we'd stop doing them."

"All the more reason we should do another one."

"Hey, losers." Carla's voice echoed down the hall, as she walked toward them with Val. Her hair shone of blond with gold highlights. She shook her head slightly, letting the loose curl drape around her face. "Like my hair? I just finished my SAT's. Pretty sure I aced them too." She crinkled her nose and kept walking. "Later, losers."

Both girls were silent. Eva wanted to send a curse her way, but with the wish magic in effect, not to mention she still had to wear her necklace, she was pretty sure anything she cast wouldn't work.

Skye glanced at her watch. "Shoot. I have to go." She collected her books and stuffed them into her backpack. "I gotta go meet Dev at the coffee shop."

"He's in school."

She picked up her backpack. "No, he dropped out."

Eva blinked a few times. "When?"

"A few days ago. He said the teachers there were always giving him a hard time, so he left." She smiled as she threw her backpack over one shoulder. "So, I get to see him every day now." She stood in front of her friend. "Wanna come?"

Eva looked down at her work. "I gotta finish this."

"Oh, come on. I'll buy you a coffee."

"Sure, why not?" She closed her books and stuffed them into her locker.

The donut shop was empty except for a couple of men at the very end of the counter. Dev sat on the last seat by the window, flecks of silver in his hair, and he wasn't alone. An older guy was with him, and he kept a close eye on the people who were in the store or coming in.

Skye sat on the opposite side of Dev, and he gave her a kiss.

"Where have you been?" Dev said, and took a sip from his small mug, "You were supposed to be here like, ten minutes ago."

"Yeah, sorry. I was doing homework and forgot you were gonna be here."

"Oh, thanks." His disapproving tone un-nerved Eva. "Hey."

Eva sat across from them. "Hi."

Dev's gaze fell on Eva's Adidas bag.

"So I hear you guys cleaned up with that hair dye stuff."

"Yeah, we did pretty good."

"Pretty good?" Skye gave her friend a strange look. "We did awesome."

Dev leaned over to his friend. "Get this shit, these two made hair dye and sold it for a dollar a pop."

The guy grinned at Eva, and it made her feel uncomfortable.

"So, got any left?"

"Just silver and a few gold."

He looked over at Dev for a moment before focusing back on Eva, then ran his fingers through his mullet.

"Why don't you spot me one? I'm in the mood for a change and I think the silver would look good."

"It looks great on Dev," Skye said, "Everyone complimented him at the party."

"It's fourteen dollars," Eva said.

Dev's friend frowned. "He just said a dollar."

"Yeah, well it costs more for the special ones."

"Special? What, are they made of gold or something?" Both Dev and his friend chuckled.

Eva's eyes narrowed. "As a matter of fact, they are."

The guy stood. "Yeah, whatever." He turned to Dev. "Catch ya later."

Dev nodded. "Sure thing." When his friend was outside the building, Dev turned to Skye. "What the fuck's wrong with you?"

Skye was shocked. "What are you talking about?"

"You were supposed to be here at one thirty, and then you make me look like a complete lying asshole in front of my friend!"

"The gold and silver *are* a different price."

"That's not what you told me." Dev turned away from her. "You told me the silver was a dollar."

"I would charge you that." She looked at Eva. "I'd put in the rest."

He reached into his pocket, pulled out a ten and threw it at Eva.

"I don't let anyone pay my way." He drank the rest of his coffee and slammed the mug down. "Don't be so fucking stupid again." He gave Eva a dirty look and headed for the exit.

"Where are you going?"

"Home."

"Are you still coming over tonight?"

He shot her a disgusted look at the doors and walked out of the building, leaving Eva confused and a deflated Skye to wonder as to what just happened.

"Skye?"

Her friend's lip trembled slightly. "That was my fault. I should have told him the real price from the beginning." She sniffed back a tear and smiled. "It's all good."

"No it isn't. He was horrible to you."

Skye didn't look at her. "But it was my fault."

"He got mad at you for stupid reasons." She sat next to her friend. "You can't let him treat you like that."

"He's not always like this." Skye turned to the huge plate glass window. "He must be having an off day or something."

"It's the weekend. Why don't you come over to my place. We can look at some more magical books. Maybe plan a protest?"

Skye tried to smile. "No, that's okay." She got up and swung her backpack over her shoulder. "I'm gonna head home. I'll see you later."

"But we've still got last class."

"Naw, I'm going to skip it and head home."

Eva sat by herself in the coffee shop and watched her friend walk toward the road in the opposite direction of the school. As much as she wanted to support her friend, this was the last straw.

All the way home it bothered Eva. Skye did not deserve to be treated like that and the more she thought about it, the angrier she got. She sat in the parlour and glared at the hearth, her mind full of ways she could torture Dev with magic. She'd have to use magic. He was stronger than her so physically hurting him was out of the question, but the only spells she knew wouldn't really make the impact she wanted, nor would they last for longer than a few hours.

The front door slammed shut and yanked Eva from her thoughts of revenge. Dom sauntered past the parlour and toward the kitchen.

"Where is everyone?"

Eva got up from the sofa.

"Mom 'n Dad had a council meeting to go to." It was then that she noticed a set of keys dangling from a key chain in his hand. "What are the keys for?"

He turned to her, a large grin on his face.

"My new car."

She blinked a few times.

"Your what?"

"Yeah, I bought a car."

"Why?"

"It was Del's idea. He thought it would be cool to have one." He walked toward the door. "Besides, with you going to a high school now, I thought it'd be cool to do some Outsider stuff too."

He swung open the front door. Eva stood in the entranceway and stared at the small red vehicle parked out front. They walked to the road. The two-door car was squared off in the front but sleek in the back, and the red colour was almost mesmerizing.

Eva was in awe as she walked around the vehicle. "This is beautiful."

"The owner called it a classic."

"What kind is it?"

"A nineteen-sixty-five Mustang Fastback." Dom's face was full of pride as he spoke. "A friend of Carla's showed it to me at a party. Said fast cars and fast women were the only way to live."

"Mom 'n Dad are gonna freak, you know that."

"Why? They've been all over me for months to do something with my life."

"So you bought a car?"

He gave her a quick wink. "It's the first step."

"To where?"

He walked around to the driver's side. "Get in. We'll go someplace."

She opened the passenger side door and jumped in. The leather seats were plush, and she sank a bit into the cushion.

"How did you pay for this?"

"Delano lent me the money, and I'm going to work for his family to pay him back."

Eva got excited. "They offered you an apprenticeship?"

Dom didn't make eye contact as he put the key in the ignition. "No, just manual labour stuff."

"Well, it's something."

He started up the engine. "Yeah, and with the exchange rate he gave me, it won't take long to pay him back either."

Eva giggled as they pulled away from the curb. "Let's see your license. I hear the pictures for them look horrible."

"I don't have a license."

"Dom, you need one to drive a car."

He snorted as they headed down the street. "Oh, look! I'm driving and I don't have a license."

She swatted him on the arm as they pulled up to the main road. He turned on the radio and music rang out from speakers somewhere in the mahogany dash. They headed toward the downtown core, and the main one-way street that ran through the heart of the city.

Eva stuck her arm out the window. She hadn't seen her brother in a good mood in a very long time, and almost forgot what it was like to get along with him. She turned his way and looked him over. He looked calm, at peace. The angry frown that had been his permanent expression was gone. Replaced with a more content, more mature look. There was no sarcastic or indignant expression, but one of maturity and wisdom. Dom was at peace with himself, and she was happy for him.

Downtown was busy and the sidewalk was full of pedestrians. The neon lights from stores lit up the warm evening as people enjoyed the first nice weather of the season.

Dom frowned as they approached a small movie house on his side of the street. "Isn't that your friend's boyfriend?"

Eva looked out the window to the sidewalk.

"Where?"

"Right there in front of the movie theatre."

Dom slowed down. Eva squinted into a crowd of people standing out front. At first, she thought Dom was seeing things, but a few people moved and revealed Dev standing with his friends, and his arm around another girl.

Dom snorted. "That's not Skye."

"No. It isn't." Eva thought back to seeing Donnie and Carla in the coffee shop. Skye made her hide that time, but Eva wasn't about to do that again. She dove over her brother and stuck her head out the drivers' side window.

Dom slammed on the breaks. "Shit! Evie!"

"Hey Dev!" Eva shouted from the window, "Nice girlfriend!"

Dom grabbed her by the shoulder and forced her back into her seat, but she leaned over him again and made a rude gesture toward Dev with her middle finger.

"Holy shit, Evie," Dom said.

"I hate him!" Eva was close to tears she was so angry. "First he treats her like crap, then he cheats on her?"

Dom turned off onto a side street and pulled along side the curb. "Are you going to tell her?"

"Hell yes! I wish I'd told Shelly about Donnie and Carla back in the fall. Maybe she wouldn't have—" She stopped short of revealing what Brad told her and stared out the window.

Dom looked worried. "Wouldn't have what?"

"Can we drive out to Skye's place?"

He nodded and turned at the next corner. Eva kept quiet all the way out. How was she going to tell Skye that her boyfriend was cheating on her? She really liked him and made excuses for his behaviour. Eva hoped she wouldn't try to make an excuse for this.

The Daniels house was dark with just the porch light on. They stopped by the pathway and Eva got out.

"Doesn't look like anyone's home," Dom said.

Eva shut the car door. "No, she's here."

She walked up to the front door and looked through the small glass windows. A small lamp on an end table was on, but it barely lit up the room. She knocked softly on the door, but after a couple moments no one came, so she knocked a second time but a little harder.

A light from the hall came on, and moments later Skye appeared in at the bottom of the stairs in the kitchen. She hurried over to the front door and opened it.

"What are you doing here?" She looked past her friend to the car parked out front. "Who's that?"

"Dom bought a car."

Skye's eyes went wide. "Dom bought a car? When did he get his license?"

"He doesn't have one."

"He can't drive without a license."

"I told him that." She paused. "I need to tell you something."

Skye rolled her eyes. "If it's something bad about Dev, please don't."

Eva took a deep breath. She had to tell her. "We saw him with another girl." She waited for Skye to burst out with some kind of excuse. How maybe it wasn't what she thought it was, or that she had to be mistaken, but her friend just stood there and kept quiet. "Did you hear me?"

"Yeah, I heard you."

"So?"

Skye shrugged. "So what?"

Eva's anger rose. "So why aren't you pissed off?"

Skye moved away from the door. "Why should I be?"

Eva followed. "You think I'm making this up?"

"I know you don't like him."

"Yeah, but you're my best friend. I care about you."

Skye turned on the kitchen light. The table was full of newspapers, some fruit in a bowl, and Skye's open backpack. Skye leaned against the side of the kitchen table and wiped at her face.

"Well, if you cared about me, why did you come out here to tell me? Why didn't you think about my feelings first?"

Eva was taken aback. "I am."

"Really?" Skye's lip trembled. "You know how much I like him, Eva, and you're always just dumping on him."

"'Cause he keeps hurting you!"

Skye broke down into tears. Eva went to her and pulled her into a tight embrace. "Please, Skye, dump him."

"I can't. He said he loves me."

Eva stepped back. "What?"

"Yeah, a few weeks ago. He said he loved me and that I meant more to him than any other girl." She stepped away from the table. "I know he's got his problems, but, he's special to me."

Eva frowned. "He treats you like trash."

"Yeah, but..." Skye looked down at her feet. "He loves me and he's my first."

"First what?"

Skye made a few awkward motions. "You know, my *first*."

It took a few moments and a few more weird looks from her friend before Eva understood what she was talking about.

"Oh."

Skye perked up a bit. "You and Brad have done it, right?"

Eva shook her head. "No."

Skye was surprised. "Really? I thought you guys would have done it by now."

Eva shrugged. "I don't know. We just haven't really thought about it."

Skye shook her head. "That's so weird."

Eva got a little closer. "So, you and Dev really did it?"

A bashful look came over her. "Yeah. Dev says it's part of being a girlfriend."

Lights flashed along the front of the house and the engine of a second car echoed outside. The girls went to the front door as it pulled up beside Dom's car and onto the front lawn. Music blared from the open windows, and before the car stopped, Dev swung open the door and jumped out.

Eva turned to her friend. "I get that you love him, but people who love each other don't treat them like crap. My dad would never say the things Dev said to you in the coffee shop. Your dad wouldn't either."

Skye stared straight ahead. "No. My dad just says things that make me feel bad." She paused. "Dev doesn't."

"But he's cheating on you. I saw him with another girl. What if he was cheating on another girl with you? Brad said he treats all his girlfriends like crap. You deserve better than that."

Skye stared straight ahead for a few moments before moving away. "I don't want to talk to him."

Eva nodded and pushed open the storm door and ran down the path. "She doesn't want to talk to you."

Dev pushed her aside. "Why? You already tell her your lies about me?"

Eva glanced at her brother, before focusing back on Dev. "I told her the truth about you."

Dev reached for the door handle. "I'm fucking sure you didn't."

Dom got out of his car. "Hey, dude, I think you should leave the girls alone."

Three guys got out of the second car. The driver stood behind the open car door and glared at Dom.

"I think you need to mind your fucking business, *dude.*"

Dev swung open the storm door and ran inside. By the time Eva got to the door he was already across the kitchen and standing very close to Skye, who was cowering in the corner by the counter. He yelled at her called her horrible names just inches away from her face, and she had her arms up trying to shield herself from his anger.

"Leave her alone!"

Eva ran up behind him and grabbed him by his jacket. She yanked hard and threw him back into the kitchen table.

Dev was quick back on his feet and grabbed Eva by the arm.

"What'd you say to me, bitch?" He twisted her arm behind her shoulder and forced it up her back. He slammed her hard into the wall and the KitKat clock fell to the floor. "You don't ever get in my way again."

Skye threw herself at Dev and all three tumbled back into the table. Eva broke free and quickly held up her hands in a defensive posture, with her left hand in a fist, and her right open wide. Her anger boiled over as she directed all her energy into her right hand and drew an 'x' in the air with the tip of her index finger. A sly smile creased across her lips. This would be such a strong spell. He wouldn't know what hit him! She slammed the palm of her hand forward the 'x'.

Nothing happened.

Dev stumbled back. "What the fuck are you doing?"

Eva froze.

The necklace!

Her anger deflated as she touched the small pendant on the chair around her neck. She didn't have any powers. It absorbed her anger and magical energy. She couldn't protect her best friend.

His eyes narrowed and he stormed forward. "You stupid—"

A wave of energy raced across the room and slammed into Dev. It threw him back onto the counter and his body crumpled onto the floor in a heap. Eva turned to the entrance. Dom stood in the doorway of the kitchen in a defensive posture. A dark look on his face. At that moment, he looked just like their father that night he gave her the pendant.

Dev lay on the floor for a moment, dazed, and slowly staggered to his feet. The front of his face was red, and he blinked a few times looking around the room.

His gaze fell on Dom. "What the fuck—"

"Get out," Dom said, in a voice so low it sent chills through Eva. "And don't ever fucking come back here again."

Dev glared at Dom. "You don't tell me—"

The room grew dark, and Skye ran behind Eva. The beams of light that shone in through the window were sucked into the darkness, like the horrible candles Eva's father burned. The girls embraced each other and backed up against the far counter.

Dev shrugged. "Fine. Whatever. I'm done with her anyway."

Dom moved away from the door and light returned to the room.

Dev took a quick look at the open backpack on the table. The remaining dye packages were visible. He reached over and grabbed a silver.

He held it up. "You fucking owe me."

The girls didn't move until the storm door slammed behind him, and even then, it was just a few minutes to make sure he was really gone. Car doors slammed shut and the girls hurried to the front door just in time to see the second car pull away from the house. Dirt, gravel and some grass spun up from the tires as it raced past Dom and his car.

As Dev and his friends spun around to leave, the corner of the car smashed into the front of the Mustang. Looking out the window, Dom swore loudly, and raised his hands in a defensive magical position, but lowered them once the other car headed toward the main road.

"Fuckers!" he yelled, as they ran outside and to Dom's car.

Eva turned to her friend. "Are you okay?"

Skye nodded. "Yeah." She wiped at her cheeks. "I can't believe how stupid I am."

"No," Eva said, and embraced her, "He's a jerk and treated you like crap. None of this was your fault."

"But—"

Eva pulled back held up her finger. "No. No more excuses for him. He's out of your life."

Skye exhaled and nodded. She turned to Dom. "I don't know what that was, but thanks."

He snorted as he ran his hand along the damage. "Yeah, you're welcome."

They went to the front of the Mustang. The left-hand side was smashed in with the light hanging from the socket.

"I'll ask my dad if he knows anyone who can do repairs for cheap," Skye said.

Dom stood back. "Thanks, but I've got a friend who knows people." He looked at Skye. "Are you okay?"

She nodded with a weak smile. "I think I will be." She turned to Eva. "You wanna stay the night?"

"Maybe you should come to my place instead." She glanced down the laneway. "In case they come back."

"No, my parents are gonna call soon." Skye wrapped her arms around her torso. "I just wanna stay here."

Eva nodded. "Cool. We'll order a pizza." She turned to Dom. "Can you tell Mom 'n Dad where I am?"

"Yeah." He walked up to the house. "But I'm putting a protection charm on this place in case those assholes do come back."

The girls went back inside as Dom walked around the house. Eva hoped this would be the last time either of them saw Dev, but the way he was, she didn't know for sure.

"Dev took a bag of silver dye." Skye said as they walked across the grass.

Eva snorted. "I don't care if he took them all, as long as we never see him again."

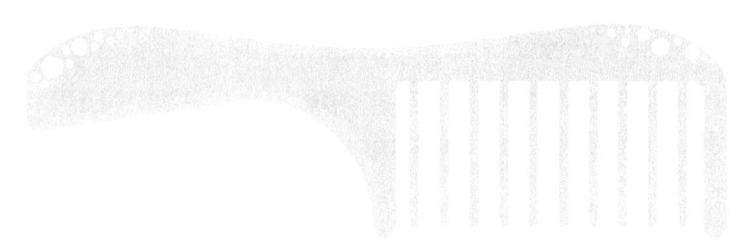

Chapter Fifteen

April warmed into May, and most of the month was quiet with hardly a dyed head of hair in sight. Carla's hair was still blonde, but they knew she had one more gold dye. Hopefully, she wouldn't use it. A few kids asked if they were going to make more of the blue for the final exams, and were disappointed when they said no.

June was busy with exam prep. It felt like old times. Eva and Skye hung out for hours and talking about everything but their schoolwork. The best thing was, Skye never mentioned Dev at all, and Keith stopped hanging out with him right after he learned what happened.

They sat in their spot in the cafeteria and picked at a plate of fries and gravy. They were supposed to be in class, but the teacher was on leave for the rest of the month, so they now finished school an hour early.

"I think you're right about the protests," Skye said, poking at the plate of food. "Mr. Jerrod screwed us around. I bet he didn't even talk to the school board."

"We don't know that," Eva said, "Maybe he did, but forgot to tell us?"

Skye gave her a sarcastic look. "Seriously? You think that? It doesn't make any sense." She popped a fry into her mouth. The red was completely gone from her hair and it was back to the natural blonde. "But I think you're right about him not talking to the school board."

"You know," Eva said, "I think we should give one of those golds to Runi."

Skye slowed her eating for a moment. "You think?"

"Yeah, I mean, the one she bought was stolen. It seems only fair."

"I guess. What about the others?"

"There's only three left, one silver and two gold."

Skye finished off the last of the fries. "So that'll leave us with one of each. Maybe we should keep it as a souvenir?"

Eva scrunched up the paper plate. "Really? After what happened with Dev, you want a memento?"

Her friend shrugged. "Why not? It'll just remind me of how much of a dork I was, and sometimes that's not a bad thing."

Eva glanced at the clock on the wall.

"Dom's gonna be here soon, and I still have to turn in my geography book."

They got up from the table and headed out of the cafeteria. The school corridors were already showing the end of the school year as many of the projects and displays were cleared of works or taken down. A few lockers were already empty and sat open. Most of the seniors were already gone, with a smattering of higher-grade students roaming the halls.

They stopped at Eva's locker, and she quickly did the lock. Her locker was almost empty except for a few binders and things that belonged to Tina. She shoved the contents around for a few moments and then backed up.

"What's wrong?"

"My geography book." Eva frowned. "It's gone."

Skye moved some stuff around inside the locker.

"Did you take it home?"

"No. I never had to."

They went to their geography class and informed the teacher of the missing book. He wasn't impressed, and suggested she check at home, but Eva was positive it wasn't there.

The teacher shook his head. "If you can't find it, you're gonna have to pay for it."

Eva sighed, as she headed back down to the main foyer.

"Well, at least I've got some money left over from the dye to cover it."

Skye looked confused. "And you're sure you didn't take it home?"

"Yup."

"Ask Tina about it."

Eva balked. "Hardly. After what she did, I refuse to even *look* at her."

Brad and Keith met up with them in the foyer right in front of the trophy case. Brad put his arm around her and gave her a kiss on the cheek.

Keith shook his head with a smile.

"God, you two are so sappy."

It was meant as a joke, but Eva was pretty sure there was some truth to it.

The mid-afternoon sun was warm and made the air warm too. A light breeze blew down the parking lot as a few kids headed off school property.

Dom was already waiting in a spot close to the main doors. He was leaning back against the mustang talking to a bunch of older kids. Eva recognized a few, and wondered just how he knew them or what he could be talking to them about. Last she knew, he didn't really care for 'outside' people.

She walked up to the car. "You're early."

"Yeah, I had a few things to do before coming here."

Keith ran his hand along the hood of the car.

"Dude, I can't believe this sweet ride is yours."

Dom beamed with pride. "Believe it."

The group of seniors said goodbye and walked off. Eva opened the passenger door and pulled the seat forward.

Brad looked wearily into the backseat.

"Are you sure we're all going to fit?"

"Don't know," Dom said, "But do you want a ride or not?"

Brad climbed in first and was followed by Skye.

"Nice car." Carla's voice came from the front of the school. Her hair was back to its original blonde without a trace of gold. "Maybe you could take me out for a spin, for old time's sake?"

Dom glared at her. "Yeah, that's never going to happen."

"Why not?"

Eva saw Shelly before anyone else.

"Because you're a fucking skank!"

She ran up to Carla and punched her in the face. The impact was hard enough that it threw Carla into Dom's car.

Keith and Dom ran to the girls and pulled Shelly back and away from Carla. She struggled to free herself, but the guys kept a tight grip on her.

Carla regained her composure and caressed the side of her face.

"What the fuck?"

"You bitch! You lying, fucking whore! I told you Donnie was screwing around, and all this time it was with you!"

"I wouldn't do that. He was *your* guy."

"Fuck off Carla. I know it was you."

Val came out the front doors and stood with a small group to watch.

Shelly pointed at her. "Val told me everything."

The focus shifted to Carla's new best friend. Val quickly looked around.

"What? I thought she already knew."

The look on Carla's face was a mixture of shock and anger, as her gaze jumped between Val and Shelly.

Shelly yanked herself free. "You bitch! I hate you. I fucking hate you!"

For the first time since Eva saw her in the foyer on that first day of school, Carla looked genuinely upset.

"Shells, I'm sorry."

"Fuck you."

"I am. Really."

"Go to hell." She stormed down the parking lot to her car.

Keith walked backward behind her. "Sorry, I need to go with her."

The small group of students that had gathered around the scene laughed and pointed at Carla and walked off. Eva got into the car with Dom but kept her gaze on Carla. She looked so helpless, but that didn't excuse her for what she did.

"I feel bad for her," Skye said, as they pulled out of the parking lot.

Eva turned in her seat. "Are you kidding?"

"She brought it on herself," Dom said, "And Donnie's not innocent in this either."

"I know, but Carla's my cousin, and I feel bad for her. She just lost her best friend."

Brad snorted. "Yeah, well Shelly's my cousin and I can tell you she's lost a hell of a lot more than Carla."

They dropped Brad off first and then headed out to Skye's home. Her brothers and sisters were playing out front when Dom pulled up on the gravel driveway. Eva jumped out and pulled her seat forward.

Skye turned to Eva. "I hope Brad isn't too mad at me for what I said."

"I don't think so, I mean, he has to know you'd feel like that for the same reason he does about Shelly."

Skye took a step toward her house. "Do you wanna come over this weekend? We can study and separate the gold dye. Make cute souvenirs or something."

"Maybe Saturday. Dom and I are going out to dinner on Friday."

Skye smiled wide. "Oh yeah, he lost the bet, didn't he?"

"Big time."

"Where's he taking you?"

"Don't know, but it better be really nice."

Skye leaned forward a bit and looked into the car.

"You hear that? Take her someplace nice."

Eva laughed as Dom rolled his eyes and looked away.

\#

The next day Keith came up to the girls at Skye's locker.

"Do you guys have any of that dye left?"

Skye rummaged through her backpack. "All we have is a gold and a silver," Skye said, and reached into her locker, "Which one do you want?"

He pulled a few bills from his pocket.

"I'll take the gold."

Eva was a little more than relieved that he took the last one.

Skye looked at her friend. "Did you give Runi that other gold?"

"Yeah, this morning. She wasn't going to take it, but I told her it was only fair, especially after what happened."

Keith took the dye and stuffed inside his jean jacket pocket. "What happened?"

"You know Val Weaver?"

"The chick that told Shelly about Carla?"

"Yeah, she beat Runi up for it, with Carla standing right there."

Keith shook his head. "Sorry, Skye, I know she's family and all, but that bitch is a nightmare."

Skye shut her locker. "I've known that for years."

"So, what are you going to use the dye for?" Eva asked.

"It's not for me, I got it for Shell. She's had such a shitty year, I thought if I gave it to her, she could actually feel good about herself for a change."

"How's she doing?"

"Good, I think. I mean, finding out your boyfriend cheated on you with your best friend is brutal."

They stopped at the stairs. Eva flicked the package in his pocket.

"Just make sure she follows the instructions."

He nodded and walked away.

It was later that day when they ran into Keith at the Grotto.

"I got that dye from you, right?"

Skye snickered. "Are you stoned?"

He looked concerned. "No, I just can't find it."

"I saw you put it in your pocket."

"Yeah, and I went to the coffee shop, and now I can't find it."

An uneasy feeling swept through Eva. "Who were you with?"

"Just me and a few guys. I thought Dev might show up since he hasn't been around in a while."

Skye's gaze softened. "Dev was there?"

"No, that's just it. He called a few nights ago, and I said I'd meet up with him, but he bailed. Thought maybe he'd be there today."

Eva was furious. "I thought you stopped hanging around him?"

"Yeah, but he wanted to talk about our business."

"What business?"

His dopey grin appeared. "Our pot business, remember? He said he was gonna talk to a supplier, but he was a no show."

"You know dealing pot is illegal, right?"

"Not forever, and when it's legal, we'll be right there ready and waiting."

Val walked up to them. She nodded at Skye. "Hey, you seen Carla?"

Skye shrugged. "Probably skipping."

"Who's skipping, losers?" Carla's hair was a bright, golden colour. More golden than before.

Eva stared at her hair. "Did you dye your hair again?"

She flipped her hair back and motioned to Keith. "Yeah, I saw it drop out of your pocket, and I *was* going to give it back, but I decided I need it more than you do." She crinkled her nose. "Besides, it's not a good colour for you."

Keith glared at her. "You bitch! I got that for Shell. Why didn't you give it back!"

Carla looked surprised. "Chill dude. I'm sure the losers here have more." She walked over to Val's side. "Heard about your buddy there. Man, that's nasty."

Keith frowned. "What buddy?"

"That Dev guy?"

Confusion came over all of them.

"What happened?" Keith asked.

"He's in the hospital" Carla leaned into them. "Word is, he got the shit beat out of him a couple nights ago. Tried to talk a bunch of bikers outta some dope."

Carla giggled as they headed to the entrance. "I guess it didn't go the way he thought."

The trio sat on a short cement wall, stunned.

"Holy shit," Keith's voice was barely above a whisper. "That's gotta be the people he was talking about." He looked at the girls, frightened. "He wanted me to go with him, but I said no 'cause of what he did to Skye." He stared off across the grotto. "Now I wish I had."

"And you'd be in the hospital right alongside him," Eva said.

Keith stood. "I'm going to see him." He turned to Skye. "You wanna come?"

She squirmed. "I don't know."

"You're not together anymore," Eva said. "You don't have to go if you don't want to."

Skye pursed her lips. "Yeah, but he is Keith's friend, and I do kinda wanna make sure he's okay."

Eva stood next to her. "Fine. I'm coming too. I know the bus to take us downtown."

It took them a good hour to get to the hospital, and they found his room with the help of a nurse. Dev shared a room with three other people who looked just as bad as he did. His face was partially bandaged up, and under his eyes were swollen and purple. A tube was in his mouth and hooked up to a machine to help him breathe. One arm and one leg were set in casts and in slings, with the flimsy hospital gown barely hiding bandages that were wrapped around his chest.

Keith stood and the end of the bed. "Jesus."

Eva stared at his hair. Flecks of silver were quite visible. She looked at Skye, and there were tears in her eyes. He was an asshole to be sure, but she loved him once. Probably still did.

Skye turned and headed for the hall but was stopped by a middle-aged woman who stood in the doorway. She held a small takeout cup in her hand and a look of worry on her face.

"Who are you?" Her gaze fell on Keith. "I've seen you before. Are you his friends from school?"

Keith nodded. "Yes, Mrs. Rogers."

She came closer. "Maybe you can tell me what he was doing downtown so late at night."

Keith looked uncomfortable. "I don't know. We haven't really talked in a while."

She looked at the girls. "Are you his friends too?"

"Yes, ma'am," Skye said, "We went out a few months ago."

A scornful look replaced the worry. "Impossible. He's been dating the same girl since public school. A nice pretty little thing. She goes to Kingston Secondary."

Skye pressed her lips together and ran out of the room.

Dev's mother focused on Keith again. "Who would do this to him?"

"I don't know, ma'am."

Her eyes narrowed. "You don't know *anyone* who wanted to hurt him?"

"No, ma'am."

Eva tugged on his jacket. "We should go."

They kept their heads low as they walked out into the hall. Eva took a last look at Dev in the hospital bed.

"I hope he gets better soon."

They met up with Skye near the elevator. She'd been crying hard. They didn't speak all the way back to the school and got there in time to get a ride home with Dom.

"We did that to him," Skye said, after they dropped Keith off.

"He did it to himself," Dom said, "From what I've heard, him ending up in the hospital was just a matter of time."

"He had silver in his hair," Eva said, "Probably the one he took from your place."

Skye looked thoughtful. "Why didn't it work?" She turned to her friend. "It was silver. He should have been able to talk those bikers into anything."

"Maybe he didn't do it right?'

"How many of those things do you have left?" Dom asked.

"One, but I don't want to sell it now, and I don't know what to do with it."

She stared out the window as they headed down the road to Skye's. What would they do with it?

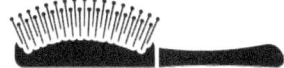

Friday was the unofficial end to the school year. Exams started Monday, and the seniors graduated two weeks after that. Most of the kids who were in school now were in the younger grades, but there were a few seniors roaming the halls or helping the teachers.

The girls' classes were mostly review and they felt longer than normal. Eva saw Brad in Geography, and spent most of her allotted study time telling him about what happened with Dev.

"No wonder I haven't seen Keith. He's probably freaked out."

"I don't blame him either," she said. "You should have seen him. They didn't just beat him up, they broke bones."

Brad shook his head. "I can't believe that's the life Keith wants."

"I don't think he does, now."

The teacher walked up to Eva's desk and hovered over them.

"Miss Shade."

359

Eva rolled her eyes and faced forward.

"I know, save it for after class."

The teacher looked amused.

"Yes, but I thought you'd like to know your textbook showed up the other day, in the book room."

Eva was surprised. "Really?"

"Yes, apparently another student tried to turn it in as hers."

"Who?"

"Vikki Harrington."

"So, I don't have to pay for the book?"

"Not this time, but I suggest you keep a better hold on your textbooks, Miss Shade. They are your responsibility." The teacher walked away without saying another word.

"Why would she do that?" Brad said, "She had to know they'd find out who it belonged to."

"Oh, who knows what she was thinking. I'm just glad I don't have to pay for it."

After class, they passed Vikki heading into the same room. Eva stepped in front of her with her arms crossed.

"Why did you steal my geography book and turn it in as yours?"

She rolled her eyes. "I lost mine and Tina said I could turn in yours."

Brad frowned behind Eva. "You had to know they'd match numbers."

"Tina said they don't do that anymore."

"Well, she's wrong," Eva said, "So they know that the book is mine and you're going to have to pay the seventy-five dollars to replace it."

Vikki's jaw dropped. "Seventy-five dollars? Tina never said it'd be that much."

Eva took hold of Brad's hand. "Then make her pay for it."

They walked to the foyer and met up with Skye and Keith. Eva liked Dom driving them all home now, and it was way better than her taking the city bus, and she got to spend a bit more time with her friends.

Outside, Shelly's little green car was parked next to Dom's. Keith and Skye were already waiting. None of them looked impressed, and every few moments one of them would glance down the parking lot.

"What's going on?" Eva asked, as they walked up to Dom's car.

"It's Carla," Skye said, and rolled her eyes, "My aunt and uncle traded in the car my grandparents gave her for a new one, 'cause she aced her entrance exams."

Brad rested against the side of Shelly's car. "Are you kidding me?"

Skye glanced over her shoulder. "Nope, and she's down there showing it off right now."

Eva squinted as she looked down to the end of the parking lot. A bunch of students stood around a red Audi Quattro, but it was the flash of gold in her hair that made Carla stand out.

"She dyed her hair again."

"Yeah," Skye scoffed, "Nice to see good things happening to bad people."

"Why would they do that?" Brad asked.

"'Cause that's what Aunt Sheila and Uncle Martin do." She looked at Eva. "I told you. They think because they have money that it makes them better than everyone else."

Shelly swatted Brad. "Hey loser, wanna ride home? I gotta stop by your place anyway. Mom wants me to pick up something from Aunt Donna."

Brad turned to Eva. "Looks like I'm riding home with them today."

"That's okay." She leaned in and kissed him. "We have all summer to hang out."

They walked hand-in-hand around to the passenger side of Shelly's car.

"Call me when you get back from dinner." They kissed for a long time, until Keith stuck his head out the passenger side window.

"Dude, come on."

She hurried back around to Dom's car and opened the passenger door to let Skye in the backseat.

Shelly smirked. "You two make me wanna barf."

Dom pulled out of the parking lot behind Shelly and followed them to the road. Eva took a quick look at Carla and her new car. As many times as she'd used the dye, and nothing bad had happened. Maybe the side effects weren't as strong as she thought? Maybe Skye's erupted because she used them all in a short period of time? Carla was being smart and spacing out the use by a couple weeks.

They pulled onto the road, windows open and the radio blaring, and when he pulled up next to Shelly's car, her radio blared the same station. They guys were singing loudly to the song on the radio, and the girls made faces pretending to be grossed out.

"All right, all right," Dom said, and forced his sister back into her seat, "I'm trying to drive here."

They turned right and headed away from the intersection, toward the lake and Skye's home. The drive out was peaceful with hardly any traffic and the sounds of the city were replaced with crickets, birds and the sound of the waves lashing against the shore.

They dropped Skye off and headed back to the main road. Dom stopped at the end of the gravel driveway and looked back at the property through the rear-view mirror.

"What is it?" Eva asked, as she took a quick look out the back window.

"You did you know there's an elemental on their property?"

"That's what it is!" She took a second look out the back window. A few of the trees swayed in the opposite direction of the others. "I knew it was something, but I couldn't figure out what."

"It's big too. Kept a close eye on me that night I put the protection spell around her house."

"It won't hurt them, will it?"

He shook his head. "If it was hostile, they'd know by now." He smirked and shook his head. "I didn't think they'd go that close to humans."

Eva grinned. "Are you kidding? The way her younger brothers and sisters act, you'd think they were half wild to start with."

Skye draped her backpack over her shoulder as Dom's car pulled onto the main road. It was hard to believe the school year was over. So much had happened over the last ten months that she didn't feel like she was the same person anymore. The protest, finding out about Eva's family, the hair dye. Dev. It was all just a blur to her now. She turned and headed for the house. Exams started next week, and she had the idea of making one more batch of hair dye—blue to be exact, just to get her and Eva through them. A gust of wind blew some of her hair across her face. All the red was gone, but the memory remained. She'd used more than she should. What would happen if she used it just one more time?

She shook her head. "Not gonna risk it."

The house was loud as the twins fought with each other and her brothers raced through the house. If she was going to pass her exams, she'd have to study all weekend and this place was going to be way too loud.

Her mother sat at the kitchen table peeling apples. "How was your last day of school?"

Skye dropped her backpack near the closet. "Okay, I guess."

"Did you say goodbye to your friends?"

Her mother picked up the dish towel that lay on the table. A red cover book lay underneath, and she slid it across toward Skye.

"Your dad bought this for you."

Skye picked up the book. It was the high school yearbook. She was speechless.

"Why would he buy this?"

"So, you'd have a memento of your first year." She got up from the table and placed a gentle kiss on the top of Skye's head. "It's not always about grades. He might not say that, but he understands."

Skye flipped through the pages. There was a picture of the aftermath of the food-fight in the cafeteria, and one of her and Eva in front of their stand, and one from her art class with her in the background. She flipped through the student pictures and snorted a laugh at the small black and white picture of her.

"Gawd, I look like such a dork."

"No, you don't."

Skye exhaled. "No, but I don't feel like that person anymore."

Melanie put her hands on her daughter's shoulders. "And you never will again, but don't be so fast to grow up. Enjoy this time you have now." She put one finger under Skye's chin and turned her head toward her. "Being an adult is a lot harder than you think."

"I know."

"Your dad just wants you to be prepared. Four years are going to fly by."

Skye nodded and put the book down as her mother walked over to the sink.

"Now go do your chores before he gets home."

Skye headed back out the front door and toward the barn. The wind was warm, and she played with the tall grass along the path to the building. The barn door was open just enough for her to slip through, and as she stepped inside, the most unusual thing met her eyes. All the animals were standing still and facing the far end of the barn. In the dim light, she could make out a tall, dark blob hovering in the corner, but as soon as she saw it, it faded into the wall and the animals returned to their noisemaking. Bessy the mule turned around and let out a long bray.

Skye walked up to the side of her pen. "Bessy, you okay?"

She looked into the animal's eyes. The long eyelashes blinked a few times, before she moved on to the far side.

Skye hurried out the door and raced around to the far side of the barn. Eva said there was something on her property, but it wasn't dangerous. She scanned the back field until her gaze fell on the tree line. An owl sat high on top of a pine tree, but it was the way the trees bent apart that got her attention. As though something were walking past, moving them out of the way. A wide smile creased her face.

"This is the best day ever!"

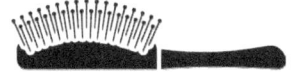

It was the night Eva had looked forward to for the whole year. She couldn't stop smiling as Dom drove them out into the township and to a hotel that housed one of the fancier restaurants in the city. Her excitement over dinner mounted and it was everything she could do to keep from screaming. She was impressed Dom took their bet seriously and had dressed up for the occasion. He wore one of their father's sleek black suits that fit Egori perfectly, but on his son, could have used a good alteration.

"Thank you," she said, watching him drive, "This is going to be the best night."

"Well, we made a deal. I'm surprised you stuck with it the whole year." He glanced at her quickly. "I'm impressed."

"To be honest, there were a few times I wanted to quit."

"No doubt."

"Having a friend like Skye really made it easy." She stuck her arm out the window and let the wind push on her hand. "But I think everyone has a hard time starting a new school. It's exciting, but scary too."

"You've really shown Mom 'n Dad how much you've grown this year," he said, and turned into the parking lot of a large, white hotel, "Are you going back next year?"

She nodded.

"I want to."

The six-story Hamlet's Inn dominated the landscape with its early seventies architecture and huge sixties sign framed in light bulbs. He parked close to the entrance and shut off the engine. He glanced at the small clock in the dash.

"Come on. Our reservation is in a few minutes."

They were taken to a large dining room with red wallpaper and dark wood chairs and tables draped in white linen tablecloths. Their table sat next to a window and gave a nice view of the parking lot and the road. A waiter immediately appeared at their table, filled their water glasses and handed them two, rather heavy menus.

"Order what ever you want," Dom said, as he took a sip of water, "I've got enough money, and after the year you've had, you deserve this."

She smiled and opened her menu. Soups, salads, and other appetizers covered one page, with a wide variety of entrées inside.

"There's so much. I don't know what to order."

Dom closed his menu and carefully placed it on the table.

"Look, I want to apologize for the way I've been acting this year." He turned and stared out the window. "That whole thing with Alisha, and then Carla, it really messed with me."

Eva lowered her menu. "Alisha was horrible to you."

"It wasn't just that. My life was set because of her. I had a shot to join the council." He looked down and picked at the corner of his menu. "I wanted to be somebody."

Eva leaned close to the table. "You are somebody. You're my brother."

He chuckled. "It's a hard job, too."

She shot him a sarcastic look. "Besides, Dad's on the council. You can apprentice under him."

He snorted. "Dad isn't on the Council. Not the way you think he is." Her confused expression made him frown. "Do you know what Mom 'n Dad do?"

"What d'you mean?"

"Mom doesn't just work at the Crypt, she's has a Legacy. She re-pots to the Regency, that's why the apprenticeship was so important to me. You're set, Evie. You'll follow Mom's path, but I have to find my own way."

She frowned. "Mom never told me about any Legacy. Do you know what is it?"

"No, but it's important enough that Dad left his family for her."

Eva always knew her surname wasn't Russian, but her father never talked about his family or where he came from. She assumed it was because his magical lineage wasn't as strong as her mothers, and surnames were passed on based on the strength of the family magic. Families with weak lineage usually ended up in a more labour intense position, like a farmer or builder, but she couldn't see her father being either of those.

"Funny though, I was never able to break the charm he had on the portal." He paused. "What does that say about my ability?"

"You're a good person," Eva said, "Maybe your job with Delano's family will lead to something."

His turned from the menu and gazed out the window. "Maybe, but what ever it is, it'll be a far cry from what I thought I was going to do." He chuckled softly. "I even thought I'd get a shot at serving on the Regency Council."

The Regency Council presided over the entire magical world, and there were more than just humans that governed. Creatures from other magical realms came together to create and enforce their laws. The Regency had the final word on everything. If what Dom said was true, and her mother did report to them, then her family Legacy was more than just a tradition. It had a global affect, and it would come to Eva one day. That's how it worked. Passed down from parent to child. If Eva was next in line, maybe that was a reason why the council was so willing to let her go to school outside their community instead of finding an apprenticeship? Global concerns weren't always restricted to the magical realms.

When their waiter returned, they had decided their orders. Dom liked the sound of the steak done medium rare, while Eva branched out and tried something new—fish. Appetizers and bread were brought to the table, and they talked more about Eva's year and what her plans might be.

"I still want to know why you got the car," Eva said, as she finished off her Caesar salad, "And don't tell me it's because Delano said to."

Dom chuckled. "I don't know. It seemed like something fun to do. I'm still trying to figure out what I want to do. Getting on the Council was everything to me, and I wouldn't let it go for the longest time."

"You're smart, Dom. You can do anything you want, and you know Mom 'n Dad will support you no matter what."

He put his utensils on the table. "I'm curious to know more about the Morozov family, but Dad won't talk about them. Says it's not our concern anymore."

"You could work at the Crypt?"

He chuckled again. "No thanks. Writing up reports of the last few moments of a dead person isn't my thing. Besides, I think that's going to be your job."

Eva scrunched up her face and made a rude noise. She hated that place. "I would, like, totally kill myself if I had to work there."

"You might not have a choice."

The waiter brought their entrées.

"Well, whatever you want to do, you have a whole world of possibilities to chose from." Eva picked up her fork and pointed it at him. "Don't forget that."

They ate and chatted the evening away. Eva was surprised at the fact that even though they were several years apart, they shared the same ideas. They hadn't had this much fun together in a long time, and hoped that this dinner, this evening, would be the beginning of a new chapter in their relationship.

It was almost ten o'clock when they left the restaurant. The traffic was sparse, and the sound of crickets was all around the parking lot. They drove down Princess toward the city and over the bridge at the railroad tracks. When they turned onto Portsmouth and headed south, the traffic was backed up.

As they slowly approached the intersection at Bath Road, red flashing lights shone up the area, and emergency lights bounced off the buildings and trees.

Dom leaned to his left. "Looks like a lot of cop cars up there. Must be a bad accident."

As they neared the intersection, several ambulances stood parked on the side of the road, with a half dozen police officers out directing traffic around the accident. A firetruck parked on the far side, had all its equipment out, but it didn't block the view of paramedics working on someone on the ground.

Eva stared at a car that had the back passenger side smashed in: a brand new red Audi Quattro. Several gurneys were headed to the waiting ambulances, and as her gaze drifted over the accident, it fell on the familiar face of a young boy lying on the ground. Two paramedics worked on him and there were medical instruments strapped to his body.

Eva stared at the boy on the ground and the realization hit her all at once.

"It's Brad!"

She threw open the car door and jumped out. Dom slammed on the brakes and went out after her.

"Eva! Wait!"

She got within several metres of the paramedics on the ground before two officers grabbed her and forced her back. She struggled against their grip, and within moments Dom was behind her, pulling her back from the scene. She pushed back against his restraint, and they fell to the ground together. Eva wailed as she stretched her arms out toward her boyfriend lying on the ground just metres away. His body limp as the paramedics worked feverishly over him.

Dom kept his arms around her as the cops stood next to them.

Eva could hear them talking to her brother, and his shaky voice ended with a question, but it sounded a million miles away and her mind was too numb to understand. She didn't take her eyes off Brad, not until a flash of gold forced her to look away. Sitting in the back of a police car, was Carla. Her head was low, but the gold in her hair radiated in the dim lights of the cruisers. Her heart pounded as she saw both Shelly and Keith being wheeled into waiting ambulances, with bandages on their bodies and covered in blood.

Shelly's car was nowhere to be seen.

A moment later, one of the paramedics slumped over. He looked defeated. The movement was duplicated by the second followed by a curt shake of his head, and a nearby officer draped a thin white sheet over Brad's body.

Eva screamed and lunged forward, but Dom kept a tight grip on her. He pulled her to her feet and embraced her tight as she cried hard into this chest. The two police officers stood close by. One rubbed her back, but it didn't stop the crushing pain that filled her chest, and no matter how hard she screamed, it wouldn't release.

A shadow passed before her eyes, and everything became a blur. Her mind was trapped in a fog that wouldn't let her focus on what was going on around her. She wasn't sure how, but she knew she was in her father's arms. She knew it was him from his scent, and he carried her down the street and away from the accident. She wrapped her arms around his neck and looked over his shoulder. She couldn't cry, couldn't move, couldn't think, and her pain felt dull and cold. They were wrapped in shadow, but she could see her brother and their mother standing in the middle of the street a few metres away from his car. Dom was broken, and their mother wrapped her arms around his waist. They stood still as the last ambulance drove away.

Everything moved in slow motion, almost to the point it barely moved at all. Her father's voice was soft and low. *"Mne ochen' zhal', doch',"*

She reached out her hand to the crash site. *"Net ya dolzhen ostat'sya"*

"Budet vremya skorbet' o tvoyem druge."

The shadows grew darker, and things moved within them. With each step Egori took, they moved several metres forward until they stood in front of their home. Eva turned and looked skyward. The gargoyles on the roof moved and gathered all together over the front porch. For the first time, she saw them clearly. Their features. Their expression. They were illuminated with a silver light that radiated and pulsed out from the centre of the house, and Eva could see, *could feel*, Sem'ya.

A soft glow emanated from the west. It wasn't the city lights, and there weren't enough buildings in that direction that could light up the night like that, but something was *there*, and she couldn't take her eyes off of it.

With two steps they were inside their home. Another two and they were in her bedroom. The walls were silver, and she could see the energy of Sem'ya moved through the walls and follow them up to her room.

Egori carefully placed her on her bed.

"Rest, little one. These next few days will be hard, and you will need all of your strength."

She let her shoes drop to the floor before climbing under the blankets. Egori placed a kiss on her forehead, and then placed his open palm over her eyes.

"Sleep."

Chapter Sixteen

They buried Brad on the following Wednesday.

It was raining.

Grade nine exams were canceled.

The cemetery was full of friends and their parents. Egori escorted Eva to the funeral. They stood next to Skye and her mother and waited for the family to arrive with the coffin. The ceremony had been private; family only, and even though Brad's father invited both Eva and Skye, neither of them went. All Eva could see when she closed her eyes was Carla sitting in the back of the police cruiser, her hair awash in a golden aura, accompanied by the horrible thought that this was all her fault.

Principal Jerrod came up to Skye's father.

"Mr. Shade, Mrs. Daniels." There was a quick nod of acknowledgment between all before he turned to Eva and Skye. "How are you girls doing?"

Neither could answer but nodded their reply.

"I'm at a loss as to how all this could have happened," he said, "From what I've heard, the girls weren't even speaking to one another anymore."

"They had a falling out over Donnie," Melanie Daniels said softly, under her umbrella behind her daughter. "My sister's lawyer said

Carla met up with them downtown, wanted to take them out for burgers to apologize. They argued about Donnie, Carla dodged in and out of traffic and wouldn't slow down until Shelly promised to not be angry with her anymore."

"She can't handle people being angry or hating her," Skye said.

Melanie placed her hand on Skye's shoulder. "Just like her mother. Somehow, she convinced them to get into the car with her."

Skye looked sorrowfully at Eva. "Yeah, because she has all the luck."

Eva knew *exactly* what her best friend meant. The gold dye. Carla must have invited them to go out and the magic took it from there. The way Shelly felt about her ex-friend, there was no other explanation.

The funeral cars pulled up and, slowly, the procession made their way to the grave site. Shelly was in a wheelchair with her leg and arm in a cast, but her brother wasn't with them.

"Where's Keith?" Eva asked.

"Still in the hospital," Principal Jarrod said. "He's still in bad shape."

The graveside ceremony passed with numbness and heartache. As people slowly walked away, Egori reached for his daughter's hand and gave her a small black stone. She glanced down at the sphere. An image of her and Brad talking at the dinner table played over and over. It was a memory of hers from the first time he came to dinner, taken and embedded within the stone. A moment in time showing what he meant to her.

She slowly crept toward the grave marker. She gripped the stone tight. Two cemetery workers carefully scooped dirt into the open grave but stopped and backed away as she came closer. Her body ached as she bent down and dug a little hole at the corner of the grave. She took one more look at the memory, and carefully placed the stone in and covered it back up. Her father stood behind her, and she buried her face in his chest and cried.

"Come, little one, your mother and brother are waiting for us at the Eternal Home. You can ask your friend if she would like to come."

Eva nodded and walked back to Skye.

"We're going to have a little ceremony in Wynden. Did you want to come?"

Skye shook her head. "No, I just wanna go home." She reached out and embraced Eva. "I can't believe this is happening."

Eva held her best friend tight as tears streamed down her cheeks. Her lip trembled. "Me neither."

They embraced one more time before Skye and her mother walked away. Eva watched as her best friend left the cemetery. Egori wrapped his arm around Eva and led her to a boarded-up doorway at the back of the church. He placed his hand on the wood, and within moments, a portal opened. He took her by the hand, and they walked into the blackness.

On the other side was a large oval room made of stone with several large cubicles embedded in the walls. Her mother and brother stood straight ahead, waiting, dressed all in black. In a large arched cubicle behind them, a lone picture of Brad sat on a small stone altar.

Venera went to her and gave her a long hug. Eva buried her face in her mother's hair with her arms around her neck and squeezed her tight. They walked up to the altar and Dom gave her a long black candle. He touched the wick with his index finger and thumb, gave it a quick twist and a flame sparked up and burned softly. He gave candles to his parents and lit flames on theirs as well before doing one for himself.

Eva stood in front of the altar and stared at the picture. She was supposed to talk about him, but the words caught in her throat and instead she cried. Eva wanted to tell them all about him, when they first met, how he was slowly growing a mustache, the way he always seemed to have the right thing to say, but none of it would come out.

"I can't do this."

"It's all right." Venera wrapped her arm around Eva's shoulder. "You don't have to. You can think about him instead if you want."

"Can I say something?" Dom asked.

Egori nodded.

Dom dribbled some wax from his candle on the altar and carefully placed the end in the pool.

"I only met him a few times, but he seemed like a good kid." He looked at his sister. "Shelly told me once he was the smartest one out of their whole family and she was pretty sure he was going to go to university and become a lawyer." He paused for a moment. "She said he didn't like people doing bad things, but he could understand *why* they did them, and sometimes, the why was more important than the crime." He nodded slowly. "When I heard that, I thought, this is the right guy for my sister." He looked at her sorrowfully. "He would have made a great addition to the family."

Soft footsteps stopped at the entrance as a young male a few years older than Eva stood holding a large silver candle holder with a black candle. The flame was a light blue and it flickered in the air current.

"Excuse me, I'm sorry to interrupt, but Mr. Nithercott wanted me to place this for your friend." The teen looked slightly embarrassed as he spoke.

"Come in, Farron," Venera said. "And please send our thanks to Mr. Nithercott."

The young teen carefully walked up to the altar and placed the candle holder in the centre of the stone slab, behind the picture. He turned to them and gave a quick nod.

"My condolences on your loss."

He kept his head low and left the Shade family alone.

Egori walked up behind Eva and placed his hands on her shoulders. "A mourning candle. How thoughtful."

Venera hugged her daughter. "You can take it to our vault and place it with the others."

Eva placed her head on her mother's shoulder. "Thank you."

The next day, Eva stayed in bed all day. With grade nine exams canceled, there was no reason for her to get up. It had been one whole week since the burial and she still didn't want to talk to anyone, but there was one thing she definitely had to do.

She pulled the blankets back and got out of bed. Her Adidas bag sat on the floor next to her fireplace. A lone silver dye package still inside. She picked up the package and stared at it. It was supposed to be fun. It was supposed to pay off their debt. Everyone loved them. Where did it go wrong?

Her grip tightened on the bag. She should have left the last four at home, like Skye said.

She should have stopped selling them when Skye lost interest.

She should have been more careful when Carla bugged them for more.

She should have been more forceful when Skye offered to use her heirlooms.

She should have been more careful with magic.

She should have—

Eva screamed and threw the bag across the room. They hit the wall and fell to the floor. She ran over and collapsed on top of it, crying and pounding her fists on the flimsy paper bag until it burst. She grabbed the torn package and ripped it more, throwing silver powder on the floor around her. She screamed with each rip, and scooped up the dye and threw it as hard as she could. She swiped and pounded on the floor dispersing it farther around her room.

Sem'ya wailed as Eva pounded harder on the floor. The door to her bedroom swung open and her father raced to her side. He grabbed her around the waist and pulled her to him. They fell back against her bed. His embrace was strong as he gently stroked her hair.

"*Pust' vse eto.*"

Eva sobbed into her father's chest.

"Oh, *papochka,* I miss him so much!"

"I know, *malen'kiy.* Death is never kind."

She pulled away from him. "It's all my fault. All of it."

Her mother came in and sat on the floor on the opposite side. "Sweetheart, none of this is your fault."

"Yes, it is." Eva said. She turned and wrapped her arms around Venera's waist. "Skye and I made magical hair dye. I infused it with magic. It was my idea. I should have known better." She buried her head in her father's chest as Venera held her tight.

Chapter Seventeen

A warm breeze blew in through the front windows and brought with it the sound of a lawn mower and the smell of freshly cut grass. Eva went to the window and inhaled. There was something about this scent that eased her mind.

It was hot and muggy in the middle of July. She hadn't been outside since Brad's funeral, and as much as it still hurt, as much as she wanted to hide from the world, she couldn't lie in bed anymore. She looked back into her room, and the small bag on her dresser. She knew what was inside; the remaining silver dye that had been all over the floor. She didn't know who, but someone had cleaned it up.

She walked through the house, the bag in her hand, until she found her parents outside looking over the backyard. Patches of grass and wildflowers covered the whole yard, and the worn dock looked worse. Her parents were discussing something about a flowering hedge along the property line, something her father didn't agree on as his arms flailed wildly and his words were more Russian than English.

"I think a fence would look nice," Eva said, walking up to them, "You can put climbing flowers all along it, and train them to cover the fence."

Her father smiled. "Agreed."

"Good afternoon to you too," her mother said, "How are you feeling?"

Eva shrugged. "Still numb?"

Egori gently kissed the top of her head. "This feeling will go away."

Eva inhaled. "There's something I have to tell you."

Her mother nodded. "The dye?"

Eva's expression turned back to sorrow. "I wish I'd told you about it, but I didn't think it would turn into anything bad."

Her father frowned. "Good intentions never do, but you can never control what other people will do. That was the only problem with your plan."

Venera nodded. "We knew months ago what you and Skye were up to, but we hoped you were mature enough that you would let us know if you needed our help."

Eva was shocked. "How did you know?"

"We are your parents," Egori said, "We know everything."

Her mother playfully slapped him. "Dom told us when you started making more than one colour."

Eva shook her head. "I should have told you about the dye. About Carla's obsession. Maybe the accident wouldn't have happened."

Venera lifted her daughter's chin with her finger. "You can tell us now."

Her lip trembled as she told her parents everything. At first it was hard, but the more she talked, the easier it was, and when she was done, her grief and her guilt felt a little lighter.

"The Regency is looking into the circumstances," Venera said. "That dye caused a lot of damage."

"I know." Eva held up the bag. "This is what's left. I know I can't just throw it away, but maybe you can do something with it?

And if you wanna ground me from ever seeing Skye again or make me quit high school, I'm okay with that."

Egori crossed his arms. "I doubt any punishment we think of will be as bad, or teach you the lesson, better than the consequences you have already experienced."

"We'll stand with you as you explain what happened to the Council." She looked gravely at her husband. "You'll have to submit a written statement about how this all happened. They'll want to know every detail, in case there are further consequences."

Eva nodded. "Okay."

"You should get on with this now," Egori said. "Best to get it down while the memories are still fresh."

She turned to the house, but then turned back to her father. "The night of the accident, you brought me home. It felt like we were going through the portal, but you weren't wearing a cloak."

Egori looked uncomfortable. "That is a discussion for another time."

Eva shook her head remembering that horrible night. "It was so weird. The world looked so different, and I saw this beam of light off in the distance."

Venera smiled and embraced her daughter. "You saw a place of strong magic."

"What place? I didn't think there were any on this realm?"

They headed toward the house. "There are some. Not many. Places that are powerful with magic and need to be protected."

"From who?"

"Let's not worry about that. Why don't we go inside and work on your statement for the Regency."

Eva put her arm around her mother. There was a good chance the Regency Council would ban her from returning when they learned all of what happened, but she didn't care. Not anymore.

It was early the next week when their doorbell rang. Eva was surprised to see Skye standing on her front porch. The girls embraced for a moment before Eva joined her on the porch.

"I can't stay long. I just came out with my dad to get some take-out." She glanced back at the station wagon parked along the side of the street. "I was hoping you'd be home."

Eva followed her down the stairs. "How are you?"

Skye shrugged. "Okay, I guess. About that last dye?"

"Taken care of."

"Really?"

"Yeah, I gave it to my mom's boss. He knows how to dispose of stuff like that."

Skye nodded. "Cool." She stared out over the front lawn. "Mom was talking to Aunt Sheila. Carla's in juvie for the summer. They're charging her with vehicular manslaughter. Her court date is sometime in late fall."

Eva exhaled slowly. Her lip trembled. "Her hair was gold, Skye."

Skye's voice cracked. "I know."

"We caused this."

A tear trickled down Skye's cheek. "I know. I can't stop thinking that we should have just kept those last dyes at my place. They would have been safe there."

Eva turned and hugged her.

"My parents knew what we were doing, you know. Knew the entire time we were making and selling it." She stepped back and sat on the stair. "I wish I'd told them what was happening with Carla."

Skye sat next to her. "Are they angry?"

"More like disappointed, and the Regency Council has set up a tribunal." She paused. "They might revoke my dispensation and not let me come back next year."

"But we'd still hang out, right?"

Eva shook her head. "Probably not. I'd have to start looking for an apprenticeship and that could take me just about anywhere in my realm, and I might not have the time to come back." She looked down at the ground. "I mean, Dom was gone for months at a time. The last one was for a whole year."

"Oh."

There was a moment of awkward silence before Skye spoke again.

"I ran into Tina and the Trio at the mall. They got their report cards. Did you get yours?"

Eva shook her head. "I don't know. I haven't looked."

Skye stared across the street. "She said she didn't do as well in her finals as she did in her mid-term. Did you know she got an A in her English exam in January?"

"Good for her."

Skye turned to Eva. "Yeah, and when I said something about the dye helping with that, she had no idea what I was talking about. It was like she didn't remember."

"It was temporary magic," Eva said. "Maybe memory loss is a side effect?"

Skye's face lit up. "So, like, if everyone can't really remember what happened, then maybe they'll let you come back?"

Eva shrugged. " I don't know."

The station wagon honked, and the girls stood.

"I gotta go." Skye grabbed Eva and gave her a tight hug. "I had so much planned for this summer. Now it's all shot to hell, and I don't even know if I'm ever going to see you again."

"I know." Eva stepped back. "And If I don't come back, I want to thank you. You were a really good friend to me."

"Maybe we can hang out at the mall before you gotta do this apprenticeship thing?"

"That'd be cool."

Skye hurried down the walkway and got into the car. Eva watched as the station wagon pulled away. She waved frantically at her friend and then collapsed back on the step.

"Things'll work out," Dom said, from the doorway.

Eva turned around. "You think?"

The look on his face made her think he wasn't sure either.

Eva watched as the car disappear around the bend. So much had happened to her. She promised herself she'd never forget, and if the Regency Council did deny her return, she at least she had a wonderful adventure. Eva and Skye's Magical Hair Solution was gone, but the friends she'd made, and the memories, would last forever.

~FIN~